OTIS ADELBERT KLINE'S
MARS SERIES

THE SWORDSMAN OF MARS
THE OUTLAWS OF MARS

OTIS ADELBERT KLINE'S MARS SERIES

by Otis Adelbert Kline

THE SWORDSMAN OF MARS

PROLOGUE

Harry Thorne opened his eyes and gazed about him with a startled expression. This was not the tawdry hotel bedroom in which he had gone to sleep; it was a small room with bare, concrete walls, a door of hardwood planking studded with bolts, and a barred window. The only articles of furniture were the cot on which he was lying, a chair, and a small table.

So the sleeping pills didn't finish me off, he thought. *Now I'm in jail for attempted suicide!*

Thorne sat up, then rose unsteadily to his feet and staggered to the window. Supporting himself by gripping the thick iron bars, he peered out. It was broad daylight and the sun was high in the heavens. Below him stretched a deep valley, through which a narrow stream meandered. And as far as he could see in all directions there were mountains, though the highest peaks were all below the level of his own eyes.

He turned from the window at the sound of a key grating in a lock. Then the heavy door swung inward, and a large man entered the cell, bearing a tray of food and a steaming pot of coffee. Behind the man was a still larger figure, whose very presence radiated authority. His forehead was high and bulged outward over shaggy eyebrows that met above his aquiline nose. He wore a pointed, closely cropped Vandyke, black with a slight sprinkling of gray, and was dressed in faultlessly tailored evening clothes.

Thorne got to his feet as his singular visitor closed the door behind him. Then, in a booming bass, the man said, "At last, Mr. Thorne, I have caught up with you. I am Dr. Morgan." He smiled. "And, I might add, not a moment too soon. You gave us quite a time—Boyd and I managed to get you out of that hotel room and down to the street, passing you off as drunk. Don't you remember a knocking at the door? You weren't quite out when we came in."

Thorne thought for a moment, then nodded. It seemed that there had been a pounding somewhere. "How did you get in? I thought I locked the door."

"You did—but I had skeleton keys with me, just in case. We took you to my apartment, treated you, and brought you out here." Morgan nodded to Boyd, who left the room, then waved his hand invitingly toward the tray. "I ordered breakfast served in your room. I especially urge you to try the coffee. It will counteract the effect of the sedatives I was compelled to use in order to save your life and bring you here."

"You've gone to a lot of trouble to save something I don't want," Thorne said. "May I ask why you are interfering in my affairs?"

"I need you," Morgan replied simply. "And I can offer you adventure such as only one other man of Earth has known—possibly glory, possibly death. But if death, not the mean sort you were seeking."

Harry Thorne frowned. "You referred to a man of Earth as if there were men not of Earth. Are you suggesting a trip to Mars?"

Dr. Morgan laughed. "Splendid, Mr. Thorne. But suppose you tackle this breakfast. It will put you in a better frame of mind for what I am going to tell you. I shall not lock the door as I leave. When you have finished, join me in the drawing room—at the end of the corridor to your right." He paused in the doorway. "You mentioned a trip to Mars, Mr. Thorne. Forgive me if I keep you in suspense for a time, but—although it is not exactly what you think those words mean—that *is* what I am going to propose."

CHAPTER 1

"You have heard of telepathy, of course—in fact, Mr. Thorne, you experimented with it at one time."

"How did you know that, doctor?"

"You wrote a letter about your experiments to the editor of a popular magazine. It was published under your own name two months ago."

Thorne rubbed his brow. "That's right, I did—been so busy I forgot all about it. But my results were negative."

Dr. Morgan nodded. "So were mine, for nearly twenty years. It was a hobby when I was in practice, but since my retirement, I've devoted my full time to it. Let me brief you on the basics.

"Telepathy, the communication of thoughts or ideas from one mind to another without the use of any physical medium whatever, is not influenced or hampered by either time or space. That is fundamental, but I had to amend it. I failed to achieve anything until I succeeded in building a device which would pick up and amplify thought waves. And even then I would have failed had this machine not caught the waves projected by another machine which another man had built to amplify and project them."

6

"You mean you can read minds by radio, as it were?" Thorne asked.

"To a very limited extent. If you had a projector in this room, and I had my receiver here, I could pick up any thoughts you sent me—but only those you consciously projected. I could not read your mind in the sense of picking up anything you did not want me to know."

Thorne took a cigarette from the box on the table to his right and lit it. "Interesting," he admitted, "but what has this to do with Mars?"

"I made only one amendment to that basic theory, Mr. Thorne. The rest of it holds true: the communication of thoughts or ideas from one mind to another is not influenced or hampered by time or space. The man who built the thought-projector is on Mars."

"Men on Mars—you mean Martians, or human beings like us? Excuse me, doctor, but that is spreading it a bit thick. I'm well enough up on present-day studies of the planets . . ."

". . . to know that the existence of a human civilization on Mars today is hardly credible," Morgan broke in. "You are quite right. None such exists."

"Then how . . .?"

"Space or *time*. I was incredulous, too, when I got in touch with someone who identified himself as a human being, one Lal Vak, a Martian scientist and psychologist. And I might add that Lal Vak found the idea of a human civilization on Earth a bit thick, too. But the explanation, fantastic as it may seem, is quite simple: Lal Vak is speaking to me from the Mars of some millions of years ago, when a human civilization *did* exist there."

Morgan raised his hand. "Don't interrupt now—hear me out. From that simple exchange of visual and auditory impressions which marked our first communications, we progressed until each one had learned the language of the other to a degree that enabled us to exchange abstract as well as concrete ideas.

"It was Lal Vak who suggested that if we could find a man on Earth and one on Mars whose bodies were similar enough to be doubles, their brain patterns might also be similar enough so that consciousness could be transferred between them. Thus, Earth of the 20th Century could be viewed through Martian eyes, while the (to us) ancient Mars culture—we cannot yet place it in time relative to Earth—could be seen at first hand by a man from Earth. First Lal Vak projected to me many thought images of Martians willing to make this exchange—so clearly that I was able to draw detailed pictures of them. But that was not enough. I could spend the rest

7

of my life without finding any counterparts of these Martians here. The second thing Lal Vak did was to tell me how to make what we call a mind-compass, and gave me the brain-patterns of his volunteers. I followed his directions and fed the first brain-pattern into the mind-compass."

Thorne leaned forward intently. "What happened?"

"Nothing. The needle rotated aimlessly. This meant that either there was no physical counterpart of this Martian now alive on earth, or any such double did not have a similar brain-pattern. I fed in the second and third patterns with the same result. But with the fourth pattern, the needle swung directly to a given point and remained there." Morgan opened a drawer in the little table and took out some pencil sketches. "Recognize this man?" he asked, handing a sketch to Thorne.

"Your assistant—Boyd, you called him?"

"Correct. Under the influence of Lal Vak's thoughts, I drew a picture of Frank Boyd. To shorten the story, I found him in an Alaskan mining camp. He was interested in the venture I proposed—he is now on Mars."

"But—I just saw him . . ."

"You saw the body of Frank Boyd, which is now inhabited by Sel Han, a Martian. On Mars, Sel Han's body is occupied by Frank Boyd, an Earthman. But I made one terrible mistake."

"What was that?"

"In my eagerness to find a volunteer, I did not investigate Frank Boyd. Sel Han has cooperated with Lal Vak and me, but once on Mars, Frank Boyd broke contact—and without his cooperation, it could not be maintained. I have learned through Lal Vak that Boyd has allied himself with a group of Martians who are out to seize power and set up an empire over the entire planet. Mars is presently in a state roughly analogous to our middle ages, socially, though in some branches of science they are in advance of us. But theirs is not a machine civilization, and an adventurer who is also a fighting man—or adept at intrigue—can go far there."

Harry Thorne grinned. "Let me see if I can guess the rest of the story. You've loosed an unsavory character on Mars and feel you've wronged your friend, Lal Vak, so you want to undo the damage if you can. You fed more brain-patterns into the object compass, and eventually the brain-pattern of . . ."

". . . This man," Morgan agreed, passing him another sketch. Thorne took it and saw a drawing of himself in minute detail.

"But that was not enough," he said. "You didn't want to repeat your error, so you spent some time investigating me first."

Dr. Morgan smiled. "And the results were most satisfactory—to me. You had a good war record in Korea, you've been on hunting expeditions to Africa, and you've been in business. Your recent difficulties, which resulted in the loss of your fiancée and your business—left you a pauper, in fact—came out of your refusal to go along with your partner's dubious (though legal) manipulations. He wiped you out and took your girl, too. . . . In short, you are a man who might well do what Lal Vak and I feared impossible."

Harry Thorne nodded. "Assuming that you can send me on this strange mission, what would you want me to do?"

"Only two things. Remain in touch with me, through Lal Vak, as much as possible, and, if you can, kill Frank Boyd—the Martian Sel Han. Otherwise, your life on Mars will be your own, to live as you choose, or as the Martians choose to let you live. If you are able to rise above your environment—as I think you will be—you will find opportunities there you could never hope for here. You will find a world of romance and adventure undreamed of outside of fiction. And if you are not equally quick with sword and wits, you will find death. Knowing you to be an expert fencer—yes, I found out that you had tried to get a job with a fencing instructor and was turned down because you beat him too easily—I don't think I need worry about you on the first count."

"The prospect appeals to me," Thorne admitted. "But I refuse to murder a man I have never seen."

"If you oppose Sel Han's designs, I assure you that you will have to kill him or be killed. There's no question of murder—it will be simple and justifiable self-defense. . . . Then—you'll go?"

"I'll at least make the attempt, with your assistance. How does this personality-transfer take place?"

"I can only describe it as a sort of phasing of similar vibrations, represented by your brain-pattern and that of the Martian volunteer. But first I must put you under hypnosis. Then I will contact Lal Vak, and we will work together. He will be on hand to meet you when you awake in the body of a Martian. Now come over here and lie on the sofa."

Thorne did as Dr. Morgan directed, and found that he was looking into a mirror painted with alternate circles of red and black. The doctor touched a button and the mirror began to rotate slowly. Morgan's voice came to him, "Now think of that distant world, far off in time and space. Think of it beckoning you."

Thorne obeyed, his eyes fixed on the mirror. He began to feel drowsy, a pleasant lassitude stealing over him. The doctor's voice faded. . . .

CHAPTER 2

Thorne opened his eyes and looked up into a cloudless blue-gray sky that was like a vault of burnished steel. A diminutive sun blazed down upon him but oddly enough, with its heat and light seemingly unimpaired.

The heat, in fact, was so great that it made him draw back into the relatively cold shade of the scaly-trunked conifer that towered above him, its crown of needle-like foliage gathered into a bellshaped tuft. Then conviction came to him. He was really on Mars! Wide awake, now, he sat bolt upright and looked about him. The tree that sheltered him stood alone in a small depression, surrounded by a billowing sea of ochre-yellow sand.

He scrambled to his feet, and as he did so, something clanked at his side. Two straight-bladed weapons hung there, both sheathed in a gray metal that resembled aluminum. One, he judged, was a Martian dagger, and the other a sword. The hilt of the larger weapon was fashioned of a metal of the color of brass, the pommel representing a serpent's head, the grip, its body, and the guard, the continuation of the body and tail coiled in the form of a figure eight. The hilt of the dagger was like that of the sword, but smaller.

Thorne drew the sword from its sheath. The steel blade was slender and two-edged, and tapered to a needlelike point. Both edges were armed with tiny razor-sharp teeth which he instantly saw would add greatly to its effectiveness as a cutting weapon. He tested its balance and found he could wield it as easily as any duelling sword he had ever had in his hand.

Replacing the sword in the sheath, he examined the dagger, and found it also edged with tiny teeth. The blade of this weapon was about ten inches in length.

Depending from the belt on the other side, and heavy enough to balance the weight of the sword and dagger, was a mace with a short brazen handle and a disk-shaped head of steel which was fastened fanwise on the haft, thick at the middle and tapering out at the edges to sawlike teeth, much coarser and longer than those on sword or dagger.

Thorne turned his attention to his apparel. He was wearing a breechclout of soft leather. Beneath this, and down to the center of his shins, his limbs were bare and considerably sunburned. Below this point were the rolled tops of a pair of long boots, made from fur and fitted with clasps which were obviously for the purpose of attaching them to the bottom of the breechclout when they were drawn up.

Above the waist his sun-tanned body was bare of clothing, but he wore a pair of broad metal armlets, a pair of bracelets with long bars attached, evidently to protect the forearm from sword cuts, and a jewelled medallion, suspended on his chest from a chain around his neck and inscribed with strange characters.

On his head was a bundle of silky material with a short, soft nap, rolled much like a turban and held in place by one brass-studded strap that passed around his forehead, and another that went beneath his chin.

Beyond a large sand dune, and not more than a quarter of a mile distant, he saw the waving bell-shaped crowns of a small grove of trees similar to the one that sheltered him. He started toward the clump of conifers.

As soon as he stepped out into the blaze of the midday sun, Thorne began to feel uncomfortably warm. Soon he noted other signs of Martian life. Immense, gaudily tinted butterflies, some with wing spreads of more than six feet, flew up from the flower patches at his approach. A huge dragon fly zoomed past, looking much like a miniature airplane.

Suddenly he heard an angry hum beside him, and felt a searing pain in his left side. Seemingly out of nowhere a fly, yellow and red in color and about two feet in length, had darted down upon him and plunged its many-pointed proboscis into his flesh. Seizing the sharp bill of his assailant, he wrenched it from his side.

The insect buzzed violently but Thorne, still clinging to its bill, reached for his dagger with the other hand and cut off its head. Flinging the hideous thing at the body, he caught up a handful of sand to stanch the bleeding of his wound. Presently, he started forward once more.

He was nearing the top of the dune when he saw, coming over the ridge from the other side, a most singular figure. At first glance it looked much like a walking umbrella. Then it resolved itself into a man wearing a long loose-sleeved cloak which covered him from the crown of his head to his knees. Below the cloak the end of a scabbard was visible, as were a pair of rolled fur boots like those worn by Thorne. The face was covered with a mask of flexible transparent material.

Thorne stopped, and instinctively his hand went to his sword hilt.

The other halted, also, at a distance of about ten paces, and swept off his mask. His face was smooth shaven and his hair and eyebrows were white.

"I have the honor of being the first man to welcome you to Mars. Harry Thorne," he said in English, and smilingly added: "I am Lal Vak."

Thorne returned his smile. "Thank you, Lal Vak. You speak excellent English."

"I learned your language from Dr. Morgan, just as he learned mine from me. Aural impressions are as readily transmitted by telepathy as visual impressions, you know."

"So the doctor informed me," said Thorne. "But where do we go from here? I'm beginning to feel uncomfortable in this sun."

"I've been inexcusably thoughtless," apologized Lal Vak. "Here, let me show you how to adjust your head-cloak." Reaching up to Thorne's turbanlike headpiece, he loosened a strap. The silky material instantly fell down about the Earthman, reaching to his knees. A flexible, transparent mask also unrolled, and Lal Vak showed him how to draw it across his face.

"This material," he said, "is made from the skin of a large moth. The people of Xancibar, the nation of which you are now a citizen, use these cloaks much for summer wear, particularly when traveling in the desert. They keep out the sun's rays by day, and keep in considerable warmth at night. As you will learn, even our summer nights are quite cold. The mask is made from the same material, but is treated with oil and has the nap scraped off to make it transparent."

"I feel better already," said Thorne. "Now what?"

"Now we will get our mounts, and fly back to the military training school, which you, as Borgen Takkor, must continue to attend. At the school I am an instructor in tactics."

As they approached the small clump of trees which Thorne had previously noticed, he saw that they surrounded a small pool of water. Splashing about in this pool were two immense winged creatures, and Thorne noted with astonishment that they were covered with brown fur instead of feathers. They had long, sturdy legs, covered with yellow scales. Their wings were membranous, and their bills were flat, much like those of ducks, except that they had sharp, down-curved hooks at the end. And when one opened its mouth, Thorne saw that it was furnished with sharp, triangular teeth, tilted backward. These immense beast-birds, whose backs were about seven feet above the ground, and whose heads reached to a height of about twelve feet, were saddled with seats of gray metal.

The tips of each creature's wings were perforated, and tethered to the saddle by means of snap-hooks and short chains, evidently to prevent their taking to the air without their riders.

Lal Vak made a peculiar sound, a low quavering call. Instantly both of the grotesque mounts answered with hoarse honking sounds and came floundering up out of the water toward them. One of them, on coming up to Thorne, arched its neck then lowered its head and nuzzled him violently with its broad bill.

"Scratch his head," said Lal Vak, with an amused smile. "Borgen made quite a pet of him, and you are now Borgen Takkor to him."

After a second prod from the huge beak, Thorne hastily scratched the creature's head, whereupon it held still, blinking contentedly, and making little guttural noises in its throat. He noticed that there was a light strand of twisted leather around its neck, fastened to the end of a flexible rod, which in turn was fastened to the ringshaped pommel of the saddle.

"Is that the steering gear?"

"You have guessed right, my friend," replied Lal Vak. "Pull up on the rod, and the gawr will fly upward. Push down and he will descend. A pull to the right or left and he will fly, walk or swim in the direction indicated according to whether he is in the air, on the ground, or in the water. Pull straight backward, and he will stop or hover."

"Sounds easy."

"It is quite simple. But before we go, let me warn you to speak to no one, whether you are spoken to or not. Salute those who greet you, thus." He raised his left hand to the level of his forehead, with the palm backward. "I must get you to your room as quickly as possible. There you will feign illness, and I will teach you our language before you venture out."

"But how can I remember all the friends and acquaintances of Borg—Borgen Takkor. What a name! Suppose something should come up . . ."

"I've provided against all that. Your illness will be blamed for your temporary loss of memory. This will give you time to find out things, and the right to ask questions rather than answer them. But, come, it grows late. Watch me carefully, and do as I do."

Lal Vak rugged at a folded wing, and his mount knelt. Then he climbed into the saddle and unfastened the snaphooks which tethered the wings, hooking them through two rings in his own belt. Thorne imitated his every movement, and was soon in the saddle.

"Now," said Lal Vak, "slap your gawr on the neck and pull up on the rod. He'll do the rest."

Thorne did as directed, and his mount responded with alacrity. It ran swiftly forward for about fifty feet, then with a tremendous napping of its huge, membranous wings, it took off, lurching violently at first, so that the Earthman was compelled to seize the saddle pommel in order to keep from falling off.

After he had reached a height of about two thousand feet, Lal Vak relaxed the lift on his guiding rod and settled down to a straightaway flight. Thorne kept close behind him.

When they had flown for what Thorne judged was a distance of about twenty-five miles, he noticed ahead of them a number of cylindrical buildings of various sizes, with perfectly flat roofs, built around a small lake, or lagoon. The oasis on which it was situated had a man-made look, as both it and the lagoon it encircled were perfectly square. The cylindrical buildings and the high wall surrounding the square inclosure shone in the sunlight like burnished metal.

Rising from and descending to the shores of the lagoon were a number of riders mounted on gawrs. And as they drew near, there flew up from the inclosure a mighty airship. No passengers were visible, but a number of small round windows in the sides of the body indicated their positions.

Lal Vak's mount now circled and then volplaned straight toward the margin of the lagoon. Thorne's gawr followed. As it alighted with a scarcely perceptible jar, an attendant came running up, saluted Thorne by raising his hand, palm-inward, to the level of his forehead, and took charge of his mount, making it kneel by tugging at one wing.

Thorne returned the salute and seeing that Lal Vak had dismounted, followed his example. As he stood on his feet a sudden dizziness assailed him. He braced himself to walk away with Lal Vak as if there were nothing the matter.

The scientist led him toward one of the smaller buildings, which Thorne now saw were made of blocks of a translucent material like clouded amber, cemented together with some transparent product.

As they were about to enter the circular door of the building, two men came hurrying out, and one lunged heavily against Thorne. Harry suppressed a groan with difficulty, for the fellow's elbow had come in violent contact with his wound.

Instantly the man who had jostled him, a huge fellow with a flat nose, beetling brows and a prognathous jaw, turned and spoke rapidly to him, his hand on his sword hilt.

Lal Vak whispered in Thorne's ear. "This is regrettable. The fellow claims you purposely jostled him, and challenges you to a duel. You must fight, or be forever branded a coward."

"Must I fight him here and now?"

"Here and now. Doctor Morgan told me you were a good swordsman. That is fortunate, for this fellow is a notorious killer."

Both men drew their swords simultaneously. Thorne endeavored to raise his blade to engage that of his adversary, but found he was without strength. His sword dropped from nerveless fingers and clattered to the pavement.

A sardonic grin came to the face of his opponent. Then he contemptuously raised his weapon and slashed the Earthman's cheek with the keen, saw-edged blade.

For an instant Thorne felt that searing pain. Then he pitched forward on his face and all went black.

CHAPTER 3

Thorne woke to a weirdly beautiful sight. Two full moons were shining down on him from a black sky in which the stars sparkled like brilliant jewels. He was lying on a bed which was suspended by four chains on a single large flexible cable which depended from the ceiling, and had his view of the sky through a large circular window.

He turned on his side, the better to look around him, and as he did so, saw Lal Vak seated on a legless chair suspended, like his bed, on a single cable which was fastened to the ceiling.

"Hello, Lal Vak," he said. "What happened?"

"I regret to inform you that you are in disgrace. If you had told me, before the duel, that you were weak from loss of blood, I could have delayed the meeting. It was only after I had brought you here that I discovered your wound, and by that time the news had gone about that you were afraid—that you had dropped your sword when faced by Sel Han."

"Sel Han! Why, that's the man Doctor Morgan wanted me to kill!"

"The same. On Earth he was Frank Boyd, a robber of mines and a jumper of claims, so the doctor informed me."

"I'll challenge Sel Han as soon as I'm up and around again. That ought to square everything, and if I win, why, the first part of my mission will have been accomplished."

"Unfortunately," replied the scientist, "that will be impossible. According to our Martian code, it would be unethical for you, under any circumstances, to provoke another duel with Sel Han. He, on the other hand, may insult or humiliate you all he likes, so long as he uses no physical violence, and does not have to stand challenge from you, for he is technically the victor."

"Then what am I to do?"

"That will rest with Sheb Takkor. As Borgen Takkor, you are, of course, son of Sheb, the Rad of Takkor. If he were to die, your name would become Sheb. As it is, you are the Zorad of Takkor. Zorad, in your language, might be translated viscount, and Rad, earl. The titles, of course, no longer have meaning, except that they denote noble blood, as the Swarm has changed all that."

"The Swarm?"

Lal Vak nodded.

"I can think of no other English equivalent for our word Kamud. The Kamud is the new order of government which took control of Xancibar about ten Martian years, or nearly nineteen Earth years ago. At that time, like other Martian vilets, or empires, of the present day, we had a Vil, or emperor. Although his office was hereditary, he could be deposed at any time by the will of the people, and a new Vil elected.

"For the most part, our people were satisfied. But there suddenly rose into power a man named Irintz Tel. He taught that an ideal community could be attained by imitating the communal life of the black bees. Under his system the individuals exist for the benefit of the community, not the community for the benefit of the individuals.

"Irintz Tel did not gather many followers, but those who flocked to his banner were vociferous and vindictive. At length, they decided to establish their form of government by force. Hearing this, Miradon, our Vil, abdicated rather than see his people involved in a civil war. He could have crushed the upstart, of course, but many lives would have been lost, and he preferred the more peaceful way.

"As soon as Miradon Vil was gone, Irintz Tel and his henchmen seized the reins of government in Dukor, the capital of Xancibar. After considerable fighting, he established the Kamud, which now owns all land, buildings, waterways, mines and commercial enterprises within our borders. He promised us annual elections, but once he was firmly established as Dixtar of Xancibar, this promise was repudiated. Theoretically, like all other citizens, Irintz Tel owns nothing except his personal belongings. But actually, he owns and controls all of Xancibar in the name of the Kamud, and has the absolute power of life and death over every citizen."

"What do people think of this arrangement?" asked Thorne. "Do they submit to such tyranny?"

"They have no choice," replied Lal Vak. "Irintz Tel rules with an iron hand. His spies are everywhere. And those detected speaking against his regime are quickly done away with.

"Some are executed, charged with some trumped-up offense, usually treason to the Kamud. Men in high places are often challenged and slain by Irintz Tel's hired swordsmen. Others are sent to the mines, which means that they will not live long. I will leave you, now. You must sleep."

"My wounds—I had forgotten them." Thorne raised his hand to his face where the sword of Sel Han had slashed him. He felt no soreness, only a porous pumicelike protrusion traveling the length of the gash. The wound in his side was covered with a similar substance.

"I had them dressed as soon as you were brought here," said the scientist. "They should not pain you, now."

"They don't. And what a strange dressing."

"It is rjembal, a flexible aromatic gum which is antiseptic, protects the wound from infection, and is porous enough to absorb seepage. Wounds closed with this gum usually heal quickly, painlessly, and without leaving scars.

"I go now. Sleep well, and to-morrow I will come to give you your first lesson in our language."

Early the next morning Thorne was awakened. He saw the white-haired Lal Vak smiling down at him. Behind him stood an orderly, who carried a large bowl which he placed on a tripod beside the bed. The orderly saluted and withdrew.

The bowl was divided into sections like a scooped-out grapefruit. In one section reposed several slices of grilled food. In another was a whole raw fruit, purple in color, and cubical in shape. In the third was a hollow cube containing an aromatic pink beverage.

Thorne sampled one of the grilled slices. The flavor baffled him, as it did not appear to be either flesh or vegetable. Having finished the strange grilled food, he tasted the pink beverage. It was slightly bitter and about as acid as a ripe orange. A sip sent an instant glow through his veins.

"What's this stuff?" he asked.

"Pulcho. A single cup is stimulating, but many are intoxicating."

Thorne finished the beverage, and Lal Vak instantly set about teaching him the things he must know in order to establish himself as Borgen Takkor.

Although Thorne's wounds healed in a few days, Lal Vak used them as a pretense to keep him in his room for about twenty. The Earthman learned the language quickly, for stored in the braincells of the Martian body which had become his were the recollections of all the sounds and their meanings.

One day an orderly came to announce that there was a man below calling himself Yirl Du, who asked to see Sheb Takkor.

"Let him come up," said Lal Vak. When the orderly had gone out he said to Thorne: "You heard what he said? He asked for Sheb Takkor."

"Yes. What does it mean?"

"It means that Sheb Takkor, father of Borgen Takkor, is dead. Hence, you are Sheb Takkor. This is one of the Takkor retainers who knows you, so call him by name when he appears before us."

A moment later, a short, stocky man entered the room. His features were coarse, but kindly. He raised one huge hand in salute, saying: "I shield my eyes, my lord Sheb, Rad of Takkor."

Thorne smiled and returned his salute. "Greetings, Yirl Du. This is my instructor, Lal Vak."

"I shield my eyes, excellency."

"You forget that under the Kamud all men are equal," said Lal Vak, returning his salute, "and one man no longer says to another: 'I shield my eyes,' 'my lord,' or 'excellency.'"

"I do not forget that I am hereditary Jen of the Takkor Free Swordsmen, nor that Sheb Takkor is my liege. From our isolated position, we of Takkor know little of the Kamud. We have submitted to it because our Rad, emulating Miradon Vil, saw fit to do so. So long as Takkor Rad rules us, though he is only the agent of the Kamud, we are content, and life goes on much as usual."

"You have come to escort your new Rad back to Takkor, I presume."

"That is my purpose, excellency."

"Then suppose you see about the gawrs while we make ready for the journey. I will accompany your Rad, and spend a few days with him."

"I go, excellency." Yirl Du saluted and withdrew.

"Strange," said Thorne, when he had gone. "He said nothing about the death of Sheb Takkor, the elder."

"His words conveyed the tidings," said Lal Vak. "A dead man's friends or relatives must not speak of him nor of his death until his ashes have been ceremonially scattered."

"When will that take place?"

"Upon your arrival. As his son and successor, you should be present at the ceremony. When it is completed, you may talk as freely as you like."

While they were talking both men had belted on their weapons and adjusted their head-cloaks. They descended to the courtyard and crossed to the lagoon, where Yirl Du waited with three gawrs attended by orderlies.

Lal Vak edged close to him. "Watch Yirl Du and me, and set your course as we do," he whispered. "You will be supposed to lead but as you don't know the way you will have to depend on one or the other of us for guidance."

In a few moments all was in readiness. The three ungainly mounts trotted forward, spread their membranous wings and took to the air.

By glancing right and left at his two companions, Thorne was easily able to gauge their course, and steer his bird-beast accordingly. They set out in a direction which he judged was due west.

Then, far ahead, Thorne saw a straight, high wall which stretched as far as he could see to the north and south. It was constructed of black stone, and at intervals of about a half mile towers built from the same material projected above it. The aqueduct which they were following led straight up to and entered this wall. As they drew near it, armed men became visible, patrolling the battlements.

Soon Thorne was able to catch a glimpse of what lay beyond the wall. First there was the glint of water in a broad canal, then the rich green of luxuriant vegetation, dotted here and there with the gleam of cylindrical crystal dwellings, and sloping in a series of terraces to a much wider canal than the first. Beyond this in the dim distance another series of terraces ascended to another elevated canal as high as the first, flanked by a wall like the one over which they were flying.

Beyond the second wall they encountered desert once more, and for several hours continued their flight toward the west. Then the contour of the ground beneath them changed abruptly. It was as if they were on the shore of a vast ocean from which the water had suddenly evaporated. First they passed over rugged cliffs, than a gently sloping beach strewn with sand and boulders. This presently dipped sharply to what was now a marshy lowland, a vast expanse of shallow water dotted and streaked with patches of green vegetation.

So absorbed was Thorne that he did not notice the menace that had crept silently up behind him. A shout from Lal Vak and a backward gesture caused him to turn in time to see a cloaked and masked warrior mounted on a swiftly flying gawr in the act of hurling a javelin at him. Behind his assailant he caught a fleeting glimpse of four more riders. He dodged just in time to avoid the barbed weapon. As it whizzed past him he whirled his gawr, then seized one of his own javelins and hurled it at his attacker.

The rider avoided Thorne's shaft with ease, and in a moment more was above him with drawn sword. Thorne whipped out his own weapon, parried a vicious head-cut, and countered with a swift slash at the neck of his assailant. The blow fell true, nearly severing the fellow's head from his body.

In the meantime, Lal Vak and Yirl Du were engaged in a lively conflict. Thorne saw the powerful Jen of the Free Swordsmen hurl a javelin with such force that it passed completely through the body of his nearest enemy. Lal Vak was fighting a sword duel with another of the attackers. The two who remained each sought a single encounter, one with Yirl Du and the other with Thorne.

The Earthman's new assailant hurled a javelin which fell short. He reached for another, and drew it back for a throw just as Thorne hurled his weapon mightily. The fellow tried to throw and dodge at the same time. He ducked low, but not low enough. Thorne's javelin struck him in the eye. His own weapon flew wide of the mark, but struck a wingjoint of the Earthman's mount.

A moment later Thorne found himself out of the saddle dangling by his safety chains, while his crippled gawr, fluttering futilely with its uninjured wing, turned over and over in the air as they hurtled swiftly toward the marsh, two thousand feet below.

CHAPTER 4

As his bird-beast turned over and over with him in the air, Thorne, swinging at the ends of his safety chains, saw that they were falling toward a small lake in the midst of the marsh with fearful velocity. As they neared the water the crippled gawr made valiant efforts to right itself, and managed to change the last few hundred feet to a glide and a dive.

They struck the water with an impact that almost robbed Thorne of consciousness. Dimly aware that he was being dragged down far below the surface of the lake, he held his breath, unhooked his safety chains, unfastened his belt and let his weapons sink. Then he fought his way swiftly to the top.

For some time the Earthman was too busy getting his breath to take note of his surroundings. Then he looked around for his mount, and saw it swimming directly away from him. Although the gawr was moving at a speed which he could not possibly hope to equal, he was about to set out in futile pursuit when a huge and terrible reptilian head suddenly reared itself between them, a scaly, silver gray head balanced on a thin, spiny neck. The monster looked first at the retreating gawr, then at the man, and began gliding swiftly toward him.

It was manifest from the start that he could not hope to outstrip his fearful aquatic enemy. As he forged ahead he glanced back from time to time, and saw that the monster was swiftly gaining on him.

With the shore but two hundred feet distant, he felt his last ounce of strength ebbing. Then just ahead of him he noticed a tiny ripple in the water, and there emerged a pair of jaws like those of a crocodile, but larger than those of any crocodile he had ever seen or heard of. There followed a broad, flat head, and thick neck, both covered with glossy fur, the head black, the neck ringed with a bright yellow band.

Hemmed thus between the two aquatic monsters, he plunged beneath the surface and dived under the oncoming beast, remaining under water until compelled to return to the surface for air.

When he had shaken the water out of his eyes, Thorne saw that the two monsters had met, and were engaged in a terrific struggle. The silver-gray scales of the one which had been following him flashed in the sun as it endeavored to shake off its smaller adversary which had seized it by the lower lip.

Suddenly it reared its head until the black-furred creature was drawn completely out of the water, and he saw that the latter was a web-footed animal about as large as a full-grown terrestrial lion, with short legs and a leathery, paddle-shaped tail which was edged with sharp spines. With the exception of the tail and claws, the body was covered with fur.

Thorne expected to see the smaller creature instantly slain. Instead, with a speed his eye could scarcely follow, it avoided the lunge of that terrible head, and turning, seized the slender, stalklike neck of its adversary in its own relatively large jaws. One powerful crunch, and the battle was over.

So absorbed had he been in this strange battle that Thorne had momentarily forgotten the peril that menaced him. Now, as the victor turned from the carcass of its vanquished enemy and swam straight toward him, he struck out for the shore, essaying the fast overhand stroke he had previously used on the surface, but his weary muscles had reached the limit of their endurance. Better death by drowning than in those horrible jaws. He filled his lungs and dived. At a depth of about fifteen feet he found a large water plant to which he clung with his last remaining strength.

But it seemed he was not even to be given his choice of deaths. Suddenly he became aware of a dark object in the green water above him. Then a huge pair of jaws closed around his waist, and with a deft twist, broke his hold on the water plant. A moment later he was lifted clear of the water.

The creature was carrying him swiftly toward the shore. He guessed that the monster was taking him to its lair, but on looking up, saw that it was heading directly toward the mouth of a narrow bayou. There, to his astonishment, he saw a small, flat boat, and standing in the boat a slender girl, who cried, "Good old Tezzu. Careful! Hold him gently."

Thorne's astonishment increased, for it was obvious that the girl was talking to the creature that carried him. Moreover, he assumed from her speech that she had sent this monster out to save his life.

The stern of the little craft sloped toward the water, and it was to this that the animal brought him. The girl seized a leg and an arm, and her efficient beast placed its snout beneath his body and rolled him into the boat.

Thorne essayed to sit up, but fell back weakly. Dimly, as through a haze, he saw the girl toss a rope to the beast, then felt the tug as the boat was towed ahead. The girl sat down, raised his head from the bottom of the boat and propped it in her lap.

"Who—who are you?" he asked.

She seemed surprised. "You do not know me?"

He stared hard. "I can scarcely see you. That haze . . ."

"Don't try. Close your eyes and try to sleep. Later we will talk."

It was easy for Thorne to obey her. It was good to lie there and relax with that gentle hand on his forehead.

Presently, opening his eyes, he saw that they were gliding through a narrow channel in the marsh. Trees hung over the water, their branches so interlaced and festooned with moss and lianas that only occasional shafts of sunlight penetrated to the surface.

Thorne glanced up at the girl. By any standard she was unquestionably beautiful, with her slightly tip-tilted nose, her glossy black hair, and her dark brown eyes shaded by long curling lashes. Though she was small and slender she was undoubtedly athletic. Her sole articles of apparel were a narrow band of soft leather which incased her small, firm breasts, a cincture of the same material about her smooth, tanned thighs, and the belt from which her sword, dagger and mace were suspended.

It was when he caught a glimpse of the clear sky through a rift in the branches that Thorne suddenly thought of Lal Vak and Yirl Du. He sat up abruptly.

"What's wrong?" the girl asked.

"I must go back at once."

The girl looked puzzled. "Back? How? Where? What do you mean?"

"Back to the lake where I left my friends fighting. If they survived they will be searching for me."

She shook her head. "It is too late. As it is we will barely make shelter before sundown. Tomorrow, if you like, I will take you back."

"But tomorrow will be too late. They will think me dead."

"Then, Borgen, they will be the more pleasantly surprised when you return to Castle Takkor."

"Not Borgen, Sheb."

For a moment she regarded him with a look of shocked surprise. Then sudden tears swelled in her eyes. "Has the ceremony been performed?"

"No. I was on my way to attend it with Lal Vak and Yirl Du when we were attacked, and you rescued me."

"Oh."

Thorne now realized that she must have been very well acquainted with Sheb Takkor the elder, and that she undoubtedly knew far more about the man whose place he had taken than he did himself. He wondered what her relationship had been with Borgen Takkor.

Suddenly the girl seized a long, barbed spear which lay in the bottom of the boat, and lunged at something she saw in the rushes. Then, before Thorne could rise to help her, she drew a huge iridescent beetle about three feet long into the boat. Plunging the point of the spear into the planking to keep it from escaping, she then put an end to the impaled insect's struggles by splitting its armored head with her mace. This done, she turned to the Earthman with a smile.

"We will fare well this evening. Now I can prepare your favorite dish."

Thorne looked askance at the beetle and began to have misgivings as to what his favorite dish would be like.

At this moment the beast towing the boat ran up on a small island, dragging it after him onto a sloping beach that bore the marks of many landings.

"Enough, Tezzu," called the girl. The creature dropped the tow-rope and came cavorting down to the boat like an affectionate dog, to be petted.

"You may bring the anuba, Sheb," said the girl. "Tezzu will carry the javelins."

Thorne judged that the anuba was the beetle. He withdrew the point of the spear from the planking while the girl handed the sheaf of javelins to her beast, then shouldered the heavy insect and followed her up a narrow path that wound through the undergrowth.

After walking about two hundred feet they came to a small cylindrical hut, made from stout posts driven into the ground in a compact circle and chinked with clay. The flat roof was made from the same crude materials, and the circular door was a thick cross section of an immense log.

"Don't you remember this camp, Sheb?"

"I . . ." Thorne was trying to frame a reply when, to his astonishment, the door flew open. A slender, spidery arm shot out and seized the girl by the wrist, jerking her through the opening. Then the door slammed shut.

Almost at the same instant a net dropped over the Earthman, jerking him backward. As he struggled in its enveloping meshes, he saw Tezzu drop the sheaf of javelins and with a roar of rage dash straight at the door where she had disappeared.

CHAPTER 5

Thorne was still carrying the beetle over his shoulder, hanging on the long spear. He thrust upward with the spear. The beetle prevented it from slipping through the meshes, and with the long handle he was able to raise the net and pitch it back over his head.

Scarcely had he freed himself when he saw descending from the branches of the surrounding trees six grotesque specimens of humanity. Not one of them was more than five feet tall. Their skins were bright yellow in color, and their spindly arms and legs branched out from bodies that were almost globular. Their Mongoloid features were surmounted by queer pagoda-shaped helmets of yellow metal and their bodies were protected by armor.

As they converged on him, shouting wildly, they brandished long, slightly curved swords with blunt ends, small oval guards and hilts long enough to be grasped in both hands.

Thorne ran his nearest foe through with the long spear which still held the carcass of the anuba beetle. The barbed point stuck, leaving him weaponless for the instant. Then he leaped forward, seized the sword dropped by his fallen enemy, and came on guard in time to meet the attack of the next.

Swiftly parrying a lightning cut at his legs which would instantly have laid him at the mercy of his attackers, he countered with a sudden moulinet which sheared down through the left shoulder of his second adversary, inflicting a mortal wound.

The four that remained seemed taken aback by this display of the Earthman's swordplay, and now approached him more warily. They were closing in on him from all sides when Tezzu gave up his attempts to tear down the door of the hut and suddenly rushed to Thorne's assistance.

A leap, a crunch of those powerful jaws, and one foeman fell with his head crushed. At the same time Thorne's sword disemboweled another of his antagonists. With shrieks of terror, the two survivors turned and fled. But the beast, despite its short legs, pursued them with incredible swiftness. One went down with his head between those relentless jaws and the last, catching a liana, scampered up for a little way only to be pulled down and as swiftly dispatched.

Thorne now rushed to the door of the hut and flung himself against it, but it remained immovable. Inside he heard the sound of clashing blades. A moment later he heard the inner bolt slide back and the door was flung open.

He was about to spring through the opening when he saw the girl framed in the doorway, dagger in one hand and sword in the other, both dripping blood. Behind her, barely visible in the dim light of the interior, lay one dead and one dying foeman.

"Why—why, I thought . . ." stammered Thorne, lowering his point.

The girl smiled amusedly and stepped out of the hut. "So you believed these clumsy Ma Gongi had cut me down. Really, Sheb, I gave you credit for a better memory. Have you forgotten the many times Thaine's blade has bested yours?"

So her name is Thaine, mused Thorne. Aloud he said: "Your demonstration has been most convincing. Yet I have not lost my ambition to improve my swordsmanship, and I should be grateful for further instruction."

"No better time than now. Still, I have you at a disadvantage, since you hold an inferior weapon."

"It is a handicap which a man should accord a girl," Thorne replied.

"Not one *this* girl requires."

She sheathed her dagger and extended her blade. Thorne engaged it with his captured weapon which, though more heavy and clumsy, was somewhat similar to a saber.

He instantly found that he had to deal with the swiftest and most dexterous fencer he had ever encountered, and time after time he barely saved himself from being touched.

"It seems your stay at the military school has improved your swordsmanship," said the girl, cutting, thrusting, and parrying easily—almost effortlessly. "In the old days I would have touched you long ere this. Yet, you but prolong the inevitable."

"The inevitable," replied Thorne, "is sometimes perceptible only by deity. For instance, this"—beating sharply on her blade, then catching it on his with a rotary motion—"has often been known to end a conflict."

Wrenched from her grasp by his impetuous attack, her sword went spinning into the undergrowth.

Instead of taking her defeat badly, Thaine actually beamed. "You have developed into a real swordsman, old comrade! I am so glad I could almost kiss you."

"That," Thorne answered, recovering her weapon for her, "is a reward which should fire any man to supreme endeavor."

"It is evident that you have mastered courtly speech as well as fencing. And now I will prepare your favorite dish for you." She called the brute. "Here, Tezzu," indicating the bodies. "Take these away."

Thorne marveled at its intelligence, when it instantly took up one of the corpses.

"A smart beast, that," he said.

"He is the most intelligent of all my father's dalfs. That's why I always take him with me when I hunt."

While Tezzu carried the bodies away and dropped them into the stream, Thaine took her mace and chopped off the two thick hind legs of the beetle. From these, she lopped the thighs, and splitting the shells open, extracted two cylinders of white meat. With her dagger she sliced these into small, round steaks, piling them neatly on a broad leaf, then carried it into the hut.

Thorne followed her in. "May I help?"

"I'd like some water," she replied. "Fill the big jar, please." She indicated a large square jar which stood beside the mud fireplace over which she now bent, placing faggots on a small heap of charcoal.

Thorne picked up the jar, and from its great weight was convinced that it was gold. He also noticed that the figures on the sides were of exquisite workmanship.

When he returned with water from the stream, the interior of the hut had grown quite dark, but a shaft of moonlight lit up the lithe figure of the girl, kneeling before the fireplace. He went in and placed the jar beside her.

Having arranged the faggots to her satisfaction, she took a small bottle of sparkling powder from a pouch attached to her belt, and emptied a few grains on the wood. Then, dipping a cup into the jar, she poured part of its contents on the powder. Thorne was amazed to see the powder and the surrounding wood wherever the water had touched it burst into instant flame.

With the fire blazing merrily, the girl now dipped several cupfuls of water from the jar into a smaller container, dropped into it a handful of red berries taken from another jar, and set the mixture against the blaze. Then she arranged the steaks she had cut on a grill made from crossed metal rods.

Tezzu came in, his immense mouth full of faggots, which he dropped beside her. Then he touched her elbow with his nose. She turned and patted his head. "Good boy. Bring more."

Obediently the beast turned and trotted out into the moonlight.

By the time the steaks were broiled, Tezzu had brought in a considerable quantity of wood. After removing her broiler, Thaine threw more fuel on the coals. From the vessel into which she had put the red berries she now filled two cubical golden cups with a steaming pink liquid. Then, using a wide leaf for a platter, she piled it high with the grilled steaks, set two other bits of leaf on the floor for plates.

"Come, Sheb. The banquet is ready for the victors."

Thorne sat opposite her and took the steaming cup from her hand. He had guessed that the beverage it contained was pulcho, and a sip confirmed this. Then came the realization that the time had arrived for him to simulate a liking for his "favorite dish."

"It is a banquet fit for a mighty conqueror," he said, reaching for one of the grilled steaks. He bit out a portion and instantly recognized the flavor. It was the same as that of the broiled food which had been served him for his first breakfast on Mars.

He had noted a swift, curious glance on the part of Thaine, when she had seen him take up his steak in his hand. Now he saw that she used her dagger as a fork to convey a slice to her leaf-plate, and that she cut off a small piece which she raised to her mouth with her fingers.

Obviously he had made a Martian social error.

Suddenly the girl leaned forward. "Just who are you, masquerading as Sheb Takkor?"

For a moment Thorne was speechless with surprise. Then he replied, "Ever since I met you I have been wanting to tell you, but the consideration of a duty restrained me."

"A duty?"

"Yes. To friends who helped me."

"And now, am I not—another friend who has helped you?"

"Decidedly! Yet, I wonder if you will believe me. I can scarcely believe myself, that I am here."

"Don't be too sure that I would not believe. I *know*. You are—Hahr Ree Thorne, and you were born on the planet, Dhu Gong, which you call Earth."

"How did you know that?"

"Borgan told me what he was going to do," she replied. "I did not believe it possible, but now I know. You are so different. And you do not understand some of our Martian customs."

"For instance, my manner of eating? Pray tell me where I erred."

"Having a dagger, you would have waited for me to take the first morsel," she said. "Lacking it, you would wait for me to hand you mine, then use it as I used it."

"I have been a boor."

"Not at all. One cannot be expected to know the customs of a new world without some instruction."

When both had eaten all they wanted, the remainder was tossed to the waiting dalf. Then the girl rose, closed and bolted the door, and selecting two large furs from a pile against the wall, gave one to the Earthman and spread the other on the floor before the fire.

"It is time for sleep," she said. Then, without another word, she lay down on the fur and drawing its folds about her, closed her eyes.

As he spread his fur and rolled himself therein, he again mentally compared his former fianceé to the girl who slept calmly there beside him, and the comparison was overwhelmingly favorable to Thaine.

CHAPTER 6

Thorne was awakened by a touch on his brow. He looked up into the eyes of Thaine.

"We must begin our journey if you would make Castle Takkor by midday," she said.

He threw off his fur and stood up. "I'm ready," he announced.

"First we will eat," she told him.

When they had finished, the girl began packing the utensils and furs together. Thorne helped her to make two large bundles of them, which Tezzu carried down to the boat.

"The Ma Gongi have discovered this camp," she told him, "so it must be abandoned forever."

"But where will you go?"

"I have many better places hidden in the marsh," she replied. "This was merely an outpost."

They gathered up the weapons and went outside. Then the girl poured a small quantity of the sparkling firepowder against the door jamb and dashed a cup of water over it. The logs instantly burst into flame, and when they reached the boat, Thorne, looking back, saw that a thick column of smoke was mounting skyward.

The morning sun was, by this time, halfway to the zenith. Most of the ice had melted in the stream. He noted, also, that many of the leaves where the sun had not yet penetrated were coated with hoar-frost that was rapidly melting into glistening beads of dew.

When they had their cargo stowed, and had taken their places, the girl tossed the tow-rope to Tezzu and indicated with a wave of her hand the direction she wished to go. He plunged into the stream and set off rapidly.

They had only gone a short distance when Thaine cried: "Look there! The boat of the Ma Gongi!"

Thorne looked in the direction she was pointing, and saw a flat boat drawn up on the bank.

"Stop, Tezzu," ordered the girl. Then: "Bring us that boat."

The beast dropped the tow-rope, and swimming in to shore, dragged the boat into the water. Then, seizing its rope he towed it out to where they drifted. Save for a bundle, wrapped in a silky covering, and a half dozen spade-shaped paddles, the boat was empty. Thorne was about to reach for the bundle when the girl checked him. "That is their food," she said, "but it will do us no good." Then she called to the dalf. "Sink it, Tezzu."

Instantly, the beast seized the side of the boat in his huge and powerful jaws. A single crunch crushed the heavy planking as if it had been an eggshell. Tezzu backed away, spitting out the slivers, and the boat filled and sank. Then he took up the tow-rope once more and proceeded on his way.

"I'm curious to know more about these Ma Gongi," Thorne said, "and this strange, forbidden food they eat."

"Legend has it that they did not originate on this planet, but, as their name indicates, on Ma Gong, the planet which now circles your world, but which revolved in an orbit of its own, between your world and mine.

"We know that there was once a mighty civilization here on Mars, and that it was destroyed in terrible catastrophe. It is just within my lifetime that our scientists have begun to uncover old records—fragments of records—and piece them together. We know now that the catastrophe came about through an interplanetary war, fought with weapons almost beyond imagination. The Ma Gongi had a cold, energy-decreasing interrotating green ray. Any substance touched by this ray would contract to less than one-hundredth of its normal size, with a corresponding increase in density.

"The toughest metals, under this ray, would become as brittle as glass and more dense than lead. But there is a limit to the contractile endurance of all matter, and once that limit is reached the atoms, which have been pushed in upon themselves, explode and disintegrate."

"And did your scientists have this weapon, too?"

"We do not know. Ma Gong was shifted from its orbit to where it now lies, and it is believed that our two moons came from some aspect of the struggle, too. We know that Ma Gong itself was rendered uninhabitable and that our own world was greatly damaged. Some of the Ma Gong must have been stranded on Mars when the war ended in mutual ruin."

"Remarkable," said Thorne.

"The Ma Gong are our enemies still," she went on. "I have often seen them. But other than them, my father, the Takkors and Yirl Du, I have seen no one except the Little People."

"The Little People?"

"They are the friends and allies of my father and me. But the Ma Gongi eat them. That is why I told you the food you saw in their boat would be useless to us. It was the flesh of one of the Little People."

"But who is your father, and why do you two live here in the marsh, instead of among your own kind?"

"My father's name is Miradon. Once he was Vil of Xancibar. There was a revolt, led by a man named Irintz Tel. In order to avoid the calamity of a civil war, my father abdicated, and fled here with me, aided by Sheb Takkor and the Jen of his Free Swordsmen, Yirl Du. These two, alone, knew where we had gone. Here my father reared me. We have been constantly harassed by the minions of Irintz Tel, and lately by the Ma Gongi as well. For three days, now, my father has been absent, and I fear that he has either been slain or captured."

"Then let me help you search for him."

"No, you must return to the castle for the ceremony, or if it has been performed, to assume your rightful place. After that, come if you will, and bring Yirl Du, but no other. He will know how to find me."

For some time now they had been gliding tortuously through a chain of shallow pools connected by narrow, half-hidden channels. Now there suddenly came into view a broad lake which mirrored at its far side an immense castle of odd and beautiful design, the translucent masonry of which gleamed like burnished gold in the sunshine. A short distance from it, and also bordering the lake, rose the cylindrical, flat-roofed buildings of a teeming city. A large number of gawrs were swimming on the lake and many boats were moored at the docks.

"This is as far as I dare take you," said Thaine. "Yonder, beside Takkor City, lies Castle Takkor. You can reach it by following the lake shore to the right."

Thorne rose and stretched his limbs, cramped from long sitting. Then he bent, took her hand and pressed it to his lips. She seemed startled. "Why did you do that?"

"On my world it is homage one pays to a lady at greeting or parting."

"What a queer custom," she exclaimed. "But I rather like it."

Thorne smiled. "Farewell, little comrade," he said. "Again I thank you for my life, for my entertainment, and most of all for the pleasure of having been with you. As soon as I have attended to my duties at Castle Takkor I will return with Yirl Du, and together we will search for your father."

"Deza go with you, and keep you safe from harm. I will be waiting for you and be expecting you."

Resolutely he turned away and stepped over the side of the boat. He stood there in the shallows watching until the little craft vanished around a bend in the narrow channel.

Keeping to the margin of the lake, he eventually reached the docks without mishap. Most of its occupants were fishermen, and those whose duty it was to tend the gawrs. But he saw a number of warriors standing about, and was surprised to note that they wore the insigne of the Kamud. As he made his way toward the gate which led to the castle, two of them stopped him.

"Where are you going, fellow?" asked one. "And whom do you seek?"

"I go to Castle Takkor," replied Thorne, "and whom I seek is my own affair."

"None of your insolence," growled the other soldier. "When you speak to us, you address the Kamud."

"When you speak to me, you address the Rad of Takkor," Thorne retorted. "Out of my way!"

"Sharp words call for sharper weapons," said one soldier. "Throw down your sword, or you die."

For answer, Thorne came on guard. Then both men attacked him simultaneously. While he could easily have bested either of them alone, he was sorely put to it to keep the two blades from reaching him. Presently, however, one soldier left his head unguarded. Instantly Thorne's sword sheared down through his brain.

For a moment Thorne's blade was held by that cloven skull; then, with a desperate jerk, he freed his weapon and easily disarmed his remaining foe, who instantly turned and fled, bawling lustily for help.

At this juncture a big man, resplendent in purple head-cloak and gold trappings came down the steps that led from the castle gate, followed by a group of lesser officers and a file of soldiers.

"What's all this?" he roared. "Must I have brawling on the first day of my arrival?"

Thorne looked up and recognized Sel Han, against whom the Martian code of honor now forbade him to raise his weapon. Instantly he was surrounded by warriors.

"This impostor who murdered Tir Hanus claims to be the Rad of Takkor," cried the disarmed soldier, "yet we scattered his ashes this morning."

Sel Han looked at Thorne. "You have heard the words of this soldier," he said. "Do you still cling to your preposterous claim?"

"You scattered the ashes of Sheb Takkor the elder. Not mine."

"We also scattered the ashes of Sheb Takkor the younger," replied Sel Han. "His two comrades, Lal Vak and Yirl Du, reported his death yesterday. He fell from his gawr, a distance that would crush him to pulp, therefore it is impossible that he could be alive to-day. Word was sent to Irintz Tel, and the Dixtar appointed me to administer the estates in the name of the Kamud. As we could not obtain the body of the unfortunate Rad, who fell in the marsh, we performed the ceremony by proxy, using ashes of the aromatic sebolis tree, as is the custom."

"Am I to understand from this that I am officially dead?"

"You are to understand from this that the Rad of Takkor is dead. Also, the title has been abolished. Hereafter the estates will be strictly administered in accordance with the rules of the Kamud. As to who *you* are, that has not been established. You came to us armed with a sword of the Ma Gongi, and impersonating the dead Rad. When questioned, you slew a soldier of the Kamud. Under the circumstances, it is my duty to arrest you and send you to Dukor for trial."

"You make yourself absurd by claiming that I am dead."

"Yield your sword, or you soon will be," promised Sel Han. "Seize him, men. If he resists, cut him down."

Seeing that resistance against such odds would be foolhardy, Thorne handed his sword to the nearest soldier. Another removed the medal that hung around his neck. Then he was led away by two warriors. They took him into the castle courtyard, where one of the large flying machines he had previously seen stood ready to take off. He was hustled up a set of metal steps and into the body of the craft, where a score of prisoners, guarded by two armed warriors, were chained by metal collars to rings in the wall. A collar was snapped around his neck.

CHAPTER 7

Thorne's journey was not a pleasant one.

Like the other prisoners, the Earthman was compelled by the lurching of the ship to keep a tight hold on his chain with both hands, and thus ease the sudden jerks on his metal collar that would otherwise have choked him. Consequently he was thankful when, after more than an hour of riding, he sensed that the ship was settling, then felt the shock of its landing.

A moment later the door was flung open by one of the guards and the folding metal steps were dropped. The other guard opened the prisoners' collars, one by one, with a key he carried, and ordered them out the door. Thorne, the third to step out, saw that they were in a large walled inclosure in which were several hundred men, some lying on the ground or lolling against the walls, others pacing up and down, or conversing in small groups.

At the bottom of the ladder an officer waited, attended by two soldiers, one of whom carried a bundle of metal rings. The officer was scanning a paper which the first guard had handed him, evidently a list of prisoners. As each man descended, he asked his name and checked the list. Then the soldier with the rings fastened one about the prisoner's neck and called the number engraved on the ring.

When it came Thorne's turn, the officer asked "Your name?"

"Sheb Takkor."

"What is your *real* name?"

"I have told you," Thorne replied.

The officer shrugged. "It will be so entered, though the report says you are an impostor. But that will be a matter for the judges."

He signed to the soldier with the rings, who clamped one about Thorne's neck and called the number. The soldier gave him a push that sent him stumbling into the yard, and the officer began questioning the next prisoner.

Recovering his balance, the Earthman walked morosely to the center of the inclosure. A glance about him at the high walls patrolled by heavily armed warriors convinced him that escape would be next to impossible. Beyond the walls on all sides he saw the upper stories of many cylindrical, flat-topped buildings. He concluded, from this, that he must be in the midst of a large and populous city.

Having completed his inspection of his surroundings, he found a place where he could sit and lean against the wall, and think. His case, it seemed, was well nigh hopeless.

As he sat there, Thorne noticed coming toward him a man with a huge chest and shoulders, long, ape-like arms, and abnormally short legs. With a start of surprise, he recognized the Jen of the Takkor Free Swordsmen.

"Yirl Du!" he exclaimed.

"I shield my eyes, my lord Sheb," said the Jen, "and thank Deza that you still live. Lal Vak and I thought you dead, and so reported at the castle."

"What brought you here?"

"My arrest came so suddenly," replied Yirl Du, "that I am still bewildered. I was sent here this morning charged with inciting the Free Swordsmen to revolt against the Kamud."

"And should they be able to prove such an absurd charge, what will be the penalty?"

"Death. In what form, I know not. The seven dread judges of the Kamud deal out death in many fiendish forms. *Their* most merciful sentence is the stroke of the sword. Then there are the mines. A sentence to the mines is really a death sentence, for few men survive their rigors for many days."

"And what sentence do you think they will pass on me?"

"Of what is my lord accused?"

"I slew a soldier of the Kamud who attacked me. Also I am to be charged with impersonating myself, because I am officially dead. Furthermore, there is some suspicion attached to me, which I cannot fathom, because I was wearing a sword of the Ma Gongi."

Yirl Du groaned. "You might have obtained an acquittal on the first two counts, but I fear this latter spells your doom. Deza grant that I, Yirl Du, Jen of the Takkor Free Swordsmen, may never live to see my Rad die in such dishonor."

"But why should a sword of the Ma Gongi constitute such damning evidence?"

"It is believed," the Jen told him, "that the Ma Gongi are plotting to overthrow the Old Race—to conquer all Mars. There have been persistent rumors that one of the archaeologists has unearthed the secret of the deadly green ray.

"Although we would not dare to publicly voice our suspicions, there are also those among us who suspect Sel Han of plotting with the Ma Gongi. He has so wormed himself into the good graces of Irintz Tel that a word breathed against him would bring instant disaster to almost any man.

"It is said, also, that the Dixtar intends to wed his daughter Neva to this arch-plotter, and that through marriage with her he will eventually succeed to the dixtarship of Xancibar."

"It is obvious that this Sel Han is indeed a menace to all mankind," said Thorne.

"I have a further suspicion," went on Yirl Du, "born when you told me of the disappearance of Thaine's father. Miradon Vil, a prisoner, would be of inestimable value to Sel Han in his plans for conquest. With the Vil in his power, he could hold the royalists as well as the Kamud in the hollow of his hand. A colony of the Ma Gongi inhabits a part of the marsh not far from Miradon's hiding place. And it may well be that they, at the instigation of their ally, Sel Han, have captured the Vil and are holding him in some secret hiding place."

Thorne was about to reply when a shrill whistle sounded.

"Come," said Yirl Du. "That was the food signal, and the last ten men in line always go hungry."

They both sprang forward to where a long line of prisoners was forming before a table containing some small cakes and cubical cups of pulcho, presided over by four orderlies who had already begun to hand a cup and cake to each man, under the watchful eyes of the half dozen soldiers with drawn swords. Thorne saw, on looking back, that there were exactly ten men behind him.

Shuffling forward with the others, he was surprised to feel a powerful hand clapped on his shoulder. Before he could offer the slightest resistance, he was spun around, and found himself walking behind the man who had previously been just behind him.

Thorne seized the brawny arm of the man who had supplanted him and swung him around. He had a swift glimpse of a glaring face, crisscrossed by a frightful pattern of livid scars. Then he drove a smashing right hook to the point of the jaw that sent the man reeling backward to the ground.

In a moment the fellow began to recover from the effect of the blow, and sat up looking about him. Suddenly spying Thorne, he shook his bullet head, then lurched to his feet, and charged.

Thorne turned at the sound, and prepared to meet the shock of the attack. With both arms outstretched, the man attempted to seize him, but a blow in the solar plexus followed by a swift uppercut downed him again.

Instantly, Yirl Du, who had drained his pulcho cup and was munching his cake, tossed the food aside and sprang forward. "Let me handle this beast, my lord. He is Sur Det, the most dreaded duelist and assassin in all Xancibar."

By this time most of the prisoners were crowding around, talking excitedly while they munched and drank.

"Swords!" some one shouted. "Bring swords!"

A group of guards came shouldering through the crowd, making way for a handsome fellow who wore the purple cloak of an officer of the Kamud.

"What's this, Sur Det?" he asked. "Fighting again?"

Sur Det scrambled to his feet and saluted. "That fellow," he said, glaring at Thorne, "has twice assaulted me. I ask settlement by swords, which is my right according to the prison rules."

The officer turned to Thorne. "What say you? Do you, also, desire settlement by swords?"

"I do," the Earthman replied.

"Obviously you have not heard of the prowess of Sur Det," said the officer. "But on your own head be your decision. Give them swords, soldiers, and let a circle be formed."

CHAPTER 8

As he stood, sword in hand, before his scar-faced opponent, Thorne was hooted by the multitude. A few who had heard of his supposed cowardice in his duel with Sel Han, quickly spread the word.

"Don't puncture him too quickly, Sur Det," called one.

"Slice him neatly," shouted another. "Let us see how good a meat-cutter you are."

They saluted. Then Sur Det, instead of engaging Thorne's extended blade as was the custom, avoided it and attacked with a swift lunge. The Earthman was barely able to save his life by side-stepping the point.

But Sur Det had left himself completely uncovered. Thorne now had but to extend his point, and the duel would be over. He started the lunge, but instead of sending the blade home, with a deft motion of his wrist cut the Martian symbol for the digraph "sh," a perpendicular line with a short hook to the right at the bottom.

A murmur of surprise went up from the crowd at this, for they knew he had his enemy at his mercy. Both men recovered. After a bewildering swirl of blades Thorne found a second opening, and instead of piercing the heart of his antagonist, slashed two horizontal lines beside the first character, the Martian symbol for "e."

"He's writing his name on the killer!" cried a spectator.

"Write him a love letter!" yelled another.

"Draw us a picture!" howled a third.

When Thorne marked his chest for the second time without inflicting death, Sur Det began to realize that this strange young swordsman from Takkor, whom he had expected to slay so easily, was only playing with him. With that realization, he went berserk with fear.

Thorne met the attack that followed, merely parrying and sidestepping until he felt his opponent's wrist begin to weaken. Then with a graceful, easy lunge, he carved the last symbol of his Martian name on that barrel chest, the "b."

At this, the crowd roared its applause, but Thorne had not yet finished; he suddenly beat down his opponent's blade with a sharp blow close to the guard—then caught it, bound it with his own blade, and with a sudden twirling wrench, sent it flashing away over the heads of the spectators.

For a moment the bewildered killer stood looking in blank amazement. Then, with a shriek of terror, he turned and fled. Thorne followed closely at his heels, spanking him soundly—with the flat of his sword until the creature fell down and begged for mercy.

"Puncture the boastful bladder and let out the wind," a spectator shouted.

"Carve your name on his craven heart," cried another.

Satisfied that the killer had been sufficiently humbled, Thorne returned to where the young officer stood, and saluted.

"I am obliged to you for this diversion," he said, tendering the sword.

"The obligation is entirely ours," replied the officer, taking the weapon. "I have never seen such marvelous sword-work, nor, I am convinced, has any one in all Xancibar. And now, to the victor goes the reward. Ho, orderly!"

At this a man came up, bearing a steaming jar of pulcho, a cup and a great platter heaped with cakes.

"What's this?" asked Thorne.

"The prize," smiled the officer, taking the jar from the orderly and filling a cup which he handed to the Earthman. "I regret that so distinguished a swordsman and so gallant a gentleman may not be more suitably rewarded. But this, after all, is a prison."

"To your long life," said Thorne, draining his cup. Then he turned to the orderly. "Distribute the cakes and the rest of the pulcho to the ten who were not served, including my defeated opponent."

At this added evidence of the generosity of their new champion, the multitude shouted its approbation. More than a half hour elapsed before Thorne was able to get away from his numerous admirers and sit alone once more with Yirl Du.

"That was a marvelous fight, my lord," said the Jen. "It will surely remove the stigma attached to your name by that unfortunate incident at the military school. The great pity of it is that it comes at a time when death by order of the Kamud is almost certain to be your lot."

"It will be certain enough if Sel Han has his way."

"We have many good reasons to kill that flat-nosed traitor," replied Yirl Du, "and there are two which I have not related to you. One is, that among the men who attacked us in the air I recognized one of his henchmen. So it was he who sent those assassins to slay us."

"What is the other?" asked Thorne.

"I have hesitated to tell you that one, as I would not give you needless pain on what may well be your last day of life. Know, then, that Sheb Takkor the elder was murdered. I was making my last round of the castle before retiring, to see if all was well, when I noticed him seated before the fireplace in his great swinging chair, hunched over in a most unnatural position. I called to him, but he made no response. I ran to his side, and saw that he was dead. A dagger had been driven into his back up to the hilt."

"And you think it was Sel Han who struck the blow?"

"More likely one of his hired assassins. He, and no one else, had much to gain by the death of our beloved Rad. And he alone profited by it."

"Perhaps there was an enemy with a grudge."

"That is not likely. The Rad never left Takkor except to hunt in the marshes or the desert, or to secretly do what he could for our deposed sovereign and his daughter. So he had no opportunity to make enemies in other than his own raddek. And I'll swear that there was not a man, woman or child among his people who did not love and revere him. Moreover, the dagger was of foreign make and delicate workmanship, not the plain sturdy kind our Takkor folk are wont to carry. I hid it in the castle, hoping that it might some day afford us proof of the identity of the assassin."

At this juncture two guards with drawn swords in their hands stopped before Thorne.

"Are you he who calls himself Sheb Takkor?" asked one.

"I am," Thorne replied.

"The Dixtar has sent for you. Come with us."

Thorne stood up, but as he did so Yirl Du flung himself between the Earthman and the guards. "Wait! Don't take him! Take me! I am Sheb Takkor!"

One of the guards laughed contemptuously. "Out of the way, O great oaf, ere I cut you down. My comrade and I sat on the wall and saw this man defeat Sur Det, the killer. Do you think you could pass for him? Moreover, have we not eyes to read the numbers on your collars?"

Yirl Du turned to Thorne. "I fear it is the end, my lord," he groaned. He saluted. "Farewell, my lord. Deza grant you life, yet if that be not His will, a brave death."

Thorne returned the salute. "Farewell, my friend," he answered.

The Earthman was led through a gate into what was obviously one of the streets of a large city. It was paved with a tough, resilient material of a reddish-brown color, and was thronged with people and strange vehicles of many descriptions. There was one thing, however, which the vehicles all had in common. They did not travel on wheels, but ran about on multiple sets of jointed metal legs shod with balls of the resilient reddish-brown substance. The smallest of these odd vehicles had only two pairs of legs, but some of the larger ones had so many that they reminded him of gigantic caterpillars, moving smoothly and swiftly along the thoroughfare.

In a moment an open vehicle with twelve pairs of legs drew up before the gate and stopped. There were three saddle-shaped seats with high backs, one in front and two side by side in the rear. A canopy overhead shaded the passengers. The front seat was occupied by a driver in military uniform. In one of the rear seats sat the Jen of the Prison Guards.

"The Dixtar has commanded that I bring you before him," he said. "Give me your word that you will not attempt to escape while in the custody of Kov Lutas, and I will spare you the ignominy of chains."

The Earthman thought for a moment. If he gave his word, once out of the custody of Kov Lutas, he could, with honor, make the attempt.

"I give my word that I will not try to escape while in your custody."

The Jen ordered the guards to remove Thorne's prison collar, and when this was done, dismissed them with a wave of his hand. "Get in," he invited.

Thorne climbed into the vacant saddle. The driver, who sat holding two levers that projected up through the floor at either side of his saddle, now slowly moved these forward. At this, the vehicle started silently and was soon moving through the traffic at a considerable speed.

Thorne saw that when the driver wished to turn to the right he advanced the left lever and drew back the right, and that he reversed the process to turn to the left. To increase the speed, he pushed both levers forward, and to decrease it drew them backward. When they were drawn back to a certain point, the vehicle came to a full stop.

Having satisfied his curiosity regarding the vehicle, Thorne turned his attention to the strange sights about him.

Noting the Earthman's interest in his surroundings, Kov Lutas said: "Apparently this is your first visit to Dukor. Perhaps you would like to have me explain some of the sights of the city."

"I should be grateful," Thorne replied.

"Dukor is divided into four equal quarters by the intersecting triple canals, Zeelan and Corvid. We are now in the northwest quarter of the city, and about to cross the Zeelan Canal into the northeast quarter, where the palace which formerly belonged to the Vil, but is now occupied by the Dixtar, is located."

"It must be a tremendous city."

"There are approximately five million people residing in each quarter," replied Kov Lutas, "or twenty million in all. Also, we have each day about ten million transients who come on commercial or state business, or simply to visit and to see the sights. Dukor is a fair-sized city as cities go. Of course it does not seem large in comparison with Raliad, capital city of Kalsivar, which commands the intersections of four great triple canals, for Raliad is said to have a population of a hundred million."

While he was speaking they came to the approach of a tremendous arched bridge, so long they could not see the farther end of it. In a moment they were out upon it, and Thorne was looking down upon the surface of the first of the three canals which collectively bore the name of Zeelan because they occupied the same huge trench. This canal swarmed with craft of many sizes and shapes, a large number of which were discharging freight into the dock warehouses which lined its banks.

The huge central canal at the bottom of the great trench, which caught the drainage from the two upper irrigating canals, was lined with bathers of all ages who wore no clothing whatever.

The canal passed, they entered a section of the city quite similar to the one they had just left. After a drive of about half an hour in this section, they drew up before an immense and magnificent edifice.

"The Palace," said Kov Lutas. "From this point we walk."

After getting down from the vehicle, they mounted a broad flight of steps which led to the vast and ornate portico. Here they were halted and questioned by guards, who readily admitted them when shown the order of the Dixtar which Kov Lutas carried. Then, after crossing an immense busy foyer and traversing a long hallway, they came before a large circular doorway, closed by two purple curtains in which was embroidered with gold thread, the coat of arms of the Dixtar of Xancibar. Here an officer examined the order carried by Kov Lutas.

"The Dixtar is expecting you," he said. Then he beckoned to one of the guards. "Announce Kov Lutas, Jen of the Guards of Prison Number 67," he said, "and a prisoner."

CHAPTER 9

When the curtain was drawn aside, Thorne followed Kov Lutas through the doorway, and found himself in the presence of Irintz Tel.

The Dixtar, his hands clasped behind him, was pacing to and fro on a plush-padded dais that fronted a luxuriously cushioned throne, which hung on four heavy golden chains depending from the ceiling. He was a small man, sparely built and quite bald. Thin-lipped, sharp-nosed and beady-eyed, his face bore the unmistakable stamp of the zealot and reformer.

Irintz Tel paced up and down for some time without taking the slightest notice of Kov Lutas and his prisoner.

After a lapse of some minutes, Irintz Tel paused midway in his pacing and, swinging on his heel, faced Kov Lutas.

"Well?" he demanded, in a high-pitched, squeaky voice.

Kov Lutas raised both hands in salute, holding them before his face. "I shield my eyes in the glory of your presence, O mighty Dixtar of Xancibar and Commander of the Kamud."

Thorne was astounded, for he had been told that under the Kamud all salutations of this sort had been abolished.

The Earthman suddenly noticed that Irintz Tel was looking sharply at him, evidently expecting him to follow the example of the Jen; but he kept his hands down.

"Who is this ill-mannered lout you have brought into our presence, Kov Lutas?" demanded the Dixtar.

"He is Sheb Takkor, whom I bring in accordance with the Dixtar's command," replied Kov Lutas.

"His manners are execrable," said Irintz Tel, "but they can be mended, and we hear that he is a good swordsman. It may be that we will find employment for him. We are both blessed and cursed with a beautiful daughter, as you are no doubt aware."

"I have heard of the great beauty of your excellency's daughter," replied Kov Lutas, cautiously.

"It is a fatal beauty that corrupts our most loyal followers and makes traitors of our staunchest patriots. And today we are constrained to part with two more of our best swordsmen. They were her guardsmen, but they chose to let their hearts rule their heads. For such a malady, where our daughter is concerned, we have a most effective form of surgery."

"What is that, excellency?"

"In order that the heart may no longer rule the head, we separate them. A bit drastic, we will admit, but it never fails to cure. We sent for you and this prisoner because we must replace the two excellent swordsmen. Our daughter, as you know, must be well guarded.

"We will first take the case of the prisoner, here. Word came to us today of his defeat of Sur Det, the killer, so we decided to personally examine into the charges against him. He is accused, we find, of impersonating the dead Rad of Takkor, of wearing a sword of the Ma Gongi, and of slaying a soldier of the Kamud, and as evidence there have come to us this Takkor family medal," lifting it from a small taboret beside the throne, "and this sword which he was alleged to have been wearing when captured. What say you to these charges, prisoner?"

"I could not impersonate the Rad of Takkor without impersonating myself," replied Thorne. "I was reported dead because my crippled gawr fell with me after I was attacked. But we fell into a small lake. After freeing myself from the safety chains and the weight of my weapons, I swam ashore. There I was attacked by a party of Ma Gongi, and after wresting the sword from one of them, beat off the others."

"We can well believe that. But why did you slay one of our soldiers?"

"Because he attacked me on my own doorstep. In answer to that charge I plead self-defense."

The Dixtar paced the dais for some time, chin on chest. Then he suddenly turned and looked at Thorne.

"We hereby declare you innocent and discharged of all liability on all three counts," he said brusquely.

"And as a recompense for the indignities which you have suffered, we raise you to the rank of Jen and appoint you night guard to our daughter Neva."

He turned to the Jen of the Prison Guards. "You also, my worthy Kov Lutas, we have decided to honor. You, henceforth, will guard our daughter by day."

The face of Kov Lutas went as suddenly pale as if a sentence of death had been passed on him.

Despite Kov Lutas's dismay, he managed to retain control of his features. "I am deeply grateful that our Dixtar has chosen to distinguish me by this honor."

Irintz Tel beckoned Thorne to him and handed him the medal. "Take back this badge of your ancient race and wear it with honor. We regret that we cannot return your title as well, but under the present social order there are no more rads. Nor can we make you our deputy, for upon hearing of your supposed death we immediately dispatched Sel Han to Takkor to represent us, as he knows our wishes and is high in our councils."

"The Dixtar is most generous," murmured Thorne.

Irintz Tel now called to the officer at the door. "Ho, Dir Hazef, conduct these two to the officers' quarters and see that they are suitably arrayed as palace Jens. On the way you will permit them to witness the fate which overtakes those who are unfaithful to their trust, and show them the Halls of Heads. Let a sword and dagger decked with the Takkor serpent be brought from the armory for the one who is weaponless, as he is entitled to carry them."

The two men saluted, and Dir Hazef conducted them to a small balcony which overlooked one of the inner courts. In the center of the court stood an officer. Dir Hazef signaled to him, and he, in turn, signaled to some one in a nearby doorway. A moment later there emerged two soldiers, driving before them two young officers

44

with their hands bound behind them. Following the soldiers came a tall fellow bearing a long, straight-bladed sword and accompanied by a boy who carried a basket.

The two prisoners were forced to kneel in the center of the courtyard. Then the tall man stepped behind them. Once, twice, his long blade flashed in the sunlight, and with each blow a head rolled to the pavement, to be garnered by the boy with the basket.

"Those two," said Dir Hazef, "were the guards of Neva, daughter of the Dixtar. They had the good taste but the bad judgment to fall in love with her and contend for her favors." He turned, and walking to a door behind them, opened it. "Enter."

Thorne stepped through the doorway, followed by Kov Lutas and their conductor.

"This," said Dir Hazef, "is the Hall of Heads, a monument to the Dixtar's justice and a warning to those who would betray him."

They were in a long, narrow room, lined with shelves on both sides clear to the high ceiling. On the shelves stood row after row of crystal jars. Each jar was filled with clear liquid, and in the liquid floated a severed human head. There were thousands of heads of young men and old; even heads of women and children.

Thorne tore his eyes away from the exhibit with a shudder, and turning, saw that Kov Lutas had already preceded him through the doorway.

After locking the door and leading them down another corridor, Dir Hazef conducted them through a room where a number of officers sat in swinging chairs, sipping pulcho and conversing, or playing gapun, a game which consisted of rolling little engraved pellets of gold or silver at numbered holes in a board, the highest number winning all the pellets risked. Although he had never before seen Martian money, Thorne recognized at once that these pellets must be the medium of exchange.

A number of apartments opened into this officers' club room, and into one of these Dir Hazef led them. "I'll leave you here to bathe and change. Vorz, your orderly, will bring your new uniforms and weapons. You, Kov Lutas, are to go on duty at once, and Sheb Takkor will relieve you at the time of the evening meal."

The apartment was plainly but comfortably furnished with a swinging bed and a swinging chair for each man, a wardrobe and an arms rack. In one corner was a metal box about eight feet in height, one side of which stood open. It was lined throughout with a gray metal resembling block tin, and this lining was perforated with many holes. Beside it was a rack on which hung a number of wisps of what looked like dry moss.

As soon as Dir Hazef was gone, Kov Lutas began removing his clothing and weapons. "I'll bathe now, if you don't mind," he said, "as I must go on duty first."

"Of course," replied Thorne. He was puzzled as he saw no sign of a tub or bathroom.

His curiosity was soon satisfied. Kov Lutas stepped into the square metal box in the corner and drew the side shut. Immediately there was the sound of rushing water, accompanied by much gurgling, blowing and gasping. A few moments later the side swung open, and the officer emerged, dripping and rubbing the water from his eyes. Then he reached for a bunch of the moss-like material and began briskly rubbing himself.

Thorne, who had meanwhile removed his clothing, now entered the box and drew the side shut. As he moved about, he accidentally trod on a round plate in the center of the metal floor. Instantly he was surrounded by a swirl of warm, scented water which came up to his chin. The water soon receded as suddenly as it had risen, and several jets opened overhead, deluging him with a fragrant creamy lather.

After about a minute of this there was a click as of some automatic mechanism, the jets ceased to spray, and the swirling water rose once more. While it rinsed off the lather this gradually grew cooler until it reached an almost icy temperature. Another click, and it drained away automatically. He opened the side, sputtering and gasping, and blindly reached for a bundle of drying material. As soon as he had the water out of his eyes he saw that an orderly had arrived with the new uniforms, and was helping Kov Lutas into his.

Thorne rubbed himself until his skin glowed warmly. Vorz, the orderly, then assisted him to don his new uniform and buckle on his weapons. His new sword and dagger hilts were fashioned like those he had found himself wearing on his first advent on Mars, but were of gold powdered with jewels instead of plain brass. And the eyes of the serpents were large rubies.

The orderly, after bustling in with a three-legged stand on which were a pot of pulcho and two cups, hurried out. Kov Lutas filled the cups, and handing one to Thorne raised the other. "May we die like brave soldiers."

Thorne joined him. "It is a strange toast. Why do you speak of death?"

"Because it is so near. To be appointed as guards to the Dixtar's daughter is equivalent to a death sentence."

"I don't see why," Thorne replied. "Certainly every man who guards her isn't going to be so foolish as to lose his head over her."

"To 'lose his head' is indeed an apt expression. More than a hundred have already lost their heads, even as those two we saw this afternoon. Neva is said to be a heartless flirt, bent on conquest. Her father wants her to marry Sel Han, but she will not have him. And it is said that she flirts with every eligible male who crosses her path, just to spite them both. She is reputed to be irresistible, and her guards, of course, can't run away from her. Nor dare they affect to despise her advances, for her anger is fully as terrible as that of her father."

At this juncture an officer entered and saluted. "Which of you is Kov Lutas?"

"I am," replied the young Jen, returning his salute.

"If you are ready you will come with me to relieve the temporary guard of the Dixtar's daughter."

"I am ready," Kov Lutas told him. "Let us go."

They went out, and Thorne, after pouring himself another cup of pulcho, sat down to reflect on the situation. But he had scarcely settled in his swinging chair when Vorz came to the door and announced, "Salute the Deputy Dixtar."

Thorne sprang to his feet and raised his hand smartly in salute. Then he let it fall to his side as he recognized Sel Han.

"Greetings, Sheb Takkor Jen," said the Deputy Dixtar with a grin. "You seem surprised at seeing me."

"And to you, greetings, Sel Han," replied Thorne coolly. "To what do I owe the—er—honor of this unexpected call?"

Without replying, Sel Han walked to the taboret and helped himself to a cup of pulcho. Then he seated himself in Kov Lutas's chair. For a time, he sat there in silence, then spoke suddenly in English. "Shut the door."

Thorne closed the door and returned to his chair.

Sel Han nodded. "I thought so. Understands English."

"Perhaps when you have finished talking to yourself, you will explain your business," Thorne said.

"Don't get stuffy with me. I can put you on the spot, or I can make things good for you. I came to make you a proposition. What do you say, Harry Thorne?"

"I say you're wasting your time, Frank Boyd."

"Ah—I figured you knew. Well, I heard about your run-in with Sur Det. Pretty handy with a sword, aren't you? There wasn't another man in this country who could have made a monkey out of Sur Det the way you did.

"He was my teacher when I came here. I saw I needed to be handy with a sword, so I picked the best teacher I could find. Since I'm younger, faster, and have a longer reach, I got so I could beat him. Then I went and started to cut my way to the top. And I'm pretty close to it now."

"Did you come to entertain me with this modest little sketch?"

"No, I came to get a line on you—and give you a break if you're willing to play ball. I can cut you in on something big."

"Such as what?"

"I'd be talking out of turn if I told you. First, you do what I want you to do, then I'll make things right for you."

"I don't think we can talk business, Mr. Boyd."

"Don't be an idiot. Get this—you're taking orders, I'm giving them. Now this girl Neva is supposed to marry me, but she doesn't see it yet. Right now, just to spite her father and me, she's flirting with every man she meets. She'll probably make a pass at you. If you don't play, she'll send you to the mines—if you do, her father will have your head. You're on the spot unless you listen to me.

"What burns me now is that she won't even talk to me—calls the guard and has me thrown out every time I drop in to see her. Now here's all I want you to do. I'm going to drop in to see her tonight before I fly to Takkor. She'll probably want you to throw me out. If she does, tell her you can't in honor lay a hand on me, because I won that duel from you at the military school. That will let you out."

At this moment the door opened and an orderly entered with Thorne's evening meal. As he arranged the dishes on the taboret he noticed Sel Han.

"May I get the Deputy Dixtar something to eat?" he asked.

"No, I'm dining with the Dixtar," replied Sel Han, rising. He swung on Thorne. "Don't forget I'm not asking you, I'm telling you—and you'd better come through."

Without replying or looking up, Thorne drew his jeweled dagger and turned his attention to the food on the taboret which the orderly had set before him. A moment later he heard Sel Han leave the room.

Soon after he finished his meal, an officer came in and saluted.

"It is time for you to relieve Kov Lutas in the apartments of the Dixtar's daughter," he said.

CHAPTER 10

When Thorne, escorted by the palace officer, reached the apartments of Neva, the sun had set, and the luxuriously furnished rooms were lighted by the soft amber radiance of the half-hooded baridium globes which hung from the ceiling on golden chains. The size and magnificence of the suite reserved for the daughter of this apostle of simplicity who would make all citizens equal, was astounding.

The chamber in which he found himself opened onto a broad terrace which led to a private garden, separated from the rest of the palace grounds by a high wall. Kov Lutas, standing in the circular doorway, smiled at their approach.

"Greetings, Sheb Takkor," he said, after exchanging salutes with the two officers. "She whom we guard is resting on the terrace. The orders are to stay always within sight and call, and when she sleeps to stand guard just outside her chamber door."

Thorne took up Kov Lutas's position in the doorway. "I'll try to carry out orders. A good dinner and a sound rest to you."

"And to you a pleasant vigil," replied Kov Lutas.

Not until both officers had gone out did Thorne steal a glance at the girl he was to guard. He was unable to suppress a gasp.

Her eyes, languorous beneath the fringed curtains of their sleepy lids, were liquid pools of lapis lazuli. Her small nose was a most exquisitely chiseled bit of sculpture. Her red lips, sightly parted, revealed teeth that were matched pearls. And her hair was spun gold and sunbeams.

For some time she was motionless, gazing pensively out over the garden. Presently she crossed the terrace and descended to the garden. Watching her, Thorne stood bemused, wondering if it were possible that the scrawny, rat-faced Dixtar could be the father of so beautiful a daughter.

So potent was the spell cast over his senses that he lost sight of her in the shrubbery before he remembered his orders, and ran down the steps into the garden.

For some time Thorne hurried blindly about in the garden. Then the nearer moon, suddenly blinking above the rooftops to the west, came to his assistance. By its pale light he saw Neva not fifty feet from him, seated on the rim of a limpid pool in the center of which a fountain babbled.

Slowly he moved closer and halted at a distance of about twenty feet. As he stood there he was recalled to mundane considerations by a burning sensation in the region of his knees. Lowering his hand to investigate the cause, he discovered that

49

heat rays were emanating from an ornate globe about two feet high which stood beside the path.

He had seen many such globes at various points around the garden and on the terrace. Although it had not occurred to him to wonder why the garden had not grown cold after nightfall, he now understood the reason.

In order to escape the discomfort caused by the proximity of the heating globe, he moved a few steps nearer the fountain. A dry twig snapped beneath his foot, and the girl looked up, a startled expression on her face.

"Have no fear," said Thorne. "I am Sheb Takkor, your new guard."

"I know," she replied. "It was the noise that startled me. You see, I am expecting some one I am not at all anxious to meet."

Though he felt quite sure he knew who that some one was, Thorne did not venture to say so.

Heavy footsteps sounded on the garden path. A shadow fell athwart the pool. Thorne glanced across to where the shadow began. Behind Neva stood Sel Han. "The Dixtar's deputy salutes his fair daughter," he said.

Without replying or even turning her head, Neva called to Thorne, "A trespasser has intruded upon my privacy, guardsman. Remove him."

The Earthman strode forward and stood facing his enemy. "It seems you are not wanted," he said quietly. "I trust that, under the circumstances, you will not have the bad taste to remain."

Sel Han laughed contemptuously. "Out of my way, worm," he ordered. "You dare not raise a hand against me." He sat down familiarly beside Neva. "Your guardsman is a spineless coward. Once he faced me, sword in hand, but grew so frightened before a blow had been struck that he dropped his weapon and fainted."

Thorne ground his teeth in impotent rage. He knew that under the Martian code he must suffer in silence any abuse which this fellow might choose to heap on him, physical violence or an assault with a weapon excepted.

"I would have you know, Sheb Takkor," Neva said, ignoring the presence of Sel Han, "that *all* the details of that unfortunate affair of yours at the training school are known to me. It was cowardly of your opponent to slash you when you were weakened from loss of blood and numbed by the virus of a desert blood-fly. And in full accord with that craven blow is his present refusal to again meet you, while he relies on the passivity which his technical victory imposes on you."

At this, the deputy forced a derisive laugh.

"Would it please the Dixtar's daughter to have her guard slain before her eyes?"

"It would please her guard," retorted Thorne, "to have the opportunity of defending himself."

"No doubt it would," grinned Sel Han. He moved closer to Neva. "Come," he said, "send away this cowardly guard who is powerless to help you. There is something I want to ask you."

Familiarly he passed his arm around her shoulders. And when, with blazing eyes, she would have leaped away from him, he held her tightly.

Thorne instantly whipped out his sword. "Release her or die," he commanded, presenting his point at the deputy's breast.

The deputy let her go, and stood erect, glaring. "Have you abandoned your honor?"

"I might ask you the same," retorted Thorne, sheathing his sword, "but I know a man is incapable of abandoning that which he has never had."

"It seems," said Sel Han, a deadly glitter in his eyes, "that you have forgotten the code—and something else."

"I am glad you have not forgotten that you are my guardsman, Sheb Takkor Jen," interposed Neva. "And since you are acting in that capacity, and not in your own personal interests, it would seem that you are at liberty to treat this trespasser as you would any other."

"I had hoped that the Dixtar's daughter would confirm me in that belief," relied Thorne. The Earthman's fist shot up in a short arc that ended beneath Sel Han's protruding chin. There was a tremendous splash as the deputy measured his length in the chilly pool.

Thorne leaped back and waited tensely, hand on hilt. His enemy came up sputtering and cursing luridly in English, then stepped over the rim. He bowed low before the girl.

"Permit me to congratulate the Dixtar's daughter on the singular efficiency of her guardsman. It is only exceeded by his total lack of honor."

Then he turned, and strode away with water sloshing in his boots and dripping from his clothing.

Thorne's hand fell limply from his sword hilt. He was bitterly disappointed, for he had felt certain that Sel Han would come out of that enforced bath raging and eager to try conclusions with him.

"The coward! The miserable, slinking coward!"

Neva was speaking, half to herself, as she gazed after the departing figure. She turned and looked up at Thorne.

"He is afraid to measure swords with you," she said, "but he will find some other way to be rid of you. He is cunning, oh, so cunning, and treacherous." She laid a slim hand on the Earthman's arm. "The deputy has considerable influence with the Dixtar, my father—but for that matter, so have I. And I will help you."

In spite of his preconceived dislike of this little beauty, Thorne thrilled at her glance and touch.

"I am honored that the Dixtar's daughter should be interested in preserving my worthless life," he replied.

"He is a strange and terrible creature, this Sel Han," she went on. "Did you notice the queer gibberish he used when he came up out of the water? Some incantation, perhaps, to a strange god. No doubt he is a sorcerer."

Recalling the deputy's lurid English curses, Thorne smiled to himself as he replied, "I doubt not that he was calling down the wrath of some deity on my head."

Neva yawned prettily. "I am sleepy," she said. "We will go in now, for I must retire. You may walk beside me."

Slowly, side by side, stepping in perfect unison, they went up the path which led to the house.

At the steps which led up to the terrace she took his arm. Again he felt the thrill of her touch, and fought it with every ounce of will power at his command.

As they entered the doorway a slave girl hurried up to take her mistress's cloak. Another moved the lever which uncapped the baridium light globes, making the room brilliant as day. And still another hurried in, bearing a tray on which was a tiny jeweled cup of steaming pulcho which she proffered to Neva.

"Bring another for the Jen," she said.

The girl hurried out, and returned a moment later with a larger cup.

"I drink to my brave and efficient guardsman," smiled Neva.

"And I to the lovely and precious jewel which he guards," replied Thorne.

CHAPTER 11

During the early watches of the night, Thorne, standing guard before Neva's chamber door, reviewed the doings of the day. Before seeing the Dixtar's daughter he had been firmly of the opinion that he loved Thaine. And he had resolved not to be overcome by the reputedly irresistible charms of Neva. But now her image was ever before him.

As he stood there, inwardly perturbed by his strangely conflicting emotions, he suddenly sensed that all was not as it should be—that some sinister, alien presence was quietly watching him.

Before retiring, one of the slave girls had pulled the levers which hooded all of the larger baridium globes, leaving only one tiny light uncovered. It shed a pale golden twilight that faintly revealed the outlines of the objects in the room.

Over all these objects Thorne's eyes now roved, yet he could discern nothing amiss. The swinging chairs and divans, depending from the ceiling by their golden chains, were obviously unoccupied. And the shadows beneath them were not so dense as to form a hiding place for a human being. There was a tall, shelved case in which many metal cylinders were kept, containing the scrolls which on Mars answered for books. But nothing could hide there. And other than these, there were only a few large pots of flowers set here and there about the room.

Once more he settled to his former position, but this time he only pretended to be preoccupied. For some time nothing happened, yet though his face was held straight ahead, he kept his eyes turned in the direction where he thought he had seen a stealthy movement. Suddenly, he saw it again. And to his astonishment, he discovered that it was a large pot of flowers which had moved. So far as he could see this pot and its contents were not markedly different from any of the others. It was about three and a half feet high and three in diameter at its center. And the two large handles projecting from its sides were of the same angular pattern as the others.

Without moving his head, he kept his eyes on this singularly mobile pot. Inch by inch it came toward him while he watched, fascinated. As it drew closer he examined it minutely, meanwhile stealthily loosening his sword in its sheath with his left hand. It seemed filled almost to the brim with rich black soil, from which the flower stalks projected.

Closer and closer it came until but a scant five feet separated them. Then it suddenly stood erect on two spindly legs and its handles turned into two spidery arms, one of which wielded a long, slim dagger. Straight for the Earthman it sprang, its weapon poised. But in that instant he had whipped his sword from its sheath, and whirling it over his head, brought it down with all his might on the amazing pot.

The hard vitreous shoulder of the pot withstood the blow of his slender weapon with ease, but the keen blade glanced downward, shearing off the spidery arm that held the dagger. At this there was a muffled shriek of pain from inside the pot, and turning, it fled swiftly for the doorway. As he set out in pursuit, Thorne shifted his sword to his left hand, and plucking his heavy mace from his belt, hurled it straight at the center of the pot.

The weapon went true to the mark. There was a resounding crash of broken crockery, and the spindle legs collapsed, precipitating everything onto the floor. Out of the tangle of crumpled flowers there rolled a round-bodied yellow man.

For some time pandemonium held sway in that quarter of the palace. Neva's frightened girls and women screamed for help, and a company of guards from the outer corridors came clanking into the room. But Neva herself, clad in a filmy wrap, came out of her sleeping room, quite unperturbed.

"What has happened, Sheb Takkor Jen?" she asked.

"That attacked me," Thorne replied, indicating the corpse, "disguised as a pot of flowers."

By this time the room was filled with soldiers and slave girls, all staring curiously at the remains. Some one had unhooded the baridium globe, and the resulting light revealed every detail.

The yellow man's disguise had been well adapted to his rotund body and spidery arms. The pot had a false bottom only two inches from the top, covered with a thin layer of soil. The flower stalks were set on narrow spikes projecting upward from this bottom. There were no handles, but holes through which the scrawny arms were thrust. Painted to resemble crockery and held akimbo, they had looked exactly like handles in the dim light. And the pot, with small holes bored in it for breathing and spying, formed an efficient body armor against sword and dagger thrusts.

"A diabolical attempt," said Neva, shuddering. Then to the soldiers, "Take it away."

Two men caught up the stiffening body and others cleared away the debris. Then, at a sign from Neva, all silently left the apartment.

She looked up into Thorne's eyes.

"You have saved me from abduction, or perhaps assassination," she said. "I am very grateful."

"Perhaps," he replied, "it is only myself I have saved. The fellow attacked me. And I have reason to believe he was the creature of Sel Han."

"What reason?"

"Because the Deputy Dixtar is said to be in league with the Ma Gongi."

"There may be some truth in that," she answered, "but don't let anyone hear you say it. My father has unlimited faith in his deputy, and has beheaded two officers who were bold enough to accuse him of that very thing."

"I am grateful for your warning," Thorne replied, "and will be discreet."

A slave girl drew back the curtain, and she reentered her sleeping room.

Morning found the Earthman exceedingly weary after a strenuous day and night without rest. Soon after he was relieved by Kov Lutas he was sound asleep in their apartment. It seemed that he had scarcely closed his eyes when the orderly awakened him.

"Your servant is commanded to prepare you to attend the Dixtar's daughter at the state function this evening," he said. "As the preparation will take some time, I was compelled to awaken you early."

CHAPTER 12

Like most of the women Thorne had known on his own world, Neva was a long time about dressing. But when, after he had waited for more than an hour before her door, she came forth, the result was most entrancing.

A tiara of pearls and pale blue amethysts woven together in a bizarre pattern on the meshwork of golden wires, bound her sun-bright hair. Beads of the same materials formed her breast-shields and supported a clinging bodice of iridescent blue silk. This vanished in a girdle of pearls and amethysts.

Thorne stood enthralled, and she smiled archly. Then she raised her arms and circled gracefully on the tips of her toes. "Like it?" she asked.

"Immensely," he replied, "even as I adore—" He stopped suddenly.

"Go on," she urged him, still smiling.

"Sorry. I said more than I intended. Perhaps you will find it in your heart to overlook my presumption."

"Perhaps I shall if you will finish." Then, "Even as I adore—" she prompted him.

"—the star-strewn firmament," he replied.

She stamped a tiny foot. "Must I command you?" She moved closer—laid a hand on his arm. "Where I might command," she said, "I will only implore."

"—the lovely jewel it adorns," he finished.

"Ah! That is what I wanted to hear you say. And now for your reward you will escort me to the reception as a gentleman and officer of the Kamud, walking at my side."

The reception of Irintz Tel, Dixtar of Xancibar, was a gorgeous affair. Held for the purpose of welcoming Lori Thool, the new ambassador from Kalsivar, largest and most powerful nation of Mars, it was a model of magnificence.

The function was held in the great central audience chamber of the palace, the ceiling of which towered a thousand feet above the heads of the assembled guests, its polished surface reflecting the rays of myriads of baridium globes, which made the place light as day.

Irintz Tel was standing with his illustrious guest on a dais in the center of the floor, presenting other visiting dignitaries and his chief officers, when the silvery notes of a trumpet rose above the hum of conversation. Instantly, every voice was hushed as a pompous major-domo announced: "The Dixtar's daughter."

All eyes were turned toward the doorway as Neva entered, walking beside Thorne. And though they lighted with pleasure at sight of the dainty little golden-haired beauty who was the first lady of Xancibar, not a few admiring glances were cast at the tall, handsome, sun-bronzed young officer.

Straight to the dais they went, the girl nodding to right and left to her many friends and acquaintances. As the little rat-faced Dixtar advanced to meet them, accompanied by Lori Thool, Thorne was once more struck by the incongruous dissimilarity between father and daughter.

The ambassador was tall, slender, and slightly under middle age, his hair just beginning to gray at the temples. He was quite handsome and elegant in his uniform and insignia of a great noble of Kalsivar.

"Neva," squeaked the Dixtar in his high-pitched voice, "this is Lori Thool, the noble ambassador from Kalsivar. Lori Thool, my daughter."

The ambassador saluted gracefully. "My homage to the most beautiful of the daughters of Mars. It must be that I have now met every one. Will you not join me in a game of gapun? I see they are setting up the boards."

"In a moment," she answered. "You have not quite met every one. This is my friend, Sheb Takkor Jen."

As he and the resplendent ambassador exchanged dignified salutes, the Earthman exulted over the fact that she had said, "my friend."

Meanwhile, Neva had beckoned a pretty little black-haired, brown-eyed beauty to her side.

"I take it that you have met the ambassador, Trixana," she said, "but not my friend, Sheb Takkor Jen."

Thorne acknowledged with a courtly salute, and a moment later found himself walking at the side of the vivacious little brunette, following Neva and Lori Thool as they made their way toward the gaming boards. From the corner of his eye, he saw Irintz Tel standing, chin on chest and hands clasped behind him. And he was quite positive that the Dixtar's look was not friendly.

A moment later he saw Sel Han slip up beside Irintz Tel and, bending, whisper some secret communication. The Dixtar nodded, and again flashed a look at Thorne.

Lori Thool and the two girls chanced much gold at the gaming boards, and Trixana won quite heavily. But Thorne only looked on. As he was standing, watching the game, he felt a touch on his arm, and turning, beheld the kindly face of the white-haired Lal Vak.

"Greetings, Sheb Takkor Jen," he said softly. "Turn and watch the game, while I deliver a message. We must not seem to be talking together."

Thorne looked back at the players, and the scientist continued: "You are in great danger. Sel Han is plotting against your life. He has denounced you to the Dixtar as being over-friendly with Neva, and her actions tonight in treating you as an equal have seemed to confirm his words. A friend has brought me news that Irintz Tel has just promised Sel Han he will turn you over to the headsman in the morning."

"What can I do about it?"

"Escape. Get away from the palace before morning."

"That I had already planned."

"How?"

"Over the garden wall."

"Splendid! It is just what we had in mind. I will have a conveyance waiting for you. Be there just after the farther moon rises and it may be that we can save you. Farewell."

When the gathering broke up, Lori Thool, after saying a lingering farewell to Neva, departed with his suite. Trixana was claimed by her father, a tall, handsome soldier in the prime of life, and Neva, left once more with Thorne, started toward the door. They had only gone a few steps when Sel Han suddenly strode up. He made a sweeping bow before Neva.

"May I have the honor of seeing the Dixtar's daughter safely to her apartments?" he asked.

She took Thorne's arm. "The Dixtar's daughter is adequately escorted."

Sel Han continued to bar her way, smiling cynically. And the Earthman noticed that the Dixtar himself was only a few feet away, looking on.

"Apparently you have not observed that the Dixtar's daughter wishes to pass," said Thorne. "Under such circumstances it should not be necessary to request any *gentleman* to stand aside."

At this, the deputy flashed a look at the Dixtar, as much as to say, "I told you so," and moved out of the way.

Back in the apartments of Neva, as Thorne stood guard before her chamber door, his mind was a mass of conflicting emotions. The time slipped by until he suddenly realized that the farther moon had risen and the hour had struck for his departure. He was about to steal softly away from his post when he was startled by a touch on his arm and a whispered, "Quiet."

Swiftly turning, he was astonished to see Neva standing there before the curtain clad in a filmy sleeping garment.

"Make no noise," she said, "and come with me. I heard someone on my balcony, and want you to surprise the prowler."

Softly they entered the sleeping chamber. For a moment Thorne stood there, accustoming his eyes to the dim light and taking note of his surroundings. Then he silently drew his sword and advanced toward the balcony, listening intently.

Reaching a window without having heard a sound, he cautiously leaned forward and peered out. So far as he could see, the balcony was deserted. He stepped out and explored. Still no sign of a prowler. Then he reentered the room.

"Did you see him?" she asked.

"I saw no one," he replied. "Perhaps you were only dreaming."

"No, no! I am positive a man was there a moment ago. Not only did I hear him, but I saw his shadow as the moon came up. I'm terribly frightened."

They were standing very close together. Her eyes, looking up into his, were wide with fear. She swayed toward him. Solicitously he threw his arms about her—felt that she was trembling. Her arms stole about his neck and clung. "Hold me tight—tight! In your arms I am not afraid."

Now it was the man who trembled; but not with fear. Their lips met.

"I love you, love you, love you!" she murmured. "Say again what you said to me this evening."

"I love and adore you," he told her, his voice husky with emotion. "Yet it is madness—a sweet madness."

"Why, dear one?"

"Because tomorrow . . ."

Suddenly the lights flashed on, and he paused, speechless with surprise.

A dozen armed soldiers rushed into the room, bared blades in their hands. At their head was Sel Han, a grin of triumph on his features. And behind them came Irintz Tel, Dixtar of Xancibar.

"Help! The guard! Release me, you brute!"

For a moment Thorne was in a daze. Then he suddenly realized that it was Neva who was speaking—that she was beating upon his breast with her clenched hands—hands that had caressed him but a moment before—straining to break from his clasp.

Mechanically he let her go. She ran to the little wizened Dixtar, buried her face in his shoulder, and began sobbing bitterly.

Thorne suddenly came to the full realization of his peril. He whipped out his sword and dagger and leaped for the door. Two warriors barred his progress.

A feint, a thrust, and one went down stabbed through the heart. He parried the thrust of the other with his dagger. Then he withdrew his blade from the heart of the first enemy and sheathed it in the throat of the second.

Other warriors leaped in close, but he bounded over the bodies of his two fallen adversaries and out of the door. Straight across the terrace he dashed, then down the steps and into the labyrinth of garden paths.

A few moments more and Thorne had reached his objective—a tall sebolis tree standing near the wall, which he had previously marked for his purpose. Pausing only to hurl his sword and dagger into the faces of his pursuers, he scrambled up the rough tree trunk, then climbed from branch to branch until he was above the level of the wall.

Walking out on the swaying branch until it sagged dangerously, he leaped. His fingers caught the edge of the wall, but it was rounded by a thousand years of weathering, and slippery with the night's accumulation of hoar frost.

With a last despairing clutch at the curved, treacherous surface, he fell to the ground twenty feet below.

As soon as he struck, a half dozen soldiers pounced on him. Weaponless, he fought them with fists and feet until Sel Han reached over and struck him on the head with the flat of his heavy mace. Then his captors, at a sharp command from the triumphant deputy, jerked him to his feet and half carried, half dragged him back to the palace.

Neva, attended by two of her slave girls, sat on a divan with a fluffy wrap around her shoulders. Irintz Tel was pacing up and down, chin on chest, hands clasped behind his back, his brow contracted in a frown and his thin lips compressed in a tight line.

Presently a tall, sad-faced man bearing a great, two-handed sword on his shoulder, strode into the room. Behind him walked a sleepy-eyed, frightened little boy who carried a basket.

"Strike the head from this despicable traitor, Lurgo," squeaked Irintz Tel, without looking up.

Lurgo the headsman lowered his huge weapon and stood leaning on the pommel, waiting while two warriors dragged Thorne to the center of the floor and forced him to kneel. Then he stepped back, carefully measured the distance with his practiced eye, and whirled the great blade over his head.

CHAPTER 13

"No, no! Lurgo! Wait!"

It was Neva who had sprung from her couch, and now stood between the sad-faced headsman and the kneeling Thorne.

Lurgo stared sorrowfully down at her, his blade still poised in mid-air.

Irintz Tel ceased his pacing for the first time and looked up. "What's this, daughter? Can it be that you care for this vile miscreant?"

"Care for him!" Neva stamped her foot angrily. "I hate him for the affront he has put upon me. For much less than this, you have caused minor offenders to suffer for days before death was finally granted them. Yet this seducer, this ravisher who has dared to lay hands on your own daughter is let off with a mere stroke of the headsman's sword. Do you hold my honor so lightly as this?"

"By the wrath of Deza, you are right!" exclaimed Irintz Tel. "I have been too hasty. Let be, Lurgo."

At this, the tall headsman sadly shouldered his sword and trudged away, the sleepy-eyed boy with the basket trailing in his wake.

"Does it not seem fair, my father," said Neva, "that since the crime of this malefactor was against me, I should be the one to pronounce sentence upon him?"

"It does indeed, daughter. It does indeed," agreed Irintz Tel. "Suppose you name his fate."

"Why, then, I'll sentence him to labor in the baridium mines," she said. "I hear that men are long in dying there, and that they suffer much."

"But," interposed Sel Han, "there are tortures . . ."

"Since when," asked Neva, facing him haughtily, "has the Dixtar's deputy acquired the right to question the mandates of the Dixtar's daughter?"

"You are right, daughter, you are right," interposed Irintz Tel. "You must not interfere, Sel Han. She has pronounced a fitting sentence, and we confirm it. Away with him, warriors."

Thorne, still dazed by the blow on his head, dimly comprehended that he had been saved from the stroke of the sworder only to be condemned to a worse fate.

As he was dragged away by the warriors, he saw the face of Irintz Tel sneering, that of Sel Han grinning malevolently, and those of the warriors stern and pitiless. But at Neva he did not look.

After conducting him through numerous passageways, the soldiers led him into a small room at one end of which a hole about three feet in diameter was cut in the wall. Into this hole they thrust him feet first, attached a tag to his arm marked "Baridium Mines," and gave him a violent push. With a speed that gave him a peculiar sensation in the pit of his stomach and caused a considerable pressure on his eardrums, he shot downward in a dark, slanting tube, the inner surface of which was as smooth as glass. Presently he glided over a series of rises which slowed his progress, then out into an open trough under a long, low shed. At the end of the trough two soldiers caught him and stood him erect.

To his surprise, Thorne now saw that he was in one of the large warehouses which lined the banks of the canal over which he had passed. After the soldiers had examined his tag he was herded with a group of other prisoners, similarly tagged, who were huddled around a large globe-heater on the dock. Here he stood, slowly turning like the others, for while the side toward the heater was comfortably warm, the one directly away from it was subjected to the freezing temperature of the early morning air.

61

Presently the sun, heralded only by a brief dawn-light in this tenuous atmosphere, popped above the horizon, its blue-white shafts instantly dissipating the cold, and swiftly melting the shell of ice which covered the canal.

Moored at the dock was a low, narrow craft about two hundred feet in length. The hull was of brown metal, and the upper structure was roofed over with iridescent, amber colored crystal curved like the back of a whale.

Through one of the doors the prisoners were now driven. As he followed along with the others, Thorne noticed the strange propulsive devices used on these craft, which were shaped much like the webbed feet and legs of aquatic birds, and were fastened at intervals along the sides.

As soon as the prisoners had been herded on board, the metal door clanged shut behind them. Shortly thereafter the craft glided away from the dock, propelled smoothly and noiselessly by its artificial webbed feet.

Thorne presently tired of the sameness of the scenery and entered into a conversation with one of his fellow unfortunates—a man who had once been high in the councils of the Kamud, but who had dared to oppose Irintz Tel. Levri Thomel was a silver-haired man in the late autumn of life. He showed no rancor against the Dixtar, but took his sentence as the decree of fate.

"At most," he told Thorne, "I would have only enjoyed a few short years of life. But you are a young man. Your case is sad, indeed, as you would have had much to live for."

For a time silence fell between them. Then Thorne asked, "What are these baridium mines like? Have you any idea?"

"There are vast workings, which require much machinery and equipment, and the labor of many slaves. The baridium ore, after being brought up from deposits far underground, is crushed and cleaned of all impurities. Then it is distilled. The liquid which passes over in the still is mixed with phosphorus and several other chemicals, and used to fill the light globes with which you are familiar. The solid residue left in the stills is calcined until it becomes an impalpable powder, fearfully water-hungry. Then it is combined with several elements, the most important of which is metallic sodium, to make the fire-powder which instantly ignites when moistened."

Thorne was about to ask him how all this affected the slaves, when the boat suddenly slowed down, then stopped beside a dock of black stone which jutted from the wall on the outer side of the canal. The metal door was thrown open, the prisoners were herded out and Thorne lost track of Levri Thomel.

They were marched through a high archway in the thick black wall, and thence into an immense building constructed of the same material. Here they formed in line, to be examined by an officer, who assigned them to various working groups. Thorne was pleased when he found that Levri Thomel was assigned to this group, which numbered about twenty men.

A guard marched them through a long corridor, lighted by small baridium globes, and thence into a broad courtyard which overlooked an immense pit, several miles in diameter, the rim of which was circled by a high black wall. As soon as they entered this court, the prisoners encountered air laden with fine dust and acrid fumes, which smarted their lungs and nostrils and set them to coughing and sneezing violently.

Meanwhile, the guard urged them onward to the edge of the pit, where he turned them over to another guard, whose face, head and body were protected by a breathing mask, helmet and air-tight suit.

This new guard spoke to them through a sound amplifier which projected from the top of his helmet.

"Down the stairway," he ordered, "and step lively. I'll make the first laggard regret his slothfulness."

The deeper they descended the more difficult breathing became, until, when they reached the bottom of the stairway, the fumes fairly seared their lungs, while the fine dust, settling on the skin, made them itch and burn. Merely being in the place without a protective suit was torment.

As these things came to Thorne's attention, he thought again of Neva. More sharply than the baridium fumes seared his lungs, the thought of her perfidy seared his heart.

CHAPTER 14

The group of slaves was ushered into a large building and set at the task of filling and sealing small phials of fire-powder. Here the laborers were seated at long benches, above which were suspended large hoppers of the powder. This was conveyed down to them by means of tubes with small valves at the bottom which could be opened or closed by the operator as the phials were filled.

Stoppers of red, resilient material like that which formed the suits of the guards were pressed into the bottles, then held for a moment against hot plates, the heat melting them down and sealing them hermetically.

The labor in this department was the lightest of any in the baridium pit. Yet it was the most dreaded of all, as the air was constantly filled with the searing powder which attacked skin and lungs alike.

With a sickening apprehension of the fate in store for him, Thorne gradually saw his own skin turning yellow from contact with the fumes and powder in the air. And despite the utmost watchfulness he was unable to avoid burning his fingers and the backs of his hands by spilling on them small quantities of powder which sifted down from the none too efficient valve.

When night came the slaves were herded into a great communal building, the only furniture of which consisted of heating globes. Here a coarse porridge was doled out to them. They were given water to drink.

In this building the air was somewhat freer from dust and fumes than outside, and therefore offered some slight relief to Thorne and other newcomers whose lungs and skin had not, as yet, been badly seared. After eating their rations, the slaves flung themselves down on the hard floor around the heating globes, many to fall asleep from utter exhaustion.

Thorne was about to fling himself down like the others when he saw, sprawled on the floor at his feet, a sleeping figure that somehow seemed familiar. The skin was yellow and mottled with many burns, yet he could not mistake Yirl Du, Jen of the Takkor Free Swordsmen.

Stooping, the Earthman shook his friend. Yirl Du's red-rimmed eyes blinked open. An angry snarl died in his throat as sudden recognition came to him. He sat up abruptly, saluted.

"I shield my eyes, my lord. I did not dream of seeing you here, and at first I did not recognize you with that yellow cast to your skin."

"You seem to have acquired considerable color yourself, old friend. How long have you been here?"

"The seven judges sentenced me the day you were taken before the Dixtar," Yirl Du told him. "The trial was a farce. There were no witnesses, and no evidence was produced against me except a letter from Sel Han."

Thorne made Yirl Du and the silvery-haired Levri Thomel acquainted, and for a time they conversed. Then the baridium globes which lighted the building here hooded, and they composed themselves for sleep.

It seemed, however, that he had scarcely fallen asleep when a small baridium hand-torch was flashed in his face, awakening him, and a guard prodded him with his foot.

"Are you Sheb Takkor?" the fellow asked in a hoarse whisper.

"I am," Thorne replied.

"Where is he who is called Yirl Du?"

"He sleeps here beside me."

"It seems you two have a powerful friend at Dukor. My superior officer has ordered me to assist you hence. Awaken Yirl Du and follow me."

The guard hooded his torch as Thorne shook Yirl Du awake and explained the situation to him. Then he thought of Levri Thomel. A touch awakened the old man.

"Come with me," Thorne whispered. "It may be that we can escape."

Then he called to the guard: "Ready."

The fellow opened the slide of his torch only wide enough to enable him to make his way among the sleeping slaves who sprawled on the floor. Then he started toward the nearest doorway, closely followed by Thorne, Yirl Du, and Levri Thomel. Once outside the building, the guard hooded his torch, and they made their way by the light of the nearer moon, which was dropping swiftly toward the eastern horizon. They presently came to a small guardhouse near the rim of the pit. Their conductor entered, and motioned them to follow.

Thorne marched in first, and found himself in the presence of an officer who sat on the edge of a swinging divan.

The officer looked up sharply. "What's this, Hendra Suhn? You have brought three of them."

The guard seemed dumfounded. "I only awakened Sheb Takkor, and told him to bring Yirl Du."

Thorne hastened to explain. "I am Sheb Takkor. These are my friends Yirl Du and Levri Thomel. It is my desire that both accompany me."

"I was only ordered to assist two, yourself and Yirl Du," said the officer. "Levri Thomel goes back."

"If he goes back, then I go with him," said Thorne.

"You refuse escape when it is offered you?"

"I decline to attempt it without my friend."

"The more fool, you," growled the officer. "Yet I have my orders to assist you, and I suppose this doddering old derelict must go with you." He arose, and stepping into another room brought two bundles of warm clothing, and two of weapons. One bundle of each he handed to Thorne and the like to Yirl Du. But Thorne instantly passed his bundles to Levri Thomel.

The officer glared for a moment, but checked himself, and went into the next room for more clothing and weapons, which he thrust into the hands of Thorne with ill grace.

"You win," he said angrily. "But this old wreck you persist in taking with you will yet cause your undoing."

Swiftly the three men donned the clothing and belted sword, mace and dagger about them. In addition to these, each was provided with a bundle of javelins in a quiver that hung by a strap across one shoulder.

"As soon as the nearer moon sets," said the officer, "and before the farther rises, you will have time to make your way in the dark up the side of the pit. The rim is guarded, but one guard has orders to pass you. That guard is stationed directly above this building. When you have passed the guard, you will proceed out into the desert until you have passed five out-cropping rocks. At the northern base of the sixth, which you will recognize because it leans as if it were about to fall to the ground, you will find supplies left there for you by your friends, because they would have been awkward for you to carry up the side of the pit."

"Who are these friends who have been so thoughtful?" asked Thorne.

"I only know that these orders came down to me from my superiors, and that they must have had them from some one high in the councils of the Kamud."

So swiftly did the nearer moon move across the sky, that only a short time elapsed ere it dropped below the eastern horizon. Then the three men set out.

Overhead, the stars were blazing jewels of white, red, pale blue and yellow, in a sky of jet. Though their combined radiance was too feeble to light the path of the three fugitives, they were still of service, for their line of disappearance marked the rim of the pit. And one constellation which Thorne fixed in his mind served as a guide to the point, directly above the house they had just quitted, where they expected to find a friendly guard.

Moving with great caution in order not to start a landslide on that steeply sloping bank, they began the ascent. It was a long, difficult climb, and they had scarcely reached the summit when the farther moon rose in the east close to the point where the nearer moon had vanished a short time before. Its light was more dim than that of the nearer and larger orb, but bright enough to reveal them to a tall guard who stood looking out over the pit. Instantly he raised a javelin and advanced threateningly.

"Who are you?" he demanded.

"Sheb Takkor and friends."

The guard stared at him suspiciously. "I can pass but two. The third must go back."

"That order was changed. You will pass three or none," Thorne told him. "We are going on at once. Raise an alarm now, and we will kill you. Raise it later, and there is one high in the councils of the Kamud who will see that you are condemned to the powder room."

"I crave pardon, Sheb Takkor Jen," he said humbly. "Pass, and may Deza guard you."

And so the three now clambered over the wall, dropped to the other side, and marched out into the desert, free men.

Carefully, now, they counted the outcropping stones of which the officer had told them. They had passed the fifth, at a considerable distance from the pit, and were just coming up to the sixth when a half dozen warriors suddenly broke from a nearby clump of conifers and charged toward them, hurling a cloud of javelins.

Thorne shouted a warning to his companions, both of whom were able to dodge the barbed weapons. He called to his two friends to support him on the right and left, then dashed straight at the advancing warriors.

There was another exchange of javelins, in which the skilled Yirl Du transfixed an enemy, cutting the attacking party down to five.

Both sides expended their store of javelins at about the same time. Then swords and daggers were drawn and the hand-to-hand fighting began. Thorne engaged the blade of the leader of the band, and was instantly beset by another warrior on the fellow's right. Over at his left, Yirl Du fought alone. Levri Thomel, on his right, was attacked by the remaining two, and showed amazing skill with sword and dagger.

For a time there was only the clash of steel on steel and an occasional grunt from one of the wounded contestants. Then Thorne thrust the leader of the band through the throat. With his chief opponent out of the way it was but child's play for him to quickly dispose of the other. Then, seeing that Yirl Du was getting the best of his assailant, he dashed to the assistance of Levri Thomel.

The old man still stood his ground, apparently unhurt, as Thorne came in to engage one of his opponents. A clumsy fencer, the fellow quickly succumbed. At the same instant Levri Thomel ran his antagonist through the heart. Turning, Thorne saw Yirl Du coming toward them, cleansing his blade with a bit of fabric cut from the cloak of his fallen adversary.

"A glorious victory, my lord. Six enemies stretched out on the sand, and we three still live."

"It was well fought," agreed Thorne. "But who could these men be? And how came they to be waiting here for us?"

"I recognized the last fellow I killed," said Yirl Du. "He was a henchman of Sel Han. The spies of the deputy evidently discovered the plot to release us, and he posted these assassins here for the purpose of ambushing us. He expected but two, and we were three—enough to defeat his cutthroats and upset his scheme."

"That is true," agreed Thorne. He turned to Levri Thomel. "It is you, my friend, who turned the tide. But for you, Yirl Du and I would now be stark on the sand in the place of these six assassins. Until I am able to express my appreciation more fittingly, permit me to merely thank you."

"It is I who owe you a lasting debt of gratitude," protested the old man. "But for you I would be down there in the pit, doomed to a lingering death. As it is, I—I . . ." Suddenly he swayed, and pitched forward on his face.

Alarmed, Thorne sprang to his side, and, turning him over asked: "What is it, my friend? Are you ill?"

"Ill unto death," the old fellow replied. "I was wounded early in the engagement and have been bleeding freely since. It is the end I would have chosen. Farewell, my comrades."

Hastily, Thorne undid his cloak, exposing a wound just above the heart. For a moment he held his hand there, but felt no pulsations.

"Levri Thomel is dead," he solemnly told Yirl Du.

"He was a brave man, my lord. And now we must look for that leaning stone, and be gone. If the morning sun finds us near the baridium pit, we too are dead men."

Sadly, silently, they gathered their javelins and moved forward. Presently they came to the leaning stone.

"It was at the north base of the stone we were to look," said Thorne, "yet there is nothing here."

Yirl Du thrust a javelin into the sand. At a depth of about ten inches it encountered an obstruction. Swiftly he dropped to his knees and began scooping out the sand with his cupped hands.

CHAPTER 15

After a few moments of digging, Yirl Du grasped something and dragged it up out of the sand. It was a pole about eight feet in length, one end of which was inserted in a cylinder six inches in diameter and four feet long. Three pairs of straps were fastened to this cylinder and a bit of stirrup-shaped metal projected from its lower end.

At the opposite end of the pole was a cone-shaped cushion of reddish-brown resilient material.

Swiftly the Jen of the Takkor Free Swordsmen unearthed three more objects like the first, and two poles about sixteen feet long. Then he dragged out two large metal water bottles and two boxes, to all of which carry-straps were attached.

Opening one of the boxes, Thorne discovered food, fire-powder and medical supplies. Among these was a bottle of jembal gum. He heated some of this by burning a small quantity of fire-powder. Then he dressed Yirl Du's wounds and burns, after which his henchman did the like for him.

"Now, my lord," said Yirl Du, "if you will be seated I will strap on your desert legs for you."

Although Thorne had no idea what the pole and cylinder combinations were for, he began to understand when his retainer brought two of them and, after inserting his feet in the stirrups, began strapping them to his legs. When they were properly fastened in place, he next strapped a box to the Earthman's back, slung his javelins in their quiver, and hung his water bottle by a strap across his shoulder. Then he handed him one of the poles.

"Now you are ready, my lord," he said, "and I'll be on my own desert legs very shortly."

It did not take Yirl Du long to do for himself what he had done for Thorne. Then, grasping his pole with both hands, he thrust one end into the sand beside him, and drew himself up until he stood on his two long stilts. Thorne followed his example. With his weight on them the tops of the stilts were compressed a little way

69

into the cylinders, which evidently contained powerful springs. The resilient, cone-shaped feet kept the stilts from sinking into the sand and added to the illusion of floating feather-like through space which the springs induced.

Yirl Du started off, walking toward the northwest. Thorne attempted to imitate his gait, but found it quite difficult, much like walking on bed springs or an aerial artist's net. At each step his desert legs threw him forward like a springboard, so that several times he was compelled to use his long pole to keep from falling on his face.

Presently he got the swing of it, whereupon Yirl Du gradually increased the pace until both of them were running. Not until then did the Earthman discover the tremendous advantage of traveling with desert legs. At each step the stilt now sank deeply into the cylinder, then hurled him upward and forward like a catapult.

The night was cold and frosty, and the exercise just sufficient to make him draw in great lungsful of the sweet desert air. What a relief after the baridium pit, with its searing, acrid fumes and its deadly clouds of corrosive dust!

As the night wore on and morning approached, the bright nearer moon once more popped above the western horizon, and hurtling forward to greet its slower, paler companion, made the sand particles and frost crystals glitter and sparkle. But long before the two moons could meet in the sky, the sun, heralded by a brief flash of silver-gray light, shot above the eastern horizon in the full blaze of its glory, and both satellites faded from view.

A few moments later, Yirl Du sighted a clump of conifers, and the two men made for it. They found a dry waterhole, but this did not daunt them with their full bottles, and the trees offered concealment and shade. Unstrapping their desert legs, they gathered firewood, brewed pulcho, and with the hot, stimulating beverage, washed down their morning meal of dried meat and hard traveler's cakes. Then, after extinguishing their fire with sand, they stretched out in the shade to sleep.

Thorne fell asleep almost immediately. Nor did he awaken until Yirl Du shook him soundly.

"The day is all but sped, my lord," he said. "I have brewed fresh pulcho and prepared our evening meal. We should eat and be ready to start as soon as the sun sets."

"What of our enemies? It seems strange that no signs of pursuit have developed."

"But they *have* developed," replied Yirl Du. "I am a light sleeper, and several times during the day as I lay awake, I saw bands of warriors mounted on gawrs flying overhead. Had they paused to search our hiding place we would have been killed or captured long ere this. Fortunately they did not."

The sun set just as they finished their meal, and they packed their belongings and strapped on their desert legs by the light of the nearer moon. Then they set out once more. Yirl Du had estimated that by traveling all night and sleeping during the daytime, they would be able to reach the edge of the Takkor Marsh in three nights. Here he would know how to find Thaine, if she were still alive and uncaptured, and they would be able to fulfill Thorne's promise to help her search for her father.

They made swift progress traveling by the light of the nearer moon, but it soon set and as on the night before there was a period of darkness during which only the stars and planets glittered overhead. This slowed them down considerably, as they were forced to proceed in the dark with extreme caution. And so, when the farther moon appeared above the eastern horizon, they welcomed it with joy, for it meant that they could set out once more at full speed.

They had traveled for some time by its pale light when Thorne noticed, over at his left, an object projecting above the horizon which he at first took for a tall, tufted conifer. But he suddenly became aware that it was moving; not like a tree swaying in the breeze, but actually traveling over the ground and coming with considerable speed in his direction. As the thing rapidly drew closer he was able to make out a huge head with a hooked beak, a long, scrawny neck, and a large, bird-like body supported by two legs, each of which was at least fifteen feet in length. The head of the monster, he judged, towered at least thirty feet above the ground.

He called to his companion. "Ho, Yirl Du. Do you see what is coming after us?"

His henchman looked around. "A koree! We must hasten, or we are dead men. It is the great man-eating bird of the desert."

They accelerated their pace from a trot to a run. Soon they had lengthened their thirty-foot steps to nearly fifty. But the koree kept coming on, and despite their utmost exertions, gaining on them.

Thorne, less skillful with the desert legs than his companion, began to fall behind, while the monster, still shortening the distance between them soon towered only fifty feet behind. It was a hideous thing—a giant bird with a crest of waving plumes, and a huge curved beak that looked fully capable of cutting a man in two with a single snap.

Its long lean neck was bare of feathers and covered with a wrinkled, leathery skin. Like the neck, the body was leathery and naked. The wings, which were short and obviously useless for flight, were featherless, but covered with sharp, horny protuberances which made them quite formidable weapons. The long legs were armored with large, rough scales, and the toes were equipped with sickle-shaped retractile claws. The monster ran with its ugly head projecting far forward and its wings sticking stiffly out from its leathery body, as if to prevent its intended victim from suddenly doubling back to the right or left.

In the meantime Yirl Du, noticing that the koree was likely to catch up with Thorne at any moment, dropped back beside him.

"We must separate," Yirl Du told him. "The bird will follow one of us. The other must then turn and follow it, hurling as many javelins into it as possible."

They separated, and the bird followed Thorne. Yirl Du instantly turned and pursued it. His first throw struck just behind the left wing, but despite his great strength and skill at hurling the javelin, he was only able to drive it through that tough skin for a little way. A second, striking below it, penetrated to a depth of about a foot. But it was enough to exasperate the monster, which turned and rushed at its persistent tormentor.

Thorne now turned and hurled a javelin. Striking at the point where the right leg joined the body it only penetrated deeply enough for the barb to hold. He tried a second cast, this time throwing with all his might. The javelin passed clear over the body of the bird and struck it in the back of the neck. Like the first, however, it only sank in up to the first barb, and therefore did not do much damage. It was enough, however, to make the monster turn and charge him.

Instantly the Earthman shot out at right angles to the course he had been following. But he made the mistake of watching the bird without looking at the ground before him, and ran straight into a tangle of desert sand-flowers. First one stilt, then the other, caught in the snarl of tough vines, and he plunged, face downward, into the sand about twenty feet beyond.

He managed to retain his grip on the long pole he carried, although it had been split when he fell, and now, after turning on his back, attempted to raise himself onto his desert legs once more.

But he was not quick enough. Already the koree towered above him, its huge beak distended for the kill.

CHAPTER 16

As the frightful head of the koree darted down to seize him, Thorne, lying where he had fallen, gripped his walking pole with both hands. Instinctively he struck at the descending horror with the pole.

The blow did the creature no injury, but it did distract the monster's attention from the man. Evidently taking the pole for a part of Thorne's anatomy, it seized it with the immense beak, and, bracing its feet like a robin drawing a worm from the ground, pulled upward.

Thorne, still clinging to the pole, was surprised to find himself standing on his desert legs once more, not three feet from the base of that leathery neck, which the bird had stretched to the utmost. Still clinging to the pole with his left hand, he whipped out his sword with his right. Then he slashed at that taut neck; the keen, saw-edged blade sheared through to the vertebral column.

As the blood spurted from the gaping wound, the Earthman let go of the pole and sprang away, almost colliding with Yirl Du, who had hurled all his remaining javelins in a fruitless effort to distract the monster's attention, and was now rushing in with drawn sword. The bird dropped the pole and plunged after them. But it had only taken a few steps when it collapsed and lay still.

Cautiously, the two men now approached the fallen giant. Yirl Du let himself to the ground, unstrapped his desert legs and set about gathering the javelins that still had sound shafts. This done, he recovered Thorne's walking pole for him. Then he donned his desert legs once more, and they resumed their journey.

Morning found them in a bleak section of the desert that was devoid of vegetation as far as they could see in every direction. As there was no fuel available, they washed their dry rations down with plain water instead of pulcho. Then they buried their desert legs, poles, boxes and bottles in the sand, dug other holes, and covered themselves until nothing showed but their transparent masks. Thus, protected from the sun as well as the prying eyes of any pursuers who might chance to fly over this spot, they slept.

As soon as the sun had set they had another cold meal and were off again. In the early hours before dawn, when the combined light of both moons made everything stand out clearly around them, they reached the top of a rugged cliff which somehow looked familiar to Thorne. Then he recalled that a line of such cliffs rimmed the ancient ocean bed in which the Takkor Marsh lay.

They paused on the brink and looked over. About a hundred feet below them was a broad ledge. At approximately the same distance below that was still another. And seventy feet farther down was the sloping, boulder-strewn beach.

Suddenly, to Thorne's consternation, Yirl Du deliberately stepped over the edge of the cliff. The Earthman uttered an exclamation of horror as he saw his henchman drop straight toward the ledge a hundred feet below. But Yirl Du alighted squarely on his desert legs, sank almost to the depth of the cylinders, and then shot forward and upward. Soaring over the rim of the ledge on which he stood, he dropped to the next, bounced onward again, and alighted on the ground below.

Thorne decided to risk the jump. Accordingly, he stepped over the edge of the cliff into empty air.

There was a vertical rush of wind past his face, then his stilts plunged almost to the tops of the cylinders, and he shot upward once more. As he had neglected to throw himself far enough forward he bounced twice before he got over the rim of the ledge. But when he next alighted he knew how to throw his weight to the front so he was catapulted over the rim. A moment later he joined Yirl Du, and together they scrambled down the sloping beach until they came to a zone of trees, vines and underbrush so thickly entangled that they made any further use of the desert legs impossible.

They let themselves to the ground, and removing these devices, hid them in the underbrush together with the poles, and continued their advance afoot.

The rising sun found them on the bank of a little stream at the edge of the marsh. Here they brewed pulcho and ate their morning meal. Then they flung themselves down for a short rest, lying so that the sun would awaken them by mid-morning.

Thorne awoke first. To his delight, he noticed that the yellow discoloration from the baridium fumes had entirely disappeared from Yirl Du's skin. He examined his own hands. They, too, had returned to their normal color. As he had no mirror in which to view his face, he went down to the stream.

He had knelt on the bank, and was just parting the rushes, when a reflection in the water before him made him look up. A huge black bat was pursuing what at first glance appeared to be a large butterfly. Apparently disabled, the smaller creature fluttered groundward, falling into the rushes not ten feet from Thorne.

In a steep spiral, the bat swooped toward its fallen prey. Leaping to his feet, Thorne saw the futile fluttering of a pair of lacy, opalescent wings above the rushes, and knew that in a moment more the bat would claim its victim. He jerked a javelin from his quiver and hurled it at the descending monster. It struck the black, furry neck with such force that the barbed head emerged from the other side.

Now it was the bat which tumbled into the rushes, only a few feet from the creature it had struck down.

Having satisfied himself that the ugly thing was dead, Thorne stepped over for a closer look at its intended prey. But as he did so, the lacy wings suddenly rose above the bushes, and he stifled a cry of amazement when he saw that they were attached to the shoulders of a slender, perfectly formed girl about three feet in height.

Save for a girdle of filmy, pale green material drawn tight at the waist by a belt of exquisitely wrought golden mesh and ending in a short skirt, she was nude. Her silky skin was a perfect flesh tint, and covered with a fine down, delicate as peach bloom. Her golden yellow hair was bound by a fillet of woven green jade links, circling her forehead just below two delicate, feathery antennae, which swept upward and backward like a pair of dainty plumes.

As he stood staring down at her, scarcely believing his eyes, she suddenly faded from his view.

The Earthman blinked and looked again. But where she had stood he now saw only the rushes which had been bent downward by the weight of her tiny body.

Faintly he heard the fluttering of wings overhead. He looked up and saw only the empty sky. Suddenly a little pixie voice, musical as a silver bell, broke the silence.

"I know you now, man of the Old Race," it said. "You are Sheb Takkor, the younger. You have saved the life of Eriné, daughter of the Vil of the Ulfi, and she is not ungrateful. Hold out your hand."

In obedient wonder, he extended his hand. A glittering something dropped into his palm. He saw that it was a tiny ring fashioned from platinum and set with a sparkling green gem.

"If you should ever need the Ulfi, rub the jewel and if there is an Ulf within scent of the ring he will be yours to command."

"Very kind of you," said Thorne, "but . . ." He suddenly realized that the fluttering had stopped. He was talking to empty air.

Yirl Du had come down the bank and was surveying him quizzically. "Your pardon, my lord. Were you speaking to me?"

"Yes. No. I was speaking to an Ulf—that is, to an Ulf maiden."

"Has one of the Little People paid us a visit?"

"Not intentionally, I guess. You see, she was struck down by that bat." Thorne indicated the carcass. "I saw her fall, thinking her only a butterfly, yet I pitied the creature and so slew the bat with a javelin. She became invisible and presented me with this." He held out the ring.

Yirl Du exclaimed with astonishment. "Why, that is indeed a precious thing, my lord, and such a gift as only the Vil of the Ulfi or a member of his family might present to a man."

"She named herself Eriné, daughter of the Vil."

Thorne was brimming over with questions about the Little People, but resolved to curb his curiosity until he could talk to Thaine or Lal Vak. Sheb Takkor, he reasoned, would be supposed to know these things. To question Yirl Du about them would be to make him suspect either that he was not Sheb Takkor, or that he had taken leave of his senses.

He kept silence while they climbed the bank to get their belongings. Thorne was about to strap his box to his back when Yirl Du said, "Wait. Let us first get our water-shoes."

"Water-shoes! I didn't see any in my box."

Yirl Du opened his box and took out a cylinder of rolled, reddish brown material. The Earthman then remembered having seen such a cylinder in his box, and extracted it. Unrolling it, he found it consisted of two hollow pieces of resilient material, to each of which was attached a small tube with a shut-off valve. He observed that Yirl Du had opened the valve on one of his and was inflating it by blowing through the tube, so he followed his example. Soon each had a pair of buoyant, boat-shaped water-shoes.

After adjusting their weapons and other paraphernalia, they carried the shoes down to the water's edge and donned them by pushing their toes under elastic bands designed to cross the arch of the foot. This done, they stepped out onto the surface of the stream.

Yirl Du started off downstream, moving with strokes much like those of a skater. Thorne, trying to imitate him, found that water-shoeing was more difficult than it looked. At the first attempt, his legs spread so far apart he came near to sitting down in midstream. Again and again he tried to glide forward as his henchman had done, but it always seemed that both feet were very definitely bent on traveling in different directions.

Observing his efforts, Yirl Du said, "I fear we should have rested longer, my lord. You have grown weak from your wounds."

"No, just out of practice," Thorne told him. "I didn't use any water-shoes while I was at school, you know. I'll get back the hang of it, presently."

And at length, by persistent effort, he did get the hang of it. By the time the sun had reached the zenith they were moving side by side in perfect unison, with long, rhythmic strokes. During this time they had traveled on a dozen winding streams, crossed six small lakes, and three times removed their water-shoes for short jaunts across the land.

At present they were gliding across the calm, mirror-like bosom of a lake much larger than any they had crossed thus far, when Thorne, chancing to notice a shadowy reflection in the placid water at his right, looked upward. To his alarm, he saw that a group of about twenty warriors, each mounted on a gawr, were gliding down toward them. And the warriors were mail-clad, round-bodied yellow men.

"Look, Yirl Du!" he cried, pointing aloft. "The Ma Gongi!"

His companion took one look. "Straight toward that point of land, quickly! It is our only hope."

They had been making for the mouth of a little stream, beside which the point of land projected. Now they turned almost at right angles to their course and made for the shore which was about two hundred yards distant.

But they had traveled only a few strokes toward their objective when a large net, hanging on four cables, was dropped by one of their pursuers. In an instant it had scooped up Yirl Du. Thorne saw him struggling futilely like some captured wild thing—saw him draw his dagger and vainly try to cut the metallic meshes.

Then the Earthman heard a swish in the water behind him, and he, too, was scooped up in a huge net.

CHAPTER 17

As soon as he felt the net swish under him in the water, Thorne instinctively dived forward in an effort to evade it. But it had traveled too far beneath him to make such an attempt successful. However, he was able to catch hold of the rim with both hands, and clung to this as he was borne aloft, so he did not sink into the toils as Yirl Du had done.

An instant later he was soaring fifty feet above the treetops, and though he well knew the risk he ran, decided on a desperate attempt at escape. Accordingly, he drew himself up until the edge of the net was on a level with his thighs, then turned a somersault and let go, falling feet foremost.

His feet were still thrust through the bands of his pneumatic water-shoes, and these helped, to a considerable extent, in breaking his fall as he crashed downward through the branches of a large tree. Straight down through the foliage he plunged, and upon striking the ground bounced upward like a rubber ball on his resilient water-shoes. After several gradually diminishing bounces, he checked himself by clutching a shrub. Then he swiftly removed the water-shoes, and, taking them under his arm, dashed away through the thick undergrowth.

So dense was the leafy tangle overhead that Thorne was unable to see his enemies, though he heard their shouts and learned that a warrior was landing. But this same dense canopy prevented his enemies from seeing him, and for this he was thankful.

He was grieved by the capture of his faithful retainer, but he could not possibly help Yirl Du, and would only render his own capture or death certain. Moreover, there was his debt to Thaine. Somehow he must contrive to escape for her sake.

It was not long before he came to a narrow stream, almost completely concealed from observers in the sky by the branches and lianas which arched and interlaced across it.

The stream, he soon found, had seemingly endless ramifications, and he traveled for several hours; in this manner he grew weary, hungry and thirsty, and decided to stop for rest and refreshment. Instead of sleeping directly out on the bank, he caught hold of a low-hanging liana, by means of this reached another, and swung himself up into a tree. Removing his water-shoes and slinging them over his back, he now traveled for some distance by swinging from tree to tree before alighting on the ground.

Wearily he flung himself down on a bed of soft moss beneath the spreading branches of an immense, aromatic sebolis tree. Then, after a pull at his water flask, he opened his box and removed therefrom a ration of dried meat and a cake. These he washed down with copious droughts of cold water. He rested there on the moss for a while, then packed up and wandered on.

As he felt that he had effectively baffled his pursuers, and knew that he was hopelessly lost, he saw no great need for haste. And so he wandered on through this strange Martian jungle, pausing at times to examine odd flowers or fruits, and marveling at its fantastic and often gigantic-insect life, as well as its many queer beasts, birds and reptiles.

Part of the time he walked on boggy land from which the water oozed at each step, and often he splashed through shallow pools. At other times he was compelled to don his water-shoes to cross flooded areas where the trees stood in the water.

There were also considerable stretches of high, dry land, usually quite heavily wooded.

Shortly after he had entered one of these he suddenly sighted a colony of pale green caterpillars, the bodies and heads of which were protected by sharp yellow spikes. There was a great diversity of size among them, the smallest being barely an inch in length, while the largest were more than three feet long and proportionately thick. All were browsing on leaves except a few of the largest individuals, which were busy spinning cocoons. He noticed many finished cocoons hanging from limbs by twisted, rope-like fastenings. They were pale green in color, and of a glistening, silky texture.

Presently he came to one hanging directly above his path, its lower tip at the height of his head. Curiously, he extended his hand to feel the silky covering, and pinched it to test its thickness. But scarcely had he done so ere a mournful, wailing cry smote his ears. It sounded much like the cry of a newborn human child, and seemed to come from the cocoon he had touched.

He jerked his hand away, but the wailing continued. Then he was suddenly aware of the whirring of a host of invisible wings in the air above him. There was a sharp twang, and a tiny arrow embedded itself in the ground at his feet. A second whizzed past his ear, and a third grazed his arm.

He realized that he was being attacked by the Little People, and suddenly thought of the ring. Snatching it from the pouch in which he had placed it, he rubbed it briskly on his palm. At this the twanging of the bowstrings ceased, and where he had only heard the beating of their wings, he now saw a number of Ulf men hovering in the air.

All of them were slightly larger than Eriné; there was as much diversity of appearance among them as there would have been in a similar sized group of humans. Their antennae were longer than those of the Ulf girl, and projected from shiny metal headpieces, notched at the front to let them through. They wore shirts of light chain-mail which reached to their thighs, drawn in at the middle by green silk belts from which depended swords and daggers. In addition to these weapons, each man carried a small bow in his hand, and a quiver of arrows strapped to his thigh.

One of the tiny warriors alighted on the ground, and advancing, saluted Thorne respectfully.

"Fleeswin, a Jen of the Ulf Archers, shields his eyes in the light of your presence, man of the Old Race and friend of Estabil, the Great One," he said. "We regret that we attacked you unknowingly, and humbly craving your pardon, place ourselves at your disposal and under your command."

"My greetings to you and your archers, Fleeswin Jen," Thorne answered, returning his salute. "Actuated by curiosity I touched this cocoon, not meaning to injure it."

"Our infants are easily frightened by the touch of strangers," Fleeswin said, "and we who guard them cannot watch them all at one time. We would lose many that might otherwise be saved if they did not summon us when menaced or interfered with."

"Then I am fortunate that your marksmanship was no better."

"Had you been one of the Ma Gongi, you would now be bristling with arrows," Fleeswin hastened to inform him. "But we saw you were of the Old Race, so only shot to drive you away. What would you with us, Bearer of the Ring?"

"If you can help me to find Thaine, daughter of Miradon Vil, I'll be grateful," Thorne answered. "I am the Rad of Takkor and her friend."

As soon as he had announced his title, every member of the little company saluted.

"We are doubly honored," said Fleeswin, "that you prove to be the Lord of Takkor as well as a Bearer of the Ring. As for finding Thaine, if she is anywhere within the Takkor Marsh, our Vil can find her for you. Permit me to conduct you to him."

After sending a warrior ahead to announce their coming, and placing another in temporary charge of the archers, Fleeswin led the way. Presently, above the drone of insects and the songs of birds, Thorne heard a haunting exquisite fantasy of sound which seemed to emanate from a carillon of no less than a thousand tiny silver-tongued bells. Yet he knew, as he drew closer, that it was not bells he heard but a chorus of Ulf voices. Soon he was able to distinguish the words of their song, and was surprised to learn that it was a paean of welcome for him.

A moment later he and Fleeswin emerged into a pleasant glen, the verdure-clothed sides of which rose steeply at his right and left. The place literally swarmed with the Ulfi, both male and female, and all were singing—some hanging suspended in the air with fanning wings, some perched in the trees or upon outcropping rocks on the hillside, some standing in cave mouths, with which the place was honeycombed, and others gathered on the mossy ground.

Fleeswin now kept to the ground, marching as if some great and honorable task had been delegated to him. As Thorne came abreast of the first singers, these began showering him with tiny, fragrant white blossoms. Then a group of two-score pretty Ulf maidens fluttered down and some draped Thorne with garlands while others strewed flowers before him.

Suddenly the music ceased, and Thorne, his body swathed with ropes of blossoms, found himself standing before a jovial looking pot-bellied old Ulf with a merry twinkle in his eyes. He sat enthroned on the lip of a large lily.

"Greetings, Sheb Takkor Rad," cried the little old fellow on the lily throne, returning his salute. "Estabil, Vil of the Ulfi, bids you welcome to Ulf-land, and desires to publicly thank you for saving the life of his precious daughter, Eriné. If there is aught that Estabil can do for you, you have but to make known your wishes."

"I wish to find . . ." Thorne began.

"I'll spare you the trouble of saying more," Estabil interrupted. "You wish to find Thaine. That we can promise to perform for you."

He leaped nimbly down from the lily throne, and continued: "Now that that is done, will you not stay to eat and drink with us?"

"Of course," Thorne assured him, "but it is important that I find Thaine, quickly. I should prefer to stay only long enough to drink a friendly cup with you, though if I were not pressed for time your hospitality would be most welcome. I'm sure you understand."

"We do. Indeed we do," Estabil replied. He turned and raised his hand, whereupon a little bearded Ulf struck a gong. Then there issued from the mouth of a cave in the hillside a figure Thorne instantly recognized. It was Eriné. Behind her came an Ulf maiden bearing a golden tray on which reposed three tiny platinum cups that sparkled with jewels, and a jar.

Thorne saluted as the Vil's daughter approached, and she smiled up at him.

"I hoped I might greet you at the banquet table," she said, "but since you cannot tarry with us, I bring you the cup of friendship and of farewell."

So saying, she filled the three jeweled cups from the jar, handed one to Thorne, one to her father, and retained one for herself.

Estabil raised his cup.

"Once there was a Rad of Takkor," he said, "who, wandering through his marshlands saw an Ulf maiden about to be done to death by a savage monster of the air. The Rad slew the monster and rescued the Ulf maiden, who proved to be the daughter of the Vil of the Ulfi. Every Ulf, from the Vil to his lowliest subject, will never forget. And in this cup we pledge to the Rad of Takkor our eternal friendship."

He and Eriné both raised their cups to their lips, and Thorne followed their example. "The Rad of Takkor gratefully accepts the pledge of friendship of the Ulfi," he said, "and is deeply sensible of the honor thus bestowed upon him. In return, he pledges his lasting friendship to Estabil, his lovely daughter, and his loyal subjects."

As soon as they had emptied their cups, Estabil raised his hand. Behind him the gong sounded twice, and a dozen Ulf warriors, flying six on a side, emerged from the mouth of a cave high on the hillside, bearing between them a rectangle of silken fabric about eight feet long and four wide. They alighted in front of the Vil, and saluted.

"The Rad of Takkor is ready to be conveyed to the house of Thaine," he said. Then he turned to Thorne. "Seat yourself in the middle of the cloth, my lord," he invited, "and you will be carried swiftly and safely to your destination."

Though he was not entirely reassured as to the safety of this fragile conveyance, Thorne did as directed.

The Vil raised his hand. The gong sounded three strokes. Then the wings of the twelve Ulf warriors began whirring rapidly, and Thorne felt himself rising. All around him the Ulfi burst into song. He waved farewell. A moment later he was gliding over the treetops, the Ulf-song swiftly dying in the distance.

Presently they flew out over a lake, in the center of which was an island. Straight to the island they took him, and set him down in the midst of it in a small clearing.

One of the Ulf warriors touched his arm and pointed. "There is the house of Thaine."

Thorne gazed intently in the direction the little fellow indicated. Presently he was able to make out what had entirely escaped his attention before—a small, irregularly shaped stone house, camouflaged with vines and creepers, and surrounded by trees.

"Ah, I see it now. I am beholden to you and your Vil for this favor. Please convey my thanks to him."

One of the little warriors rolled the cloth into a bundle and thrust it beneath his arm. All twelve of them saluted and swiftly faded from view.

He crossed the clearing, and entering an opening in the vines, found a large circular doorway cut in the stone. The door stood open, revealing a large room with several swinging chairs, suspended divans, and a fireplace. Three circular doorways cut in the walls led to other rooms.

"Thaine," he called, then waited expectantly.

There was no answer.

He was about to call her a second time when he suddenly heard a low growl from one of the rooms beyond. Then, out of that room streaked a huge black-haired beast with short legs, webbed feet, a paddle-shaped tail armed with spikes, and a cavernous mouth as large as that of a crocodile. He instantly recognized it as a dalf.

There was but one thing to do, and that quickly. Thorne seized the handle of the great door of thick planking, and swung it shut. A moment later he felt the impact of the heavy beast on the other side. He kept his hand on the latch, and it was well that he did so, for he suddenly felt that it was being pressed upward from the other side. Recalling the remarkable sagacity of these creatures, he was convinced that the beast was trying to open the door.

He was looking around for something with which to brace the latch, when he suddenly heard another growl, this time behind him. Turning, he beheld a second dalf, black with a ring of bright yellow fur circling its neck, swiftly bearing down upon him.

CHAPTER 18

When he saw the second dalf charging toward him, Thorne whipped out his sword and raised it to defend himself. But he lowered it again.

"Tezzu!" he exclaimed.

At this the demeanor of the beast suddenly changed. Instead of charging, it now bounded playfully up to him, then began skipping and leaping around him and making little purring noises deep in its throat.

And now, in the same leafy opening through which the beast had appeared, he saw a slender, girlish figure carrying a basket of fish and a trident.

"Thaine!" he cried.

"Hahr Ree Thorne! It's really you! I'm so glad!"

Dropping basket and trident, she ran forward, flung her arms around his neck and, much to his amazement, kissed him.

"I thought you would never come. I feared they had killed you."

"They tried hard enough," he replied, "but I got away and came as soon as I could."

"I'm sure you did. Let us go inside while I prepare something to eat. Why do you stand there holding the latch?"

"Because one of your dalfs is on the other side, trying to get at me."

"That's Neem. He won't molest you, now that I am here."

Thus reassured, Thorne opened the door. Neem, the great black dalf, waddled out to meet his mistress, but paid no attention to the Earthman. The latter picked up the basket and trident, and they went in.

Thorne insisted upon helping Thaine prepare the meal, and they soon had pulcho brewing, fish grilling, and fresh cakes baking.

"From your floral decorations, I judge that you have been among the Little People," said Thaine, as she turned a browned slab of fish.

"You judge correctly," Thorne replied. "In fact it was a dozen of their warriors who brought me here. Then they saluted and disappeared. Do you know anything about that strange power of theirs—making themselves invisible?"

"I've seen them do it many times," she told him, "yet how they do it remains a mystery. Our scientists believe they are able to surround themselves with auras of photo-electric force which cause light rays to bend around them and anything within the auras, such as their weapons and clothing. Since we see objects only by means of light rays reflected from them into our eyes, if the rays miss them or bend around them they are invisible to us."

"Sounds reasonable enough," said Thorne. "But what is this force?"

"One might as well ask, 'What is electricity, or magnetism, or gravity?' We know that when they are very weary, or weakened by wounds or illness, they are unable to generate this strange force."

"That explains why Eriné was visible when pursued by the bat. She must have been exhausted."

"The bat?"

Thorne told her how he had saved the life of the daughter of the Vil of the Ulfi, and showed her the ring.

"It is a precious gift, and one not lightly bestowed," said Thaine. "I have one like it, and so has my father, but only because he once saved the life of the Vil of the Little People."

"You remind me, that we were to go in search of your father. Have you had any word from him?"

"None. Even the Ulfi are baffled, and they know almost everything that takes place in this marsh. I fear I shall never see him again."

Thorne saw the tears gathering in her eyes. "We'll find your father, never fear," he said reassuringly. "And now that the food is ready, let us eat, and I will tell you of my adventures since I last saw you. I owe you an explanation for staying away so long."

When he had finished, she pounced on that very part of the story which he most wished to forget. "This Neva, is she very beautiful?"

"Very, even though she is deceitful and cruel."

"You love her?"

"Would you love a person who had tricked you—then condemned you to a horrible, lingering death?"

"That," said Thaine, refilling his pulcho cup for him, "is not an answer but an evasion."

"Well then, if you must have it, I wish I had never seen her. But I bore you with these troubles of mine. Let us speak no more of them."

"My poor Hahr Ree Thorne," she said. "You do not bore me. Your troubles are my troubles, for are we not true friends?"

"Thaine," he said, "you *are* a real friend."

"I am glad," she said softly, and laid her cheek against his shoulder.

Presently she leaned forward, half turned, and gazed up into his face. "Look at me, Hahr Ree Thorne. Is this Neva really so much more beautiful than I?"

"What a question!" he exclaimed. "It's just like a woman to think of a poser like that."

"Another evasion," she countered, "but it tells me what I wanted to find out. She *is* more beautiful."

He studied her smilingly. "I wouldn't say so. She is a blonde, you are a brunette. She is a great beauty of her type, and you of yours. You and Neva are gems of equal luster, but different."

"Why, then, perhaps I can make you forget this Neva."

Before he was aware of what she was about, she had turned still more—was lying back across his arm. Her eyes were dark wells of enchantment. Her red lips, half parted, drew him seductively.

"Why don't you kiss me?" she pouted.

"You little witch!"

Fiercely he bent down—crushed those warm red lips against his own.

For a moment, she suffered his caress, unresisting. Then, with a little frightened gasp she broke from his embrace—returned to her place beside the pulcho jar. Mechanically, she filled their cups. Tears trembled on her long, dark lashes. Her lips quivered ever so slightly as she handed him his cup.

"Why, Thaine, what's wrong?" he asked.

"I—I didn't know it would be like that," she quavered.

"You don't really love me, then?"

"I wish I really knew."

At this juncture there was the noise of huge wings flapping overhead, followed by a thud. Thorne knew from the sounds that a gawr had just flown over the house and landed in the clearing. Both dalfs sprang up, growling ominously, but Thaine silenced them.

Then, accompanied by Thorne, she ran to the door and peered through the leafy screen.

CHAPTER 19

When Thorne looked out through the leafy screen that camouflaged the door of Thaine's island home, he saw that a warrior in the uniform of an officer of the Kamud had dismounted in the clearing. The fellow was leading his gawr beneath the branches of a large, spreading tree, where the bird-beast would be concealed from observers flying overhead. The newcomer walked with the peculiar, rolling gait of a man whose legs are abnormally short in proportion to the rest of his body.

"It's Yirl Du!" Thorne exclaimed.

Keeping cautiously beneath the trees which fringed the clearing, Yirl Du circled toward the house. A few moments later he entered the opening in the screen. To Thorne he rendered the usual salutation, but to Thaine, the royal salute. This surprised the Earthman until he remembered that she was the daughter of Miradon Vil, and therefore entitled to the homage due a princess.

"I have news—momentous news," said Yirl Du as he entered the hut.

"Have—have you news of my father?" Thaine asked, anxiously.

"Ill news," he replied. "His majesty is in the clutches of Sel Han, who has imprisoned him in Castle Takkor."

"We must find a way to rescue him," exclaimed Thorne.

"Wait, I have not told you all," Yirl Du said. "Perhaps I had best begin at the beginning. After I was netted by Sel Han's Ma Gongi, they searched a while for you, my lord. But at last they gave up the chase and flew with me to Castle Takkor. I found the castle garrisoned entirely by Ma Gongi, with Sur Det and a few of his cronies in command. Sur Det had been rescued from the prison pen by Sel Han.

"It seems that some time ago the yellow scientists rediscovered how to generate the deadly green ray used in warfare by their ancestors. Since then they have been building large ray projectors, not as yet being able to manufacture small hand projectors powerful enough for efficient use. With four of these projectors and an army of Ma Gongi mounted on gawrs, Sel Han yesterday flew to Dukor, overawed the army and the people with the weapons he had brought with him, and took over the government. He captured all the high officers of the Kamud, and it is said he intends to proclaim himself Vil of Xancibar in a day or two. These officers, among whom are Kov Lutas and Lal Vak, together with the Dixtar and his daughter Neva, were sent to Castle Takkor, where they are now prisoners, guarded by the Ma Gongi warriors.

"Miradon Vil, who had previously been captured by Sel Han's Ma Gongi scouts, was at first held in the secret camp where they were making the ray projectors. But as soon as the government had been over-thrown, Sel Han ordered him brought to Castle Takkor, where he could be guarded with the other important prisoners.

"Sur Det ordered me imprisoned in a room in one of the towers, to await the arrival of Sel Han, who would then decide what my fate should be. But, unfortunately for his plans, he had me put in a room in which there was a hidden panel which communicated with a secret passageway that led to the underground cellars, and thence out under the docks.

"I lost no time in making use of this means of escape, but ran into one of Sel Han's officers. I caught him by the throat before he could make a sound, and hung on until he ceased to breathe. Then I donned his uniform and weapons, and boldly ascended to the dock. There, by virtue of the authority vested in my borrowed uniform, I demanded and received a gawr from one of the attendants, and flew away unmolested."

"Do you think it would be possible for you and me to return to the castle, enter by way of the secret passage, and rescue Miradon Vil?" Thorne asked.

"I fear it would not, my lord," Yirl Du answered. "His majesty is too well guarded. He is an even more important prisoner than Irintz Tel. Sel Han holds him as a hostage to prevent any uprising among the royalists, just as he holds the Dixtar to keep the loyal Kamudists from revolting."

"How many ray projectors are left at the castle?" Thorne asked.

"There are none," Yirl Du told him. "All four are in use in Dukor. Where Sel Han goes, there go the projectors, also. He will not leave them in the hands of his most trusted officers, for they are his very lifeblood. Without them he could be easily defeated by a handful of regular soldiers. And so far as I know, no others have been completed."

"Why, then, perhaps we can take the castle," mused Thorne. "You told me once that the Free Swordsmen would revolt against the rule of any but a rad of the Takkor blood."

"I'm sure they are loyal, my lord," Yirl Du said. "You have but to command, and they will fight to the last man to recover your castle for you."

"Good. I think it can be done without heavy losses. I have a plan."

That afternoon, shortly after Thorne had outlined his plan and given his instructions to Yirl Du, the latter flew away in the direction of Takkor City.

Some time later, when the shadows had begun to lengthen, Thorne, who had been snatching forty winks on one of Thaine's divans, was awakened by her hand on his brow.

"The time has come," she said.

Thorne sat up, drank the cup of freshly brewed pulcho she proffered him, and sprang to the floor.

"Now if you will be so kind as to lend me Tezzu and a boat," he said, "I'll be off."

"Why do you say 'lend,'" she asked, "when I am going with you?"

"You are to remain here. There will be fighting—bloodshed. It is too dangerous."

She drew herself up proudly. "I am a warrior, and as good a swordsman as the man you just sent to rally your followers. If you won't take me with you I shall go in a separate boat."

Seeing the impossibility of dissuading her from her resolve, Thorne set about making preparations for their journey. They then took Tezzu with them, leaving Neem, the other beast, to guard the house, and went down to the boat.

Tezzu, with the tow-rope in his huge mouth, swiftly took them across the lake and into a narrow stream where the foliage arching overhead concealed them from the sight of flying enemies. After traversing a veritable network of these tiny streams and crossing a number of small lakes, they reached the shore of Takkor Lake just before sundown.

At the command of his mistress, Tezzu dragged the boat up out of the water, upon which ice crystals were already beginning to form, and into a place of concealment, where he was left to guard it. Then the man and girl set off along the lake shore, following the same route that Thorne had followed upon his first disastrous visit to Castle Takkor, and carefully keeping out of sight among the trees.

They had not traveled far before the sun set, so they were forced to pick their way through the undergrowth by the light of the nearer moon. Shortly thereafter, Yirl Du appeared in the path before them.

"Everything is arranged," he said softly. "I have been waiting to lead you to the rendezvous."

They paused only long enough to draw up their boots and let down their head-cloaks for warmth. Then Yirl Du led them away through the glittering, frost-coated jungle. Presently they came to a large clearing where several hundred warriors, mounted on gawrs, were assembled, and more were arriving constantly from all points of the compass, singly and in small groups. There was also a group of fifty warriors who were unmounted.

"In a little while there will be five hundred mounted warriors here, my lord," said Yirl Du. "My son, Rid Du, has assembled a thousand more afoot. They are scattered about in the city, seemingly only amusing themselves, but will rally to him at the signal, half to capture the gawrs on the wharf and the other half to rush the castle gate."

Shortly thereafter the last flying warrior arrived.

After a brief final conference with Thorne, Yirl Du led his foot-soldiers away. They were picked men, for they were to follow Yirl Du through the secret passageway into the castle and then capture and throw open the gates, so the soldiers under Rid Du could rush in.

Thorne was to lead the air attack which was calculated first to draw the attention of the defenders from Yirl Du's little party, and later to assist in crushing the Ma Gongi guards.

After he had waited for the length of time agreed upon with Yirl Du, Thorne gave the signal to his men, and one by one the great bird-beasts left the ground. With the Earthman in the lead, they formed a long line which ascended for about two thousand feet, then straightened out to fly directly for the castle. Once above his objective, Thorne led the way downward in a swift, descending spiral which, as it neared the upper parapets, flattened into a great circle that followed the outline of the walls.

An alarm had been sounded at the first approach of this flying host, and now, as they drew nearer, javelins flew up at them, hurled by the defenders on the walls. Assisted by the force of gravity, while their enemies were impeded by it, the flying warriors were able to reply to good purpose, and soon there were many dead and wounded Ma Gongi on the ramparts. But it seemed that as fast as they fell more rushed up to take their places.

At the first alarm, five hundred of Rid Du's warriors had swarmed down over the docks where the gawrs were kept. As they were guarded only by a few soldiers and orderlies, the bird-beasts were soon captured. In the meantime, led by Rid Du, the other half of his little company assembled before the gate and began hurtling javelins up at the defenders.

Now was the time for Yirl Du to strike, and Thorne watched tensely. Presently he saw the little company emerge from one of the castle doors, quickly form a flying wedge with Yirl Du at the apex, and charge across the courtyard, cutting down or scattering the surprised Ma Gongi in their way. Just before the gate the two wings of the wedge divided, and each column ascended into one of the watch towers which guarded the gateway. A moment later the gates swung open, and in poured the Free Swordsmen from the town, with Rid Du at their head.

Now Thorne's flying warriors swooped down into the melee, abandoning their javelins for fear of injuring their comrades, and fighting at close range with sword, mace and dagger. The slaughter was appalling. The Ma Gongi, most of whom had been slaves and were unaccustomed to warfare, were no match for the disciplined Takkor swordsmen.

The ramparts and courtyard were thickly strewn with their bodies as Thorne, with Yirl Du, Thaine, and a small contingent of Takkor swordsmen, cut down the warriors who guarded the entrance, charged into the castle, and began their search for the prisoners.

Yirl Du led the way to the great central tower, then fought their way up the winding staircase, the yellow defenders stubbornly contesting each step of the way.

Thorne and Yirl Du were ever in the front as they climbed the stairs, and both were soon covered with wounds. When they reached the flight which led to the top story, they met with the most desperate resistance they had yet encountered. But the swiftly flashing blade of the Earthman backed up the swords of Yirl Du and Thaine, and the javelins of the warriors who came behind them soon cleared the stairs of living enemies, and the few who remained above to contest their way were quickly cut down.

Thorne tried the door and found it barred on the inside. Reversing his bloody sword, he beat upon the panels with the pommel.

"Who is it?" came a cautious call from within.

"The Rad of Takkor," Thorne replied. "Open quickly."

At this, there was the sound of a sliding bolt, and the door swung open. A tall, broad-shouldered man whose shaggy hair and flowing beard gleamed golden yellow under the baridium lights stood in the doorway.

At sight of him, Yirl Du and the other warriors instantly raised both hands before their eyes and muttered the royal salutation, while Thaine, with an exclamation of joy, ran forward and flung her arms around his neck.

"Father!" she cried. "I'm so glad we found you safe."

Gently he took her face between his huge hands, and bending, kissed her forehead. "Little daughter!" he murmured. "This was man's work. You should not have come."

"Did you not train me to do a man's work? And have I not done it well? Ask Sheb Takkor."

Thorne, who had instantly sensed that this regal looking personage must be Miradon Vil, had only been a shade behind the others in rendering the royal salutation. He now stood, respectfully waiting for the Vil to speak.

"It is a question I need not propound," said Miradon. "I know you have fought nobly, or you would not be here. But, come, Sheb Takkor Rad, and you, Yirl Du Jen. There are those in other apartments who will be glad to thank their gallant rescuers."

He led the way down the hall and tapped on a door. From within came a little squeaky voice, which Thorne immediately recognized as that of Irintz Tel. "Who is there?"

"Miradon Vil with friends who have rescued us. Open."

The bolt slid back, the door swung open, and the little rat-faced Dixtar stepped out, followed by Kov Lutas and Lal Vak.

"Where's Neva?" squeaked Irintz Tel. "Have you found my daughter?"

"She should be in one of these apartments," replied Miradon Vil.

"Open the doors! Break them down!" ordered the Dixtar, with a wave of his hand. "Why do you all stand there, staring?"

Thorne regarded him coldly. "You forget, Irintz Tel," he said, "that this is my castle and these are my warriors. They take orders only from me."

At this, the Dixtar turned deathly pale, but Thorne, ignoring him, warmly greeted the handsome young Kov Lutas and the white-haired Lal Vak, both of whom profusely thanked him for coming to their rescue.

In the meantime, Miradon Vil had gone on to the next door and rapped. Thorne's heart gave a great bound as he heard the voice that answered—the voice of Neva.

Irintz Tel rushed to the door and embraced his daughter as she stepped out, followed by two of her slave-girls. Kov Lutas and Lal Vak instantly crowded forward to greet her, and the latter ceremoniously introduced Miradon Vil.

Thorne held aloof, watching them, his breast seething with conflicting emotions. Despite his resolve to put Neva forever from his thoughts, he now found that sight of her had suddenly reawakened all the old longing with redoubled intensity.

Suddenly he realized that Neva had seen him—was coming toward him—holding out her arms to him. His heart throbbed wildly. Yet he resolutely steeled himself to break the subtle spell she had again cast over him—forcing his flagging will to recall her betrayal of him and the hideous death to which she had condemned him.

"Sheb, beloved!" she murmured. "The time has been so long . . ."

"The Dixtar's daughter," he said with frigid politeness, "honors the lowly castle of the Rad of Takkor by her charming presence. The Takkor retainers will have instructions to do all in their power to make her stay a pleasant one."

With this he saluted stiffly, and walked to where Yirl Du stood awaiting his orders. "See that these, my honored guests, are given the best the castle affords."

"Yes, my lord."

For a moment Neva stood bewildered. Then a sudden flush suffused her lovely face. Turning, she reentered her apartment, head held high and eyes flashing.

Without even glancing at the door through which she had vanished, Thorne addressed Yirl Du. "I understand that the chief officials of the Kamud, including the seven judges, are confined here."

"They are in the west wing, my lord."

"Have them brought here, Jen," cut in Irintz Tel imperiously. "We would speak with them."

"They are to be kept in their quarters, and well guarded," continued Thorne. "Also, you are to search for Sur Det, and if he still lives, bring him to me. I would question him."

"Yes, my lord."

The Earthman now turned to the little Dixtar. "I trust it will not be necessary to again remind you that my warriors take orders only from me."

Irintz Tel shot him a venomous glance. Then he swung on his heel and entered Neva's apartment.

Thorne looked at Miradon Vil with an apologetic smile. "I hope that your majesty will excuse me, as I have pressing duties. Preparations must be made at once, so we can all leave the castle before morning. Sel Han may return at any moment with his ray projectors, and if he finds us here our case will be desperate, if not entirely hopeless."

The Vil returned his smile. "I understand. Can I help?"

"No, I thank your majesty."

Thorne hurried down the corpse-littered stairs, and out into the courtyard. Here he set about making immediate preparations for flight, ordering that all available weapons and provisions be brought out and loaded onto the gawrs. He planned to leave the Vil and Thaine in their secret hiding place, and to find another for Irintz Tel and Neva. Then he would lead his warriors far out into the marsh and hide from Sel Han and his fearsome new weapons until he could devise some plan for successfully combating him.

He was overseeing these preparations some time later, when Yirl Du came and asked to speak with him aside.

"My lord," he said, "Sur Det cannot be found among either the dead or the living."

"Then he has escaped. We must hasten our preparations, for he has undoubtedly gone to Dukor, and will bring Sel Han and his ray projectors down upon us."

But the words had scarcely left his mouth when a guard called from one of the towers: "A vast host of warriors mounted on gawrs is approaching. Also there are a score of the great metal gawrs."

Instantly, confusion reigned in the castle. A frightened warrior leaped on the back of a half-loaded gawr and jerked the guiding rod. The bird-beast flapped awkwardly up out of the courtyard. But it had scarcely cleared the castle walls when a strange and terrible thing happened. A green ray shot out from somewhere beyond the wall—struck the fleeing warrior and his mount. For an instant they were visible, bathed in that weird, green light. Then they seemed to suddenly shrivel and disintegrate. Where they had been there was nothing at all. The ray winked out and consternation settled over the courtyard.

CHAPTER 20

Thorne knew that Sel Han, with his powerful ray projectors, could not only cut off any attempt at flight, but could destroy the castle and all in it at his pleasure. Yet he resolved that he, his friends and his followers should not succumb without resisting to the utmost. He accordingly rallied his panic-stricken warriors to the defense of the walls, then mounted to the ramparts to survey the movements of the enemy.

Sel Han, it seemed, was not disposed immediately to storm the castle. All of his flying machines had alighted well out of javelin range of the walls, and from the interiors of these, Ma Gongi foot-soldiers were pouring. A ray projector had been mounted on the flat roof of a nearby house, and Thorne stared at it curiously. It looked much like a large telescope on a conical stand. The flying warriors were circling the castle, but the great bulk of these were alighting on the ground. Soon only a few remained in the air as scouts and observers.

Glancing out over the lake, the Earthman saw that a second projector was mounted there on a large boat. He walked around the walls and descried a third on the roof of a building to the landward side, and still farther, a fourth, mounted on the ground to command the remaining sector of the wall.

Having completed his inspection of the disposal of the enemy troops and projectors, Thorne returned to a parapet beside the gate which opened on the dock, and before which Sel Han had massed his chief officers.

As he stood there on the battlement, watching every movement of the enemy, he heard a group of people coming up behind him. Turning, he beheld Miradon Vil and Irintz Tel walking side by side. Though they had always been deadly enemies it was evident that they had united to make common cause against the man who not only threatened them, but all of Mars as well.

Behind the two ex-rulers of Xancibar came Neva escorted by Lal Vak, and Thaine escorted by Kov Lutas. All carried weapons.

"We sought you out, Sheb Takkor Rad, hoping that we might be of some assistance in the defense," said Miradon Vil.

"I fear there is little we can do save surrender or die, your majesty, though I have resolved that I, personally, will fight to the death rather than surrender to Sel Han."

"Your resolve coincides with my own," replied Miradon Vil.

"And mine! And mine!" chorused the others, with the single exception of Irintz Tel.

The ominous silence that followed was suddenly rent by the clarion notes of a trumpet. Hurrying to the wall, Thorne saw that a man had detached himself from the group around Sel Han, and walked to a point before the gate just out of range of a hurled javelin.

Once again the herald sounded a ringing call on his trumpet. Then, resting his instrument on his hip, he cried: "His Imperial Majesty, Sel Han the Invincible, Vil of Xancibar, Vil of Vils, and Vildus of all Mars, commands that Sheb Takkor and his warriors instantly lay down their weapons and come forth from the castle gates unarmed. His majesty has it in his power to utterly destroy the castle and every soul within it. Witness!"

He paused dramatically, and as he paused a pencil of green light stabbed out from the projector on the house-top. It flashed to the top of one of the lesser towers, and where the ray touched, the crystal blocks and mortar shriveled and vanished, leaving a jagged hole in the battlement.

The ray winked out, and the herald continued: "There will be no terms of surrender, other than such conditions as the Vildus of Mars shall see fit to impose."

With a farewell flourish of his trumpet, he turned and walked back to where Sel Han and his officers stood waiting.

Thorne turned to an officer who stood near by. "Get me a herald."

The officer ran to the gate tower and immediately emerged with a youth who carried a trumpet. Thorne gave him his instructions, and mounting the wall, he blew a ringing flourish. After waiting for a moment, he announced: "The Lord of Takkor, his warriors and his friends, defy Sel Han of the empty titles, and his bandits, who have invaded the Takkor domain. Here is Castle Takkor, and here are its defenders unafraid, for Sel Han to come and take if he can, or to destroy if he has aught to gain by wanton destruction. The Lord of Takkor further states . . ."

The speech of the herald was suddenly cut off, along with his life, by a green flash from the ray projector on the house-top.

A roar of rage went up from the Takkor swordsmen. If Sel Han had thought to frighten them by this demonstration he had a poor conception of the caliber of these men.

But though this had made the Takkor warriors more steadfast in their purpose, there was at least one occupant of the castle upon whom it had worked the opposite effect. Chancing to look toward Irintz Tel, Thorne noticed that he was trembling violently.

Presently there came two more blasts from the trumpet of Sel Han's herald.

"His Imperial Majesty, the Vildus of Mars, could destroy the castle and all it contains," shouted the herald, "yet he is just and merciful. He realizes that the warriors of the Takkor Rad and the prisoners are respectively under the command—and in the power of a man who is willing to sacrifice them all to satisfy his own empty vanity and make good his puny defiance of Sel Han, the Invincible.

"Wherefore, his imperial majesty gives you, each and every one, a respite from death, during which you may have time to depose this foolhardy leader and save your own lives. And to the man who will bring him the head of Sheb Takkor, the Vildus of Mars covenants to present the Raddek of Takkor with all its lands. His majesty decrees that your respite from death shall last from now until the planet has completed one turn upon its axis. If, by that time and at that very moment, you have not obeyed his edict, then will the castle and all in it be utterly destroyed."

Having said his say, the herald returned to the group of officers.

"Looks as if things have quieted down for the present, at least," said Thorne, turning to the others. "I suggest that we all get some much needed sleep."

"One moment, Sheb Takkor," interposed Irintz Tel. "I suggest that before we retire we hold a council and decide just what we are going to do. It is only fair that we should all have some say in the matter."

"I quite agree to that," Thorne replied. "Thus far I have been acting under the belief that I was carrying out the wishes of the majority in defying Sel Han. If I have erred, there is yet time to rectify the mistake. Let us go into the castle."

They gathered, a few moments later, in the apartment which Thorne had chosen for himself. The Earthman had asked Yirl Du to attend as the representative of the Free Swordsmen. The others were Neva, Thaine, Miradon Vil, Irintz Tel, Lal Vak, and Kov Lutas.

Thorne stood at a taboret in the center of the room, filling cups with steaming pulcho, a jar of which had just been brought in by Yirl Du. These he passed to his assembled guests. Then he said to Irintz Tel, "Since it was at your suggestion that this council was assembled, I will call upon you first to address us."

The Dixtar took a dainty sip of pulcho, then carefully held the cup before him.

"My good friends and comrades in adversity," he began, "I, for one, see the hopelessness of our position here, and the futility of further resistance to the decree of fate. After all, it is better to be live prisoners than dead heroes, blasted into nothingness by the awful weapons of the Ma Gongi. I suggest that we surrender to Sel Han while he is inclined to be merciful, thus not only saving our own lives, but those of the brave Takkor swordsmen who sought to rescue us from the conqueror."

"You have all heard the suggestion of the Dixtar," said Thorne. "Will you surrender or resist?"

"Resist!" they cried unanimously.

Then the Dixtar, who for ten long Martian years had never been gainsaid in anything, went suddenly pale. "I fear," he said, "that you will all regret this rash decision when regret comes too late." Then he turned, clasped his hands behind his back, and with his chin sunk on his chest, strode out of the room. The others soon followed to go to their several apartments.

The Earthman, left alone, prepared to retire. One thing kept recurring to him as he hooded the baridium globes and crept into bed. It was the fact that as Kov Lutas walked out between the two girls, he had seemed more attentive to Thaine than to Neva. Yirl Du had told Thorne that the young officer avowed undying love for the beautiful daughter of the Dixtar. Thorne was puzzled.

He soon fell asleep, but it seemed to him that he had not slumbered for more than a few moments when he was awakened by a sharp tug at his coverlets. He looked up sleepily.

"Yirl Du!" he exclaimed. "What's wrong?"

"I have made a startling discovery, my lord," Yirl Du replied, "else I should not have disturbed your rest."

"I'm sure of that," said Thorne. "What is it?"

For answer, his henchman drew a scroll from beneath his cloak. After passing it to the Earthman, he walked to the lever and unhooded the baridium globes, flooding the room with light.

CHAPTER 21

Thorne glanced curiously over the scroll given him by Yirl Du. Then he threw back the covers and leaped out of bed.

"Where did you get this?" he demanded. "Where is Irintz Tel?"

"The traitor is in his own bed, and probably asleep by now," replied Yirl Du.

"But what of Sel Han? Did Irintz Tel get a message through to him, and was there a reply?"

"He did, and I have the reply also." Yirl Du plucked a second scroll from beneath his cloak and handed it to Thorne, who perused it carefully, then re-read the other message.

The correspondence went in this order, the first letter full of hasty revisions:

> To Sel Han, Vildus of Mars,
> Salutation and submission:
> With my help you can take Castle Takkor and all in it, sustaining but trifling losses. Tomorrow night, in the period of darkness between the setting of the nearer moon and the rising of the farther, quietly mass a thousand men near the lake gate. Have another group of fifty warriors bring a long stout rope, knotted for easy climbing, beneath the point where I stand when I hurl this note. I will drop a cord to draw up and make fast the rope for them. Then we will cut down the guards and throw open the gates. With a thousand of your foot-soldiers in the courtyard and your mounted warriors attacking from above, there can be but one outcome. I seek to make no terms, but align myself wholeheartedly with your cause, and now await your reply and your commands.
> Irintz Tel

To Irintz Tel,

Salutation and greetings:

Your plan pleases me. As soon as the sky grows dark, lower your cord with a muffled weight at the end. When you feel two tugs on the cord draw up the rope which we shall tie on the other end, and lash it to a merlon. As soon as it is secure, tug twice, and we will do the rest.

If, through your efforts, we are able to capture the castle, I will make you Vil of Xancibar or any other vilet of equal size which you may choose, and Neva shall share with me the throne of all Mars.

SEL HAN VILDUS OF MARS.

"Ah! So that's their game. They will capture the towers, throw open the gates, and take us by surprise during the dark interval."

"They will unless we prevent Irintz Tel from drawing up their rope for them. Shall I place him under arrest?"

"No. Let him sleep. There is nothing he can do before tomorrow night, and I already have the glimmerings of a counter plan. In the meantime, tell me how you got these documents."

"It was quite simple, my lord. As you know, I am familiar with every secret passageway in this castle. When Irintz Tel left the conference I suspected him of some treachery, so I followed. Seeing him enter his apartment, I slipped into a hidden passageway which leads to a panel in the central room of his suite. There, through a small peep-hole, I spied upon him. He seemed quite agitated, and finally went to the writing board and composed this letter. He made a copy, probably because, as you see, the original is full of corrections and crossed-out words.

"Next, he unraveled the silken lining of one of his garments and wound the long cord he obtained therefrom into a ball. He thrust the ball of cord and the copy of the corrected scroll under his cloak, and went out. On the way out he hurled this original letter into the fireplace. Luckily I was able to open the panel, run to the fireplace, and rescue it before it caught fire.

"I read the note, and followed Irintz Tel. I saw him tie the cylinder to the end of his silken cord and hurl it out toward the enemy camp where it was picked up by a yellow warrior. Some time later Sel Han's reply came, and Irintz Tel drew it up on the wall.

"With a false beard and tattered cloak, I disguised myself as a castle menial. Again I spied upon Irintz Tel in his room. Presently I saw him place Sel Han's answer on the writing board, and resolved to attempt to get it without arousing his suspicion. Accordingly, I went into his room with a load of wood, managed to upset the writing board, shake the scroll out of the cylinder, thrust it into my belt, and hand him the empty cylinder, which he immediately tossed into the fire."

"Obviously Irintz Tel thinks both of these documents were burned, and so imagines himself safe from discovery. That fits in splendidly with my plan."

"But aren't you going to arrest him and punish him?"

"No. I have a more subtle scheme than that. Say nothing about these notes or the Dixtar's treachery to anyone. Leave all to me. Tomorrow, go about your duties as if nothing is amiss. And now get yourself some rest. I'm going back to bed."

Thorne was up with the sun, and instantly set about his task. First he put his men to work cleaning up the place and tending the gawrs. Then, accompanied by Yirl Du, he explored the underground chambers of the castle. It was not long before he had mapped out a route leading through the largest doorways and archways to a point near one of the concealed entrances of the secret passageway, through which Yirl Du had previously escaped, and which led underneath the docks. After investigating this passageway and the space beneath the docks, he returned to the castle cellar.

"Bring me six skilled masons," he told Yirl Du, "and have them conceal their tools on the way so there will be no suspicion of what we are about to do. I'll wait here."

Yirl Du hurried away, and presently returned with six members of the Free Swordsmen, carrying tools and mortar concealed in two large food hampers.

Thorne addressed them. "I want you to remove the blocks from the wall at this point, until you have made an opening large enough for a gawr to pass through. Then wait here with your tools for further orders, which will not come until tonight. Food and pulcho will be sent you."

Accompanied by Yirl Du, he crossed the room and stepped through the large doorway, carefully closing the door after him.

"Keep this door closed with two guards before it," he said, "and give them orders to admit nobody but you or me. You, yourself, will take food to the workmen at meal-times."

After the two guards had been posted, Thorne and Yirl Du paid a visit to the tower where the officers of the Kamud were imprisoned. These, the Earthman ordered transferred to a dungeon in the cellar. When this had been accomplished he returned to the battlements to direct the work there, and to keep watch over the enemy.

That afternoon, after Irintz Tel had retired to his apartment, Thorne issued secret instructions to his various officers. These, in turn, transmitted instructions to the men in their charge.

Miradon Vil, Kov Lutas, Lal Vak and the two girls were told nothing. Thorne did not want the Dixtar's daughter to know of the perfidy of her father until his own plans had been carried out.

Night came at last, with the transient brightness of the nearer moon. It was at the setting of this orb that all of Thorne's forces were to go into action. In the meantime, a secret watch was kept on Irintz Tel.

Presently Thorne, standing in the shadow, saw the Dixtar cross the courtyard, walking unconcernedly and saluting the officers and men he encountered. Leisurely he mounted to the wall and a moment later disappeared in the shadow of the tower.

Thorne softly called to Rid Du, who stood waiting. "Start out with the gawrs, and warn the men to be careful about making any unusual noise."

Led by a man who had been coached for the purpose until he thoroughly knew the route through the castle and cellar which had been mapped out by Thorne, the great bird-beasts, each carrying a rider, began forming in line and marching into the castle.

By the time the moon had set nearly two-thirds of the gawrs had entered the castle. At this moment all the warriors on the walls and in the towers began silently stealing from their posts, with the exception of the few who guarded the towers that controlled the lake gates. These had instructions to remain until the first attackers appeared, then flee down the inner stairways which led to the cellars, and join the others.

Thorne kept his post at the doorway until the last huge bird-beast had lumbered through. Then he closed and bolted the door on the inside, and ran up the steps of the central tower where, one by one, he aroused Neva, Thaine, Miradon Vil, Lal Vak and Kov Lutas.

"Come with me quickly, and make no sound," he told them. "The enemy is about to attack, and I have a plan to frustrate them. But we must be quiet."

They followed him down the stairway unquestioningly, Neva escorted by Miradon Vil, who seemed strangely solicitous of her safety; Thaine, attended by Kov Lutas, and Lal Vak walked with the Earthman. Thorne closed and bolted every door after them as they followed the route where the gawrs had walked through the castle and descended to the basement. Here, after passing through several rooms, and bolting each door behind them, they caught up with the end of a line of warriors, among whom Thorne recognized the guards from the gate towers. This line was swiftly and silently filing through the hole opened in the wall by the masons, who, since all the gawrs had passed, had begun to fill it up under the direction of Yirl Du.

Thorne bolted the last door and told his companions to follow the warriors through the opening. Then he approached Yirl Du. "Have you shown these men the secret passageway?"

"Yes, my lord. And I have instructed them to completely wall up the hole as soon as the last warrior has passed through, then follow by way of the passage."

"Good. Come with me, for we still have the most difficult part of our task to perform."

They hurried out to where the men and bird-beasts stood under the dock, amid the supporting pilings, and now heard the flapping of many wings above and around them.

"Sel Han's flying warriors are attacking the castle. Now is our chance, but we must work swiftly."

In accordance with his previous orders, a hundred of Thorne's warriors had divided themselves into four groups of twenty-five men, each under the command of an officer. The members of one of these groups, all young fellows under the command of Rid Du, had stripped themselves to their loin-cloths and were plastering each other from head to foot with a thick coating of heavy grease, working in the dim light of a small baridium torch held by another warrior. Stacked near them was a pile of large crocks made from transparent material.

As soon as they were thoroughly greased, each man belted sword, mace and dagger about him, then took up a crock, inverted it, and lifted it over his head, so it rested upon his shoulders. They marched down to the water's edge, and Rid Du, who was in the lead, chopped a hole in the thin ice with his mace, then stepped into it and disappeared from view, still holding the crock over his head. His companions followed him, one by one, until all had dropped out of sight.

"Do you think they'll make it?" Thorne asked anxiously. "Looks as if they might run out of air before they reach the boat."

"Don't worry, my lord," Yirl Du replied. "All are trained divers. Every one of them could walk out to the boat and back again without danger of suffocating. And when they break through the ice around that boat the crew of the ray projector will have short shrift, with the exception of the operator whom you ordered kept alive."

"I hope you are right," said Thorne, "and you should know if any one does. Now, it is time for us to attack the other projector crews. I'll take the one on the west, you the one on the north, and Ven Hitus the one to the east. Come!"

He leaped into the saddle of a gawr held ready for him, and swiftly led the way to the west end of the dock, the great bird-beasts of his twenty-five warriors lumbering after him on the frozen ground. At the end of the dock a large ramp led up under a warehouse, open toward the lake after the manner of a lean-to. He rode out through the front of this and reconnoitered for a moment. By now there was a tremendous commotion in the castle. Baridium torches were flashing all about, and by their light he could see the warriors milling on the walls, while others mounted on gawrs circled the towers and battlements.

But what chiefly concerned him now was the ray projector which he was to capture, and which Sel Han had mounted on a house-top. He marked its position by the faint glow of the light on its instrument board. Then, with a whispered "Now!" to his fighting men, who had assembled around him, he pulled up on the guiding rod, and his bird-beast launched itself into the air.

In a few moments they were soaring above their objective, which was only about five hundred yards from the dock. Then they dived downward in a steep spiral.

The crew of the ray projector had paid no attention to the sound of gawrs flapping above their heads, evidently taking these to be the mounts of their own warriors. And so, when the great bird-beasts alighted on the roof around them, and Thorne's fighting men sprang upon them with drawn swords, they were taken completely by surprise.

Thorne made straight for the operator, who leaped up to meet him; the Earthman's blade quickly sent his weapon spinning, and he clapped his hands over his eyes in token of surrender. The Takkor swordsmen made short work of the others.

Setting two men to guard his prisoner, Thorne raised his baridium torch above his head and unhooded it three times in succession. A moment later he saw it answered by three flashes from the projector on the north, and knew that Yirl Du had succeeded in capturing it. Then came a signal from the one on the east, announcing the success of Ven Hitus, and shortly thereafter another from the projector on the boat, now under the control of Rid Du.

Thorne called a warrior to his side.

"Fly back to the dock," he ordered, "and tell them they can all come out now. Send fifty men to capture the airships, but let them go on foot. I want no one in the air except the man who is to carry dry clothing to Rid Du and his warriors on the boat. And let him return as soon as possible."

Thorne turned his attention to the instrument board of the ray projector. Though it held a half dozen dials with numbers and pointers on them, evidently to tell the operator how much of this or that charge or substance the mechanism contained, he was at present concerned only with the parts intended for manipulation by the operator.

These consisted of two small cranks and a lever. One crank, he soon found by testing it, elevated or lowered the muzzle of the projector, and the other turned it to the right or left. He pointed the muzzle upward where it could do no damage, and pulled the lever. A green flash shot skyward. He swiftly shut it off, and having mastered the weapon without the operator's assistance, ordered him bound.

A moment later the farther moon rose, flooding the scene with its pale light. After making sure that his men were in charge of Sel Han's airships, and that his warrior had returned from the boat, Thorne turned his attention to the castle.

Evidently Sel Han was still unaware that his projectors had been captured. Fully a thousand of his riders still circled above the walls on their bird-beasts. Thorne aimed the projector into the thick of these and pulled the lever. Instantly the green ray flashed out, cutting a great gap in the circle of flyers. And now from the north, south and east, the other projectors went into action.

The panic stricken riders who remained quickly dived for the nearest shelter—the castle courtyard. The Earthman instantly shut off his ray, and the others followed his example.

Calling two of his warriors before the instrument board, he instructed them in the use of the projector. He told them that if any of Sel Han's men should attempt to fly up from the courtyard they should be instantly annihilated. And finally he ordered them to watch for him to raise his hand, at which signal they were to blast a hole through the base of the castle wall directly in front of them, then shut off the ray.

These instructions completed, he mounted his gawr, and flinging the bound Ma Gong operator across the front of his saddle, flew to the dock where the main body of his swordsmen waited.

Dismounting, he turned his prisoner over to two guards and called an officer.

"Get me a herald," he commanded.

The officer hurried away, and reappeared in a few moments with a youth who carried a trumpet. Thorne gave him his instructions and he walked toward the gate.

As the Earthman stood looking after him he felt a touch on his arm. Turning, he beheld Neva, who had just come up behind him.

"I cannot find my father," she said. "I've looked for him everywhere. Do you know where he is?"

"I am sorry to say," he replied, "that the Dixtar saw fit to open the castle gates to the enemy. I haven't the slightest idea where he is—probably with his good friend, Sel Han."

She appeared distinctly shocked. "You don't mean—you can't mean . . ."

"That he could have betrayed us? Why not? It seems to run in the family."

She went pale at this, then looked up at him with flashing eyes. "Sheb Takkor Rad," she said, "some day you will regret those words. There are certain things of which you are ignorant, which I hoped you would eventually come to understand. But now—now I don't care. I hate you! I never want to see you again!"

As she flung away from him the notes of the herald's trumpet sounded before the gate.

"The Rad of Takkor," cried the herald, "calls upon Sel Han and his bandits to lay down their arms and march out of the castle. If they fail to comply they will be destroyed utterly, and the castle with them. As a token of surrender they will immediately throw open the gates."

Thorne waited for some time, watching the gates expectantly. They remained closed. He called to the herald. "Continue."

Again the herald sounded his trumpet.

"The Rad of Takkor is inclined to be merciful," he cried, "yet you try him sorely. Behold!"

Thorne raised his hand. A green ray flashed out from the house-top, drilled through the base of the wall, then winked off, leaving a gaping black hole. From within the castle there came the sounds of a mighty tumult—shouts, groans, curses, and the clash of weapons. Suddenly the gates swung open, and there emerged a rabble of yellow warriors, weaponless, thrusting before them two white men whose arms were bound behind them, and carrying on their shoulders the bodies of a dozen more. It was obvious that the Ma Gongi, facing destruction by their own dread weapons, had mutinied to save their lives.

Leaving his gawr in charge of a warrior, Thorne hurried forward. As he drew near the prisoners he recognized the tall, broad-shouldered figure of Sel Han, and the wizened, rat-faced Dixtar. The first corpse, borne by four yellow warriors, was that of Sur Det.

"Surround the Ma Gongi," Thorne shouted to his swordsmen. "Be on the lookout for treachery. And bring me the two white prisoners."

Under the watchful eyes of the Takkor fighting men, the horde of yellow warriors continued to pour from the castle until it was emptied of enemies. Then, at a command from the Earthman, the swordsmen closed in behind them and a small detachment entered the castle to look for stragglers.

"Bring the prisoners and follow me," Thorne ordered.

He led the way to where Miradon Vil stood with Neva, Thaine, Lal Vak and Kov Lutas.

Rendering the imperial salute to the Vil, he said, "Your majesty, I bring you two men who have usurped the throne of your empire, one for a generation, the other for a day. They are your prisoners, to do with as you will. And since the weapons with which Sel Han set out to conquer Mars are in the custody of my swordsmen, you are once more Vil of Xancibar. As for the nest of this would-be world conqueror and his fellow conspirators, which is said to be somewhere on my estate, every prisoner here knows where it is, and I am sure that at least one of them can be persuaded to tell."

"Sheb Takkor Rad," replied Miradon Vil, his voice shaking with emotion, "I find it difficult to express . . ."

He got no further, for at this moment there came a sudden and unexpected interruption. Thorne's first intimation of it was the sound of a sword being whipped from its sheath. He turned in time to see Sel Han, who had managed to slip off his bonds and snatch the sword of the man who guarded him, leap across the space which separated him from the two girls, catch up Thaine, fling her over his shoulder, and dash away.

Drawing his own blade, the Earthman was the first to spring after the fugitive. Only a short way off stood Thorne's gawr, held by a warrior. Sel Han split his head with a blow of the sword and leaped into the saddle.

Still clutching the struggling, kicking Thaine, and holding both her wrists with his left hand, he pulled up on the guiding rod with his right. The great bird-beast lumbered forward and took off, flapping noisily because of the double burden it carried, while Thorne and his companions looked on helplessly, not daring to use their javelins for fear of injuring the girl.

The gawr, obedient to the guiding rod, flew swiftly out over the lake.

CHAPTER 22

Before the sound of Sel Han's derisive laughter died out, Thorne turned and sprinted for the nearest gawr.

"Send five hundred swordsmen after me," he ordered as he sprang into the saddle. "This may lead to an ambush." Then he lifted the guiding rod and was off.

As his bird-beast rose in the air, Thorne saw that Sel Han was already halfway across the lake, and circling toward the northeast, a direction that would carry him over the heart of the marsh and into a terrain altogether strange to the Earthman. A glance behind him showed a horde of his riders coming across the lake. Fearing they might not have marked his course, he raised his baridium torch over his head and flashed it thrice. His signal was answered, almost immediately by three flashes from a rider in the front ranks.

He did not doubt that Sel Han was making for his secret lair, which was believed to be somewhere in Takkor Marsh. But league after league of marshland unrolled beneath them, with the fugitive showing no signs of halting. And gradually, Thorne's swift bird-beast gained on the other. The nearer moon rose, its bright rays accentuating the details of the scene.

Presently, when it seemed that the two moons were about to meet, Thorne noticed a change in the topography of the country ahead. They were nearing a broad, flat-topped mountain with a sloping base of sand and boulders that led to rugged, frowning cliffs.

Sel Han's destination was obviously those frowning cliffs, but as he approached them Thorne noticed that his bird-beast had reached the limit of its endurance. With its beak almost over the rim, it fell, fluttering weakly and pecking ineffectually at the sheer cliff face with its hooked bill in an effort to save itself. Fortunately there was a shelf of rock only fifty feet below, and on this the creature alighted.

Thorne arrived on that shelf not five seconds later, but Sel Han had already sprung from his saddle, and with Thaine still slung helplessly over his shoulder, was sprinting away along that narrow ledge. Whipping out his sword, the Earthman leaped down and set out in hot pursuit.

Abruptly the ledge curved around a sharp bend in the cliff wall, and for a moment Thorne lost sight of his quarry. Then, as he rounded the bend, he saw them again. They were now in an indentation of the cliff face about an eighth of a mile deep, and the cliff opposite him was honeycombed with baridium-lighted caverns and terraced with ledges that swarmed with Ma Gong workmen. On the top of the cliff above them a troop of mounted yellow warriors sat on guard. This, then, was the hidden nest of the conspirators.

Though not more than five hundred feet separated Sel Han and his followers, he was unable to reach them, for the ledge ended suddenly only a short distance farther on. But if he could not cross to his men, he could call them to him, and this he did.

"Ho, warriors! Your Vildus is beset! To me!"

Instantly there came a chorus of answering cries, and the flapping of their mounts' wings as they took off. Almost at the same moment the vanguard of the Takkor swordsmen rounded the bend in the wall.

Though he had noted all these happenings, Thorne had not slackened his pace; he turned and called to his men.

"Capture those caves," he shouted, pointing across the inlet with his sword, "and everything in them."

Again he turned and dashed forward, then suddenly cried out in consternation. Sel Han and his precious burden had disappeared.

The Takkor swordsmen and the Ma Gong warriors now clashed in midair, but Thorne ran on breathlessly until he reached the very end of the ledge. Then he saw the explanation—a circular doorway hewn in the solid rock at his left.

Fearing an ambush, Thorne stepped warily through that opening. He found himself in an immense cavern, lighted and ventilated by a hole in the roof through which the bright moonlight was streaming. Immediately beneath this hole a narrow wooden bridge crossed a wide chasm which split the floor of the cave from side to side. At the opposite end of the bridge was Sel Han. He had flung Thaine to the floor, and was hacking desperately with his sword at the two slender poles which supported the farther end of the bridge.

Thorne sprang forward, but the wood splintered and the bridge sagged, then fell into the chasm.

Thorne paused on the brink of the chasm. It was fully fifty feet across, and about two hundred feet deep, reaching clear to the smooth walls on both sides.

The Earthman glared at his enemy, who laughed mockingly. Behind him, on a pedestal at the rear of the cave, was a stone colossus with a sardonic grin on its repulsive features, evidently the forgotten god of some vanished race. It almost seemed as if the god had laughed.

"Now if you had a pair of wings . . ." bantered Sel Han, grinning maliciously.

Thorne had no intention of replying, but at this moment he noticed something which made him change his mind. Thaine, lying on the floor behind his enemy, sat up and opened her eyes, looking about her in bewilderment. She still wore her weapons.

"Sel Han, the mighty swordsman," he mocked. "The irresistible Vildus of Mars. I am alone, yet you run away. It must be that you fear me."

"I am too great a man to engage in a common brawl," Sel Han replied. "As soon as my warriors have defeated yours, they will come and cut you into small pieces. Then . . ."

He paused suddenly, having detected a sound behind him. Thaine had sprung to her feet and drawn her sword.

Sel Han still clutched his own weapon. "Put down that sword, you little fool!" he growled. "Do you think you can beat *me*?"

For answer, she extended her blade in a swift lunge that would have stretched an ordinary swordsman on the stone floor. But her abductor was no ordinary swordsman. He parried with a quick riposte.

Thorne realized that Sel Han was thoroughly angry and in deadly earnest. The thrust he had aimed at Thaine's heart was meant to kill!

Suddenly, above the clashing of the blades and panting of the contestants, Thorne heard the sound of footsteps and the clank of weapons behind. Turning, he saw Yirl Du and a dozen Takkor swordsmen.

"The traitors' nest is captured, my lord," announced Yirl Du. Then he saw what was taking place at the other end of the cavern . . . "Why—why!" he stammered.

But on the instant, Thorne had conceived a plan. "Follow me!" he cried. "We can do no good here."

He ran out of the cave, Yirl Du and the warriors at his heels. Their gawrs were perched on the ledge.

The Earthman leaped into a saddle and pulled up the guiding rod. "Come with me, and bring ten men," he told Yirl Du.

Thorne guided the bird-beast up over the rim of the cliff and came down beside the hole in the roof of the cavern. Unhooking the two safety chains from the saddle, he fastened them together. Yirl Du and his ten men alighted around him a moment later.

"Bring me all your safety chains," Thorne ordered.

They brought them, and he swiftly fastened them together, end to end, until he had a chain nearly a hundred feet in length. He hooked one end of this in his belt ring.

"Now let me down that hole and swing me toward the ledge on which they are fighting."

They seized the chain and let him down swiftly. He was directly above the appalling depth of the chasm.

Leaning down over the rim of the hole, Yirl Du set the chain in motion—a pendulum with a slender linked shaft and a human weight.

Nearer and nearer Thorne swung toward his objective, and Sel Han, who had heard the rattle of the chain, broke away from Thaine for a moment, to try to impale the Earthman as he spun helplessly at the end. But Thaine, seeing Thorne's danger, instantly went to his rescue, attacking her abductor so furiously that he was forced to devote all his attention to her.

At last Thorne's feet touched the ledge. The chain slackened, and he reached around to unhook it from his belt ring. This done, he looked up just in time to see a sight that drove him berserk with rage and grief. Two feet of Sel Han's steel were projecting from Thaine's back. With an agonized gasp, Thaine crumpled to the floor.

Thorne sprang furiously to the attack, but rage and grief are poor allies in a contest with swords. The Earthman, fighting his opponent, and little caring what happened to himself, constantly risked desperate lunges which left him dangerously exposed to counter thrusts.

Only when he was bleeding from no less than a score of wounds and felt himself growing weaker did his common sense reassert itself. Resolutely, purposefully, Thorne now began to fence.

Sel Han instantly noticed the change in his antagonist's swordsmanship, and a look of fear came over his flat features. Yet he fought savagely.

Thorne was fencing coolly now, thrusting and parrying with ease and precision. So lightly did he hold the skill of his opponent that on hearing the clank of weapons he took time to glance across the chasm to see who had entered the cave. With a start of surprise he recognized Neva, Miradon Vil, Kov Lutas and Lal Vak. Miradon Vil, he saw, was reaching out for the end of the chain which Yirl Du was swinging toward him. But it was Neva, beside the Vil, who grasped the chain and swung across the chasm.

Thorne was so surprised that he was not quite quick enough in parrying a cut for his head. Sel Han's blade parted his head-strap and bit through into his skull.

He saw a myriad dancing stars, then the blood spurted down into his eyes, half blinding him.

But for all that, he sprang to the attack, forcing his opponent back, back, until he stood on the very edge of the chasm. Again Sel Han tried that headcut which had worked so well before, but this time Thorne saw it coming. He parried, then countered with a sweeping moulinet to the neck—a drawing cut that sheared off the still-grinning head. It fell at his feet, and the body toppled backward into the chasm.

Staggering drunkenly, Thorne kicked the leering head after the body. Then he lurched forward . . .

CHAPTER 23

Thorne opened his eyes slowly, blinked, then opened them again and stared in astonishment. He was looking up at a frescoed ceiling on which was depicted a Martian battle scene—a beleaguered city fighting off the attack of a vast army. Four golden chains depended from the ceiling, supporting the divan on which he lay beneath silken covers of peacock blue embroidered with a design in gold. Swiftly he glanced around, and saw that he was in a luxuriously furnished chamber, lighted by three large circular windows through which the bright sunlight streamed, their crystal segments opened like flower petals to admit the crisp morning air.

111

Seated in a swinging chair nearby, a man with white hair was poring over the contents of a large scroll.

"Lal Vak!" Thorne exclaimed.

The old scientist turned and smiled. "Ah, you know me at last," he said. He put down his scroll and walked over to the divan.

"Where am I?" Thorne asked him.

"Why, in the palace, of course." He pointed to the silken cover and the embroidered design. "These are the colors, and this the design of the royal family of Xancibar."

"But I don't understand. The last I remember, I was in that cave."

"Precisely. Neva pulled you back from the brink of the chasm. You had lost a deal of blood and fainted in her arms. Yirl Du left guards at the captured nest of the conspirators. Then we picked up five hundred more of your Takkor swordsmen at the castle and flew here. They easily cleared the palace of Sel Han's followers, and Miradon Vil was received and acclaimed by the people with great rejoicing. They were heartily sick of the atrocities of Irintz Tel and the Kamud. But all that took place six days ago. You have been delirious since. Yesterday the royal physician removed the jembal from your wounds and pronounced them healed. And last night you fell into a deep, healthful sleep which he believed would restore you."

Thorne raised his hand, and felt the scar on his head reflectively. Again he saw the horror of the struggle in the cave . . . "Poor Thaine," he murmured.

"But Thaine is better," said Lal Vak. "The physician says she can be up and around in a day or two."

"What! I thought her dead."

"The wound was high—painful, but not dangerous."

Thorne threw back the covers and swung his legs over the edge of the bed. His head reeled dizzily.

"Where are you going?"

"To Thaine," Thorne replied.

"But you can't get up yet."

"Can't I?"

Thorne stood erect, swaying uncertainly. His legs were very weak and he felt light-headed. A jar of pulcho and several cups stood on a near-by stand. Lal Vak filled a cup and handed it to him. He drank it off at a gulp and called for another. Then he staggered to the bath box, declining the assistance of his white-haired friend.

Stepping out of his sleeping garment, he entered, closed the door, and trod on the plate. A few moments later he emerged, dripping and brushing the water from his eyes. When he opened them he saw a familiar figure standing before him with two great wisps of dry moss.

"Vorz!" he exclaimed.

"The same, my lord," replied the little orderly, and proceeded to give him a brisk rub-down. "His majesty granted me leave to serve you, and I trust you will not send me away."

"Not I," Thorne replied. "If his majesty permits, I'll take you back to Takkor with me."

"Thank you, my lord."

Vorz had laid out his clothing and weapons for him, and these he now proceeded to don. There was a magnificent cloak of orange trimmed with black, the colors of nobility. Then there was the Takkor medallion to hang about his neck. And a jeweled sword and dagger with Takkor serpent hilts.

"Do I look all right to go calling on a lady, Vorz?" he asked.

"Magnificent, my lord," was the reply. And Thorne thought of the last time Vorz had groomed him, the night of Irintz Tel's reception, when he and Neva had plighted their troth and she, when they were discovered, had condemned him to the baridium mines. But now there was another picture to add which puzzled and somehow comforted him. It was the memory of Neva swinging across the chasm at the risk of her own life and drawing him back from the brink just in time to save him.

"Come," he said, taking the arm of his old friend. "Let us find the apartment of Thaine."

They strode through the hallways in silence for a time. Then Thorne thought of Irintz Tel. "What has become of the Dixtar?"

"I'll show you," replied Lal Vak.

Presently they came to a door; the scientist drew a large key from his belt, unlocked the door, and threw it open.

"Enter," he invited.

Thorne stepped inside and recognized the Hall of Heads. There were the shelves, reaching to the ceiling, with their thousands of grisly relics. Then he saw that a pedestal had been set up in the center of the hall. On the pedestal was a jar; a pair of small, beady eyes, glazed with the film of death, looked out at him sightlessly from a wizened, ratlike face.

"Irintz Tel!" he exclaimed. "Well I can't say that I blame Miradon Vil."

"You wrong his majesty," said Lal Vak. "The Vil had nothing to do with this. In fact he had granted the Dixtar full pardon, and bestowed on him a magnificent estate on the Zeelan Canal. But the next day Irintz Tel disappeared. An anonymous note was received that night suggesting that we look here. And we found this. We think it was the work of relatives of some of his victims. But no search is being conducted. The thing is done, and cannot be remedied. After all, they were certainly justified."

They quitted that place of horrors and came to the apartment of Thaine. A guard saluted and admitted them; a slave girl bade them be seated while she went in to announce them to her mistress.

"I'll wait here for you," said Lal Vak, "since I have already paid my respects to the young lady this morning."

Thorne went in alone. On a luxurious divan beneath fluffy blue silk coverlets lay Thaine.

"Hahr Ree Thorne!" she cried a trifle faintly, and held up both arms to him. He bent, and the arms went around his neck—drew his face to hers. Their lips met.

"You should not be up," she said reprovingly, "for you were worse injured than I."

"My scratches have healed," he laughed, "and now I'm ready to leave—to go back to Takkor. I don't care for cities—or palaces."

"Nor I," she told him. "This is such a big lonesome place. Already I am homesick for the marsh—for the hunting and fishing, and the blazing log fires in the evenings."

It suddenly occurred to Thorne that, since he had put Neva forever from his mind, life would be far more worth the living with Thaine by his side.

"Thaine," he said, "do you remember that day in your father's cabin when you tried a certain experiment?"

She smiled up at him. "How could I forget?"

"And you said you must have time to think."

"Since then I have thought—much. I was so inexperienced—I thought love was a thing which might be cultivated, little knowing that it is a flower which springs up spontaneously in the heart."

"Thaine! You can't mean that at last . . ."

"Yes, Hahr Ree Thorne. At last I have found true love. It came to me so unexpectedly, when I met Kov Lutas, that it left me weak and breathless."

"Kov Lutas!"

"Why, yes. We are to be wed as soon as I am well. Hadn't you heard?"

Thorne achieved a smile, but in his heart there was a feeling of emptiness—of desolation. He forced his lips to say the conventional things, to wish her joy and to proclaim Kov Lutas the luckiest man on Mars. But to himself he thought: *First Sylvia, then Neva, and now Thaine! It is my destiny to be alone and loveless.*

Rising, he said: "I must go now and prepare for my journey. Farewell, and Deza grant you much happiness."

Once outside her door, however, he could dissemble no longer. Lal Vak remarked his woebegone expression.

"Why so sad?" he asked. "I trust you found the lady well."

"Perfectly," Thorne replied. Then added: "Old friend, I'm a fool ever to have anything to do with women. From now on, I'm through, and I mean it."

"Why, what's this?" asked the scientist. "Do you fall in love with every woman you meet?"

"Well, not exactly that. But since Neva betrayed me . . ."

"Betrayed you! What talk is this? Why she has twice saved your life! What are you talking about, boy?"

"You should know as well as I," Thorne said bitterly. "Was it not she who sent me to the baridium mines?"

Lal Vak looked at him quizzically for the moment. "You are a greater fool than I thought, my boy. She sent you to the baridium mines to save you from the headsman. And who do you think it was who aided you to escape from the mines? There were only three people in Xancibar with the power to do so. The other two were Irintz Tel and Sel Han. Do you think *they* did it?"

"Why I thought it was you."

"I had a small part," Lal Vak admitted, "but it was she who engineered everything—who pulled the strings and moved the officials in high places, so the thing could be accomplished. You should have seen her, tearful and apprehensive that next day, as she connived with Kov Lutas and me to win your freedom. And after the thing had been done, she was beside herself with worry for fear you would be captured. Every day she besought me to try to obtain news of you. You should know, also, that the tales of her heartless flirtations were utterly false, invented by Sel Han and spread by his henchmen to keep off powerful rivals. She was no more a murderous siren than our little Thaine. That I can attest, and I have known her all her life."

Thorne was stunned. "I have done her a great wrong, old friend," he said, "and not only in my heart. I openly cut her when she held out her arms to me that night in Takkor Castle. I have lost the only woman I ever really loved through my own lack of faith."

"She saved your life in the cave at the risk of her own," Lal Vak reminded him. "Is that the act of one who has ceased to care?"

"I don't know," groaned Thorne. "The more I see of women the less I understand them."

"At least, you should call on her and apologize."

"That I will do. Let us go to her apartment."

As they approached the door of Neva's apartment, two guards saluted smartly and stood aside for them to enter. In the reception room a slave girl met them. "Tell your mistress Sheb Takkor is calling," Thorne told her.

The slave girl returned almost immediately. "My mistress is not receiving callers, my lord," she said.

Thorne turned to Lal Vak. "You see, I was right," he said. "But it is no more than I deserve for my little faith. Come. Let us go back to my apartment. I must prepare for my journey."

CHAPTER 24

Back in his apartment with Lal Vak, Thorne notified Vorz that they were leaving. Then he went to the writing board, spread a scroll, and composed a letter. Then he rolled it, placed it in a wooden tube, and handed it to Lal Vak.

"Give this to Neva after I am gone," he said, "and I shall be grateful to you. I have apologized for my boorish conduct and thanked her for having twice saved my life—a life that has become empty and purposeless without her. But it is, as you have said, the least I can do, and unfortunately, the most I can do, as well."

Lal Vak thrust the cylinder under his belt. "I'll be glad to deliver this for you," he said. "Now I'll go out and arrange for your transportation."

Presently he returned. "A flying machine awaits you on the roof," he said, "and his majesty is ready to receive you."

Thorne emptied his pulcho cup and arose. The scientist conducted him to a reception room where Miradon Vil, resplendent in his royal cloak of peacock blue trimmed with gold, was standing on the dais before the throne addressing a number of his nobles. But when the Rad of Takkor was announced, he dismissed them all and stepped down to receive his guest.

"My boy," he said, "I am happy to see you well, and with your memory and reason restored."

"And I," replied Thorne, "am equally happy to see your majesty restored to the throne of your ancestors; but no happier, I am sure, than every citizen, high and low, in Xancibar."

"Some time ago," said Miradon, "I rendered you the empty thanks of a deposed Vil. Today I am in a position to show my gratitude more tangibly and practically. First, I free you and Takkor from all allegiance to Xancibar. This makes you the supreme ruler of the raddek, and the collector and dispenser of all Takkor revenues.

"Second, I have conferred with the Vils of the other great powers of Mars, and we have decided that you shall be the arbiter of our destinies. You captured the weapons and the laboratory with which Sel Han sought to conquer Mars. In unscrupulous hands they could do much harm. But we have faith in you. We want you to keep them, to protect us against any other ambitious plotters who may arise, so that we may fight our wars and settle our differences with the weapons of honor and chivalry we have always used. So, in effect, we make you the custodian of our liberty."

From a taboret which stood beside the dais, he took a golden medal, set with sparkling jewels and hung on a heavy golden chain. "This commemorates our resolution, and is the badge of your high office."

Inscribed on the medal Thorne read:

SHEB TAKKOR
Supreme Arbiter of Destiny
and
Custodian of Liberty
by the will of the
Associated Vilets
of Mars

The Vil snapped the chain around Thorne's neck, so the new medal flashed and scintillated on his chest just above the Takkor medallion.

"I am overwhelmed, your majesty," said Thorne. "The nations of Mars have placed too high a value on my poor services."

Miradon smiled and stroked his silky golden beard. "There is but one more thing, and I will give you leave to go."

He raised his hand, and a flourish of trumpets sounded from the doorway. Two heralds entered, trumpets resting on hips. Behind them came six pages, carrying a gold-embroidered cloak of peacock blue like that worn by the Vil. Following the pages was another, bearing a jar of pulcho and a gem-encrusted golden cup.

The heralds separated, and stood, one at each side of the dais. The pages held the cloak spread before the Vil.

"Permit me," said Miradon, unfastening Thorne's head straps and removing his cloak of orange and black. He handed the cloak to a slave, and taking the one which the pages had brought, fastened its jeweled straps about Thorne's head. Then the last page came up with the pulcho and the cup.

Filling the cup, the Vil drank half its contents, then passed it to Thorne. "Drink," he commanded.

Thorne drained the cup and returned it to the tray.

The Vil raised both hands before his face. "I shield my eyes to the Zovil of Xancibar," he said.

Thorne raised his hands and responded to the salutation.

"That is all," said Miradon. "And now, since you insist on leaving us so soon, Lal Vak will conduct you to the roof. I will be there to see you off in a few moments."

In the company of the scientist Thorne left the presence, and climbed the stairs toward the roof.

"Tell me something, Lal Vak," said Thorne. "What is the significance of this cloak? And what is a zovil?"

"A zovil," replied the scientist, "is a vil's son, just as a zorad is a rad's son. The cloak, and the ceremony that went with it, made you a prince of the imperial house of Xancibar."

"I seem to have gotten almost everything on this planet but the one I want the most," said Thorne morosely.

"I presume that you refer to Neva," said Lal Vak. "Well, don't consider her totally lost to you, yet. Women have been known to change their minds, you know."

On the roof of the palace a great metal flying machine stood waiting. Standing around it was a group of the most exalted nobles and officials of Xancibar.

A moment later the leonine head of Miradon Vil appeared above the top of the stairway. As he stepped out on the roof the courtiers again rendered the imperial salute. He walked up to Thorne and placed his huge hands on his shoulders.

"Farewell, my son," he said, "and take good care of that which I have entrusted to you."

As he spoke, it seemed to Thorne that his voice broke slightly, and there was a suspicion of tears in his eyes.

"Farewell, your majesty," Thorne replied.

The warrior went up to the forward cab with Vorz and the pilot, and closed the door after him. Thorne turned to select a seat. Then he gasped in amazement.

Seated near a window was Neva, clad in a most becoming costume of peacock blue, embroidered with gold. She smiled up at Thorne as he hurried to her side and bent over her. "You!" he exclaimed. "I can't believe my eyes!"

"Lal Vak brought me your note," she said. "After I had read it I decided to forgive you."

"But—but, how came you here, and wearing the colors of royalty?"

"Since I am the only daughter of Miradon Vil, there is no one who has a better right to these colors."

"But what of Thaine?"

"Thaine," replied Neva, "is the daughter of Irintz Tel. Miradon Vil—my father—when he went into exile, was determined to insure my safety, and to give me the advantages which were rightfully mine. So he exchanged me for Thaine when we were babies. Thaine doesn't know, yet, and I only learned the truth five days ago."

Looking at her, Thorne decided that he must have been blind not to realize the resemblance between the fair-haired Vil and this girl before.

"Then—then his majesty, your father, knows you have come with me?"

"Of course. Why else should he have performed the ceremony that made you Zovil of Xancibar?"

"I'm sure I don't know."

"Because, stupid, he could only make you a prince of his house by making you my husband. There is no other way."

Full realization suddenly came to him. He caught her in his arms, sought and found her yielding lips. "Neva, beloved!" he murmured. "Are you really my wife?"

"Unto death, Deza help you!" she replied archly.

But there was a starry light in her glorious eyes which he could not fail to understand.

THE OUTLAWS OF MARS

As THE powerful car plunged up the mountain road Jerry Morgan wondered what sort of reception awaited him at the end of this drive. Would the mysterious, eccentric man who was his uncle, and who lived in this mountain retreat which his nephew had never been permitted to visit, turn him away now?

It was not until he had reached the highest limit of timber growth that he came upon a log habitation built against the mountainside which rose steeply behind it, rugged and bare of vegetation. He stopped the car in front of the log porch, off the road enough to avoid blocking it. No one was around; no one appeared as he slammed the car door shut, climbed the steps and crossed the veranda. No one answered his knock; the door swung open at the impact and Jerry entered.

He found himself in a large living room, finished and furnished in pioneer style, the walls decorated with trophies. Despite the chill at this altitude, there was only cold, gray ashes mingled with bits of charcoal in the fireplace. Jerry had the feeling that the place had not been lived in for some time.

Exploration confirmed his initial impression. Shelves in the kitchen were empty save for a few dishes and utensils. There was no sign of food, and a thin film of dust had settled over everything, even the sink.

Puzzled, he returned to the living room and seated himself on a birch settee before the cold fireplace. Obviously, though this was the nominal residence of his uncle, Doctor Richard Morgan did not really live here. Where, then, did he live? As far as Jerry had been able to see in every direction there had been no sign of a building of any kind, save this one.

As he sat there, reflecting on these mysteries, he suddenly heard the door open, and turning, saw his uncle.

Like his nephew, Richard Morgan was tall and powerfully built. The remaining black among the silver hair and beard was as jet as Jerry's, and though he did not look like a military man, his presence radiated authority. His forehead was high and bulged outward over shaggy eyebrows that met above his aquiline nose; and he wore a pointed, closely cropped Vandyke.

"Glad to see you, Jerry," boomed the doctor in his resonant bass voice. "I've been expecting you."

Jerry Morgan stared in amazement as he took his uncle's proffered hand. "Expecting me? Why, I told no one-intended to surprise you. It sounds almost like thought-transference."

"Perhaps you are nearer the truth than you imagine," replied the doctor, seating himself.

Jerry brushed this aside, mentally, as he groped for the proper words with which to frame his next speech. "I'm afraid you're not going to like what I have to tell you, Uncle Richard," he began. "The fact is, I've disgraced . . ."

"I, know all about it, Jerry," said the doctor gently, and then proceeded to give a detailed account of the episode the young man had been about to tell. He ended with: "You knew the colonel would never believe a story about your being framed in a manner reminiscent of nineteenth century melodrama, so you had no choice but to resign. What you didn't know was that it was not Lieutenant Tracy, your rival, who arranged the affair but Elaine herself."

"Impossible, uncle. . ."

"Think, Jerry. Had you told anyone-anyone but Elaine-that you were not going directly back to your quarters as usual, but were stopping at the drugstore in town first? Someone had to know you would be in town at a certain time that night in order for the plan to succeed. It couldn't have worked in any other place, although it could have happened at a later time. And Lieutenant Tracy was in the field that night, and could not have been privy to it. In fact, he knew nothing of it at all."

"Then I misjudged them both-Tracy and Elaine."

"Not too badly in Tracy's case, I should say. He just wouldn't have done it that way though. He couldn't have been as sure of the colonel's reaction as the colonel's daughter was, you see. Well, don't fret about them my lad. They're two of a kind and they richly deserve each other...And now will you believe me if I tell you I know everything you've done since? Good." He stood up. "You have guessed that I don't live here-that this place is only a dummy habitation to keep the folk who live hereabout from prying into my affairs. Follow me."

He led the way through the kitchen, and thence down a stairway into the garage. At the back was a tier of shelving. The doctor reached behind a shelf and pulled. Instantly, the whole tier swung back from the wall, revealing a dark passageway, hewn from the rock, leading into the mountainside.

"Enter," said the doctor.

At the end of the tunnel they came to a sliding door, which the doctor pushed back. Behind it was an automatic elevator. They entered; Morgan touched a button and they rose noiselessly. At the end of the ascent, they stepped out into a large, airy hallway, into which filtered sunlight streamed through irregularly shaped skylights of frosted glass.

"Seen from the outside, those skylights simulate the drifts and ridges of snow which surround us," said Morgan. "We are now at the peak of the mountain, and this building is so constructed that, viewed from near or far, it appears to be a part of it."

"Amazing!" exclaimed Jerry. "I pictured you in a little cabin, perhaps with a small laboratory."

"I have other surprises for you," said the doctor. "In the meantime, Boyd will show you to your room. He has already installed your luggage and drawn your bath. I'm sure you will want to freshen up' after your journey. See you at breakfast."

"Before I tell you of my life's work," said Morgan, as they attacked the viands before them, "let's talk about you. I know precisely how you feel. You have lost your career and the woman you wanted, and you have come to me for the rest of your patrimony, with which you expect to embark on a certain desperate adventure. The odds are a thousand to one against your coming out alive, but this means little to you the way you feel now."

He proceeded to relate full details of Jerry Morgan's plans.

"You seem to read my innermost thoughts, uncle, as if they were a printed page spread before you. I can't imagine how you know all this, but you are right."

Morgan sighed. "If you are determined to go on with this, I'll do all in my power to help you. Yet it is my hope that I may be able to offer you a new interest in life-new adventures that will serve a most excellent purpose, and beside which the one you have planned will pale to insignificance.

"You have said, half in jest, that I appear to read your mind. I do; I have always read your mind, since the death of, your parents put you under my guardianship-which took place after I had perfected my experiments with telepathy. Telepathy, one of the most remarkable powers of the objective mind, is not affected by time or distance. It acts instantly, once contact has been established.

"I started out trying to build a device which would pick up and amplify thought waves. This led to contact with a man on Mars who was experimenting in transmitting thought-waves-but not the Mars of today," he added, seeing the expression on Jerry's face. "Lal Vak, the Martian, spoke and still speaks to me from the Mars some millions of years ago, when a human civilization did exist there. We found that personalities could be exchanged between certain Martians and

Earthmen who were nearly doubles physically, and whose brain-patterns were similar. Since that time, we established contact with a Venusian, Vorn Vangal who is contemporary with Lal Vak. I am presently in contact with both of these men who, to our niche in space-time have been dead for millions of years. I was able to send two Earthmen to Mars and two to Venus, through personality exchange. The two men on Venus are still alive, and in communication with me. Of the two I sent to Mars, only one remains; the other, who was a criminal, was slain by his fellow-Earthman. This leaves me with only one representative on Mars."

Had it not been for the demonstration he had already received in relation to Morgan's intimate knowledge of his own affairs, Jerry Morgan would have been far from credulous. Under the shock of what he had learned, it seemed somehow believable. "It sounds interesting," he said, trying not to be carried away. "How about sending my personality to Mars."

"Lal Vak, Vorn Vangal and I have worked out improvements," Morgan said. "I am now prepared to send you on a journey through time and space in the flesh."

"Then you must have some sort of space-time vehicle."

"Follow me, and I will show you," replied the doctor, rising.

CHAPTER II

IN THE center of the high, dome-roofed shed stood a huge globe, more than fifty feet in diameter. It was covered with thick asbestos, held in place by a meshwork of steel cables. A circular metal plate, studded with bolts, and apparently the lid of a doorway or manhole, was on the side facing them.

"I am indebted to the people of Olba, a nation on Venus, for the mechanism which makes this space-time vehicle possible," said the doctor. "I do not pretend to understand it myself, and can only tell you that it has made several trips successfully-though without any human cargo. The power which propels it either comes from or is tapped by the human brain, and what you may have heard of as telekinesis is as good an explanation as any. I already have contact with the mechanism. Now watch the metal plate and see what happens."

Jerry watched, then uttered an exclamation as it began to turn swiftly, projecting farther and farther from the surface of the sphere with each turn. It was threaded, and when it unscrewed itself for a distance of about five feet, it suddenly fell forward with a loud click, and hung suspended by a heavy metal hinge, revealing a dark hole in the sphere. Then a ladder of flexible steel cable uncoiled itself from the dark depths, and dropped to the ground.

Jerry sprang up the ladder and crawled into the hole. After following a narrow passageway for about twenty feet he came to a small circular room about ten feet in diameter. The walls, floor, and ceiling of the room were thickly padded and suffused with soft light. He turned as a shadow blocked the 'light from the tube.

"How do you like it?" asked Morgan.

"Fine," replied Jerry. "Why not let me start now?"

"I had that thought in mind when I brought you here. However, landing on Mars will have difficulties because of the rarer atmosphere-not as rare as the Mars of today, but noticeably more so than what you're accustomed to. Because of this, and the lesser gravity, your heart and lungs will have to make readjustments, and it will take time to become acclimated. Go slowly, when you leave the sphere."

"How long will it take to get there?"

"I cannot calculate precisely, but it will not take long."

"And do you know on what part of the planet I will alight?"

Morgan nodded. "While you were crossing the United States by train, Lal Vak was traveling from his home in the city of Dukor, to Raliad, largest city of Mars. He is now housed in the imperial palace of Raliad, and is in contact with meso the globe, directed by our minds, will travel straight to the palace. When you arrive, he will be there to greet you, and to teach you the language of Mars. After that, you will have to shift for yourself."

"Fair enough. But what do you want me to do on Mars? I gather that I can be of help to science, or something of the sort."

"If you succeed in living on Mars, you will be the first Earthman to do so in the flesh. After that, my thought-recorder will be in contact with you, day and night, making a record of what you see and do. Alighting in Raliad, greatest city of Mars, you will communicate much valuable knowledge regarding this mighty city. From the moment you land, you will be an explorer, automatically relating your adventures to us here."

The doctor raised the lid of a case which Jerry had previously noticed, fastened against the wall. It contained a repeating rifle, a Colt forty-five in a shoulder holster, a hunting knife, a camp axe, a canteen, and a number of boxes of ammunition and provisions.

"For emergency," said the doctor, "just in case you should happen not to alight at the imperial palace in Raliad." He closed the lid and secured it. "Now let me strap you to the center of the floor, and you will be ready to start."

A few minutes later, warm farewells had been made, the doctor departed, and the outer door screwed into place.

The globe lurched unsteadily for a moment, then Jerry found himself forced suddenly against the floor as it shot swiftly upward. Gradually the intense pressure against his body grew less and was followed by a feeling of lightness. This feeling lasted for only a few moments; then he felt himself growing heavier, but the sensation was most peculiar. For instead of pressing against the floor, his body was now pulling away from it-tugging against the straps as if in an effort to rise toward the ceiling.

The strange pressure of the straps gradually lessened. Then he felt a slight jolt, and the floor began wobbling unsteadily beneath him. Evidently the globe had landed-but on what?

Hastily unfastening his straps, he got to his feet, but the effort shot him up against the ceiling of the cubicle. When he stood on the swaying floor again he saw that the door was unscrewing itself. A moment later it dropped down from the opening, and bright daylight came in through the hole.

His first look outside convinced him that he had really landed on Mars. The sun, though it appeared much smaller than when viewed from Earth, blazed brightly with a peculiar, blue-white light. It hung just above a horizon of weird and grotesque plant growths. Looking downward, Jerry saw that the globe had alighted on the shallow, sandy margin of a small lagoon, and its rocking was occasioned by the wash of waves driven by a stiff breeze.

His heart pounded wildly as he gazed about him at this strange landscape, and a giddiness assailed him. Believing this to be due to the lessened gravity of the planet on which the globe now rested, he waited for his circulatory system to adjust itself. Slowly, cautiously, he inhaled the air. It was cool and sweet, but somehow it did not satisfy him. He filled his lungs to capacity, again and again, but his heart resumed its wild pounding; there was a feeling of pressure in his eardrums. A gray haze obscured his vision, he fought against it, but to no avail.

He fell back, gasping for breath, then all went black.

CHAPTER III

JERRY'S senses returned slowly.

His lungs ached from their unwonted exertions, his throat was dry and parched, and his heart was drumming in his ears.

Slowly, cautiously, he sat up. His fingernails, he saw, were still quite blue, evidence that he had escaped suffocation by a very narrow margin. The sun had risen at least twenty degrees, proving that he had been unconscious for more than an hour.

For some time he sat there, inhaling the cool, sweet air; then he got up cautiously, and went back into the cubicle. Here he opened the case which contained his weapons, equipment, ammunition and provisions. He loaded the rifle and pistol, and filled his pockets with ammunition for both weapons. The balance of the ammunition and provisions he placed in a heavy canvas bag provided for the purpose, and fitted with straps so it could be slung over his back.

After strapping the pistol, camp axe, knife and canteen in place, he slung the pack over his back, took up the rifle, and creeping through the narrow passageway, turned and descended the ladder. The shallow water at its foot only came to his ankles, and he splashed up onto the sandy beach.

As he stood there, scanning the strange trees and shrubbery before him, he heard a sharp click. The ladder had been withdrawn into the globe, and the door was screwing itself into place. A moment more and it was tight; then the globe rose, water dripping from beneath it. It soon became a tiny speck which rapidly faded from view.

Resolutely he turned away, and climbing the sloping beach, strode in among the strange, treelike growths which fringed the shore. Now Jerry felt an exhilarating sense of lightness and freedom of movement. The weight of his supplies, equipment and weapons was but trifling; and it seemed as if the metal parts of his rifle were made of aluminum rather than steel.

As he passed through the first fringe of trees, Jerry found that he had stepped into a cultivated garden, laid out with paths of resilient, reddish-brown material as springy as rubber, which wound among beds of bright, weird blooms of grotesque forms and patterns, clumps of shrubbery, and shady groves of trees.

After walking for a distance of about a mile he reached the edge of the garden, bounded by a wall about fifty feet in height, which stretched in a gradual curve to the right and left, as far as he could see. It was constructed from immense blocks of translucent, amber-colored material, fitted together so cleverly that the seams were all but invisible. At regular intervals, curving stairways led up to the top of the wall, and he made his way to the nearest one.

A short climb brought him to the top of the wall, which was more than a hundred feet thick. He walked across it and peered over the edge, then drew back dizzily. He was looking down on the busy streets of an immense city, so far below him that the scurrying people and speeding vehicles looked like tiny insects. The wall on which he stood edged the roof of what was the largest building in sight, and the roof itself was covered by the garden through which he had just come. As far as he could see, there were other buildings formed from translucent blocks of various colors, taller by far than the mightiest skyscrapers on Earth, and all topped by roof-gardens.

From his point of vantage, Jerry now surveyed the garden through which he had just passed. He saw many scattered individuals at work, caring for the plants and harvesting the fruits-muscular, nut-brown men who were naked save for turban-like head-pieces, leather breech-clouts, and high boots with the tops rolled down below the knees.

Except for their strange apparel and the fact that their chests were, on an average, larger than those of Earthmen, they did not show any marked difference from terrestrial peoples. He descended to the garden once more and walked in the direction where he had last seen the nearest worker.

He had not gone far when he found himself face-to-face with a girl. She was slight, slender and white-skinned, with large brown eyes, raven-black hair, and an ethereal beauty of face and form. A fillet of woven gold links set with polished bits of lapis lazuli bound her glossy hair. A band of the same materials supported her small breast shields of beaten gold. And from a belt of gold links powdered with amethysts, depended a tight cincture of shimmering peacock blue fabric with a texture like that of satin.

Though Jerry was merely startled at this sudden meeting, he saw by the look in her eyes that the girl was frightened. She half-turned as if about to flee but evidently reconsidered, and once more faced him resolutely.

Resolving to try to calm her fears, he said, "Good morning."

Then he smiled, and started what was meant to be a step in her direction. But the result, instead of a mere forward step, was something in the nature of a leap which landed him not two feet in front of her.

The effect of this performance on the girl was instantaneous. Before he had recovered his equilibrium, she screamed and shrank back.

Scarcely had he regained his balance, when Jerry's attention was attracted by a new sound-a terrific roar which came from a huge beast that was bounding toward them along the path. With a yawning, tooth-filled mouth as large as that of an alligator, a furry black body fully as big as that of a lion, short legs, and a hairless, leathery tail, paddle-shaped and edged with sharp spines, the oncoming monster certainly looked formidable.

Jerry thought and acted swiftly. His first duty was to get the girl out of the path of the charging monster.

Gripping his rifle in his left hand, he bent and encircled her slender waist with his right arm. Then he leaped to one side, just in time to avoid those gaping jaws. But the spring he male carried him clear over the hedge, and into a carefully-tended bed of tiny flowering plants.

For the first time since he had landed on Mars, he realized the tremendous advantage of his Earth-trained muscles. The short-legged beast, unable to leap over the hedge, was crashing through it. So he turned, and still carrying the girl beneath his arm, bounded away with tremendous leaps.

The slender form of the girl was feather-light, and impeded him scarcely at all. On Earth she would have weighed about ninety pounds; on Mars she weighed about thirty-four.

Glancing back over his shoulder, he saw that although he had a good start on the beast, it was following him with a speed that was amazing in a creature with such short legs. Soon the stairway loomed before him, and he bounded up it, five steps at a time. As soon as he reached the top of the wall he put the girl down and turned to face their pursuer, which had meantime reached the steps.

Snapping his gun to his shoulder, he took careful aim between the blazing green eyes, and fired. Without a sound or a quiver, the beast sank down on the steps.

At the sound of the shot the girl had sprung erect. For a moment she peered down at the fallen beast. Then, her eyes flashing like those of an enraged tigress, she turned on Jerry with a volley of words that were unmistakably scornful and scathing.

Suddenly her hand flashed to her belt and came up with a jewel-hilted dagger. Jerry noticed that the blade was straight and double-edged, with tiny, razor-sharp teeth. For a moment he did not realize what she intended doing; but when she raised her weapon on aloft and lunged straight for his breast, he caught her wrist just in time.

As he stood there holding her wrist to keep her from reaching him with that murderous blade, he became aware that men were coming through the garden, converging on them from all directions and scrambling up the stairways. These brown-skinned men, whom he had previously seen working as gardeners, were all armed with saw-edged, straight-bladed swords and daggers, and heavy maces with disk-shaped heads.

There was no chance to escape, so he stood his ground, still clutching the struggling girl's slim wrist with one hand, and leaning on his rifle with the other.

Suddenly the girl wrenched her wrist from his grasp, and sprang nimbly away from him. And in a moment he was surrounded by a circle of menacing, saw-edged sword blades.

CHAPTER IV

As HE stood there, ringed by hostile swordsmen, Jerry thought rapidly. Obviously, the brown men understood that his rifle was a dangerous weapon, for they were approaching him cautiously. Accordingly, he bent and laid it at his feet. Then he unstrapped his other weapons piled them on top of it, and raised his hands above his head in token of surrender.

Instantly two men leaped in and took possession of the weapons. A third cast a loop of tough, flexible leather around his wrists and drew it taut.

The girl spoke to one of the men, evidently an officer, who saluted her by holding both hands before his eyes, and issued a sharp command to the others. Then she turned and descended the steps to where the dead beast lay. As his captors dragged him after her, Jerry was surprised to see her stoop and throw her arms around the great shaggy neck. When she arose, tears were trickling down her cheeks.

She led the way through the garden. Behind her, walking at a respectful distance, was the officer; following him was the man who held the thong which bound Jerry's arms. On each side of the Earthman strode a brown warrior, sword in hand, and behind him walked two more, bearing his arms and equipment. The others dispersed.

They followed a path of the resilient brown paving material which presently led to the mouth of a tunnel which yawned from one side of a tree-covered mound. At either side of the tunnel mouth stood a white-skinned guard, who in addition to sword, dagger and mace, was armed with a sheaf of wicked-looking multi-barbed javelins.

At sight of the girl, these guards saluted respectfully. Then one hurried into the tunnel and emerged a moment later, followed by a vehicle which made Jerry gasp in astonishment. It moved smoothly and silently on six pairs of jointed metal legs shod with balls of resilient reddish-brown material like that used in paving. In lieu of seats, it supported twelve saddles, set three in a row. And in the foremost row, at the extreme right, sat the driver, who manipulated the multiped conveyance by means of two vertical levers, on either side of his saddle.

The girl climbed into a saddle beside the driver, and Jerry was placed in the central saddle of the next row, a guard on each side of him. The man who held the thong that bound his wrists, and the two who bore his equipment, seated themselves in the next row. The vehicle started as the driver pushed the two levers forward.

The tunnel which they entered led downward in a steep spiral. It was lighted by small globes filled with a thick, luminous liquid which he later learned was derived from a radioactive substance called baridium. They were suspended on short chains from the ceiling, and shed a mellow, amber light. Swiftly they sped down that spiral ramp, and Jerry caught flashes of small level platforms at regular intervals, leading to arched doorways. Presently, the vehicle slowed down and came to a sliding stop before one of them.

The girl sprang out onto the platform, and Jerry was dragged after her by his captors. She led the way to a tremendous arched door before which stood a score of armed and uniformed guards. These guards were white. They saluted respectfully, and parted their ranks to let the party pass.

The splendor of the room they now entered left Jerry spellbound with awe. It was a tremendous circular audience chamber, at least a thousand feet in diameter, and as high as it was wide. Its ceiling of burnished gold was supported by huge pillars, fifty feet in diameter, each seemingly cut from a single piece of pale blue crystal.

The floor was of hexagonal, orange colored crystal blocks, between the interstices of which molten silver had been poured, and the whole polished to a mirror-like luster. Suspended from the ceiling on thick golden chains, and hanging about two hundred feet above the floor, were huge light globes, twenty feet in diameter, filled with the luminous liquid he had previously observed.

At spaced intervals around the circular wall, uniformed guards stood, leaning on their tall spears.

In the center of the room, toward which they were walking, stood a circular dais, consisting of three disks placed concentrically one above the other. The top disk was of blue crystal, the middle one of orange crystal, and the bottom one of black.

Suspended above the center of the highest disk, on four thick golden cables, was a massive golden throne, upholstered in blue. And on this throne, Jerry saw a big man, with handsome, regal features that were as expressionless as stone. His thick, iron-gray beard had been braided into five long plaits which hung down to his wide golden belt, in which a thousand jewels sparkled. His arms and torso were bare, save for his jeweled golden armlets and wrist-guards, and a gem-encrusted medallion which hung on his chest. A close-fitting casque of burnished gold was on his head, and a single huge gem blazed above his forehead with a blue-white light.

Two young white men wearing blue, one a blond and the other a brunet, stood on the top disk at either side of the throne. Below these, on the orange disk, stood a tall, broad-shouldered fellow with nut-brown skin, his clothing orange trimmed with blue, and a girl slightly lighter colored, who likewise wore orange and blue. Jerry saw that she was slight, slender and beautiful.

On the lowest disk were a score of white-skinned men and women who wore orange trimmed in black. And surrounding the disks were at least a thousand more who exhibited a variety of colors, though the majority of them wore black. But every one, other than the warriors from the garden who had captured the Earthman, and the man and girl who stood on the middle disk, was white-skinned.

Those who stood around the throne stepped aside and saluted respectfully as the girl came up with the guards and prisoner. But she ran swiftly up the steps and threw her arms about the monarch's neck, tears streaming from her eyes.

The big man picked her up as easily as if she had been a doll, and seated her on the wide throne beside him. For some time they conversed. From time to time she looked at Jerry as she talked, and he knew the conversation related to him.

Presently, in the midst of her story, the girl stepped down from the throne and took Jerry's rifle from one of the brown guards. She brought it to her shoulder, exactly as he had done, and he was alarmed to see her finger on the trigger.

"Wait!" he cried, and sprang forward, to snatch the rifle away from her. But at the moment the weapon went off. The girl was hurled backward by the unexpected recoil of the heavy rifle, and fell to the floor. The bullet struck one of the crystal pillars.

Instantly, pandemonium reigned. The girl was picked up by the monarch, who hastily sprang down from his throne as she fell. Then, still holding her feather weight in his arms, he issued a sharp command.

Jerry was astounded to see a circular section of the floor rising before the throne, supported by three stout pillars. When it had risen to a height of about twenty feet, another floor was disclosed beneath it. As this one came to rest, three huge black men stepped from it, carrying a large circular rug made from the resilient reddish-brown material. They spread this on the floor.

Then two of them seized Jerry and dragged him to the center of the rug, where they forced him to his knees. The third, who carried an enormous, two-edged sword in a sheath strapped to his back, drew the weapon and looked inquiringly at the monarch. The latter nodded.

CHAPTER V

HALF-STUNNED, Jerry waited for the executioner's keen blade to descend. But at that instant the blond, blue-clad youth who had stood beside the throne rushed up, sword in hand and struck aside the blade of the executioner.

A moment later, another man came running up-a white-haired man who wore orange and black; and on his beardless countenance was a look of calm benignity. He smiled encouragingly at Jerry, then turned and addressed the pokerfaced monarch. The latter issued an order to the two black giants at the Earthman's sides, whereupon they permitted him to arise.

In the meantime the girl in the monarch's arms revived, and he put her on the floor, where she joined in the discussion. Jerry noticed that there was considerable wonder written on her face, as the white-haired man talked to her and the ruler. Four others joined in the discussion the two young men in blue who had stood at either side of the throne, and the dark-skinned girl and man who had stood on the central dais.

Although he could not understand a word that was spoken, Jerry saw that this latter personage was urging his execution. The girl, however, evidently sided with the white-haired newcomer and the blond youth.

Presently, the ruler rumbled a curt order. The thongs were removed from Jerry's wrists, and the white-haired man after saluting the ruler, took the Earthman's arm and led him away.

"You are Dr. Morgan's nephew, are you not?" he asked in English.

"I am," gulped Jerry, "but how did you know? And who are you?"

"I am Lal Vak," was the reply. "I was unavoidably delayed. As I am a stranger in Raliad, and there is a revolt in the provinces, I was accused of being a spy. My arrest came this morning, and I had some difficulty in clearing myself of the charge, despite my credentials from the Vil of Xancibar. A stranger is usually accounted guilty until he is proven innocent."

While they talked, they threaded numerous passageways, and Jerry noticed that every one they met stared curiously at his army uniform.

Presently they came to a spiral runway, and Lal Vak, stepping out on the signal platform, pulled a cord which unhooded a large light globe overhead by drawing up the four quarters of its metal covering as the petals of a flower open. A moment later one of the vehicles skidded to a stop before the landing.

Then they climbed into the saddles, the scientist spoke a word to the driver, and they shot swiftly upward. After passing eight platforms, the vehicle came to a stop before the ninth, and they got out. Threading another hallway, they came at length to a large door which an attendant, on seeing Lal Vak, threw open for them.

They entered, and Jerry found himself in the central room of a large and luxurious apartment, lighted by a single circular window that extended from floor to ceiling, its crystal panes opening outward to admit the afternoon breeze. The furniture, consisting of chairs, divans, and a table, was legless, and suspended from the ceiling by flexible, silk-covered cables.

"Let us sit on the balcony and talk," said Lal Vak.

Jerry stepped through the window and followed Lal Vak out onto the balcony. He looked over the railing. Far below him was a broad street, thronged with darting multiped vehicles and scurrying people. Other balconies, he observed, jutted out above, below and around this one, and from the buildings across the street.

Seating himself on the bench beside the scientist he mechanically took out a cigarette and lit it. A look of astonishment crossed the features of Lal Vak.

"What's wrong?" asked Jerry.

"For a moment I thought you were on fire," replied Lal Vak. "I remember Dr. Morgan's telling me about this curious custom of Earth-people, but it startled me. Tell me, why do you do it?"

"Just a habit, I guess. But a habit I won't have very long," said Jerry, looking at his half-empty cigarette case, "as I don't suppose there is such a thing as tobacco on Mars. May as well quit now." He was about to toss the case ever the railing when Lal Vak caught his arm.

"Wait," he said. "Save those little white cylinders. They may prove valuable to you."

"How?" Jerry wanted to know.

"As evidence of your advent from another world. The Vil of Kalsivar suspects that you are an enemy spy, who arrived on the palace roof with an outlandish costume and strange weapons in order to deceive him in case of capture. It is thought that your purpose was to kidnap Junia, daughter of Numin Vil."

Jerry said, "Just a moment. Let me get this thing straight. I take it that Numin Vil is the ruler, who sat on the throne."

"That's right. He is what you might call, the Emperor of Kalsivar, mightiest nation of Mars."

"And that girl I rescued from the wild beast is his daughter?"

"She is. The Sovil, or Imperial Princess of Kalsivar. Unfortunately, you did not rescue her from a wild beast. It seems that you met her on the roof garden, and attempted to abduct her. Her favorite dalf came to her rescue, and you slew the beast with one of your strange weapons."

"What's that? You mean the creature I killed was a pet?"

"Not only was it a pet, but she loved it almost like a member of the family. She got that dalf when a cub, and raised it herself."

"Hm. Sort of watchdog, eh? I'll apologize to the lady, of course, and if possible, get her a new dalf."

"Apologize, yes, but don't mention a new dalf. She has many, but to speak of replacing this one would be almost equivalent to offering to replace her brother after you had slain him."

"I think I begin to understand."

"You certainly succeeded in getting into plenty of trouble, and you are far from out of it yet. With the assistance of Her Highness, Junia Sovil, I was able to get you a forty-day stay of execution, but at the end of that time you must stand trial. The

135

Vil granted this clemency so you would have time to learn the language, and thus be able to speak in your own behalf, as well as to hear your accusers."

"What accusers?"

"I mean, in particular, Thoor Movil, Junia's cousin, who is head of the spy system of Kalsivar. He is the tall, dark-skinned fellow who wore orange trimmed with blue. Blue, on Mars, is the exclusive color of royalty. A Vil, or his descendants of unmixed royal blood, may wear it with gold. A noble, closely related to the royal family, may trim his orange garments with blue. Thoor Movil is the son of Numin Vil's younger brother."

"He appears to be of a different race," said Jerry.

"His mother was of the brown race," Lal Vak explained, "which is a mixture of the black and white races, according to our ethnologists. It is believed that Kalsivar was founded by a black race, which was later conquered by a white race, that intermarriage occurred for many generations, and the brown race resulted. A few of the blacks, however, retained their racial purity. Within historical times, about five thousand years ago, Kalsivar was reconquered by a white race which did not intermarry with the other two, and whose leader was the founder of the present dynasty."

"And this revolt you speak of. Who is fomenting it?"

"The origin of the leader is shrouded in mystery," replied Lal Vak. "For at least a thousand years there has been a prophecy among the brown people to the effect that a man of their own race, of the old royal blood, would arise to lead them to victory over their white rulers. Less than a year ago a stranger appeared among a large group of them, who had gone into the desert to perform religious rites as is their annual custom. This person wore a hideous mask, fashioned in the likeness of the chief of their ancient gods, Sarkis the Sun God, and claimed that he was the reincarnation of that god, returned to lead them to ultimate victory.

"Many fell down and worshiped him, remaining to form the nucleus of a rapidly growing army of outlaws, who raid our agricultural districts, and harass our shipping. Many punitive expeditions have been sent out against these outlaws, but they invariably break up into small bands which scatter over the trackless desert, to reform later at some unexpected point for fresh raids. Their mysterious leader has come to be known as Sarkis the Torturer.'

"Does this Sarkis constitute a menace to the present ruler of Kalsivar?"

"Decidedly," was Lal Vak's reply. "His ranks are being rapidly swelled by deserters from the imperial army. And the roving desert tribes, many of which are of the brown race, have unanimously espoused his cause."

At this moment a brown-skinned slave appeared in the window opening and spoke with Lal Vak. Then the latter turned to Jerry. "I doubt not that you are hungry, and our regular time for eating has arrived. Let us go inside."

They went in and sat down on one of the swinging divans. The slave brought a large bowl, mounted on a tripod, which he set before them. The bowl was divided into six segments, and in each segment reposed a different kind of food. Mounted on a single shaft in the center of the bowl was a small, circular disk, on which stood a flask and two cubical cups, all of gold, exquisitely carved and set with sparkling jewels.

The servant poured a steaming liquid into the cups. It was pink in color, and gave off a fragrant aroma.

Lal Vak took up a cup and extended it to Jerry. "I believe you will find it easy to like our favorite Martian drink, though you may find it difficult to accustom yourself to some of our foods."

"What is it?"

"We call it pulcho," Lal Vak replied. "Taken in moderate quantities it is a pleasant stimulant. When drunk excessively, it is intoxicating."

The Earthman took a sip, and found it as the scientist had said, both pleasing and stimulating.

The brown-skinned servant hastened forward to refill his cup, and the Earthman noticed that he took it up in such a way that for a moment the palm of his hand was held over it.

The man handed him the brimming cup, but before he could raise it to his lips, Lal Vak snatched it from him. Springing to his feet, he whipped out his dagger and presented its point to the breast of the servant, addressing a few sharp words to him.

With a trembling hand, the fellow took the cup and drained its contents at a single gulp. A dull, glazed look came to his eyes. He slumped to the floor, then lay still.

"I thought I saw him drop something into your cup," said Lal Vak, "but I wanted to make sure. As you see, I was right."

"You mean that the fellow tried to poison me?"

"Precisely," Lal Vak replied. "He is only a tool, of course. You have an enemy in Raliad, it seems, and one who occupies a high place."

"But who could it have been?"

"That is what we will try to find out-later," the scientist told him, turning toward the door. "I go now to call the guard. Under the circumstances, we had best keep our own council. I beg you, for your own good to remember, after I have taught you our language, that this impudent fellow had the bad taste to commit suicide in our presence."

CHAPTER VI

STUDYING assiduously under the efficient tutelage of Lal Vak, Jerry rapidly learned to read and write the Martian language.

The scientist also instructed him in Martian manners and customs, and described to him the immense city without.

"Raliad," Lal Vak told him, "is truthfully called the 'City of a Million Gardens.' Here every house, from the imperial palace down to the lowliest hovel, has its roof garden. It is so immense that, within its confines live more people than make up the entire nation of Xancibar, whence I come. Its resident population is well over a hundred million, and its floating population daily numbers at least twenty-five million more. More canals verge here than in any other six cities on the planet, and the canals are the main arteries of travel and commerce."

Some five days before the date set for his trial, Jerry was enjoying his evening meal in company with Lal Vak, when the latter told him:

"I have arranged a surprise for you. Her Imperial Highness, the Sovil, when I told her that you had mastered our language, and that you had a petition for her ears, graciously consented to grant you an interview."

"Great! When do we start?"

"Patience, and finish your meal," smiled Lal Vak. "We have plenty of time. A guard will be sent for you at the appointed hour, for you are still a prisoner, you know. To show proper respect for her highness, I think we had best dress you for the audience."

"This Army uniform is getting rather seedy looking," said Jerry.

"On Mars we dress according to our stations in life. I understand that you are of noble blood."

"On the contrary," Jerry replied, "there are no nobles in the nation from which I came. We have our great men-our leaders in finance, in war, in science, and in the arts-but no nobility."

"That I know. Yet Dr. Morgan told me he was descended from the nobility of another nation-Ireland, I believe he called it. This will entitle you to wear orange, trimmed with black, on Mars."

"True. I had forgotten that my first American ancestor was an Irish viscount. But he renounced his title, so that lets me out."

"It doesn't change the blood:"

"That's true, but I think I'll be loyal to his ideas, just the same."

"Then you will have to wear the plain black of a commoner."

Lal Vak summoned a servant, and ordered that a suit of commoner's clothes be brought. Some time later, Jerry surveyed himself in the burnished gold mirror. He wore a cincture of glossy black velvet, which left his legs bare. On his feet were black boots of soft leather.

There was a broad belt of woven silver links about his waist, from which depended an empty sword scabbard on his left, and a dagger sheath on his right. The weapons had been removed because of his status as a prisoner. His arms and torso were bare, save for a pair of silver wrist guards, a pair of armlets of the same metal, and a medallion which depended from around his neck. On his head was a black turban, held in place by a band and chin strap of finely woven silver links. This turban was made of a tenuous but extremely strong and wind-proof material, which could be unbound and dropped about his shoulders to form a cloak that would reach to his knees.

A few moments later the guard flung open the door and a page entered.

"Her Imperial Highness, Junia, Sovil of Kalsivar, commands the presence of Lal Vak and Jerry Morgan."

They returned his salute, and followed him out into the hallway, where two armed guards fell in behind them.

The page led them to the nearest runway, where they took a multiped vehicle to the second floor above them. Here they walked back along an almost identical hallway, and Jerry realized, as they paused before a blue-curtained door guarded by two warriors, that Junia's apartment was directly above his own.

The page went in first, to announce them, then returned and bade them enter. In a large, magnificently furnished room, Junia reclined on a swinging divan of blue plush, surrounded by a bevy of her ladies.

As Jerry stood before her and rendered the royal salute by holding both hands before his eyes, he caught his breath at sight of her loveliness.

"I shield my eyes in the glory of your highness's presence," he said.

She returned the salute by raising one slender hand before her eyes-the salute rendered to those of other than royal blood. Then she turned to Lal Vak.

"You have made a mistake, I believe," she said. "This afternoon you requested an audience for a nobleman from another world, and I granted it. Now you bring a commoner before me-an affront which even the Zovil, my brother, would not have dared."

"I can explain in a few words, your highness," said Lal Vak. "Jerry Morgan's noble ancestor renounced his title. Though nothing can rob him of his noble blood, he hails from a country where there are no titles, and so prefers to appear as a commoner."

"It is a churlish preference I should expect in him, after his actions when first we met. It seems he would add insult to injury."

Lal Vak was about to reply, but Jerry forestalled him.

"I fear your highness misapprehends my intentions. Since I came to apologize for those same blundering acts of mine, I wore the black of a commoner in token of humility."

"Why, this is better," she said, with a faint smile. "I had not expected so quick a wit in one whose blunders have been so lamentable."

"It is charitable of you to allow them to pass as blunders."

"Had I not accounted them so, you would not have been granted this interview," said Junia.

"You lead me to hope that the forgiveness for which I have come to sue will be granted."

"It is already granted."

"I am profoundly grateful," he said with almost undue eagerness.

She said no more, but her brown eyes dropped, and a slow blush suffused the lovely features.

For a moment Jerry stood thus, unconscious of everything about him save the allure of this maiden. Then Lal Vak touched his arm, and the spell was broken.

"Come," he said softly. "The interview is ended."

As one in a daze, Jerry saluted and withdrew, accompanied by the scientist and followed by the two guards.

Lal Vak speaking English so the two guards who followed would not understand, said, "I saw that look which passed between you two. If you would live, even to the day of the trial, you must never attempt to see her again; never let any one know the depth of feeling which you have betrayed and to which she involuntarily responded this evening.

"To know that I should never see her again would be to lose all zest for life. But why do you say I must put her from my mind?"

"Because to do otherwise will be to align yourself against forces that can only compass your destruction. Already you have made one powerful enemy, whose name I believe I can guess. And now, would you align Manith Zovil, your friend and protector, and even the Vil himself against you?"

At this moment they entered their apartment, and the two guards took up their positions before the door.

"As I have previously told you," Lal Vak went on, "Manith is the Zovil of Nunt, one of the major powers of Mars with which Kalsivar is on friendly terms. He was sent here by his father, Lom Harr, Vil of Nunt, for the express purpose of courting Junia Sovil. And I have been given to understand that the two young people are not at all averse to the idea."

"That does put me in an awkward position. I can't prose cute my own interests without interfering with those of my friend and benefactor."

"Precisely. And although we have not definitely discovered the identity of your secret enemy, I believe that he will come out into the open very shortly. Strangely enough, what he believes to be his own interests, are opposed to those of Manith Zovil, as well as to your recently awakened desires."

"And his name?"

"Thoor Movil, whose father was the Vil's brother, but whose mother was a sovil of the ancient royal family of the brown race. He urged your instant execution on the day Manith saved you. There are but two people between him and succession to the throne of Kalsivar-Shiev Zovil, Junia's brother, and Junia herself. If he could accomplish the death of one and marry the other, his succession would be assured, save for one thing-that no man of the brown race has occupied that throne since the conquest by the white race, five thousand years ago. However, it appears that Sarkis the Torturer is the tool of Thoor Movil, as he demands, that Kalsivar shall be ruled by a man of the ancient brown royalty.

"The entire plot is clear enough to me, but Numin Vil would not believe me. And Thoor Movil would quickly set his assassins on my trail if the Vil should fail to act against me."

"And just where do I fit in?"

"I have tried to make it plain," said Lal Vak, "that Thoor Movil is both fearless and unscrupulous. What, then, would happen to you if you were to reveal your true feelings toward Junia, and such revelation were to come to his ears? He would treat you as a pestiferous insect which one crushes beneath his foot."

At this instant one of the guards at the door drew back a curtain and announced: "A messenger from His Highness, Thoor Movil."

Lal Vak paled beneath his coat of tan. "It has come, and sooner than I expected," he told Jerry in English. Then he spoke to the guard in the Martian tongue: "Admit him."

A brown-skinned page entered.

"His Highness, Thoor Movil, is entertaining His Imperial Highness, Shiev Zovil, at gapun," announced the page, "and commands the attendance of Lal Vak and Jerry Morgan."

"Await us outside while we make ready," Lal Vak told the page. The latter stepped out beyond the curtains, and the scientist spoke in English: "Let me warn you, my son, that Thoor Movil bids you to a more dangerous game than that of gapun. You will best be able to defeat him by being scrupulously careful to offend no one, and by passing unnoticed any insults save only those which may amount to an actual challenge, and which no Martian gentleman may ignore and retain his honor."

CHAPTER VII

As HE and Lal Vak followed the page into Thoor Movil's large and luxurious apartments, Jerry saw that the party was a small and select one, consisting of about twenty men. Three of them, Shiev Zovil, Manith Zovil and Thoor Movil, wore the blue of royalty. The others, with the exception of the Earthman, wore the orange of nobility.

Four gaming boards set on a large swinging table served the gapun players. These boards contained numbered holes, and the game consisted of rolling Martian money-small engraved pellets of gold silver, and platinum-into the holes, the first pellet into the highest numbered hole winning the entire stake from each roll.

Pulcho, which was being imbibed by the gamblers, was being poured by a dozen brown slaves.

As Jerry knew Thoor Movil for his enemy, he was surprised when the latter did them honor by rising to receive them. The brown prince found a place for Lal Vak first, then he turned to Jerry with a sarcastic smile, and said in the hearing of all the company: "You are our latest and most distinguished gambler, since you wear the darkest clothing of any one present."

Jerry returned his sarcastic smile with a cheery one. "That I am the latest is plain to be seen," he said, "but I protest that I am not the most distinguished. You do me too great an honor."

"How so?" asked Thoor Movil.

"It is your highness who is our most distinguished gambler, since you have the darkest skin of any present."

The two princes, Shiev and Manith, laughed uproariously and some of the nobles ventured to smile, but most of them looked exceedingly grave. And gravest of all was Lal Vak.

"Is it customary in your country for a guest to insult his host?" asked Thoor Movil, fingering his sword hilt.

"On the contrary," Jerry replied, "I should say that it is as great a rarity as for a host to insult his guest."

Thoor Movil's frown deepened, but Manith Zovil interposed. Taking Jerry's arm with one hand, and that of the brown prince with the other, he said, "Come. You two are delaying the game. Let us on with the play."

Before they could seat themselves, however, a tall, broad-shouldered player who wore the orange and black of the nobility, rose and said: "I, for one, do not care to play, so long as this commoner is present. His appearance is offensive enough, but his manners are a stench and an abomination to sensitive nostrils."

Jerry paused and regarded him coldly. "I have not the honor of your acquaintance."

At this, Lal Vak plucked at his arm, and said in English:

"Beware. This is the trap Thoor Movil has set for you. This man is the most dangerous swordsman in all Kalsivar."

"I am Arsad, Bad of Moor," said Jerry's new-found enemy. "You are standing in my way."

Recalling his preceptor's warning to avoid a quarrel at any cost, Jerry stepped aside.

But again the fellow turned and faced him. "Have I not said that you stand in my way?"

With this, Arsad struck the Earthman a sharp blow on the cheek with the back of his hand.

Jerry saw red, and he struck out straight from the shoulder, his fist landing full on the mouth of his adversary. Arsad stumbled backward and crashed across the gaming table, sending the gapun boards flying. For a moment he lay there as if dazed. Then he sprang up with a roar, spat out three teeth and a mouthful of blood, and whipped out his sword.

Jerry felt a jeweled hilt thrust into his hand, Manith Zovil, Crown Prince of Nunt, had again befriended him, this time by lending him his sword.

Swiftly Jerry came on guard parrying a thrust for his heart. He found his own return thrust parried with ease, and soon realized that he was up against a master swordsman. But Arsad must have come to recognize this at the same time, for he began to fence very cautiously.

Meanwhile, the spectators, who had formed a ring around the two contestants, were treated to such an exhibition of swordsmanship as they had not seen for many a day. For, though Arsad was known as one of the best swordsmen on Mars, Jerry had likewise been regarded one of the best swordsmen in the American Army.

Arsad had not exhausted all his tricks. And Jerry learned a new one just after he had parried a particularly long lunge to his body. For the Bad of Dhoor, in recovering, turned the edge of his saw-toothed blade against Jerry's side, and as he drew it back, cut a deep gash from which the blood spurted freely. It was a trick which could not have been performed with any but a saw-toothed Martian blade.

Clutching his side to stanch the flow of blood, the Earthman now took the offensive with such vigor that time and again his opponent was forced to give ground in order to save himself. Still Arsad remained unwounded.

But the Martian had, by this time, discovered that he was in danger of losing his life. Snatching his turban-like head-cloak from his head, he hurled it into Jerry's face, blinding him for an instant. Then he lunged.

Jerry's earthly muscles saved his life by a split second, as he leaped back a full ten feet. Then he brushed the blinding fabric aside and gave a fierce leap forward, sword out, straight at the charging Arsad. In sheer surprise the latter tripped and fell, an easy target for the Earthman's point.

But instead of administering the coup de grace, Jerry struck the sword from the hand of his tricky opponent, then presented his point to his breast.

"Wait! Would you kill an unarmed man?"

"Unless you yield!"

But Arsad sprang backward, and to one side; he seized the weapon which the Earthman had beaten from his hand, and coming up to catch Jerry with his blade low, slashed swiftly for his neck.

Jerry dived straight forward, under that whistling blade, at the same time extending his point. The sword of Arsad flashed harmlessly over his back, but his own plunged clear through the body of the Martian, projecting a full two feet from his back.

With a look of horrified unbelief on his face, the Rad of Dhoor dropped his sword and slumped to the floor.

Two surgeons, who had been sent for at the beginning of the duel, now came forward. One pronounced Arsad dead. The other dressed Jerry's wound by drawing it together and covering it with a thick gum called jembal which quickly hardened into a flexible, porous covering that was antiseptic, permitted drainage, and kept out infection. A slave took the bloody sword from Jerry's hand, cleansed it, and returned it to him.

His wound dressed, the Earthman returned the sword to the Zovil of Nunt. "For the second time I am indebted to your highness."

"A trifle," Manith Zovil replied. Then taking a cup of pulcho from a slave who waited nearby, he handed it to the Earthman. "Drink," he commanded. "It will help to restore your strength. You have lost much blood."

Jerry tossed off the beverage and felt refreshed. In the meantime, the body of Arsad had been taken away, and all traces of the duel removed by the slaves. The gapun boards were replaced on the table, and several of the nobles resumed their interrupted gaming, drinking and laughter as if nothing had happened.

Most boisterous of all was Shiev, Zovil of Kalsivar. The crown prince was a slight, spare youth, and something of a fop. That he had drunk overmuch pulcho was plainly evident.

"Come," he cried, beating on the board with a handful of platinum pieces. "Let us on with the game. I would see if this black-clad commoner can play gapun as well as he can fence."

"If it pleases your highness," said Jerry, "I should prefer not to play tonight. I have lost much blood, and feel the need of repose."

Shiev flushed. "You refuse the honor—refuse to play with the heir to the throne of Kalsivar? You are exceedingly impudent for a commoner."

"And you are exceedingly ungracious for a prince."

His words were like a bombshell in the room. The face of Shiev Zovil went deathly white. His hand flew to his sword hilt, but ere he could draw the weapon, Manith Zovil had interposed.

"Wait, Shiev," he said. "This man is from another world, and does not know our customs."

"Then he needs teaching."

"Not with the sword," Manith answered. "He has demonstrated that on the body of Kalsivar's greatest swordsman."

"Now, by the wrath of Deza!" exploded Shiev. "Are you intimating that I fear to fight this clumsy oaf? Have a care how you presume on our hospitality, or it may be that only your ashes will be back to Nunt."

"Do not presume too much on the fact that I have come to woo her highness, your sister. I am your royal equal, and my sword shall answer further insinuations from you."

At this, Shiev lurched drunkenly to his feet and whipped out his blade. Manith Zovil drew his own weapon, but to Jerry's surprise, Lal Vak stepped between them.

"Before you go on with this duel, highnesses," said the white-haired scientist, "I beg you to pause and consider the consequences. Many things are done in the heat of anger that bring regret when the blood cools. If you fight, one of you may be killed. You are both brave men and fearless, and this does not weigh with either of you. But no matter which one dies, there will be an immediate result—a war between Kalsivar and Nunt that will cost millions of lives and use up the resources of both nations."

At this, the nobles immediately sided with Lal Vak, and begged the two princes to sheathe their swords. Jerry, who had joined those attempting to cool the wrath of Manith Zovil, noticed there was one man in the room who held aloof from all

146

this-as soon as he saw that the swords were to be sheathed, he added his voice to those of the others in crying for peace.

The two princes were brought to the point of saluting each other, though the eyes of both still flashed ominously. Then Manith Zovil saluted his dark-skinned host, thanked him for his hospitality, and took his departure. Jerry and Lal Vak did likewise, and came upon the prince as he waited for a multiped vehicle on, the signal platform.

"Again I have your highness to thank for interposing in my behalf," said Jerry. "Won't you join Lal Vak and me in our apartment for the rest of the evening?"

"Sorry, but I am going now to take leave of Numin Vil and quit this country," replied Manith. "Junia is glorious, worth fighting and dying for, but I am not of the stuff that can brook these constant insults from her popinjay brother.

"As for the obligation, my friend, there is none. I only did that which any man worthy of the name might do under similar circumstances. This is not the first time Shiev Zovil has insulted me, and I am convinced that it is because his cousin has poisoned his mind against me. Unfortunately, I can find no pretext for seeking a quarrel with Thoor."

At this moment, a multiped vehicle stopped at the platform. Manith Zovil bade Jerry and Lal Vak farewell when they reached their platform, and invited them to visit him in his own palace. He would be leaving, he said, as soon as he could pay his respects to Numin Vil.

When they arrived at their apartment, followed by Jerry's two guards, Lal Vak suggested that the Earthman retire immediately, as he would need rest after losing so much blood. As for himself, he was going to visit a friend in another part of the palace, and would probably return quite late.

The scientist gone, Jerry removed his headcloak, and was about to do the same with his other clothing, when a guard drew back the curtain and announced: "A page from Her Highness, Nisha Novil."

Jerry replaced his headpiece, and said: "Let him enter."

A brown-skinned page stepped into the room, saluted, and said: "Her Highness, Nisha Novil, commands the immediate presence of Jerry Morgan."

"Bear my excuses to her highness," replied Jerry. "Tell her that I am weakened from loss of blood-that I . . .

"This is a command, Jerry Morgan. There can be no excuses."

Jerry pondered for a moment, and heartily wished that Lal Vak was here to advise him what to do. Because Nisha Novil was the sister of Thoor Movil, he sensed a trap of some sort. Yet the page would accept no excuse-apparently had been so instructed.

He turned to the page, and said: "I am ready. Conduct me to her highness."

CHAPTER VIII

Tim roomy apartments of Nisha Novil were furnished with a splendor that was almost barbaric, and Nisha herself was the most ornate object of all. Lying on a swinging divan upholstered with alternate stripes of orange and blue plush, she shot a languishing smile at Jerry from beneath her long, curved lashes, as he was ushered in before her.

The only cloth upon her shapely body was a silken cincture of orange trimmed with blue. Her small breast-shields were of blue and amber beads. By any standard she was undeniably beautiful.

With a wave of her hand she dismissed the page. Then she spoke, her voice low, with a purring quality, like that of a kitten that is being stroked.

"You are prompt, Jerry Morgan, but why have you brought the bodyguard? Were you afraid I might injure you? As you see, I am unarmed."

"Your highness forgets that I am a prisoner under suspended sentence of death. The guards . . .

"Yes, to be sure. I had forgotten." She addressed the two. "My slaves will give you pulcho in another room. Wait there until I send for you. I will be responsible for your prisoner."

With respectful salutations, the two guards followed a brown slave-girl through a curtained doorway. Then Nisha waved a slim hand, and the other slave-girls who stood in attendance behind her filed out of the room. As soon as they were alone, the princess rose with feline grace, and stood before Jerry, smiling up at him beneath languorous lids. She was no bigger than Junia, and much like her in appearance. Yet there was something about her, an untamed feral something in her every look and gesture.

"Come," she said, taking Jerry's hand and leading him to the divan. "You must be weary after your dual with Arsad. Come and rest here beside me while we talk."

"I did lose some blood," Jerry replied. "That was why I was about to ask your highness's indulgence. . ."

"But since I am dispensing with formality," she cooed, drawing him down upon the divan, "you may rest here as well as in your own apartment. And what I have to say cannot wait, for there are those who plot against your life, and I would save you. Tomorrow will be too late."

"Your highness is most generous to take an interest in my life."

She snuggled against him. "On the contrary, I am most selfish. From the very day when I first saw you, standing before the throne of Numin Vil, I have desired you.

"I heard of the suicide of the slave in your apartment, but did not grasp the significance at the time. However, when I learned of your duel with Arsad today, I knew that you had done something to displease my brother, and that where Arsad failed, another of Thoor's tools would eventually succeed. So I had a talk with my brother."

"I don't know what I ever did to him," said Jerry, "except that I turned one of his own sarcastic remarks against him, this evening."

"That had some weight, but it is not the true reason for his bitterness against you," she told him. "It began when our cousin, Junia, begged your life from Numin Vil after you had slain her dalf. I may add that those of whom Thoor becomes jealous never survive long."

"It seems that I have been exceedingly fortunate, then."

"Your skill with the sword saved you tonight," she answered, "but other means of compassing your death have already been planned. Thoor Movil's spies are everywhere, and when he heard of the look which Junia gave you in her apartment today, you were marked for death.

"And just what can you do about all this?" Jerry asked.

"Everything," she replied. I have made a pact with my brother. Your life is to be spared to me on condition that you never again cast your eyes toward our fair cousin."

"So you have arranged the whole thing between you. Thoughtful of your highness. But did it not occur to you that I might have some ideas of my own on the subject?"

To his surprise, she flung her arms around his neck-pressed her warm lips to his.

Had he never seen Junia, it is quite possible that the Earthman might have capitulated. Gently he disengaged the clinging arms from around his neck, and arose.

Nisha fell back on the divan, panting. Then she sprang straight for the Earthman. Screeching curses, she beat upon his breast, scratched his bare flesh until the blood welled forth. And through it all he stood immobile, hands at his sides, teeth clenched in a grim smile.

Her fit of fury passed almost as suddenly as it had begun. With horror in her eyes, she stood limply before him.

"Deza help me!" she moaned. "What have I done?"

"Have I your highness's leave to go?" he asked, with studied calm.

"No, wait! You must not leave me thus!"

She turned and ran into another room, reappearing a moment later with a basin of water, a handful of soft moss, and a bottle of jembal. Jerry stood like a statue while she washed away the blood and applied the healing gum to the scratches she had inflicted. Her ministrations finished, she looked up at him, tears swimming in her large black eyes and pearling the long lashes.

"Forgive me, my dear lord," she begged, contritely. "Strike me! Break me with those strong hands of yours! But do not leave me with anger in your heart. Only say that you forgive me, and Deza will grant me strength to go on, knowing that I may some day win your love."

"It is I who should ask forgiveness," Jerry told her, "since you have only wounded my body. But I, it seems, have unwittingly wounded your heart."

"You are generous, my lord," she cried, and flinging her arms around his neck, crushed her lips to his. "Now go. But remember-Nisha loves you, and will be waiting."

Without a word, he turned and left the room. He had taken the multiped vehicle to his own floor, the one below, before he noticed that his two guards were not following him. But he reasoned that they knew the way to his apartment as well as he.

Passing into the apartment, he hooded all the baridium light globes but one, preparatory to retiring. But, strangely enough, he no longer felt tired or sleepy. Feeling that a breath of air would do him good, he pushed open the two lower segments of the window, and stepped out onto the balcony. The night was unusually cold, even for Mars at that season.

Jerry threw back his head and inhaled a great lungful of the cold, sweet air. But he checked the inhalation with a gasp of amazement, for he saw, looking down from the second balcony above him, the lovely face of Junia. As she stood there, wrapped in her light, soft furs, he wished that he might bridge the gap between them.

She smiled, and Jerry returned her smile. Then she turned away and he saw her no more. But a plan had come to him. He could bridge that gap, with the aid of his Earthly muscles. Less than eight feet above his head hung the tough coils of the vine which decked Nisha's balcony. And he could see, by craning his neck outward, that the vines on Junia's balcony hung even lower.

A few moments later, he stood on Nisha's balcony. Fortunately for his plan, the vines on Junia's balcony hung lower, and he was able to reach the lower most of these by a vertical jump, thus avoiding the necessity of running past the window.

The loop held and he easily made the balcony above. Like the other two, it was edged with potted plants, and at first he did not notice the figure standing at the opposite end in the shadow of an aromatic sebolis. But as he crept over the railing, he noticed a slight movement in the shadow, and his heart leaped to his throat. Could this be a guard-and he unarmed?

Jerry was unable to more than make out a muffled form standing immobile before him. Silently, he crept forward, and as silently sprang, flinging one hand about the arms and body of the figure and clapping his left hand over the mouth.

To his astonishment, he found that he clasped a woman. A muffled scream came from the girl as he dragged her out into the full light of the nearer moon.

"Junia!" he exclaimed, releasing her and standing shamefaced before her. "I thought you were a guard."

"Just what are you doing on my balcony?" she asked. "And why would you have attacked a guard of mine?"

"I had to see you. There was no other way to see you alone. Oh, Junia, it seems that I am doomed to blunder each time I approach you-that the fates have conspired to make you hate me."

"I-I don't believe I could ever bring myself to hate you, Jerry Morgan," she said softly. "But you are so clumsy. One scarcely knows what to do with you or how to restrain you."

As she stood there looking up at him in the moonlight, Jerry reflected that this girl could do more to him with her eyes alone than could Nisha with her arms and lips-with her whole body.

"You have said that you had to see me," she told him presently. "Why?"

"Because I love you."

"You are bold to approach me thus, and bolder still to make such a declaration," she said. But there was no hint of anger in her eyes.

"You are right, highness," he said dejectedly, "With your leave I will depart, and never trouble you more."

But as he turned away, she laid her hand on his arm. "Wait, Jerry Morgan," she said. "What if I were to tell you that I also care?"

"Junia! You can't mean id"

"But I do, Jerry Morgan."

Gently, reverently, he took the tiny, fur-clad form in his arms. She raised her lips.

A moment they stood thus-a moment during which, for Jerry, all time stood still. Then she drew away.

"You must leave me, now. It grows late, and we may be discovered." There was a catch in her voice that sounded like a stifled sob, as she added: "May Deza keep you safe, and bring you back to me, unharmed."

Then she stepped into the darkness of her apartment.

For a moment Jerry stood there looking after her. Then he lowered himself over the railing, went down the vines hand over hand.

He found the apartment deserted, just as he had left it. Going to the door, he parted the curtains to see if his two guards had returned. They had not, and he was about to turn back when a man wearing the blue of royalty suddenly came running around a bend in the hall toward him. With a start of surprise, he recognized Manith Zovil. The Prince of Nunt carried a bloody sword in his hand, and blood was trickling from a wound on his breast.

Springing forward, Jerry caught him and helped him inside.

"What has happened, highness?" he asked. "Were you attacked?"

"Attacked, yes!" panted Manith. "I have just slain that drunken fool, Shiev Zovil. For the love of Deza, help me get rid of this blood, or my life will be forfeit, and there will be a war more vast and deadly than Mars has ever seen before!"

CHAPTER IX

WITH water and a handful of moss, Jerry cleansed the wound of Manith Zovil. Then he closed it with jembal. As it was only an inch in width and centrally located, the Prince of Nunt was able to hide it completely with the heavy medallion which hung on his chest.

Having cleansed his benefactor's sword and returned it to his sheath, Jerry mopped up several drops of blood from the floor, then went out onto the balcony and flung the telltale moss over the railing, and far out to his left, so no one below could accurately judge from which balcony it had fallen.

This done, he returned to where Manith sat panting on a divan, and poured him a cup of pulcho.

"Drink this, and try to compose yourself, highness. There is no cause for alarm, now. You and your weapons are free of blood, and your wound is dressed and concealed. Rather a bad one, too. A little more to the left, and you would not be alive."

Manith tossed off the drink and put down the cup.

"You are right, my friend," he said. "I met the drunken popinjay in the hallway. He was carrying his sword in his hand, and evidently bound for your apartment. As soon as I came near him, he lunged at me without a word of warning, and before I had a chance to so much as grasp my hilt.

"As you see, his design failed. Having dodged away that treacherous stroke, I drew my own sword and thrust him through the throat with as little compunction as if he had been a dalf."

"And you are sure he is dead?"

"If not, he soon will be."

"But why should any blame attach to you? You killed him in a fair fight, after an unprovoked assault."

"Because there were no witnesses. A duel with witnesses is legal; without them, is it murder."

"Did you meet anyone in the hallway before or after the duel?"

"No one."

"Then you are safe. Only you and I know what occurred, and I pledge you my word that I will never tell."

"I believe you, for though you wear the black of a commoner, you are a gentleman."

"And now," continued Jerry, "the best thing for you to do is to go on as if nothing had happened. You have taken your leave of the Vil, and were about to depart for your own country. I suggest that you go on, unhurriedly, as planned."

"In that case there should be no suspicion..."

He halted his speech suddenly, as the tramp of feet and the clank of weapons sounded without. Then rising, he seized the pulcho flask, and filling two cups, handed one to Manith and took up the other. Behind him, he heard the steps of men entering the chamber, but disregarding it, held the cup aloft, and said: "A safe and pleasant journey to you."

A sword flashed out from behind him, striking the cup from his hand and spilling the contents on the legs of Manith Zovil. Turning, he looked into the glittering eyes of Thoor Movil. Behind the brown prince stood a dozen warriors, swords in their hands.

Jerry forced himself to smile at his enemy. "Rather a boisterous way to announce your visit, highness," he said, picking up the cup, "but you are welcome, nevertheless. Manith Zovil and I were just drinking to his safe and pleasant journey. Won't you and your men join us?"

"It comports with your every action since you first came to Kalsivar, that you should choose to be facetious at a time like this."

"Since your highness chose to be playful, I merely fell in with your mood," Jerry replied, still smiling. "Courtesy to a guest, you know."

"But I am not playful, as you will learn soon enough. I am in deadly earnest. Where are your guards?"

"How should I know?" Jerry replied. "They were set to guard me, not I, them."

"What were you doing in the hallway a few moments ago?"

"Nothing. I have been in my apartment for some little time. Manith Zovil and I have been sitting here chatting. He is leaving for Nunt, you know, and dropped in to say farewell."

Thoor turned to the visiting prince.

"Did you notice anything unusual in the hallway when you came here?"

"Nothing," Manith replied. "Why?"

"Because Shiev Zovil has just been murdered there."

"Why, that's ghastly," said Manith. "I must tender my condolences to the prince's father and sister. Who do you think did it?"

"I believe," said Thoor Movil, "that the spy who occupies this apartment is the one who committed the crime."

"That would be impossible," said Manith. "He could not commit a murder and sit here talking to me at the same time. And I believe you do him an injustice in calling him a spy."

"How was the prince slain?" Jerry asked.

"Stabbed through the throat, as you well know," replied Thoor Movil.

"Perhaps you have not noticed that I am without weapons."

"True. But you may have a sword concealed about the apartment."

"I invite you to search it."

"We will do that without your invitation. Ho, men, see if you can find the weapon for me."

The soldiers went to work peering behind all movable objects and ripping upholstery, but the search was futile.

"Just as a matter of form," said Thoor Movil to Manith Zovil, "may I look at the blades of your sword and dagger? I do not suspect you, of course, but I must be thorough in the line of my duty."

"I understand perfectly," Manith replied, and tendered his weapons.

Thoor Movil examined the sword minutely, and returned it without comment, gave the dagger a cursory glance, and handed it back, also.

"They are clean, and your highness is absolved," he said. "But there is something suspicious about your friend, here. I go now to make further search, but I will leave four men on guard. Would you care to go with me?"

"Of course," Manith Zovil replied. "I must go back to his majesty the Vil, at once, to offer my sympathy before I leave." He turned to Jerry. "Farewell, my friend. I am sure you are innocent, and that his highness, here, is sure to find the guilty one and clear you."

He departed with Thoor Movil, and Jerry heard the dark prince post guards outside. He sat down on the ripped and rumpled divan to think.

Unless he could find some way to escape from Kalsivar, Jerry reasoned that nothing could save him except the intervention of Nisha in his behalf. And he did not want to feel obligated to her.

There was one, however, in that vast nation, in whose good graces Jerry particularly wished to remain. He felt sure that, sooner or later, Thoor or his agents would go to Junia with insinuations regarding him. Best go to her himself, he thought, ahead of any one else.

Once more, Jerry went out on the balcony. It had become colder as it grew later. And the farther moon had risen in the east, while its nearer, swifter companion, hurtled forward from the west to meet it, the two making visibility much better than before.

He leaped up, caught the trailing vine, and pulled himself up to Nisha's balcony. But scarcely had his feet touched the floor when a heavy cloak was thrown over his head, strong arms pinioned his arms to his sides, and he was half carried, half dragged through the window. He kicked and struggled in an effort to free himself from his unseen assailants, but in vain. His hands and feet were swiftly and skillfully bound, and with the cloak still over his head, he was deposited on a divan.

Then something sharp pricked his side, and a gruff voice said: "If you know what is good for you, you will remain quiet."

CHAPTER X

JERRY succumbed to the inevitable and gave up his struggles. Then suddenly, to his surprise, he heard a throaty contralto voice that was strangely familiar-the voice of Nisha.

"Remove the cloak, Jeth," she said, "and cut his bonds. My brother's men have gone."

The cloak dragged from his head, Jerry blinked in the unaccustomed rays of alight globe which hung above him, and flexed his numb limbs. He was in a small chamber, evidently the dressing room of Thoor's sister.

A burly, brown-skinned guard stood beside him, and another stood watch at the door. Nisha, herself, was looking down at him.

"I hope my men have not injured you," she said solicitously. "They acted in the emergency, under my commands, in order to save your life. The emergency has passed, but you are still in great danger. However, if you are willing to do as I tell you, it may be that I will be able to save you."

"You have been most kind," Jerry told her. "What do you want me to do?"

"Thoor's men are searching the palace-in fact, the whole city-for you. I guessed that you would try to escape by way of the balcony, and set my two faithful men, here, to watch for you and bring you to me unharmed but incapable of attempting to escape. And it is well that I did so, because Thoor's soldiers came through my apartment a moment later and searched the balcony. By telling them I had not seen you, which was true enough, I prevented their searching this dressing room.

"I have planned an escape for you, but it will involve a complete change in your appearance."

Going to a dressing table nearby, she selected two small flasks which she handed to Jerry. "This," she said, indicating the first, "will dye your hair jet black. And this," pointing to the second, "will make your skin the same shade of brown as my guards'. I will go outside while they help you."

As soon as she departed, the two men assisted Jerry to strip from head to foot. Then one set about applying the black dye to his sandy hair, while the other painted his skin with the brown liquid. Gazing into the burnished gold mirror, Jerry was astounded at the transformation; he was, to all appearances, a racial brother of the two brown men.

One of them brought him a coarse gray breech clout and headcloak and a pair of gray boots-the clothing of a slave. Quickly donning these, he again surveyed himself in the mirror. He looked exactly like one of the thousands of browned-skinned slaves he had seen employed in the palace. A small blue and orange emblem, stitched to all of his garments, announced that they, and their wearer, were the property of Nisha Novil. After be had transferred the contents of the pouch attached to his former belt to the plain gray pouch he now wore, he was ready.

One of the guards went out and a moment later Nisha entered the room. She dismissed the other guard, and glanced at Jerry.

"Your disguise seems perfect," she said after a careful inspection. "Your name is now Gudo. As Gudo, the slave, you'll shortly be conducted hence in a band of fifty of my slaves, who go to work on the new canal that Numin Vil is building. Every slaveholder in Kalsivar is required to send one-tenth of his male slaves to work for one senil, or tenth of a Martian year, on the project. It fortunately happened that they were to leave tonight, to relieve the fifty who have been working there for the last senil, and who will return to my service."

"Your highness is most kind," said Jerry.

"At the end of the senil," she went on, "you will be returned to my country estate on the Corvid Canal. I will be waiting there for you, and together we will make plans for the future. Please understand that I am not pretending altruism or a disinterested friendship. I would rather see you dead than in the arms of another. You will have one senil in which to think it over."

She spoke so calmly that Jerry could scarcely believe this was the girl who had alternately caressed and clawed him a short time before. She handed him a full flask of the black dye, one of the brown stain, and a third which contained a clear liquid.

"You may find it necessary to change your disguise," she said. "A few drops of this liquid added to a basin of water will make a solution that will instantly restore your hair and skin to their natural color.

"In a moment more you must leave. You will be going into danger, perhaps to your death, though Deza knows I have done everything possible for your safety." She moved closer. "Can you-will you take me in your arms-hold me for just a moment? Let me feel your lips on mine just once-willingly? A senil is so long-and if fate should take you from me, there will be, at least, this memory."

"I can and will, Nisha," he replied, suiting his actions to his words. "I like your candor. You're a girl in a million. It is a pity that love is not a thing we can command like a slave, or call to heel like a dalf."

"I know," she replied. Then she turned and called the guards. When they entered she said: "You have your instructions, and will carry them out at once."

"Come, Gudo," said one, taking Jerry's arm.

"Goodby, highness," said Jerry.

"Farewell. I will always love you," she replied, with a look of longing in her eyes.

Then he passed out the door between the two warriors.

Jerry's conductors led him through a series of rooms and corridors into a large chamber, where an aggregation of gray-clad, brown-skinned slaves waited, guarded by a company of white warriors. A scribe took down his assumed name and the name of his owner, and he was herded in with the others.

They were kept standing there for some time, their ranks constantly swelled by newly arrived slaves. But presently Jerry noticed some sign of activity at the other end of the hall. Then he saw that a group of soldiers was painting a number on the foreheads of the slaves, with red pigment, and thrusting them, feet first, into a hole in the wall.

He was greatly puzzled by this at first, but presently his own turn came, and the riddle was solved. With the painted number still wet on his forehead, he was thrust into the dark hole. Instantly he shot downward at a steep angle, with a rapidly increasing acceleration, in an incredibly slippery tube about four feet in diameter.

At first he descended in a series of spirals, but presently this changed to a steep, straight incline. Then, gradually, this leveled out, slowly checking his momentum, until he presently shot out under the roof of a low shed, to land on a padded platform. Here two guards, waiting to receive him, glanced at the painted number on his forehead and turned him over to another guard, who conducted him to a place where a group of his fellows waited.

By the dim light of the farther moon-for the nearer, brighter luminary bad now set-he saw that they were on a dock which fronted a canal. Moored to the dock, directly in front of him, was a strange craft. It was long and low, arid roofed over in the manner of a whaleback steamer, but with blocks of translucent material through which the rays from its baridium globes shone forth. But the strangest thing about it was its propulsive mechanism, the visible part of which consisted of eight pairs of huge-jointed metal legs, each tipped with a webbed foot like that of a duck. Obviously the craft actually swam on the surface of the canal like a waterfowl.

He saw a demonstration of this a moment later when a similar boat passed, and was astounded at the smoothness and speed with which these mechanical legs could propel the craft over the water.

For some time he and his fellow slaves stood shivering on the dock. But presently they were herded aboard the vessel and into several large compartments, each of which was heated by a globular contrivance which stood in the middle of the floor.

As soon as they entered there was a rush to get near the heating globe, and those who succeeded lay down to sleep in its genial warmth. Jerry, wearied by his adventures and exertions and weakened by his wound, was glad to curl up against the outside wall and close his eyes.

CHAPTER XI

JERRY was awakened by a sharp kick in the ribs. A guard was standing over him. "It is time to eat, slave," he said gruffily.

Following the guard came a line of slaves bearing large trays of food and drink. The food consisted of a stew in which were combined fish, flesh and vegetables cut into small pieces and seasoned with a peppery condiment. The beverage was the omnipresent pulcho. Jerry ate his stew in the manner of his companions, by drinking the thin gravy and scooping up the rest with his fingers. Then he slowly sipped his cup of pulcho, and was ready with the others to hand cup and bowl back to the slaves who came to collect the dishes.

The heating globe had been turned off, but its place was more than taken by the sun, which was already halfway to the zenith.

Jerry arose and looked curiously out at the passing scenery. On one side of the canal he saw a wall, topped by small buildings at regular intervals, and patrolled by sentries. On the other side a series of broad terraces led downward to another canal, and another series progressed upward to a third. The terraces were covered with cultivated gardens and orchards, and dotted here and there with cylindrical buildings, evidently the dwellings of the Martian agriculturalists.

The purpose of these three canals in a single excavation was plain enough. The two upper and outer canals each watered the system of terraces below it. The total excavation was about fifteen miles in width. Each canal was approximately a mile in width, and each system of terraces six miles.

The canals were dotted with craft of various sizes and kinds. All of the larger boats were propelled, like the one on which he rode, by mechanical webbed feet, but some of the smaller ones had sails, and others were paddled like canoes.

The smaller craft seemed mostly to be engaged in the occupation of fishing, in which nets, lines and spears were all employed. And Jerry was startled to see some of the fishermen leave their boats, carrying their spears or nets with them, and walk on the surface of the water.

Presently, when he came near enough to one to observe how it was done, he saw that the fellow wore inflated, boat-shaped water shoes, on which he glided about with the ease of a skilled terrestrial ice skater.

The sun had reached the zenith when the canal on which they were traveling suddenly came to a junction with another. Jerry judged that they must be quite near the equator, and verified this by looking at his shadow, which had shortened to almost nothing. The junction of the triple canals was effected by connecting the two upper channels of each by means of four viaducts in the form of a square. These viaducts, each fifteen miles in length and a mile in width, were supported on tremendous arches high above the terraces and the two intersecting drainage canals.

The boat on which they rode turned to the left in the farthest transverse channel, and after skirting the wall for several miles drew up at a dock. The doors were flung open and the guards herded the slaves out onto the wharf, where they were turned over to a new group of guards who had evidently been waiting to receive them. Here an officer took the records and called the roll.

This done, they were marched through a tunnel in the thick wall. They came out on a rather fragile wooden platform, fully two miles above the ground. Directly below them was the waterless central channel of a great triple canal, still under construction.

As far as Jerry could see, this tremendous excavation stretched northward. He saw men at work on the terraces, evidently leveling them off and getting them into shape. But the excavating, at this point, had all been completed.

Supported and reinforced by thick steel cables, a causeway of the resilient red-brown material used in paving, slanted down from the platform to the bottom of the depression; on this some two-score multiped vehicles waited. Under the direction of the guards, the slaves mounted the saddles; when all were aboard, the vehicles scampered down the swaying, trembling causeway.

Despite the skill of its driver, the one in which Jerry rode would have been jounced off into the yawning abyss beneath had it not been for the cables which formed a protecting railing on either side. He heaved a sigh of relief when they were once more on solid footing. They were now in the dry bed of the central drainage canal, which was composed of solid rock, so smooth that it looked almost as if it had been planed. And here, the multiped vehicles gave an example of the speed of which they were capable. The banks of the canal, and the terraces with their busy workmen, literally hurtled past them.

Mile after mile of dry channel and barren terraces reeled past them with a monotonous sameness, until mid-afternoon. Then the vehicles suddenly slowed down and Jerry caught his first glimpse of the digging of a Martian canal.

At first he thought; he saw two lines of huge beasts converging from the center of the excavation in a huge, extended V, snapping and tearing at the wall of earth, rock and sand before them. But in a moment he saw that they were not beasts, but machines, with jointed metal legs and mighty steel jaws. These huge machines, each operated by a single slave mounted in a saddle on its back, bit and swallowed until they had filled their capacious interiors, then turned and climbed the banks to disappear over the tops, while others returned empty and voracious once more.

Interspersed among the machines at regular intervals were armed overseers, directing the work, each driving a small six-legged vehicle.

Behind the line of devouring metal beasts was another Tow with the same type of body and legs, but with shovel-shaped, under-slung lower jaws. These jaws created a terrific din as with sharp, rapid blows like those of trip hammers they planed off the jagged fragments. When filled, they, like the others, backed away from the line and climbed the slope to get rid of their loads, while other, empty machines scuttled in to take their places.

Some distance behind the scene of operations and pitched upon the newly planed terraces at either side of the central channel the work camp was situated. It consisted of about a thousand large, round portable dwellings with dome-shaped tops, made from furry pelts which would turn back the heat at night.

The vehicle in which Jerry rode turned and scrambled up the bank to the tent city at the right. It was followed by nine others. The remaining machines climbed the left bank.

They came to a halt in front of a tent, before which a man wearing the orange and black of nobility sat on a swinging divan. An officer handed him a sheaf of papers, which he conned for a few moments. Then he returned them and waved his hand.

Instantly, the guards ordered all the slaves out of the saddles. Then they were drawn up in squads and marched through the camp, up the side of the terrace to the very top. Here they crossed a temporary bridge, stretched on steel cables across the empty upper channel. There were four more similar bridges for the use of the digging machines, which swarmed across them in endless chains. They emptied their loads of rubble on the outer bank by the simple expedient of opening their metal mouths, lowering them, and tilting their bodies up at the rear. This done, they turned about and scampered back for more provender.

The Earthman and his companions were issued implements and put to work at once, reducing and leveling the piles of rubble regurgitated by the machines. The implement given Jerry was a heavy pole about eight feet in length with a thick iron disk on one end. This was used like a rake or hoe, to spread the material about. Then, with the shaft held perpendicularly, it was employed to tamp and pack the surface.

It was hard work, even for Jerry with his Earth-trained muscles. And he could realize how much more difficult it must be for the slaves around him. The sun's rays beat down relentlessly upon them, and the guards urged them on with spear points whenever they lagged.

Men who dropped from exhaustion and were unable to rise were kicked down the embankment, to be buried beneath the constantly growing deposit of rubble.

Jerry worked at the end of his squad, every member of which was a brown man. Next to him was a squad of white men, and one of them, a tremendous fellow over seven feet tall and muscled in proportion, was his nearest neighbor. This powerful giant made play of his work, laughing and chatting with guards and workmen alike. Presently he called out to Jerry:

"Ho, slave of Nisha Novil. At last you palace dalfs will have to do a man's work."

Jerry grinned back at him. "It must be that you like it, since you call it man's work."

"Not I," said the giant, "but because necessity compels..."

He paused in the midst of his speech and looked upward, a startled expression on his face. At the same instant a shadow darkened the sun above them. Then something struck Jerry behind the knees and he fell backward into a large net with metal meshes. The giant turned to flee, but the net caught him also, and he was swept back on top of the Earthman.

As the two men sought to disentangle themselves, the ground receded rapidly beneath them.

Looking up, Jerry saw that the net which held them hung from two chains which depended from both sides of a grotesque flying monster with membranous wings, a fur-covered body, long legs covered with yellow scales, and a flat, duck-like bill armed with sharp triangular teeth. The chains were fastened to the sides of a saddle of gray metal, on which sat a brown warrior who was hurling javelins at the guards below.

A glance around showed that at least five hundred of these flying monsters had attacked the camp, and all were now rising with slaves and guards struggling in their nets.

"What is this? Where are they taking us?" Jerry asked his companion.

"A slave raid," the latter replied. "Deza help us, for we are in the clutches of Sarkis the Torturer!"

CHAPTER XII

THE raiding party flew rapidly away, its victims dangling helplessly in the nets. "I have heard of this Sarkis the Torturer," Jerry said. "An outlaw, I believe. But what can he want with us?"

"He wants fighting men, and victims for sacrifice. This raid will provide both."

"How both?"

"The captives will be put to the test. Those who can use a sword and are willing to join the outlaws and worship the Sun God will be spared. The others will be reserved for sacrifice. But why do you ask all these questions?" He glanced sharply at Jerry for a moment, then exclaimed: "Ah, I see the reason now! You are a white man in disguise. Who are you?"

Jerry looked down at his chest, and saw what had betrayed him. Two of the strips of jembal applied by Nisha to the scratches she had made on his body had been rubbed off in the scuffle. And along the edges of the scratches his unstained white skin showed. "Since you know this much, I may as well tell you all," he said. "I am Jerry Morgan of the planet Earth, which you call Dhu Gong. I got into trouble in the palace, and had to leave hurriedly in this disguise."

"I have heard of you," said the big man, a look of admiration in his eyes, "and of your duel with Arsad, Rad of Dhoor. Since you slew the best swordsman in all Kalsivar, I do not think you will have difficulty qualifying for the service of Sarkis-that is, if you care to join the outlaws."

"I hadn't thought of it," Jerry told him, "but it might not be a bad idea. I'm an outlaw, myself, sentenced to be flayed alive and sprinkled with fire powder, whatever that is."

"Fire powder is a material we use to light fires with," said the giant. "It is made from baridium, the same substance used in manufacturing our lights, and ignites when wet."

"Odd stuff," replied Jerry, "and scarcely a comfortable thing to have sprinkled on one. But tell me, who are you, and how did you happen to be doing a slave's work?"

"I am Yewd, the fisherman," said the giant, "and was accused of stealing a boat. I was innocent, but an enemy brought false witness, and the seven judges sentenced me to work a year on the excavations with the band of felons you saw me with."

"Then I presume that you have no cause to love the government."

"You are a man of sound judgment and rare discrimination," laughed Yewd. "In a nation where justice is a mockery, on what side should any real man fight? But unfortunately, I have not the skill with the sword which is likely to save me from becoming a sacrifice to the Sun God."

"Perhaps I can find a way to save you from that fate," said Jerry. "And I hope you will be willing to forget that I am Jerry Morgan, and remember that I am Cudo, the slave."

"That I will," said Yewd, heartily. "But what are you going to do about those white streaks?"

"I'll fix them easily enough," Jerry told him. He took the bottle of brown liquid from his pouch and stained all the white lines. "How does it look?"

"A perfect match, Gudo," said Yewd. "That is great stuff if you want to change your complexion. At present I am satisfied with mine."

His disguise completed once more, Jerry looked down at the landscape beneath them. It was a vast rolling desert of ochre-yellow sand, sparsely dotted by patches of thorny creepers with large red flowers. "Wherever they are taking us," he told his companion, "it must be a long way into the desert."

"The Torturer and his outlaws have many secret lairs," said Yewd, "and some of them must be in the desert. But gawrs require much water, and I'll wager that this time we are being taken to one of the wild marshes of the district."

"Gawrs?"

"Yes. The creatures that are carrying us. Have you noticed their webbed feet? They swim as well as fly."

It soon became evident that Yewd's prediction was correct, for the flock sailed over a sheer precipice which edged what had evidently once been the shore of an ancient ocean. Now it was a sloping sandy beach which led down to a marsh, in which a number of small lakes reflected the slanting rays of the afternoon sun. Around the shores of several of these lakes were the portable fur huts of a large armed encampment, dimly seen through a haze of smoke from the thousands of cooking fires.

The lakes were dotted with swimming gawrs with their wings chained down to prevent their flying away. Armed sentinels were posted on the bluffs and in a wide circle all about the camp. And a score of them constantly soared high overhead, keeping watch.

At sight of the returning raiding party, a great shout went up from the camp. Then a number of warriors caught up their spears and hurried to an open space among the huts, where they formed a large ring. One of the raiders dropped to the center of this ring until the net rested on the ground, while the gawr hovered overhead.

Two soldiers, who had detached themselves from the ring, came forward and ordered the three captives out of the net. One by one the gawrs descended, hovered and flew away, until all the nets had been emptied.

The captured men were a motley group, consisting of white, brown and black men. But the spearmen who surrounded them were equally diversified as to color, and more so as to their clothing and ornaments. Jerry noticed, however, that they had one thing in common. Hanging suspended on the chest of each was a clear crystal disk about six inches in diameter.

The Earthman nudged his giant companion. "What are those disks for?"

"Symbols of their religion," Yewd replied, "and magic instruments with which they light their fires in the daytime. They are worshipers of Sarkis, the Sun God. At night they must use fire powder like the rest of us."

Magic instruments-and for lighting fires. Jerry instantly recognized them for large magnifying glasses, but he said nothing to his companion. He noticed a stir in the crowd behind the spearman, and heard cries of:

"Way for His Holy Majesty! Shield your eyes from the blinding glory of Sarkis, Lord of the Day and Vil of the Worlds."

A path opened up in the crowd of warriors, all of whom instantly raised their hands before their eyes to salute a most repulsive-looking thing. It was on a divan that topped a gilded platform, borne on the backs of a score of slaves. The thing was obviously a man, large and muscular. But his face was concealed by a most hideous mask of burnished gold, fastened to a headpiece on which a thick mat of golden threads formed a bristling, leonine mane.

The sharp hooked nose of the mask was covered with red lacquer, and the lips were blue against a background of yellow fangs. From behind the oval slits in the black-ringed eye-sockets a pair of glittering eyes looked forth. The garments were of royal peacock blue, and those parts of the body which would normally have been exposed-torso, legs, arms and hands-were covered with a finely woven golden mesh. He wore a richly jeweled, gold hilted sword and dagger. And on his chest there hung a large crystal disk, fully twelve inches in diameter.

At a sign from the masked figure on the divan, the slaves lowered the platform to the ground and stood with folded arms on either side of it.

The Torturer rose, and standing in front of his divan, spoke in weird, sepulchral tones that echoed hollowly in the golden confines of his mask.

"The sacrifice comes first," he said. "Then we will make trial of the prisoners."

At this, a number of the spearmen herded the prisoners back to a spot at the left of the divan. Then a lane opened in the lines opposite it, and through this came a hundred slaves, staggering under the weight of a large metal platform on which five broad steps had been built. On each step reclined a man, bound in place by chains tightly drawn around neck, waist and ankles. Suspended above them on two poles by means of short shafts which allowed it to be turned in any direction, was a tremendous crystal disk.

This disk, as the slaves lowered their burden to the ground, had its edge turned toward the sun. But as soon as the platform had been placed in position, the

Torturer raised his hand, and at this signal two men in yellow robes sprang up beside the poles and swung the disk around, manipulating it until they had focused the sun's rays in a brilliant spot of blue-white light, on the floor of the platform just in front of the lowest step.

This done, the masked figure raised both hands. Instantly the surrounding multitude began a slow, eerie chant which reminded Jerry of a dirge. The metal floor of the platform had already become red hot at the point where the light focused.

With an expression of horror on his features the man on the lowest step watched the oncoming spot. As it drew close to him, his skin was seen to redden from the heat it radiated. Suddenly he shrieked, as the white-hot light touched his side. The chanting grew louder, and in a moment more the agonized shrieking ceased, as the concentrated sun rays burned through a vital spot.

The brilliant, blinding spot traveled onward. One after another the remaining men shrieked and were silent. The chanting ceased. The smoking platform with its grisly burdens was carried away.

The two yellow robed men advanced so they faced both the masked figure on the platform and the sun.

"Thus, O Sarkis, Lord of the Day and Vil of the Worlds, do thy humble servants greet thee at thy rising, bail thee at thy meridian, and speed thee at thy setting, in accordance with the ancient custom," they said, raising their hands before their eyes.

The Torturer dismissed them with a gesture. "Now we will examine the prisoners," he announced, seating himself once more upon the divan.

Four men, bareheaded and naked to the waist, emerged from behind the platform. They stepped in front of the divan and saluted. Two were white, one wearing an orange cincture trimmed with black, and the other a plain black cincture. The third and fourth men were brown-skinned and wore the gray of slaves. A short, squat black man, also wearing the gray of a slave, now approached the man in orange and black, and held out to him a sheaf containing a dozen swords. The fellow selected one, and Jerry saw that its sides, instead of being saw-edged, were smooth and dull, while its point was tipped by a small oval bulb. The black passed similar swords to the other three men.

In the meantime, one of the captives, a brown slave, was marched up in front of the Torturer. He saluted, and took a sword from the black.

The Torturer leaned forward and looked at him appraisingly.

"We have here swordsmen of the first, second, third and fourth grades," he said. "If you would avoid the sacrificial altar you must defeat at least a fourth grade swordsman. This will make you a common warrior, and you need go no farther. But if you are ambitious and would be an officer, a barb, then you must defeat our swordsman of the third grade. Defeat the swordsman of the second grade, and you will be made a jen. And if you can best our swordsman of the first grade, you will be made a jendus. Defeat at any stage will render you a victim for the sacrifice. Which swordsman do you choose to fight first?"

"I choose the swordsman of the fourth grade, may it please your holy majesty."

And as soon as the two contestants had crossed their weapons Jerry saw that there was good reason for the slave's diffidence. His antagonist had him at the second thrust, marking him over the heart with a spot of red pigment which squeezed out of the bulb on the end of the sword.

"To the sacrifice pens," ordered Sarkis, in his hollow, sepulchral tones, "and bring the next prisoner."

Man after man was brought forward. Some were unable to defeat the swordsman of the lowest grade, and so went to the sacrifice pens. Most of those who won the first duel were satisfied to stop there and enlist in the army of Sarkis as common soldiers. But there were a few who aspired to higher honors. One of these became a barb, and stopped there. Another aspired to be a jen, but was defeated by the swordsman of the second grade.

When the fourth grade swordsman had fought ten duels, he was replaced by another. The swordsmen of the upper grades had so little fencing to do that it was unnecessary to relieve them. Some fifty-odd men had fought, and a sixth swordsman of the fourth grade was testing, when Yewd, who stood just in front of Jerry, was called.

"Farewell, Gudo, my friend," he whispered. "If it were to be a spear or javelin, I would have a chance. But with a sword I am all but helpless."

A shout went up from the crowd at sight of Yewd's giant thews, but as soon as he had a sword in his hand, his unfamiliarity with that weapon was instantly apparent. His brown-skinned opponent grinned, played with him for a moment, and then marked him twice on the chest.

Jerry's turn was next. The surrounding warriors hooted him as derisively as they had Yewd. But when he selected a weapon, tested its balance, and whipped it about with the ease and grace of a practiced swordsman, they grew silent.

The swordsman of the fourth rank advanced with weapon in readiness, but Jerry held up his hand. "Wait. I would not waste the time of his holy majesty."

"What is this, slave?" asked the masked figure on the throne.

"With your majesty's permission, I will engage only the swordsman of the first grade. I have seen the fencing of these others, and they would furnish but poor sport for me. But none has yet tried the mettle of this jendus."

"Why, this is bold talk," said Sarkis. "But braggarts who cannot make good their boasting do not long survive among us. Have at him, then."

CHAPTER XIII

JERRY found his antagonist a swordsman of unusual talent. And as he fought, there were many times when he was only able to save himself from the touch that would have sent him to the sacrifice pen by the agility which his Earth-trained muscles afforded him on Mars.

And it was this same factor which, in the end, gave him the advantage. For his opponent, evidently fearful of the derision of the horde, pressed so fiercely that he tired himself. Soon Jerry was only playing with the man who had been the idol of the Torturer's warriors. But he quickly put an end to it by marking the chest of the jendus just above the heart.

The face of the latter was a study in mixed emotions-surprise, chagrin, and hurt vanity. But Jerry's attention was distracted from him by the voice of the masked man on the divan.

"You have made good your boast, slave," he said, "and we are ready to appoint you a jendus in our army if you will prove your devotion to our cause by truthfully answering any questions I may put to you. Fail to do so, and there is still the sacrifice pens. What is your name?"

"Men call me Gudo, the slave."

"Slave of whom?"

"Of Her Highness Nisha Novil."

"Ah! And you mean to tell me that her highness would send a swordsman of your ability to work on the canal?"

"That was where she sent me, your majesty."

"Are you of the brown race of Kalsivar?"

"If I am not," said Jerry with a smile, "what am I?"

"That is what I mean to find out-in a moment," said Sarkis. He turned to a slave and issued a curt order. The latter dashed away, returning a moment later with a large basin of water. The Torturer took a small flask from his pouch, and uncorking it, poured several drops of a clear liquid into the water. After stirring it with his dagger he beckoned to Jerry. "Come and stand before me," he commanded.

The Earthman did as directed.

Taking the basin from the slave's hands, Sarkis commanded: "Remove our headcloak."

As soon as he had complied, Jerry was drenched from head to foot by the contents of that basin. To his surprise and horror, he saw that wherever the water had touched, his skin had resumed its normal color.

"And now," said the Torturer, a note of exultation in his hollow tones, "who are you?"

"I am Jerry Morgan of Earth."

"And not the slave of Nisha Novil?" No."

"Nor yet a member of the brown race of Kalsivar. Nor do men call you Gudo. You have lied to me, and you know the penalty. To the sacrifice pens with him. And see that he is the first victim to greet the great Lord Sun at his rising tomorrow."

Jerry was hustled away through the jeering crowd to the gate of a large inclosure, surrounded by a stone wall thirty feet in height. A guard opened the gate, and he was hurled through by his burly conductors.

A big hand reached out to help him. It was the hand of Yewd, the fisherman.

"I did not think to see you here," said the giant, "and with your rightful color restored. This Sarkis must be a wizard, in very truth."

"At least he is a good guesser," replied Jerry, "or what is more probable, is someone who saw me at the court of Numin Vil.."

"There may be some truth in that. I have heard that the Torturer spends much time away from his army, and that he comes and goes alone in his great metal flying machine. Each time he leaves, he flies straight toward the sun until his craft is lost to view, and gives out that he is returning to his home in the sun."

"I'm afraid he would need a better insulated suit and mask than the ones he is wearing for a visit to the sun," said Jerry. "Can his people actually believe he goes there?"

"Many of them do," replied Yewd. "Others, I am convinced, only pretend. They have joined forces with him because he has always been victorious, and because his raids afford much loot."

While they were talking the last of the victims from the raid was thrust into the pen. And shortly thereafter, night fell with the suddenness common to Mars, where there is little light refraction in the thin dry atmosphere, and no perceptible twilight. The pen was plunged into instant darkness.

In the deeper shadow of the wall, Jerry was carrying on a whispered conversation with Yewd.

"You say the pen is on the edge of the lake, and that the gawrs swim riderless only a short distance from the shore?" he asked.

"If they remain as they were before I was brought hither. But I don't see how it will be possible for you to leap to the top of the wall."

"That is a detail you must take on faith. In any event, we are all doomed men, and an attempt to escape cannot put us in worse case."

"You are right," agreed Yewd. "Let us then pass the word among the others, and see who is willing to make the attempt with us."

"Tell them to take off their belts and give them to you," Jerry said, "and I will do likewise. Twenty belts will easily reach over the top of the wall and to the ground on the other side. I'll meet you here when we have made the rounds."

A few moments later Yewd and Jerry collided in the darkness. "Have you some belts?" asked the Earthman.

"More than we need," the giant replied. "I have twenty-seven."

"And I have thirty-two," Jerry told him. "We will construct two lines. Every man is coming with us, and thus we will be able to get them over the wall with more speed."

As soon as the two long chains of belts had been fastened together, Yewd cleared a path for Jerry. Absolute silence had been enjoined upon all, but there was a subdued murmur of wonder as they heard the Earthman run and spring, and a moment later saw him outlined against the stars as he drew himself up onto the wall.

The end of each chain of belts had been hooked to the back of his own belt. But he left them there for a moment, as he paused to cast a swift, cautious look around him. There were no guards between him and the water's edge. Most of the campfires had burned down to beds of glowing coals, but the sounds of revelry were loud and there was the mixed medley of songs, and drunken quarrels.

Assured that the way was clear, Jerry swiftly unhooked the two chains of belts, and lowered one on each side of him until ten belts had passed each hand and he knew that the ground had been reached. Then he gave one line a gentle shake, after which he gripped it with both hands and braced himself on the opposite side of the wall. A heavy weight was thrown on that chain of belts, but Jerry's powerful Earthly muscles were more than capable of supporting it. And in a few moments Yewd was on the wall beside him.

Yewd jerked a signal to the men beneath him, and as soon as the line grew taut, descended on the other side, where he grasped the ends of both lines.

Retaining his seat on the top of the wall, Jerry directed operations by signaling to those below each time a man had reached the top of the wall on either line, until he had counted sixty, and the pit was emptied. Then, drawing up the ends of the lines, he dropped them on the outside, and letting himself down as low as possible by hanging onto the outer rim of the wall, dropped after them.

Silently the men resumed their belts, and then, forming a great human chain by clasping hands in the dark, they silently advanced to the water's edge. Here they paused for a moment, while Yewd whispered the final instructions.

"Remember, not a sound or a splash," he cautioned. "It may be that we will become separated from one cause or another. If so, our place of rendezvous will be the southern end of the Tarvaho Marsh. Pass the word along, then swim out, seize the gawr nearest you, and fly straight north."

The human chain broke into its units, with the exception of Yewd and Jerry. Because the latter knew nothing whatever about managing a gawr, the two had decided to attempt to make their escape on the same bird-beast.

A short swim brought them to the side of a great bird-beast which snorted and shook its head as the two men climbed to its back. Yewd, seated in front, unsnapped the ends of the two chains which trammeled the creature's wings by being hooked through perforations in the membrane around one of the wing-bones. The double purpose of these chains became evident to Jerry when, a moment later, the giant fisherman snapped one to his own belt and the other to that of the Earthman.

"It is customary for a rider to attach both chains to his belt each time he mounts a gawr," explained Yewd, "to prevent his falling to the ground in case he slips from his saddle. But since there are two of us, we must be content with one chain each."

There was a light rod, fastened at one end to a short rope which was hooked around the gawr's neck, and at the other, to the pommel of the saddle. The giant now raised the rod, whereupon the great bird-beast swam swiftly forward, then took to the air with a mighty flapping of wings. This was the signal which had been agreed upon for the others to take off. And their advent into the air was followed by a mighty splashing and flapping all about them.

It was followed, too, by shouts from several of the sentinels who had heard the noise and thought the bird-beasts had been attacked by some of the monster saurians which were known to inhabit the marsh.

But before the mounted guards had reached the remainder of the herd, the sixty stolen gawrs were silently winging their way northward in the darkness, high above the marsh. Pursuit parties were instantly organized, to fly in all directions, as it was impossible to tell which way the fugitives had gone.

In the meantime Jerry and his party flew steadily toward the north, unable to see each other in the darkness and guided solely by the blazing stellar constellations overhead, with which every Martian is familiar.

Presently, however, the nearer moon popped above the western horizon, and by its light Jerry saw that the gawr which he and Yewd bestrode had fallen quite a distance behind the other bird-beasts.

"Looks as if we are going to be late for the rendezvous."

"The creature has a double, nay a treble burden," replied Yewd. "I weigh as much as two average men, and you are not small, by any means."

They lagged farther and farther behind until their fellow fugitives were out of sight. Shortly thereafter the beast fluttered groundward despite Yewd's frantic tugs at the guiding rod. Although they were now flying over the desert, far to the north of the marsh where Sarkis was encamped, the bird-beast had selected a small, tree-covered oasis at which to land.

As soon as it alighted it folded its wings, ran in under the trees and splashed into a shallow pool, where it knelt, taking sips of water and refusing to rise or move.

Yewd unsnapped the ends of the chains from his and Jerry's belts-then fastened them to the gawr's wings.

"We may as well dismount and get some rest, ourselves. It will not stir from this place until it has fully recovered from its fatigue."

They accordingly got down from the saddle and stretched themselves out on the sand beneath the thick canopy of trees. Scarcely had they done so when Jerry saw baridium torches flashing overhead, and looking up, saw a large party of flying warriors.

"Deza be praised!" exclaimed Yewd. "We have been preserved from capture by the sudden weariness of our bird-beast, and the thick foliage above this oasis. Had it continued to fly with us at the rate we were traveling sae should soon have been overhauled."

When the last of their pursuers had passed, Jerry settled down once more in his bed of sand.

He was awakened by a slanting shaft of bright sunlight, which had penetrated the surrounding foliage and shone directly in his face. Sitting up and looking about him, he saw that Yewd had already arisen and was standing beside the pool looking at the gawr, which had slumped over in a most unnatural position.

"What's wrong?" he asked.

"Come and see for yourself," Yewd told him. "We are in sore straits."

Hurrying to the giant's side, Jerry saw that the bird-beast was dead. Blood had drooled down from the corners of its beak to form a congealing, bluish red pool upon the bank.

"What killed it?" Jerry asked.

Yewd pointed to the place where neck and body joined. From this spot several sharp spines projected through the skin.

"It swallowed a dagger fish. Must have been dying when we mounted it back at the marsh. The wonder is that the creature carried us this far."

"Looks as if we'll have to walk the rest of the way," the Earthman observed.

"It looks as if we are doomed. For between us and the Tarvaho Marsh is an immense stretch of trackless desert, inhabited by fierce beasts, hostile tribes and deadly insects."

CHAPTER XIV

JERRY smiled grimly. "Last night we were in the sacrifice pen of the Torturer," he said. "Every man in that pen considered himself doomed. Don't give up hope."

"Although I can see no ray of hope, you somehow give me courage," said Yewd. "At least we have weapons. There is a sheaf of javelins fastened to the saddle. I modestly confess that few men are my equal with spear or javelin. One has to be quick and accurate to spear fish."

He climbed up, removed the sheaf of javelins from the saddle, and after passing one of the multi-barbed weapons to Jerry, slung the rest over his back.

"It is unfortunate that we have no water bottles to take with us," said Jerry. "But we had best drink our fill from the pool before we start, blood or no blood. And now shall we start?"

"I am ready," said the giant.

And so they set off across the rolling dunes of ochre yellow sand.

When noon arrived both men were tired and thirsty, but there was no sight of an oasis and pool.

Presently they came to a gently sloping hillside, strewn with gray boulders, and by mutual consent, decided to pause for a rest.

Jerry sank down on one of the boulders, and to his surprise, found it soft and yielding. With suddenly aroused curiosity he pricked it with the point of his javelin and a clear viscous liquid welled forth.

"Look, Yewd!" he exclaimed. "Here is a stone that bleeds."

The giant looked, then dipped a finger into the sticky liquid and tasted it.

"Deza be thanked!" he exclaimed. "These are not stones, but fungoid plants that we call torfals. Had you not made this discovery we might have died from hunger and thirst in the midst of plenty. But this liquid supplies a balanced ration of food and water."

Jerry tasted the liquid. It was sweet and slightly acid, with a syrupy consistency, and a flavor that reminded him both of bananas and muskmelons. Pressing on the skin around the incision he had made, he drank his fill. Yewd, meanwhile, had tapped another torfal, and was drinking thirstily.

When both had finished they arose, refreshed, and each taking as many medium sized torfals as he could conveniently carry, they plodded on into the afternoon.

The sun was midway toward the horizon when suddenly, upon crossing an unusually high ridge of sand they came to a large oasis where the waters of a small lake gleamed among the tree trunks. With glad cries, they hurried toward it. But they had scarcely entered its grateful shade, when they heard shouts, cries, and the clash of weapons from some distance beyond. They judged from the sounds that a considerable force of men was engaged in some sort of cavalry battle, but because of the intervening trees and shrubbery, were unable to see the contest. Here was a serious situation for Jerry and Yewd. They were hidden for the moment, but they were in grave danger of being discovered.

Cautiously Jerry and Yewd crept forward in the concealment of the shrubbery, until Jerry, parting the branches ahead of them, saw two parties of warriors, each numbering about a thousand men, in deadly combat.

Those nearest the oasis were mounted on the backs of large, two-legged creatures that were neither true birds nor reptiles. They stood about five feet high at the shoulder, but their long necks, covered with bright green scales, held their ugly reptilian heads to a height of ten feet. These heads were much like those of large serpents, except that they were tipped by crests of curling white plumes and there was a sharp, straight horn on the snout of each. Their birdlike bodies were covered with thick yellow down, and the legs, like the necks, were armored with bright green scales. The wings were merely short bunches of white plumes attached to tiny useless stubs.

They were fitted with saddles somewhat similar to those used on the gawrs, and equipped with large quivers that held the javelins of the riders.

The riders were obviously of the white race, though well tanned by the sun. Their clothing consisted of cloaks, evidently made from the downy hides of creatures like those which they bestrode, headdresses of the white plumes, which were attached to the back of the head and spread out, fanwise above the face, and cinctures and boots of leather. Their thighs, arms and torsos were protected by scaly plates, evidently made from the leg coverings of their mounts. And in addition to javelins, sword, dagger and mace, each was armed with a long shaft like that of a lance, but tipped with a pair of sharp tongs.

Their enemies were similarly mounted and armed, with the exception that their mounts had black plumes instead of white, and they used these for their headdresses. All the riders of both warring factions wore the crystal disks which marked them as worshipers of the sun.

The battleground was strewn with dead and dying warriors, whose comrades on both sides fought above them. Although they were using every type of weapon, their favorite seemed to be the strange shaft tipped with tongs. With these, riders on both sides seized their enemies and dragged them from their saddles, the sharp points piercing them deeply.

The chief purpose of the things, as was plainly evident, was not to kill, but to capture enemies. On each side, Jerry noticed a detail of warriors guarding wounded prisoners who had been dragged from their mounts to the back of the lines.

"Who are these people?" Jerry asked his companion.

"Wild desert lorwocks," Yewd replied. "They are ferocious fighters and slave-raiders. Perhaps you have noticed that the tuzars, the long weapons they carry, are admirably adapted for slave taking."

"Rather hard on the slaves, I should say. But when those things once grip them, they have to come."

While they watched, the battle surged nearer and nearer the oasis. Jerry's attention was attracted to one of the white-plumed lorwocks, evidently the chief. And though his force was being driven steadily backward by their black-plumed opponents, he charged again and again into the lines of the enemy, each time dragging back a limp, bleeding prisoner at the end of his tuzar, while he fended off hurled javelins with his sword blade.

But presently, as he returned to the fray, a cloud of javelins descended upon him simultaneously from many directions. Some he parried and some he dodged, but there was one that pierced his neck, whereupon he went limp in the saddle. His mount wandered erratically for a moment, then turned and charged straight into the bushes where Jerry and Yewd were concealed. They leaped aside just in time, but the thing stopped and looked inquiringly at Jerry as if asking him to relieve it of its limp burden.

Yewd sprang in and caught the guiding rod, while Jerry examined the stricken chieftain. He was quite dead.

"Here are weapons, and a mount for one!" exclaimed Yewd. "If we only had another rodal, we would not need to walk or fear to encounter armed enemies."

At this instant, another riderless mount dashed into the bushes. With a swift spring, Yewd seized the guiding rod and leaped into the saddle.

"Come, let us be off before the warriors see us," he said.

"No, wait. I have a more ambitious plan," Jerry told him.

Swiftly he removed his own clothing, and stripping that of the dead chieftain from him, donned it, along with his weapons. The tuzar had been lost, but the other weapons were intact.

"By the power and glory of Deza!" exclaimed Yewd, when he had finished and leaped into the saddle. "You seem a very lorwock chief. But come, let us start before we are detected."

"I have a better plan," Jerry told him. "From what I have seen, I am convinced that we could not travel far without being traced by these tribesmen. But if we join them they may accept us as friends and allies. Will you follow me into that battle?"

"With all my heart."

Jerry handed him all of the javelins but two from his own quiver.

"You prefer javelins-I the sword. Follow closely, keeping off enemies from my sides and back. I will attend to those in front. Let us see if we cannot turn the tide of battle."

By this time the black-plumed lorwocks had driven their closely pressed adversaries into a defensive semicircle by executing an encircling movement at each end of the line. And the horns of the great crescent thus formed were swiftly drawing together.

One horn of the crescent had just reached the oasis when Jerry pushed forward on the guiding rod. His rodal charged.

The Earthman steered his swift mount so that instead of charging with the other white-plumed warriors, he was riding behind the attacking line of black-plumes. As these warriors had their tuzars extended toward the line of white-plumed warriors, they could not use them on him, but could only turn in their saddles, snatching out their swords or javelins for defense.

Some who thus turned their attention away from enemies in front of them were instantly dragged from their saddles by the tuzars of the white-plumes. Some fell beneath Jerry's flashing blade; the others were pierced by the javelins of Yewd.

As a result, the line of black-plumes was thrown into confusion. In less than five minutes the entire right horn of their crescent had been shattered and put to rout. But Jerry continued on through the center and around to the left horn, cutting and thrusting as he rode, while the deadly javelins of Yewd kept off enemies from his sides and back.

The Earthman's unexpected coup completely turned the tide of battle and won the day for the white-plumed lorwocks. With shouts of triumph they pursued the shattered remnant of their fleeing enemies, dragging them from their mounts with their tuzars, while others captured and herded together the riderless rodals. Jerry estimated that at least seventy-five per cent of the black-plumed warriors had been killed or captured. The rest were fleeing for their lives.

When the last enemy and rodal had been rounded up, the white-plumed warriors and their lesser officers crowded around Jerry and his giant companion. Then one of the jens, who had evidently been constituted spokesman by his fellow officers, said:

"Though we know not who you are nor whence you came, riding the rodal of our jendus and wearing his garments, my comrades and I salute you and your slave, and bid you welcome." So saying, he raised both hands before his eyes, and all the others followed his example.

"There has been a prophecy among you that a fighting man would come to lead you to victory," said Jerry. "An impostor, who hides his face behind a mask, and blasphemously calls himself the reincarnation of Sarkis the Sun God, has gathered a considerable following. But I tell you now that I am he who has come in answer to your prophecy. I learned the art of war on another planet; I am that leader for whom you have been waiting."

When he had finished he calmly took out his cigarette case, selected a cigarette, and lighted it. The effect on the lorwocks when they saw smoke ensuing from his mouth and nostrils was instantaneous. To a man, they clapped their hands over their eyes and bowed to their saddle horns.

"As I told you," said Jerry, when the warriors ventured to look up once more, "I do not claim to be the reincarnation of Sarkis. I am Jerry Morgan of Dhu Gong, and will be so called. I have come to gather the desert hordes beneath my banner. And those who ride after me now will have the honor of being the first to do so. For the present, I ride north."

So saying, he wheeled his mount, and with Yewd following close after him, rode away. To a man, the lorwocks fell in behind him with their prisoners and captured rodals.

CHAPTER XV

Two DAYS after he had achieved command of the white-plumed lorwocks, Jerry led them down the side of a steep declivity and across an ancient, boulder-strewn beach, to the shore of a small lake at the southern end of the Tarvaho Marsh.

"This," he told his jens, "will be our chief camp for the present. From here we will send messengers to the desert hordes, announcing that a new leader has come, and that the days of the Torturer are numbered."

At the opposite side of the lake, Jerry saw the gawrs that shad been captured by the escaped prisoners. And on the shore, in their improvised camp, he saw the prisoners themselves. He called Yewd to his side. "Ride around the lake," he commanded, "and tell our comrades to cross the lake and join us."

A half hour later the two forces were joined, and Jerry found himself in command of eight hundred mounted lorwocks, fifty-nine gawr riders, and three hundred prisoners. After a conference with his jens, he called the black-plumed prisoners together and addressed them, telling them he was going to release them and send them as messengers of good will to the black-plumed tribes, inviting them to join him.

After he had made his speech he smoked a cigarette to impress them, and sent them on their way.

In ten days, his forces augmented by thousands of desert tribesmen and escaped slaves, Jerry made his first raid on the central camp of Sarkis. Five thousand of his newly recruited men crossed the marsh with water shoes in the dead of night. Then, while a number of the Earthmen's lorwocks created a disturbance on the bluffs above the Torturer's camp, Jerry's men mounted and escaped with five thousand gawrs. As he had anticipated, Sarkis had placed a guard around the sacrifice pens, but had thought his flying bird-beasts safe.

When the Torturer learned that it was Jerry Morgan's men who had raided his camp, he swore that he would bring the Earthman and all of his followers to the torture platform; and on learning of his camping place, set out with a huge armed force to crush him.

But Jerry's flying scouts quickly reported the movement of Sarkis's immense army, and when the Torturer reached the Tarvaho Marsh he found it deserted.

The Earthman's forces reassembled at a new rendezvous, but not before they had raided two of the Torturer's lesser camps, in one of which they captured, in addition to many slaves and much rich loot of all descriptions, fifty large metal flying machines. Each would accommodate fifty warriors in addition to the pilot. The glazed windows could be opened to admit the air, or covered with metal shutters to keep out enemy projectiles.

When he reached his new rendezvous and distributed the loot, Jerry found, among other things, several thousand suits of clothing. Among these were many outfits of rich black material intended for sale to wealthy commoners. The Earthman selected a number of outfits that suited him as to size and cut, with appropriate silver mounted weapons and silver trappings. And though he might have worn the peacock blue of royalty, he chose rather to be known as the Commoner.

He also caused pennons to be made of black material, each edged with silver fringe and centered with a single silver star.

As the days passed, Jerry's army swelled rapidly. Not only was he joined by the desert hordes, escaped slaves, outlaws, and deserters from the Torturer's army; even the great nobles of Kalsivar, who were dissatisfied with the policies of Numin Vil, began throwing in their lot with him. The fame of his exploits spread rapidly, all over Mars.

But despite his rapid rise to power and unprecedented series of victories he was still an outlaw, with a price upon his head. Numin Vil now believed the Earthman to be the murderer of his son, and even Junia was convinced by the evidence Thoor Movil had brought forth, Jerry heard.

Numin Vil, further angered by the desertions of many of his nobles, gave orders that the army of the Earthman should be crushed, his followers slain without quarter, and himself brought in, dead or alive.

Though he might have brought the expedition sent against him to grief, Jerry rather chose to avoid it. Deep in his heart was the hope that some day he might again be in the good graces of Junia-that he might be able to prove to her that he was innocent of her brother's death.

The Torturer, who had no such scruples as Jerry regarding the imperial forces, met and surrounded the first expedition, then annihilated it, killing or capturing every man and officer present. In this battle the Torturer kept himself well out of sight and ordered the black-and-silver standards of the Commoner to be shown. Then, at the conclusion of the battle he permitted several prisoners to escape to Raliad with the story that the army had been crushed by the forces of the Earthman.

Among those in the imperial palace who listened with bated breath to the recital of each new exploit of the Commoner, was Nisha Novil. The princess had never for a moment given up hope of making him her own.

Accordingly she ordered her luxuriously appointed flying machine one bright morning, giving out that she intended to visit her estate on the Corvid Canal. But before she started she had a brief conference with her brother, Thoor Movil.

"I will make a bargain with you," she said. "Accompanied by your spy, Wurgul, to show me the way as we had planned, I will visit this Commoner in his main camp. If he accedes to my wishes I will spare his life. If not, I will use my dagger. But in case I spare his life, you are to intercede for him with the Torturer and the Vil. And when you have become Vil of Kalsivar, you are to spare him. Do you agree?"

"On the one condition that you persuade him to give up his command and go with you to your country estate. As long as he has an army at his back he remains a menace."

"I will accept that condition. And now, farewell."

"Farewell, and may success reward your undertaking," said Thoor, rising and walking to the door with his sister. But he smiled to himself, for he had already issued special instructions to Wurgul, who was to conduct her to Jerry's camp.

Nisha was amazed at the size and orderliness of the outlaw camp. It was a city of portable huts, laid out around a central plaza from which all streets radiated like the spokes of a wheel. And in the middle of this plaza was a large hut of black fur.

As soon as the flier had passed over the bluff, two others out of a score circling above the camp flew up and challenged them. When the colors of the princess were shown, her pilot was ordered to descend at a cleared place on the edge of the camp.

The machine alighted, then came to a stop. The ladder was dropped, and Nisha Novil stepped out, followed by Wurgul the spy. She was met by an officer and a squad of men, who accorded her the royal salute. In answer to her inquiries, they told her that the Commoner was in camp, conferring with his jens, and summoned a multiped vehicle for her.

Accompanied by the officer and Wurgul, she rode along one of the streets of the camp until they came to the central plaza. Here they were challenged by a guard, who insisted that both the princess and her follower deposit their weapons with him before going farther.

Nisha protested, but when she saw that it would be impossible to proceed without complying with this order, surrendered her jeweled dagger, and ordered Wurgul to give up his sword, dagger and mace.

A soldier raised the silver curtain which draped the central doorway of the black hut. And the officer who had come with the two visitors, announced: "Her Royal Highness, Nisha Novil."

Nisha swept into the room with Wurgul at her heels, and caught sight of Jerry. Seated among his officers, his black clothing and plain silver trappings contrasted oddly with their brightly colored garments and their gold, platinum and flashing jewels. Yet, as he rose to greet her, she saw that he was easily the most striking figure in that assemblage.

"This is an unexpected honor and pleasure, your highness," he said, rendering her the royal salute. "May I present my nobles and officers?"

"Later, Jerry Morgan. At present I am wearied by my journey. And I have a message for your ears alone."

"It shall be as your highness wishes," he told her. Then he addressed his men: "The meeting is adjourned until I send a new summons."

The nobles and officers arose and filed out, each saluting the princess as he passed her. When the last man had gone, there remained only Jerry, Nisha and Wurgul. The Earthman looked significantly at the spy, whereupon the princess ordered him to wait outside the door for her.

"Won't you be seated and have some pulcho?" invited Jerry. He indicated his own swinging divan and a small taboret beside it on which stood a steaming flask of freshly brewed pulcho, surrounded by a dozen jewel-encrusted, platinum cups.

Nisha sat down and Jerry filled a cup for her. After she had accepted and tasted it he filled another for himself, and stood before her.

"You need not be formal, Jerry Morgan. Come and sit here beside me."

"Indeed, I prefer to stand for a while," he replied. "I have been sitting in conference all morning. And now won't you tell me in what way I may be of service to you?"

"You-you make it so difficult for me, with your formal ways."

"I'm sorry," he answered. "My intentions are quite the reverse."

"When last we parted," she told him, "you were to think over a certain matter, for the space of one senil. At the end of that time we had arranged for a rendezvous at my country place on the Corvid Canal. But the rendezvous was not kept, nor have you vouchsafed me an answer. I have been so lonely for you-so hungry for even a small sight of you.

"Once more I offer you all that any man might desire-myself, my love, and the wealth position and power which will fall to the lot of my husband. Think, Jerry Morgan. Before another senil hag passed I will be sister to the Vil of Kalsivar. Give up this futile life of outlawry and come with me to my country estate. There we can be quietly married, and I can promise you that within a senil your power in Kalsivar will be second only to that of the throne, itself, for you will be the brother-in-law of the Vil."

"I hope you will believe me, highness," replied Jerry, "when I say that it grieves me more than I can say to decline your offer. As you say, I am an outlaw, under sentence of death. And furthermore, I am indebted to you for life itself. But somehow, marriage is a thing I have always associated with love. And unfortunately, love is a thing which cannot be coerced or commanded. Where love enters, it commands. We who are its subjects can only obey, no matter where its dictates lead us."

At this Nisha's black eyes flashed and Jerry expected another outbreak. But it did not come. Instead, she arose and said meekly: "Then this is the end. It is farewell forever. Let us not part in anger."

Slowly she walked up to where he stood, arms outstretched.

"One last kiss," she whispered.

Her hand hovered above the silver mounted hilt of his dagger. With a sudden, snake-like movement she seized it, wrenched it from its sheath, and lunged for his breast. But the Earthman was too quick for her. He caught her wrist in a grip of iron, wrenched the weapon from her grasp.

In the meantime Wurgul, who had been standing outside the silver curtain, engaged the guard who stood there in a conversation. While they conversed, he managed to move against the curtain in such a way as to push it back, permitting him a glimpse into the room. He saw that Jerry was standing with his back to the doorway, holding the wrists of the raging princess.

For an instant, he fumbled in the folds of his headcloak. Then, with one hand still concealed, he raised the other and pointed skyward. "What strange craft is that?"

As the guard looked up, Wurgul's other hand came out from beneath the folds of his headpiece, clutching a short, straight dagger. The blade flashed downward-plunged into the guard's back up to the hilt.

Wurgul turned, flipped back the curtain, and ran noiselessly up behind the Earthman. Nisha saw him coming, but save for a widening of her eyes made no sound or sign. He lunged straight for the unprotected back of the Earthman.

CHAPTER XVI

As JERRY held the raging little princess away from him, he suddenly noticed that her eyes had gone wide, as if she had seen something startling behind him. He flung her back across the divan, and whirled around just in time to see Wurgul lunging at him.

There was no time to seize a weapon, but Jerry blocked the stroke with his left hand against the wrist of the assassin. Then he drove a smashing right to the point of Wurgul's jaw. The spy slumped to the floor, unconscious. At the same moment an officer and a half dozen guards rushed into the room.

"This murderer just slew Shuvi, the guard," cried the officer. "Stabbed him in the back."

"Put him in the prison pen. I'll attend to his case later."

As two warriors carried out the still unconscious Wurgul, Nisha came to her feet. "I suppose I, too, must go to the prison pen," she said defiantly. "Or perhaps you will order my execution at once."

Jerry smiled grimly down at her. "Neither," he answered. "You sought only to take that which you once saved for me-my life. I have not forgotten, and I am not ungrateful. You are free to go."

At this Nisha laughed bitterly.

"You are a generous fool, Jerry Morgan," she said. "If you were wise, you would keep me here-make me your slave. I warn you that once I am free, I will leave no stone unturned to compass your ruin."

Jerry turned to the officer, who stood with his four men, awaiting orders. "You will conduct her highness to her flier."

Nisha walked out with head held high, and in her black eyes was the feral gleam which the Earthman knew meant trouble.

Jerry sat among his officers, conferring on future plans of campaign until a late hour. One thing they had all urged upon him was that he should select from among his followers two men who would be his constant companions night and day, in addition to the regular guard.

He chose Yewd, the giant fisherman, and a black dwarf named Koha, a queer, misshapen creature whose brawny arms were longer than his legs, and whose great shoulders were as broad as those of the giant. He could throw daggers with deadly accuracy, and carried a heavy, long-handled mace with which he had bested many a swordsman by the simple expedient of smashing through guard and skull.

The Earthman had dismissed his officers, and was preparing to retire for the night, with Koha stretched across his doorway, and Yewd standing guard behind his divan, when a messenger came running up to the doorway.

"A herald has arrived from Sarkis the Torturer," he announced.

"Admit him," said Jerry.

With Yewd standing on guard at one side of his divan, and Koha at the other, Jerry awaited the herald, who said: "I bear a challenge from His Holy Majesty, Sarkis, Lord of the Day and Vil of the Worlds. Tomorrow afternoon, when the great Lord Sun has spanned three-fourths of the sky, his holy majesty will leave his entire army on the Heights of Zokar, which overlook the Plain of Ling, and will ride along to the center of the plain.

"If Jerry Morgan is the leader that he claims to be, he will leave his own army on the Heights of Lokar, which overlook the plain from the opposite side, and ride down alone to do battle with the Lord of the Day. And there, within sight of the two hosts, let the issue of single combat determine who is the true leader foretold in the prophecy, and who the imposter."

"You will await my answer outside," said Jerry. Then, as the herald passed through the curtained doorway, he turned to the giant fisherman. "What think you of this, Yewd?"

"Though my poor wits fail to read the riddle," replied the giant, "they plainly tell me that there is one. Perhaps this Sarkis honestly believes he can beat you in single combat. But it is not his way to take such a risk."

"And what think you, Koha?" asked Jerry, turning to the dwarf.

"I think the Torturer wishes to bring the two armies together so there may be a great battle, which, by some trick, he is confident of winning, though there be little difference in strength," said the black man.

"And yet," said Jerry, "I cannot do otherwise than accept this challenge. To fail to do so would smack of cowardice."

"That is true," agreed Yewd.

"It would seem that the Torturer has put us in a position where we must walk into his trap. Let the herald remain outside, and call a conference of the officers."

This was done, and for some time Jerry was cloistered with his men. Then he sent for the herald. When the fellow entered, he said: "Tell Sarkis that Jerry Morgan accepts his challenge."

The herald saluted and departed. But as soon as he had gone, the camp began to dissolve away in the moonlight. Piece by piece, the portable fur huts came down, were rolled up and stowed on the backs of the pack-rodals, along with all other camp articles and utensils.

Before the night was an hour older, a vast cavalcade, shadowed by a flapping host of gawr riders, climbed up onto the plain, and started in the direction of the Heights of Lokar.

"Always do what the enemy expects you not to do," Jerry bad told his officers. "Sarkis will expect us to leave tomorrow morning, so we will leave now. Thus, we will be the first on the field, and in a position perhaps to thwart him, or to leave if a trap is revealed."

Jerry's army reached its objective without incident, and pitched camp. Save for the sentinels on duty, all the men were permitted to sleep late the following morning, so they would be fresh for battle. But to Jerry's surprise, morning and noon came and went without a sign of the Torturer.

Presently, however, near midafternoon, his gawr sentinels announced the approach of a vast horde. Shortly thereafter the army of the Torturer took up its position on the Heights of Zokar, facing them across the Plain of Ling, and the black cloud of gawr riders which accompanied it settled to the ground.

After a delay of more than two hours, during which the Earthman watched with bated breath, a lone warrior mounted on a rodal came trotting down the hillside toward the center of the plain. The slanting shafts of the late afternoon sun were reflected by the burnished gold of his mask.

Yewd had his rodal and weapons in readiness, and it was but the work of a moment to mount and ride down the hillside at full charge toward the gold-masked champion.

The latter, on seeing Jerry, halted his beast near the middle of the plain and waited, evidently in no hurry to begin the engagement. He carried a tuzar, but Jerry, who had not mastered this weapon, carried a long, stout-shafted lance, instead.

As soon as the Earthman came within a hundred feet of his enemy the latter lowered his tuzar and charged. Jerry couched his long lance, and with it pointed at the breast of his adversary, urged his beast forward.

The masked rider, however, swerved his mount, and while Jerry's lance encountered only empty air, the sharp points of the tongs clamped into the Earthman's hips. He was jerked from the saddle, and his enemy rode swiftly toward the enemy lines, dragging Jerry over the rugged ground.

A mighty cheer went up from the lines of Sarkis, at sight of this easy victory for their champion.

In the meantime, Jerry seized the tongs and dragged himself to a standing posture. Then, still clinging to a tong with his left hand, and sailing over the ground with tremendous leaps, he unhooked his heavy, saw-toothed mace from his belt and brought it down with all his strength on the shaft of the tuzar.

The tough wood cracked, but the long fibers still held. Again and again Jerry hacked at that stubborn shaft. It seemed ages before the last fiber snapped, and he fell free, his mace flying from his hand, while the tongs released their hold and clattered after him.

Half stunned and covered with blood, bruises, scratches and dust, Jerry lay on his back, breathing heavily. From the corners of his eyes he saw his adversary wheel his mount, and flinging away his useless shaft, draw a sharp, multibarbed javelin from the sheath at his back.

Cautiously, the masked man rode toward his fallen and motionless antagonist, his javelin in readiness. Jerry was breathing more easily, now, and felt his strength returning. Suddenly he saw the javelin arm fly back-the deadly barbed missile hurtling straight toward him.

In a flash he had rolled over, just out of reach of that keen point. And then, before his enemy had divined what he was about, he sprang to his feet and bounded straight for the hideously masked figure. The mounted warrior reached for another javelin but before he could withdraw it from the sheath the Earthman had sprung up behind him and caught him with an elbow crooked about his armored neck.

Now it was the turn of the masked man to be jerked from his saddle. Jerry, while they fell, had released his hold on his enemy and alighted catlike on both feet. He whipped out his sword and turned to face his adversary. The latter got up and drew his own sword.

For some time both contestants fenced cautiously. Then Jerry, after a swift feint, found the opening he sought, and lunged straight for his opponent's breast. His point went true to the mark, but his blade bent double and snapped in two. In an instant he realized that the masked man wore a metal breastplate. With a triumphant laugh his enemy drove a savage blow.

Jerry saved himself from death by a quick leap to one side. Then, before the masked man could draw back from that lunge, he struck again with the broken stump of his sword. But this time, he plunged it with unerring accuracy, through the right eye-slit of the golden mask-through the eye and into the brain of his enemy.

At this, a tremendous shout went up from the army of the Earthman. It was answered by jeers from the army of the Torturer, and Jerry, looking in the direction of this strange demonstration, saw the reason. For the Torturer himself was being borne on his platform of state, straight down toward the front of his own lines.

Jerry wrenched the stub of his sword from where it was wedged in the bony orbit of his fallen foe. Then he tore the mask from the lolling head. The dead face that looked up at him was that of the jendus he had defeated in the Torturer's camp.

Hurling the hideous mask from him, Jerry turned and walked back toward his own lines. Two riders dashed down to meet him, Yewd and Koha. The white giant led a saddled rodal. The black dwarf brought him a new sword and a flask of steaming pulcho.

After a copious draught from the flask, he mounted and rode back to his headquarters. Here his chief surgeon awaited him, and cleansed and dressed his wounds while he held conference with his officers.

Despite the furious anger of his men, however, Jerry ordered his officers to hold the men in check.

"Have I not always counseled you," he said, "to do what the enemy expects you not to do? If we go into battle with the army of Sarkis now, we will be doing precisely what he expects us to do. We will sit quietly for a time-and see what happens. When the time comes, we will make some plans of our own."

Scarcely had he finished this pronouncement when one of his gawr scouts came sailing down out of the sky. Dismounting, he ran up before the Earthman and saluted.

"Numin Vil is coming up behind us with a vast host," he cried excitedly, "which outnumbers our force at least two to one! We are trapped between two mighty armies!"

CHAPTER XVII

THERE was consternation on the face of the officers, but Jerry, standing in their midst, smiled confidently. "Just as I suspected. It is well that we did not attack the army of Sarkis, for then, weakened by our losses, we should have fallen an easy prey to the forces of Numin Vil."

As a matter of fact, this was the last thing Jerry had suspected. But now he must think, and think fast, if his command was to be saved from annihilation. He knew, also, that his men must be given something to do to keep up their morale.

"Pack equipment," he ordered, "but do so in such a way that the enemy will not notice. For the present, leave the huts standing. But have them ready to pack at a moment's notice."

As his officers hurried away to carry out his orders, Jerry sat down and poured himself a cup of pulcho.

"Why not march south or north?" suggested Yewd. "We are only hemmed in from the east and west."

You surprise me, Yewd. What do you think our enemies would be doing, in the meantime?"

"I don't know."

"Nor do I. But I believe they could and would march south or north as fast as we, in the meantime gradually converging upon us from both sides. And they might corner us in a much worse place than this hilltop, where we have some advantage of position."

"But even our lofty position will not avail us against such superior numbers," said Koha.

"If it could, we should have no problem," Jerry said. "But since we have a problem, I am seeking to solve it. Fetch me a gawr, and I'll have a look about."

The dwarf waddled hurriedly away, returning a few moments later with a saddled bird-beast. Jerry mounted, pulled up on the guiding rod, and soared aloft. First he flew out over the Plain of Ling, and had a look at the army of Sarkis. There was considerable activity among the hordes of the Torturer.

190

He turned, and soaring higher, flew back across his own camp toward the forces of Numin Vil. As he urged his great flapping bird-beast onward, the sun dipped suddenly beneath the horizon, and the rolling desert below him was lighted only by the pale rays of the farther moon.

Presently, he described the advancing army of the Vil of Kalsivar. It was a formidable host, and he knew that it would be disastrous to pit his smaller force against it. He calculated that, unless Numin Vil struck with his aerial forces first, he would not be able to attack, for at least a half hour. Accordingly, he turned and flew back to his own camp as fast as his bird-beast would carry him.

Before he reached his headquarters the farther moon had set. But campfires had been lighted both in his own camp and in that of the Torturer, and by these he was able to locate his own hut, and descend.

Here he found his chief officers clustered, more panic-stricken than before. But he had made his plans now.

First, he ordered all fires quenched. Then the huts were dismantled and packed with the other equipment. As soon as this had been done, all in pitch darkness and with a minimum of noise, he formed his little army into a great triangle, with the pack-rodals in the center, the rodal cavalry forming the three sides, and the gawr riders and metal fliers flapping in wedge formation overhead. Though he might have ridden on a gawr, or in one of the metal flying machines, he chose rather to lead the main body of his army, and so rode at the point of the triangle which faced the position of Sarkis, with Yewd riding close at his left, and Koha at his right.

It was difficult for the men to see each other's positions in the gloom, and there were some collisions as they charged straight for the position of the Torturer. Scarcely had they crossed the plain when the vanguard of Numin Vil appeared on the heights they had just deserted, carrying his baridium torches.

Urging his men to greater speed, Jerry led them up the hill. At any moment, he expected a counter-charge from the forces of Sarkis, and was puzzled when it was not forthcoming. The twinkling campfires were burning as brightly as ever, and he could see men moving back and forth before them. But as he drew closer, he saw the reason. Not one of the vast city of huts which had been there that afternoon was standing, nor were there any rodals in sight.

The giant Yewd saw the situation almost as soon as the Earthman, and burst into noisy merriment.

"By the might of Deza! The Torturer played a neat trick on us. And had you not decided to give him battle, we would now be back on the Heights of Lokar, vainly striving against the powerful forces of the Vil."

"We haven't escaped yet," said Jerry. "Numin Vil is close behind us, and the nearer moon is due to rise soon." He called to the officers who rode nearest to him. "Pass the word along to break up into small groups, and scatter. Let all lorwock warriors return to their own tribes, and remain with their families and friends for the space of ten days. At that time, our meeting place will be the Marsh of Atabah. Let those who have no tribes or families to return to, live where they will in small groups until the time for our rendezvous arrives.

"I go, now, to the Atabah Marsh, with my fliers."

He signaled a large airship which had been flying overhead, and it settled swiftly to the earth before him. Then he dismounted and entered, accompanied by Yewd and Koha.

Swiftly and quietly his orders were carried out. So that by the time the forces of the Vil had passed the Heights of Zokar and the nearer moon had risen, the trail they followed had split up into many, which spread out fan-wise, and gradually grew more tenuous as they advanced, until there were a thousand small trails, no single one of which it would be worth the while of an army to follow.

Jerry led his flying contingent straight to the Atabah Marsh. A few portable buts which had been stowed in the airships were set up. But most of the gawr riders bivouacked under the clear sky, wrapped in their furs. Later, their pack-rodals, if uncaptured, would be in with the rest of the huts and supplies.

As the Earthman sat in his but, eating a meal which Koha had hastily prepared, and sipping his pulcho, the more he thought about it the more he was convinced that the Torturer had some purpose beyond that of involving him in a battle with the forces of Numin Vil.

Accordingly, he called in the jen of his scouts, and ordered that a hundred gawr riders take the air at once, flying in all directions, to bring him news as to the locations of both Sarkis and Numin Vil.

As soon as the jen of scouts had gone out, he sent for his jen of spies. After a brief conference it was decided that twelve spies, each starting alone and leaving at irregular intervals, should fly to Raliad and attempt to learn what was taking place there.

Early the following morning Jerry was awakened by the black dwarf, who proffered him a cup of steaming pulcho, and said: "A spy has just returned from Raliad with important tidings. Will you see him now?"

"Admit him," said Jerry.

A small, mild-mannered brown man in the garments of a slave entered on Koha's invitation. "What have you learned, Eni?" asked Jerry.

"Sarkis is in Raliad."

"What! You mean he has been taken prisoner?"

"Far from it. While Numin Vil was pursuing our army, the Torturer led his forces to the west gate of Raliad. His appearance was a signal for those in sympathy with the revolution to fall upon the loyal soldiers and guards who remained. The gates were thrown open to him by traitors, and he marched straight to the palace with almost no opposition.

"All the members of the white nobility who were unable to escape were either slain or made prisoners. The brown nobility have been assigned their ranks, titles and estates and the brown prince, Thoor Movil, has been proclaimed Vil of Kalsivar."

"But Junia! What of her?"

"She is a prisoner in the palace. And the Torturer has offered her the choice of marrying Thoor Movil, or dying under the burning disk."

"And has she made a choice?"

"That I have not heard."

"But what of Numin Vil?"

"He returned to Raliad late last night, but the gates were closed to him, and the warriors of Sarkis manned the walls. He attacked repeatedly, but each time was driven off with heavy losses. Early this morning he withdrew his forces and pitched his camp on the Plains of Lav, within sight of the city."

"You have done well, Eni," said Jerry, "and I will see that you are suitably rewarded. Await my further orders outside."

As the spy saluted and backed out of the doorway, Jerry turned to his two guards and counselors.

"At last we begin to see the depth of the Torturer's cunning," he said.

"This time it seems he has outguessed me, though I was able to defeat part of his plans. It was his intention to dispose of me, to wipe out my army, and to weaken the army of Numin Vil, all this while he was capturing Raliad."

At this instant a guard drew back the curtain and announced: "Algo the spy, from the camp of Numin Vil."

"Let him come in," said Jerry.

A tall, soldierly white man of middle age, dressed in the uniform of the Palace Guard, entered and saluted.

"Eni has told me what befell last night," Jerry told him. "Who set Numin Vil on our trail?"

"It was Nisha Novil," said the spy. "Yesterday afternoon she came hurrying into the audience chamber, and asked for an immediate hearing on a matter of grave importance. It was granted, and she told the Vil a slave of hers, returning from her country estate on the Corvid Canal, had flown near the Heights of Lokar on his gawr, and had seen your army encamped there.

"Numin Vil sprang down from his throne, ordered a force assembled, and set out at the head of it, bent on annihilating us."

"She said nothing about the force of Sarkis being encamped opposite us on the Heights of Zokar?"

"Not a word."

"Ah!"

Jerry sprang up from his divan.

"That will be all, Algo. You may return to the camp of the Vil, and report in two days."

As Algo saluted and withdrew, Jerry turned to Koha.

"Fetch me the clothing of a palace slave, I am going to the Imperial Palace in Raliad."

CHAPTER XVIII

DISGUISED as a brown-skinned palace slave with the crystal disk of a sun-worshiper on his breast, and mounted on a swift, sturdy gawr, Jerry flew toward Raliad, unheeding the picturesque scenery which unrolled swiftly beneath him.

On sighting the imperial palace, Jerry soared high above it in order to select the best place for a landing. He saw that the Torturer had stabled a number of his gawrs in the lagoons of the palace roof garden, something Numin Vil had never permitted. However, this made it easier for Jerry to reach his objective; he decided to land on the roof of the palace itself.

He accordingly selected the lagoon which was nearest that side of the edifice on which he knew Junia's apartments to be situated, and soared down to the sloping beach. A brown-skinned attendant, who wore only a leather breechclout, came hurrying up.

"You cannot alight here slave," he said, gruffly. "Only the warriors of Sarkis and Thoor Vil may stable their gawrs in these lagoons."

Without replying, Jerry untied and tossed him the thong which held the end of the guiding rod to the saddle. Then he sprang to the ground.

"Have I not said that you cannot land here?" demanded the attendant.

"Fool!" said Jerry. "I'm the bearer of important tidings for his holy majesty. Would you like it known that you have delayed me? For such as you there is the burning eye of the Lord Sun."

"Forgive me, my lord," said the attendant, abjectly. "I did not know you for a messenger of the holy one."

"See that my mount is well fed and watered, and hold him here in readiness for my coming, as I may be leaving soon, in a hurry."

"I hear and obey, my lord," replied the attendant, saluting respectfully.

Jerry swaggered away in the direction of the nearest vehicle tunnel. But as soon as a turn in the walk took him out of sight of the attendant, he slipped off through the shrubbery toward the thick wall that edged the roof. Here he mounted a stairway, and, going to the edge of the wall, peered over the balustrade.

It took him but a moment to identify the balcony of Junia, which was in the upper row, by the swinging divans with their golden chains and cushions of peacock blue, flanked by taborets of gold inlaid with lapis lazuli, which could only adorn the apartments of the Vil or his immediate family.

Reaching beneath his headcloak, Jerry now took out a coil of light, tough rope. Going to a point directly above one end of Junia's balcony, he made one end of the rope fast and dropped the coil. It fell among the potted shrubs, and the Earthman noted that it reached all the way, with a good twelve feet to spare.

After a swift glance around, to make sure that he was not observed, he swung over the balustrade and slid down the rope, alighting on the balcony without a sound. Cautiously, he made his way among the plants to a point opposite the window, and peered between them into the apartment.

His heart pounded wildly as he caught sight of the girl who meant more to him than life itself. Junia was seated before a small taboret, loaded with a variety of dainties. A brown-skinned slave girl was urging her to eat, but she would only sip a little pulcho from a tiny jeweled cup.

As he crouched there in the shrubbery, deliberating as to the best way to approach her, he suddenly saw a look of loathing come over her features. She was gazing toward another part of the room which he could not see. Someone had entered an armed man, evidently, for he distinctly heard the clank of weapons.

Then Jerry recognized the hollow, sepulchral tones of Sarkis the Torturer.

"I have come for your decision, princess. The great Lord Sun nears the zenith, and the time for the noon sacrifice is near at hand. You will give me your word, now, that you will wed with Thoor Vil at once, or you will go beneath the burning eye."

Again there was the clank of weapons, and the Torturer stepped into view before Junia. Behind him came two burly black warriors.

The girl stood up, and said defiantly: "You have asked for my answer. Take it then, nameless one who hides behind a mask lest his face be identified with his own evil deeds. I will not marry the false Vil, my cousin, and your puppet. You have offered me two choices, but Deza presents a third."

So saying, she suddenly turned and sprang through the window.

"Seize her!" shouted the Torturer. Before she was halfway across the balcony one of the burly blacks had her.

At this Jerry whipped out his sword and sprang from his hiding place. A single bound brought him directly in front of the astounded guard, and a sweeping cut sheared through the fellow's head from crown to chin.

"Courage, highness," he said, as Junia jerked her arm free. He whirled to confront the second warrior, who ran at him with his point extended. Deftly the Earthman parried the thrust, then caught the charging black on his blade.

The masked Torturer was now running toward the door which led to the hallway, bawling for the guard. Jerry snatched his mace from his belt and hurled it with all his might. It flew straight to the mark, smashing into the rear of the golden helmet and flattening the Torturer upon the floor.

Leaping over his foe, Jerry reached the door and shot the bolt, just as a considerable body of men came rushing up from the outside. When they found the door locked they began hacking at it with their weapons, but Jerry knew it would be some time before they could break through.

Sheathing his sword, he caught up his mace and replaced it in his belt. He was tempted to tear the mask from the face of the recumbent Torturer, but knew that he must make every second count in order to carry out his plans. Snatching a blue-and-gold curtain from a doorway, he ran out onto the balcony. Junia was standing near the railing.

"Who are you?" she asked. "Don't come near me or I'll jump."

For answer, he cleared the space between them at a single bound and flung the curtain over her.

"I know you now, Jerry Morgan," she said, "for there is no other man on Mars who can jump like that. Release me."

"You must trust me, highness," he said, bundling the fabric more tightly about her slender figure, "for I have come to save you. If you resist you will only put us both in peril."

"How can I trust the murderer of my brother?"

But Jerry had no time to reply. Flinging his bundle over his shoulder, he hurried to where the rope trailed on the balcony. With his dagger he cut off a twelve-foot length, and quickly made a sling by which he swung the girl across his back. He could hear the door of the apartment splintering as he started to climb, hand over hand, toward the balustrade above.

The attendant, seeing the strange bundle upon his back, looked surprised, but Jerry said, sharply: "Bring me my mount quickly, fellow! Can't you see I'm in a hurry?"

Evidently still puzzled, yet afraid not to obey him, the man waded into the shallows and led the great bird-beast out onto the sand.

Jerry climbed into the saddle, made the thong of the steering rod fast, and, unhooking the safety chains from the gawr's wings, hooked them through the rings in his belt. At this instant there was a shout from the nearest tunnel mouth, and a group of warriors came running out.

"Stop him!" called an officer. "Stop that slave! He has stolen the princess!"

The Earthman lifted the guiding rod and the huge bird-beast, after running clumsily along the beach a few feet, spread its great wings and took to the air.

As soon as he was out of javelin range above the palace roof, Jerry turned his mount's head toward the Plains of Lav beside the Corvid Canal, where he had heard that Numin Vil was encamped. He planned to restore Junia to her father, then escape before his identity was discovered.

Scarcely had he flown across the palace area when a score of warriors mounted on gawrs rose in pursuit. The Temple of Mercy lay directly in his path, and on this he saw that one of the Torturer's immense burning glasses had been placed. This was surrounded by a group of yellow-robed priests, who were encircled by a company of brown warriors, some of whom led gawrs.

As he flew straight toward them, one of the warriors chanced to look up. Instantly he called the attention of his companions, and in a moment they had mounted and soared aloft to head off the Earthman.

Jerry was now faced with the necessity of flying across the city, almost at right angles to the course he would have chosen. Some time passed before they flew over the great wall which marked the edge of Raliad. Jerry knew that sooner or later, with his doubly laden bird-beast, he would be overtaken and slain unless he could reach a body of his own flying warriors. Accordingly he tried, by turning the head of his mount a little at a time, to steer a course toward the Marsh of Atabah.

He had flown thus for some time when he suddenly noticed that the sun no longer beat down upon him. Looking up, he was astounded to see that it was obscured by the upper fringe of an immense, red-dish-brown cloud which, trailing backward and downward like a ragged, twisted garment, reached clear to the ground.

Never, in all his experience on Mars, had Jerry seen a cloud but he had been told of the terrific sand storms which sometimes swept the face of the planet.

There could be little question but that the cloud now bearing down upon him with such amazing speed was a cloud of sand and other debris picked up from the surface of the land by tremendously powerful winds. He saw a ragged streamer creep up on his pursuers. It caught them. For a moment they were tossed about like leaves in a gale, then the cloud swallowed them up.

Swiftly Jerry let down his headcloak and drew the transparent, flexible mask with which it was equipped across his face. Tucking the cloak down around the precious bundle on his back, he awaited the onslaught of the storm. He noticed that his mount dropped a transparent inner eyelid over each eyeball, and a thinly perforated membranous flap over each nostril.

There was a roaring, rumbling noise behind him now, that swiftly increased in volume until the sound was deafening. Then the storm struck.

At the first impact of that giant force the gawr turned completely over, and for a moment Jerry hung from his safety chains. Whirling, hurtling particles of sand beat against his clothing and mask, sifting into the interstices and getting into his eyes, ears and nostrils. The gawr righted itself, and he dragged himself back to the saddle, gripping the horn and clinging with all his strength.

The world above, below and around him was blotted out by a maelstrom of flying sand.

Hours passed thus, and still the storm showed no sign of abating. Presently the gawr began fluttering weakly, and turning over and over, sank rapidly groundward.

Suddenly it struck a solid object with a terrific impact. Jerry was hurled forward with such force that the safety chains tore out his belt rings.

CHAPTER XIX

WHEN Jerry regained consciousness someone was shaking him, calling his name. "Jerry Morgan, speak to me! O Deza, grant that he still lives!"

He opened his eyes and looked up into the frightened face of Junia, bending over him as he lay on his back in the sand. The slanting rays of the afternoon sun shone brightly down from a clear sky.

"Junia!" he exclaimed. "Are you all right?"

"Yes. And you?"

He sat up and his head throbbed painfully. Exploration with his fingers revealed a lump that was sore, but not dangerous.

"Apparently I collided with something as hard as my head," he said, getting dizzily to his feet, "but there are no permanent injuries."

Junia did not reply. As soon as she had learned that he was not badly hurt her manner had altered perceptibly. And Jerry guessed the reason. She could not feel other than antagonistic toward the supposed murderer of her brother.

"Highness," he said, "I wish I could prove to you in some way that I am not guilty of the-the crime which you seem to think I committed."

At this she turned on him and said, almost fiercely: "I wish to Deza that you could! But mere assertion proves nothing."

He walked over to where the bird-beast was lying, half-buried beneath a drift of sand. It was breathing heavily, with its great membranous wings outspread, and its head stretched out upon the ground. He pulled up on the guiding rod, but when he released it the head dropped back as before.

With the flat head of his mace he scooped the sand away from one side. Suddenly he noticed blood in the sand around the wing, close to where it joined the body. An examination revealed the fact that the bone was snapped asunder. The gawr would never fly again, and he realized that it must be suffering horribly.

Resolutely he walked to where the head lay on the ground anal, raising his mace, drove the keen saw-teeth down through the creature's skull into its brain. "We will have to walk," he called to Junia.

"Apparently," she replied, "since you have just destroyed our only other means of transportation."

"If you will look at the gawr's left wing you will see the reason."

At first she seemed determined to do nothing of the sort, but presently her curiosity got the better of her, and she walked over and looked.

"Oh, the poor creature!" she cried. "And you slew it to end its suffering. Forgive me, Jerry Morgan."

"Willingly," he answered. "And now have you any idea where we are?"

"I'm afraid I can be of no help," she said, "for this terrain is as strange to me as to you. And the desert, after all, is much alike all over Mars."

He removed the sheaf of javelins from the saddle of the bird-beast and slung it over his shoulder. Then he rolled up the hanging in which he had carried the girl, wrapped the rope about it, and slung it beside the sheaf.

"Come on," he said. "Let us climb to the highest sand dune we can find. Perhaps we will be able to sight something besides desert."

The highest dune in sight lay to the northwest of them, and toward this they plodded through the soft sand. Upon mounting to its top they made out, far to the south, a chain of low hills sparsely dotted with vegetation. In every other direction there were only barren dunes of ochre-yellow sand.

"Where there is vegetation there may be food and water," said Jerry. "Our best plan will be to go south."

A walk of some five miles brought them to the foot of the hills they had descried from a distance. On close inspection they did not look so inviting. The sparse clumps of vegetation were mostly thorny shrubs that offered neither food nor shelter. And there was no sign of water.

They reached the top after a short climb, and Junia cried out in pleased surprise at the sight which lay before them. They were looking down into a green valley, through which a narrow stream meandered. Here was water, and perhaps food, for plants and shrubs which grew along the banks of the stream made it probable that there would be edible fruits or nuts.

With renewed hope in their hearts they hurried down the hillside, and made straight for the stream. Rinsing his folding cup, Jerry offered it to Junia. But she declined it, and drank from her cupped hands. They remained beside the stream for some time, drinking and bathing their faces in the cold water. Then Jerry arose.

"I think we had best be going," he said. "The sun is low, and as yet we have found neither food nor shelter."

Without a word she arose and followed him along the river bank. Presently, he noticed a fin cleaving the water near the shore. He drew a javelin from his sheath and cautiously stalked it. Presently it came close under the bank, and he drove the multibarbed weapon straight down through the water in front of that fin. It struck something solid.

But scarcely had he driven the point home when the half was wrenched from his hand. An immense and hideous head on a long scaly neck reared itself high above him, taking the javelin with it, and he saw that he had speared the neck of a huge saurian.

The giant water lizard opened an immense mouth that was armed with a triple-row of sharp, back-curved teeth, and, with a loud hiss, darted straight for this thing which had had the presumption to annoy it with a javelin.

For a moment Jerry stared, too astounded to move. But when he saw it darting toward him his Earth-muscles carried him straight back in a tremendous flying leap to where Junia stood.

The saurian floundered up out of the water on two immense flippers, hissing angrily, and dragging an amazingly huge body out onto the bank.

Jerry caught Junia up as if she had been a child and, turning, sprinted away at his best speed. The saurian turned back toward the river, still hissing its anger and shaking its neck to dislodge the annoying javelin.

When he had placed a good mile between himself and his pursuer, Jerry stood Junia on her feet once more, and paused for a short breathing spell.

"I thought I had speared our dinner," he said, "but I came near furnishing a dinner, instead. What do you call that thing?"

"It is a histid," she replied. "They are quite common in wild marshes and lakes."

"Well, this histid has made a vegetarian out of me," said Jerry. "I no longer have the craving for fish that I had a few moments ago."

They moved on once more, following the curving bank of the stream. Presently the ground grew soft and boggy beneath their feet, the water oozing up around them at each step. Then suddenly, with a peculiar sucking sound, a round trapdoor in the bog flew open just in front of Jerry, and a long, slimy thing as large as a boa constrictor darted out. At the end of the thing was a white sucking disk, which clamped itself to the Earthman's chest. He was lifted off his feet, then dragged downward to the very rim of the hole beneath the trapdoor, which was about three feet across.

Jerry bridged himself across that hole. The slimy thing that had seized him threshed about beneath him, almost tearing the skin from his chest in its efforts to drag him down. Then he heard a scream from Junia.

Supporting himself with his knees and left hand, he snatched his long dagger from his belt with his right. Then, with the keen edge, he cut through his slimy enemy, just below the sucking disk, and sprang erect. Junia was being fought over by two of the things, which had both seized her simultaneously.

Transferring his dagger to his left hand, Jerry whipped out his sword with his right, sprang forward, and simultaneously severed the two snaky necks. Then he sheathed his dagger and, throwing Junia over his shoulder, ran across the sucking ooze toward the higher ground.

The two severed disks still clung to Junia, one on each side of her waist. Drawing his dagger, he slit one from side to side with the point, then peeled it away. Beneath it, the blood had begun to ooze through a thousand little punctures in the soft white skin. Swiftly he removed the other, and then slashed and ripped off the one that clung to his own chest.

Taking a bottle of jembal from his belt pouch, he applied the antiseptic gum to her wounds. Junia was pale and trembling.

"Once again you have saved my life, Jerry Morgan," she said. "If only..."

Yes, I know. Somehow, some day, I'm going to prove to you that I am innocent."

"Deza speed the day!" she said. "And now, let me dress your wound."

She took the bottle from his hand and deftly applied the liquid gum. She had finished dressing his wounds and was handing him the bottle when suddenly her eyes went wide.

"Look! Look behind you!" she exclaimed.

CHAPTER XX

AT JUNIA'S cry Jerry whirled around, then gave a low whistle of amazement. A monstrous thing was wading toward them across the narrow stream. As he gazed, it emerged upon the bank, a gigantic and hideous bird, fully forty feet in height.

Its long lean neck and scrawny body were leathery and bare of feathers. On its huge head was a waving crest of plumes. Its beak, which was four feet in length and two in width at the base, was hooked like that of an eagle. The short wings were covered with sharp spines in lieu of feathers. The long scaly legs were adaptable either for wading or swimming, and there were leathery webs between the toes, which were armed with immense, sickle-shaped talons.

"What is it?" Jerry asked.

"A koroo," Junia told him. "The aquatic cousin of the koree, the great man-eating bird of the desert. Like its desert relative, it is fond of human flesh. But the koroo is much larger and considered far more formidable."

"It's certainly big enough," he replied. "We would just make about one mouthful apiece for it. Do you think it has seen us?"

"I think not. Let us move away as slowly and quietly as possible, and seek a place of concealment."

Slowly, cautiously, they crept up the stony bank. Jerry, meanwhile, kept a sharp watch on the monster, which raised its plumbed head to its full height and cocked an eye in the direction of the fleeing couple. At sight of them its crest rose and its horny wings, which had been hanging at its sides, were suddenly elevated to a horizontal position. Then, with a peculiar booming cry, it charged swiftly toward them.

"It sees us!" said Jerry excitedly. "We may as well spring for it, now."

He caught up Junia, flung her over his shoulder, and started up the hillside with huge leaps that almost matched the giant strides of the bird.

Jerry ran as he had never run before. But the fifteen-foot legs of the monster koroo shortened the distance between them with alarming rapidity. Soon the Earthman could hear it stertorous breathing behind him. Then he noticed a dark hole in the hillside, just in front of him. Like a hunted animal seeking cover, he plunged into it.

He took his baridium torch from his belt and unhooded it, flashing it about to assure himself that there was no formidable creature lurking there. He was in a roughly circular cave, about thirty feet in diameter, with a twelve-foot ceiling. Swiftly he ran to the opposite side of the cave and faced about.

The koroo was now peering into the hole, its head cocked to one side. Seeing its intended prey standing in the back of the cave, it lunged forward. But its long neck would only negotiate about half of the distance, and the opening was not large enough to admit its shoulders.

Temporarily baffled, the monster backed out and began scratching and tearing at the opening with its immense talons. After it had enlarged the hole considerably, it again lunged forward. This time its shoulders passed through.

Jerry took a javelin from the sheaf he carried and, running up close to the hideous head, plunged it into one huge, glaring eye.

With a squawk of pain the koroo backed out of the cave, shaking its head and clawing at the shaft of the weapon in an effort to dislodge it. The barbs held, but the shaft was snapped off like matchwood. Blinded in one eye, the man-eater again hurled itself into the hole. Once more Jerry ran forward, and this time threw a javelin with all his strength into the other eye.

Again the giant bird backed out, shaking its head and clawing at the shaft. Then it lost its balance and rolled end over end down the steep hillside, loosening a small avalanche of stones and gravel. About halfway down it brought up against a huge boulder with a crash, and lay still.

Drawing his sword, Jerry half slid, half ran, down the hillside to where the koroo lay. He pricked it with the point, but it did not respond. Sheathing the larger weapon, he took out his dagger, and, after laying back a section of the leathery skin on the breast, cut out a large slab of meat. With this he returned to where Junia waited in the cave mouth.

"At last we have food," he said, depositing the meat on a flat boulder.

"I have never heard of anyone eating koroo," she said.

"Nor I," replied Jerry, "but I'm hungry enough to eat crushed rock."

Swiftly he gathered a pile of dry brush and dead leaves, and powdering a small quantity of the latter, lighted them by focusing the rays of the setting sun on them with his crystal disk. Soon he had an efficient cooking fire crackling, and when it had burned down to a bed of glowing coals, grilled several slices of the meat.

Politely he passed the first slice to Junia. She attempted to bite off a piece, but was unable to So much as dent it with her teeth. Jerry tried another with similar results.

It tasted like a slab of sole leather flavored with fish oil, and was neither palatable nor chewable.

"There seems to be an excellent reason why you never heard of anyone eating koroo," he told Junia.

"Apparently," she replied. "Yet the flesh-flies seem to enjoy it."

She nodded in the direction of the carcass, and Jerry, following her gaze, saw that virtually nothing remained but the picked skeleton. A half dozen huge insects still walked about it, as if looking for stray morsels.

"They are welcome to my share," he said. "After all, I believe I should prefer to tackle crushed rock. But if we may not eat, we can at least sleep. The sun is low, and we had best make our preparations for the night."

When Jerry awoke in the morning his first thought was of Junia. How little and helpless she looked, sleeping there wrapped in her blue curtain! A fiercely protective feeling surged up in him as he turned to face this strange and hostile world.

Cautiously he removed a stone or two of the barrier he had erected the night before, and peered out. But there were no enemies in sight, so he soon had the opening cleared out.

The sound of his labors awakened Junia, and she quickly joined him. Together they went down to the stream to drink and wash.

"Shall we hunt upstream or down?" Jerry inquired. "I think we would do well to keep near the water."

"Down," Junia voted. "We would be going in the general direction of Raliad."

Their hopes rose as they rounded a bend in the little stream, for it emptied into a large river. In the middle of the river was a very sizable island, and Jerry scanned the shore attentively.

"Junia, does that look to you like a boat?"

"I believe it is."

"That means human beings, and food. I'll swim across and find out."

"Don't leave me behind!" she pleaded; she followed him into the water, leaving the curtain robe behind.

They struck out firmly for the island, breasting the slight current, and landed near the object they had spied from the other shore. It proved indeed to be a boat, wide, flat and wooden. In it lay two wooden paddles, a net, and a multi-pronged fishing spear. And there was the remnant of a narrow path leading up from the shore, where the ground was so packed by footsteps that the weeds which had grown over it were stunted.

"Maybe the people who left this boat here also left an empty dwelling we can use," said Jerry. "Shall we investigate?"

"By all means," Junia replied. "It will be bitterly cold after sunset, and neither of us is equipped for it. If there is a dwelling of some sort, we can at least build a fire and keep warm."

They were suddenly startled by a terrific roar, followed by a crashing in the underbrush. Then a huge black dalf burst into view, and charged at them with bared fangs.

Stepping in front of Junia, Jerry whipped out his sword and awaited the beast. But when it came quite near him, it stopped suddenly, sniffing in his direction and growling softly. Then he noticed that it had a tarnished, gold-plated collar around its neck, on which was the inscription:

Neem, the dalf of Thaine

Evidently, thought Jerry, this beast was half minded to be friendly.

"Quiet, Neem," he said.

The great beast pricked up its ears and ceased growling.

"Come here, Neem," Jerry went on, lowering his sword and holding out his hand.

The dalf came forward slowly, evidently still suspicious. Then Junia spoke to him, at the same time stepping from behind Jerry. As soon as he saw her, Neem gave violent manifestations of an exuberance of joy. Soon she was rumpling his head, while Neem stood, leaning lightly against her, with his eyes half-closed, the picture of contentment.

"I must resemble his former mistress," said Junia. Then she went on musingly: "I wonder who this Thaine could have been."

"Perhaps we can solve the riddle if we find the house of Thaine," said Jerry. "The sun is due to set in a very short time. Let us start searching."

He led the way up the path, with Junia and the dalf following closely behind. But presently, when he emerged in an open glade in the center of the wood, the trail disappeared entirely. And a careful look around disclosed no sign of a house.

CHAPTER XXI

As JERRY and Junia stood in the little sunlit glade, Neem, the great black dalf, stood between them, gazing up at, first, one and then the other. Apparently he wondered why they had stopped.

"No sign of a house here," said Jerry.

At the word "house," Neem pricked up his small ears. Then he seized a fold of the headcloak which Junia wore, and began tugging gently.

"Go ahead. Show us the house, Neem," she said, encouragingly.

At this, the beast turned and trotted toward a vine-covered mound, his flat, spiked tail proudly elevated. He led them through a small opening in a leafy screen of tangled vines, and behind it they saw a door cut in the supposed mound, which turned out to be an irregularly shaped house covered with vines and creepers.

"The place is certainly well concealed," said Jerry. "Thaine must have been hiding for some reason."

Rearing up, the dalf pressed on the latch with one huge paw, then shouldered the door open and went in. Jerry and Junia followed him into a large room, comfortably furnished with swinging chairs and divans. There were three circular doorways cut in the walls, leading to the other rooms. And at one end was a large fireplace, around which were various utensils, and beside which a shelf held a number of dishes, cups, and the like, all of which were of gold, skillfully engraved and set with jewels. A shelf on the other side held a number of covered jars, such as the Martians use for the storage of foods.

"Evidently the lady was quite wealthy," said Jerry. "Those dishes and jars look as if they came from a palace."

"They did. On each is the mark of the royal house of Xancibar. It must be that Thaine had some connection with the house of Miradon Vil."

"Or perhaps with a gang of burglars. In any case, we eat!"

And eat they did. It was some time before they troubled to examine the three other rooms. One was obviously the sleeping room of a man-a mighty huntsman, judging from the weapons and the collection of trophies.

The second room was used for storage. In it they found considerable quantities of dried and preserved provisions, as well as boxes of clothing, sleeping furs, fire powder, and other necessities.

The remaining room was unmistakably the boudoir of a girl, with its many chests of feminine apparel, and its dainty jeweled boxes of cosmetics. There were weapons here, also, but smaller and lighter than those in the sleeping room of the man.

Junia immediately took possession of this room, and Jerry retired to the room of the hunter. He bathed, then took the bottle of depilatory which he had long since substituted for his razor and went to the mirror to remove his beard. Putting down the depilatory, he returned to his belt pouch, and getting the bottle of clear liquid, filled a jeweled gold basin with water at the bath box, added a few drops of the chemical, and removed the dye from his skin and hair.

He got out the bottle of black hair dye, and with it redyed his hair and eyebrows and stained his beard jet black. Then he opened several chests until he found what he wanted-boots, cincture and head-cloak of brown, pliable leather like those worn by huntsmen. These he speedily donned.

His toilet completed, Jerry opened the door to the living room and saw, to his surprise, that Junia was there before him. She had kindled a fire in the grate, and had a pot of fragrant pulcho brewing. Like Jerry, she had chosen huntsman's leather in preference to the blue and gold raiment which was at her disposal. She was bending over close to the fire, preparing a pot of hunter's stew, a mixture of dried meats, berries and vegetables.

Hearing the sound of his footsteps behind her, Junia turned, took one look at him, and uttered a piercing scream. Instantly, Neem the dalf, who had been lying stretched near her, sprang up with a roar, and plunged straight for the Earthman.

Neem, after charging up to within three feet of Jerry, suddenly stopped, sniffing the air. Then he hung his head, the bristles on his back receded, and with a most crestfallen manner he returned to his place by the fire.

"Sorry to have startled you," said Jerry. "I thought I made sufficient noise coming into the room."

"It wasn't the noise, but the change in your appearance," Junia said. "I should never have known you.

"Then perhaps my plan will work," Jerry told her, continuing: "Junia, I want to take you back to your father, and when I do, I would like to remain and help him. Without my help, and that of my army, it is probable that he not only will never be able to retake Raliad, but that the Torturer may completely crush his army."

"Just what is your plan?"

"I would go as I am, disguised as a huntsman from Xancibar, who found you in this marsh. As a reward, your father should be glad to give me a post in his army. I am a soldier by profession-have made a study of the art of war. With my help, and that of my warriors, who I am sure I could persuade to reinforce the Vil's army, your father will be able to drive the Torturer from Raliad and retake his empire."

"I suppose you realize," she said, "that if my father should recognize you, or if you should be betrayed by someone else, he would have you put to death without compunction. And even with the-the barrier that stands between us, I should not want that to happen."

"I know," he agreed. "And for a crime I did not commit."

"That remains to be proved," she reminded him. "And I have prayed every night that you may prove your innocence."

"Bless your heart!" For a moment Jerry laid his large brown hand over her small one.

They sat there before the fire, toying with their pulcho cups and making their plans for the morrow.

"I found a map which shows our location," said Junia. "We are in the midst of the Takkor Marsh, on the rim of which is situated Castle Takkor. The Raddek of Takkor is within the Empire of Xancibar, and subject to its ruler."

"Then how far are we from Raliad?" asked Jerry.

"I have computed the distance at four thousand jahuds," she replied.

"May I see the map?" he asked.

She rose and went into her room, presently reappearing with a roll of waterproof silk, which she spread on the taboret. "Here is our location in the center of the marsh," she said, pointing to a tiny red dot on a small island.

He looked at the map more closely. "It appears that we are about two hundred jahuds from the Corvid Canal," he said. "That will take us straight to Raliad. We are five hundred jahuds from Dukor, capital of Xancibar, and only fifty from Castle Takkor. Why not go to the castle and ask the Rad for the loan of a couple of gawrs?"

"I am surprised at you, Jerry Morgan," she said. "Have you forgotten that Sarkis is in Raliad, and that Thoor has been named Vil?

"We know not what treaties may have been concluded between Kalsivar and Xancibar during our absence. It may be that the Rad of Takkor would place us under arrest and send us to Raliad. Perhaps Thoor and Sarkis have offered a fabulous reward for our return."

"I bow to your superior judgment," he said, "and apologize for being so thick-witted. Naturally, if it would not be wise to go to Castle Takkor, it would be equally unwise to go to Dukor. But if we go straight to the Corvid Canal, disguised as a huntsman and his sister, it may be that we can take passage on one of the boats for Raliad."

"Have you thought of the matter of passage money?"

"No," Jerry admitted. "And I suppose the boatmen won't take promises. Perhaps we'll have to steal a boat."

"Fortunately not," she replied. "I found a well-filled purse in the bottom of a chest in Thaine's sleeping room." She put a small, gold-embroidered silk bag on the taboret, and opening it, disclosed a considerable sum of gold and platinum pieces stamped with the mark of the Vil of Xancibar.

"Take the purse," she went on, "and if we succeed in reaching my father I will learn the whereabouts of this Thaine, and reimburse her."

Jerry pushed the purse back to her. "You take charge of it," he said. "And now, how about what I asked you? Will you permit me to assist your father in my character as a huntsman?"

"I'll sleep on that," she told him, rising and yawning prettily. "Good night."

CHAPTER XXII

THE EARTHMAN arose early, and went down to the bank of the stream to prepare the wooden boat for their journey across the marsh.

The fragrant aroma of boiling pulcho greeted him as he opened the door, and Junia cheerily called him to breakfast. This consisted of several kinds of dried fruits, which she had stewed, and the inevitable pulcho.

Their breakfast over, they carefully selected the provisions and supplies which they would take with them, with a view to keeping their packs as light as possible, for they would have to walk across the desert a distance of about seventy miles before reaching the Corvid Canal. Then it might be necessary to walk ten or fifteen miles farther before reaching a boat station.

When they .bad loaded and strapped on their packs, with a rolled sleeping fur attached to each, Jerry went into the huntsman's sleeping room and got his weapons. After replenishing his supply of javelins from a large sheaf on the wall, and pouching a half dozen bottles of fire powder, he was ready.

Neem accompanied them down to the boat, and when they were ready to push off, Jerry called to him. But instead of getting in with them, he took the tie-rope in his mouth, and plunging into the water with it, pulled them out into the middle of the stream, then stopped, looking back at them.

"Why, I believe the beast wants to tow us!" exclaimed Jerry.

"Of course," Junia told him. "That is what all marsh-reared dalfs are trained to do. I'll guide him."

She sat down in the front of the boat, and unrolling the map, spread it over her dimpled knees.

"To the right, Neem," she said.

The dalf obediently turned and started away, dragging the boat after him with a speed which Jerry could never have equaled with a paddle.

A two hours' ride through the marsh brought them to a wide sandy beach strewn with boulders, behind which towered a row of rugged, frowning cliffs.

"The desert starts at the edge of those cliffs," said Junia, glancing at her map. "And a hundred and forty jahuds beyond lies the Corvid Canal."

They left the boat on the beach, and shouldering their packs, climbed up among the boulders to the base of the cliff. Here they consumed a laborious hour in scaling the precipice, then emerged into the desert.

After a brief rest, they started off across the ochre-yellow sands. Presently, a growl from Neem attracted Jerry's attention, and he looked in the direction toward which the dalf was gazing. He saw that several rodals were coming swiftly toward them.

They were riderless, and had obviously run thus for some time. It was apparent that these were the survivors of a clash between desert tribesmen. The rodals came to a halt a short distance away from the travelers. Jerry turned to the girl.

"Suppose you wait here with Neem to guard you, and I'll see if I can catch a couple of rodals. I'm accustomed to handling them."

The nearest rodal had stopped at a patch of sand flowers about half a mile away, and Jerry walked slowly toward it. As be drew near, he saw that it was engaged in hunting the large insects and small rodents and reptiles which make up the diet of these desert steeds. It raised its plumed, snaky head at his approach, and stood staring at him. At this, Jerry made a sound used by the desert lorwocks to call their mounts, while he continued to saunter closer.

The rodal was puzzled. It looked around several times, as if half minded to sprint away. Again Jerry called. This, and his slow, careless approach seemed to reassure it. Almost before the creature was aware of it, the Earthman had his hand on the guiding rod, and had vaulted into the saddle.

Once on the rodal's back, Jerry was in complete command. And the matter of capturing a second mount for Junia was easily accomplished. Soon they were speeding across the sands on their tireless desert steeds, with Neem loping along beside them.

At noon they halted in a small oasis for rest, food and pulcho. Then they pressed onward, and late that afternoon sighted the black stone wall which, topped by sentry towers at intervals of one jahud, or approximately a half mile, guarded the Corvid Canal.

They now took a course parallel to the wall, and just out of sight of the sentries, until they came to a tower above which was a small replica of a ship. This indicated that it was a station where boats stopped for passengers and freight. Here they abandoned their rodals and waited until sunset.

A short walk in the dim moonlight brought them to an arched opening in the wall. A sentry on the wall above the gate flashed his baridium torch in their faces and challenged them.

"Who are you, and what do you want?"

"I am Jandar the Hunter, with my sister Thaine, and her dalf. We have left our but in the Takkor Marsh, to seek passage for Raliad."

"Have you passage money?"

"We have saved a little from the sale of our furs," replied Jerry, "and would see the wonderful sights in the greatest city of all Mars."

The sentry called to someone below him, and a moment later the two massive doors beneath the archway swung outward. A voice called: "Enter."

They went in side by side, with Neem trailing at their heels, and traversed the dimly lighted passageway which led through the wall. This brought them up before a corpulent, red-faced officer in the uniform of Xancibar, at whose back stood two stalwart guards. The officer sat on a swinging chair before a taboret, with a baridium torch dangling above his head. A scroll of waterproof silk was unrolled before him. Beside it was an ink pot, and in his hand was a writing brush.

"Name?" he rasped at Jerry.

"Jandar the Hunter."

"From?"

"Takkor Marsh."

Dipping the brush into the pot of ink, he made the entry on the scroll. Then he turned to Junia with the same questions. She replied that she was Thaine the Huntress, also from the Takkor Marsh.

Having entered this, he glanced at the name plate on the dalf's collar, and wrote it down on the scroll. This done, he said:

"It is not strange that there should be two dazzlingly beautiful Thaines in Xancibar, nor yet that there should be two black dalfs named Neem. But that there should ever have been two such Thaines, each with a black dalf named Neem, is passing strange. Also, I have heard it said that her highness, the Vil's adopted daughter, lost her black dalf Neem in the Takkor Marsh some time ago. I wonder if this could be the same beast."

"I see nothing strange in the fact that my sister was named after her highness, nor that she should name her black dalf after the beast which belonged to the Vil's adopted daughter," said Jerry. "And," he continued, laying his hand on the hilt of his sword, "I resent the insinuation of theft which your words seem to imply. I wait to hear you retract them."

"You take a strange tone for a mere hunter," said the officer, looking the Earthman over with the practiced eye of a military man. And though the officer was not accounted a bad swordsman, the cool self-assurance of the young man who stood before him did not make him at all anxious to press matters further. He sat down heavily, and continued: "But after all, hunters have their rights, as does every citizen of Xancibar, however humble, under the just role of our mighty Vil. And as his majesty's representative, it is my duty to see that you get justice. I, Hazlit Jen, retract the insinuation, and wish you and your sister a pleasant trip to Raliad. Shortly after the rising of the nearer moon a large passenger boat going your way will dock here. In the meantime, there is a small cabin boat tied at the wharf. If you care to pay the price, it might be that you could charter it for the trip."

Jerry removed his hand from his hilt and saluted. "We are beholden to you for your kindness. Come, sister. Let us interview the boatman at the dock."

At this, the bulky officer arose.

"Permit me to interview Padrath for you," he said. "I know the fellow. If he thinks you are in a hurry, he will want to charge you double or perhaps treble fare."

Intuition instantly told Jerry there was something amiss. "Don't trouble yourself. If we find the boatman unreasonable, we will wait for the passenger ship."

"Ah, but I insist," wheezed the officer, crowding past them and waddling down to the dock, where a small narrow craft with a cabin of iridescent crystal was moored.

With a whispered warning to Junia to remain quiet and keep the dalf with her, Jerry softly stepped upon the deck, and tiptoeing to the cabin door, crouched there, listening. For the most part, the conversation was indistinguishable, but he did make out the words: "Junia, Crown Princess of Kalsivar," "Thoor Vil," and "a reward of ten thousand platinum tayzos."

Noticing that one of the bulky shadows inside had gotten up, he quickly stepped back to the dock.

A moment later, the door opened and the red-faced officer squeezed through.

"All is settled," he wheezed, "and at a great bargain for you. I, myself, am going with you and will pay half of the charge, which my friend Padrath has made very nominal for my sake. I had intended going tomorrow, but tonight will do as well. Bear with me but a moment, and I will be with you."

He waddled off hastily in the direction of the tower.

"What did you hear? What does it all mean?" asked Junia.

"It means," replied Jerry grimly, "that the fat, red-faced jen has recognized you, and has conspired with the boatman to take us to Raliad, that they may collect the reward of ten thousand platinum tayzos which Thoor Vil has offered for your return."

And knowing this, you mean to go with them?"

"We have no choice in the matter. To attempt an escape over the wall, patrolled as it is, would be extremely dangerous and would only put us back where we started if successful. This way the danger will be equally great, but at least we will have the satisfaction of knowing that we are drawing nearer to our destination. And some opportunity for escape may present itself before we reach Raliad."

CHAPTER XXIII

So FAR as physical comforts went, Jerry and Junia were pleasantly installed on a pile of cushions in the cabin of Padrath's swift little boat. The boatman himself sat in the front of the cabin on a saddle-like seat, manipulating the two driving levers which controlled both the speed and direction of the craft. The corpulent, red-faced officer occupied a cushion across from them, and Neem, the black dalf, snoozed at their feet.

Under any other circumstances it would have been pleasant to glide swiftly and smoothly over the placid waters of the canal, leaving a wake of ripples that sparkled in the mellow light of the farther moon.

Presently, some time after the nearer moon had risen, Jerry said: "You are weary, little sister. Close your eyes and sleep."

"And what of you, big brother?"

"I would watch this strange scenery," he told her.

"It is no more strange to you than to me, and not a bit less interesting."

Near midnight, Hazlit Jen brought a pan of charcoal, ignited it with a pinch of fire powder and a splash of water, and brewed pulcho. After passing a cup to the boatman and one to Junia, he filled one for Jerry and handed it to him. But the Earthman noticed that before he picked it up, he held the palm of his hand over it for a moment. Accordingly, he held the cup without tasting it, and then as the officer filled his own cup, said:

"A whim of mine, Hazlit Jen. Among huntsmen it is a custom for good friends to exchange cups." He pressed the cup into the officer's left hand and took the one he had poured for himself.

The man's face grew redder, and he flashed a suspicious look at Jerry.

"To a swift journey and a safe arrival," said the Earthman.

Having gone this far, Hazlit Jen was forced to raise the cup which Jerry had handed him. But as he slid so, it slipped from his hand.

"Clumsy of me," he wheezed, catching up the cup and hurling it through the porthole as if his temper had got the better of him. Then he filled another cup.

Shortly thereafter, Hazlit Jen settled back among his cushions and was soon snoring lustily.

"We must get some sleep," Jerry whispered to Junia, "for a long journey lies ahead of us. You sleep first, and I will watch. Then, when you awaken, I will get some sleep."

When the Earthman awoke, the sun was at the zenith. And Junia was busily engaged over the charcoal pan, preparing their noon meal. The appetizing odors made Jerry ravenous, and he did full justice to the meal, paying extravagant tribute to the skill of the cook.

They invited Padrath and Hazlit Jen to join them, but both declined, saying that they were not hungry, and would prepare their own food later.

After they had eaten, Jerry and Junia went out on deck where Neem was basking in the sunlight, and fed him the remainder of the anuba steaks. Then they sat down to enjoy the sunshine and the scenery that was slipping past them.

Far below them was the drainage canal, swarming with boats and fishermen. And across the thirteen mile chasm was the other irrigation canal which watered the opposite terraces, its larger craft plainly visible in the clear air.

At intervals of about two hundred jahuds, cross canals bridged the chasm on tremendous arched structures of metal and stone, connecting the two upper canals and making it possible for boats to cross directly from one to the other without using the slower systems of locks which occurred at equal distances, and connected both with the lower drainage canal.

The sun was low in the west when Padrath turned into one of these transverse channels and crossed to the irrigation canal on the opposite side.

As they turned into the other canal, the sun set, and night fell suddenly with its blaze of sparkling stars in a black velvet sky, and the pale farther moon preparing to follow the sun beneath the western horizon.

Lights flashed on in the teeming craft that swarmed on the canal, the houses that dotted the terraces, and the watch towers upon the wall. And Padrath unhooded the baridium torch that lighted the small cabin. The boatman then rose, and turning over the control levers to Hazlit Jen, sauntered out upon the deck, closing the door after him.

For a time he stood looking at the passing towers and stroking his bushy beard. Then he said: "We should make the border of Kalsivar before the farther moon sets. I suppose you two have passports."

"Why, no, we haven't," replied Jerry. "I didn't know they would be required."

"They are. But a few platinum pieces will serve as well. I know an officer."

"How much will it cost?" asked Jerry.

"Five tayzos should be enough."

"My sister carries our money," said Jerry. Then he turned to Junia. "Pay the boatman five tay..." he began. But at that instant something descended upon his head with terrific force, felling him to the deck. Fortunately for him, he had coiled the leather lasso inside his headcloak to conceal it, and this saved him a crushed skull.

216

Almost as soon as the blow fell, there was a low growl from Neem. Then the big dalf, with a quickness that was surprising in a creature of such great bulk, leaped straight over the fallen Earthman, There was a muffled shriek, and a crunch of shattered bone. Then Padrath fell to the deck with the dalf on top of him, his head crushed like an eggshell.

Jerry sprang dizzily to his feet, and grasping Neem by the collar, pulled him off his fallen assailant. A single glance told him that the boatman was beyond all human aid.

Feeling sure that Hazlit jen, who had tried a more subtle method of assassination only a few hours before, was in on the plot, Jerry tiptoed to the cabin door and softly opened it. The officer sat at the controls, looking straight out through the front windows and piloting the craft through the canal traffic with undiminished speed.

Jerry quietly closed the door. Then he returned to where the corpse lay, and tearing off a piece of the headcloak, heaved it into the water. With the fabric he mopped up the blood, then dropped it overboard.

He turned to Junia.

"I am going into the cabin to try to learn the plans of Hazlit Jen," he said. "First give me five tayzos. I will leave the door open. If you see me raise my hand to my head, rush into the cabin, saying that Padrath has snatched your purse with a thousand tayzos in it, and leaped overboard."

"But what are you going to do? He may kill you."

"Have no fear, and trust me," said Jerry, pressing her hand as she passed him the money. "Is all clear?"

"Yes."

Jerry went to the cabin door, and opened it noisily. Then be walked in, and toward the front.

"I dislike to trouble an officer with what must seem a most trivial matter," Jerry began, "yet to a poor hunter a matter of five tayzos is of considerable importance. To me it represents many dangerous hunts, and many trips to the City of Takkor, where the grasping fur merchants pay us less than a tenth of the prices they receive from the tanners in Dukor. I hope that you understand."

"I understand fully, my poor fellow," said Hazlit Jen. "Go on."

"I have not forgotten that you warned me against the cupidity of our boatman," continued the Earthman. "Just a moment ago he approached me and asked if we had passports. Since we had none, he said he would have to have five tayzos with which to bribe the officials at the border in order that we might pass into Kalsivar. He claimed he was well acquainted with one of the officers, and could arrange everything for us."

"The amount he mentioned was correct. But if he told you he could arrange things with the officials, he lied. Only I can do that. And it is to me that you must pay the money."

"Indeed I am glad I consulted you in this matter," Jerry told him, handing over the five platinum pellets with a look of relief.

The officer dropped the money into his belt pouch. "Leave everything to me, and you will be safe and sound in Raliad before sunup."

Jerry raised his hand, as if to adjust his headcloak. This movement was followed by a most convincing scream from Junia. Then she rushed into the cabin.

"What happened? What's wrong?" asked Hazlit jen, paling.

"The boatman!" she panted. "He snatched my purse and leaped overboard. Our life savings-our thousand tayzos-are gone with him."

Jerry sprang to his feet, simulating anger, but the anger of the red-faced officer was not simulated. Moving both levers back to neutral, he turned and asked: "Where is the scoundrel?"

"He must be on shore, and well away with the loot by this time," said Junia.

Hazlit jen plunged across the cabin, through the door, and out upon the deck. Jerking his baridium torch from his belt, he flashed it over the placid waters.

"Gone!" he wheezed angrily. "Gone with a thousand platinum tayzos! Oh, the blackguard!"

"After all," said Jerry dryly, "there are more platinum pieces where those came from. The fool has only cheated himself."

"Eh? What do you mean?"

"Since the low-born villain has decamped, there is no reason why two officers and gentlemen should not be perfectly frank with each other," said Jerry in a confidential tone. "Let us drop all pretense. I realized that you had recognized her highness, from the start. What you have evidently not realized is that I an in the employ of His Majesty, Thoor Vil. Of course she doesn't know that. And I thought it best not to tell her until we arrive. She might offer absurd objections, or attempt to escape."

"Quite right," said Hazlit. "But what of the reward?"

"I'll split it with you" Jerry told him. "I had intended dividing with you and the boatman. But since he took the purse, there remain larger portions for both of us. It is he who is the greatest loser."

"Why, so he is," said the officer. He was still holding his baridium torch, unhooded, and the rays were shining on the deck. For a moment, the little pig-like eyes paused and widened at sight of a small, red splotch.

Jerry saw it too, and quickly looked up to see if the jen had noticed it. But the officer looked away unconcernedly.

"Let the fool boatman go with his ill-gotten gains," he said. "We will have ten thousand tayzos to divide between us."

He hooded his baridium torch, and replacing it in his belt, started toward the cabin.

During this conversation, the boat had been drifting slowly forward under its own momentum, the driving mechanism having been set at neutral.

"We are almost at the Kalsivar border," said Hazlit Jen, resuming his seat between the two control levers. "You two had best remain in the cabin. I will dock the boat and attend to interviewing the officers, alone."

He pushed both levers forward a little way. A cunning look came into his eyes as he smoothly guided the boat up to the international dock. He drew the levers back to neutral, and stood up.

"Await me here," he said, "and leave everything to me. I won't be long."

CHAPTER XXIV

JERRY kept his place among the cushions in the cabin when Hazlit jen went out to moor the boat. But he had no intention of leaving the officer unwatched.

The Earthman watched through a porthole while Hazlit jen tied the boat to the dock and walked to the tower doorway. As soon as the officer entered, Jerry strolled unconcernedly out on the deck and across the dock after him. Guards were stationed at regular intervals along the dock, as well as upon the black wall, and in the open windows of the tower. And there were four swift patrol boats of Kalsivar anchored at equidistant points across the canal, facing four similar boats belonging to Xancibar.

Instead of entering the tower doorway, Jerry paused just outside it, and a little to one side. Hazlit jen, with his back toward him, was standing before the commander of the border guards, who sat on a swinging chair with writing materials on a taboret before him.

"The hunter murdered the boatman," Hazlit jen was saying, "and threw his body into the canal. Then he told me his victim had robbed his sister and leaped overboard. I will take the girl on to Raliad, for she is innocent, but I should like to have you hold this assassin here until I come back. Then I will return him to Dukor in chains, to stand trial for murder.

"I don't know why you wish to leave him with me, instead of the Xancibar officer," said the commander, "but since you have paid me five tayzos, I can see no objection to holding the assassin for you." He turned to a soldier who stood behind him. "Take six men and arrest the hunter on the small boat at the dock," he ordered.

Jerry waited to hear no more. Springing across the dock, he whipped out his sword, slashed the tie-rope, and leaped aboard the boat. Then he plunged into the cabin, seized the two control levers, and pushed them forward as far as they would go. The boat tore away from the dock with a rush, just as the two nearest guards came running up.

Jerry kept his eyes ahead and his hands on the control levers, while Junia watched from the rear deck.

"The patrol boat is drawing up to the dock," she said, "and Hazlit jen is getting aboard. Now they are starting after us."

It looked as though their capture would be only a matter of minutes, when Jerry, who had noticed the farther moon just ready to settle below the western horizon, suddenly thought of a plan. Zigzagging through the traffic toward the outer bank, he presently reached a position only a few feet from shore. By this time the patrol boat was but two hundred feet behind them, its prow lined with warriors ready to leap upon their afterdeck.

Presently the moon dipped below the horizon. Instantly Jerry hooded the baridium torch that lighted the cabin, plunging the boat into darkness. Then he set the levers so the craft would turn about in a narrow circle. Grasping Junia's hand, he hurried her out onto the deck.

The dark bulk of the shore loomed beside them, and the boat began curving away from it. Gathering the girl in his arms, Jerry jumped, his Earth-trained muscles easily carrying him beyond the water's edge. Swiftly he ran up the bank in the darkness. And a moment later, he knew that part of his plan had worked out, for there was a terrific crash, and the shouts of men struggling in the water, as the small boat, turning in a circle, rammed the large craft amidships.

There were stairways for the use of defending warriors at regular intervals along the inner side of the wall, and Jerry presently groped his way in the dark to one of these. Climbing it without noise, he saw a guard approaching, outlined against the sky. At this moment, Jerry, who had completely forgotten Neem the dalf, felt a wet muzzle pressed against his arm.

"Get him, Neem," he whispered.

While Jerry and Junia crouched in the shadow, the great shaggy beast crept over the edge of the wall. The guard saw him and raised his javelin. But ere he could draw it back for a thrust, the furry body shot through the air, the huge jaws closed on his head with a single crunch, and the sentinel expired without a sound.

Jerry caught up Junia once more and ran to the edge of the wall. Uncoiling the rope beneath his headcloak, he passed it around her slender waist and let her over the edge. The lasso did not grow slack until most of its length had been paid out so he knew there was a drop of about thirty feet beneath him.

"Release the rope," he called down to Junia softly.

She instantly complied, and fastening it around Neem, he pushed the beast over the edge, snubbing the lasso on the parapet in order to hold the great weight of the dalf.

As soon as the beast had alighted, Jerry let himself down as far as he could by hanging from both hands, then dropped, alighting in the soft sand without injury.

Recovering the rope, he caught up Junia and hurried away.

For some time the darkness favored them. Then the bright nearer moon suddenly popped above the western horizon, almost at the point where the farther moon had set, flooding the desert with light. By this time they were more than a mile from the wall, and Jerry found that by keeping to the hollows behind the sand dunes, they could travel without danger of being seen by the enemy.

The bright nearer moon was high in the heavens when a black shadow suddenly swept across its face and fell upon the fugitives. It was followed by another and another, and Jerry, looking up, saw that a party of a hundred gawr riders was passing high overhead.

Junia, who had also been watching the fliers, clutched his arm. "They've seen us! What shall we do?"

"I'm afraid there is nothing we can do," he replied. "It is too late to hide, we can't outrun them, and it would be hopeless to try to fight a hundred warriors."

The sound of flapping leathery wings grew louder as the flying warriors spiraled lower, and in a few moments they had landed in a circle completely surrounding the fugitives.

Stationing himself in front of Junia, Neem bristled up, and ominous rumblings issued from his cavernous throat.

Then suddenly the leader of the warriors flung himself down from his steed. He was short and bow-legged, with long ape-like arms and tremendously broad shoulders. Instead of a javelin, he carried a heavy, long-handled mace.

"Koha!" Jerry exclaimed.

"I hoped it would be you, master," the black dwarf cried, saluting. He turned to the others, whirling his mace aloft. "Ho, warriors! It is the Commoner!"

At this a cheer broke from the throats of the entire company.

"We have been searching for you day and night, since your disappearance, master," continued Koha.

"The lady with me is Her Imperial Highness of Kalsivar," said Jerry. "You will salute her, and provide a gawr for each of us."

Instantly the entire company sprang from their saddles, rendering the imperial salute to Junia and proffering their mounts. Jerry selected one for the princess and another for himself.

Mounted on their swift bird-beasts, it took them less than a half hour to reach Jerry's camp, where he and the princess received a tremendous ovation. Here, after providing Junia with a portable hut, and recommending that she get some sleep, the Earthman called his officers together.

"It is highly probable," he said, "that there will be desperate fighting for all of us in a few days. And strange as it may appear to you, we will probably be fighting as allies of Numin Vil. As you all know, the Torturer is in Raliad, and has put the dark-skinned prince on the throne for his puppet. By joining forces with Numin Vil, we will be assisting him in combating a mutual enemy, and if we win, there will be suitable rewards for all. Are there any questions or objections?"

No one spoke.

"There being no objections," Jerry continued, "you will send out riders at once to summon the tribesmen, and the other units of our army that are in hiding. Let the Atabah Marsh be the rendezvous, and be ready for matching orders by tomorrow. I go now to inspect the work of our armorers and smiths."

Rising, he strode through the circle of officers, followed by Yewd and Koha, and crossing the sandy, boulder-strewn beach to the base of the cliff, entered a dark doorway.

Unhooding his baridium torch, he followed a winding passageway deep into the cliff. He emerged in a tremendous natural cave, where a night shift of two thousand men was at work, forging and welding small octagonal metal turrets, each large enough to hold one man. The turrets were fitted with thick crystal panels, each of which could be opened or closed by a lever in the hands of the occupant.

"How many are ready?" Jerry asked.

"Eight hundred are finished," Koha replied. "And there will be two hundred more by morning."

"Good! And now let us see what the workmen in the next cave have accomplished."

As they passed through the huge workshop, Jerry paused from time to time to inspect a turret or say a few words to a workman. A second passageway led them into another tremendous cave, where five thousand workers, men and women, were busy. The men were molding hollow metal shells of cast iron. The women were filling them with measured quantities of fire powder, and inserting small, stoppered globes of water. Some of these were fitted with percussion plungers which would break the globes on contact, and others with tiny clockwork mechanisms that would jerk the stoppers from the glass globes in from one to ten seconds, depending upon how they were set.

"You made the tests as I ordered?" Jerry asked, turning to Yewd.

"All of them," replied the giant. "The large globes, when dropped, excavate holes in the ground that will contain a hundred mounted men. The smaller ones make craters proportionate to their size."

"How many are finished?" Jerry asked.

"A hundred thousand of the small, and ten thousand of the large."

"You have done splendidly, all of you," said Jerry. "Keep it up, and if nothing happens to prevent, I will return tomorrow. I go, now, to return the princess to her father, and to perfect our alliance with him."

Yewd said: "Deza grant that you may find Raliad a safer place this time than you ever have before."

CHAPTER XXV

As HE drew near his own camp, some hours later, Jerry saw that the preparations for war which he had ordered were well under way. Already the city of portable huts had grown to thrice its former size, and his forces were still being swelled by large companies of rodal cavalry, and by thousands of flying warriors. The lakes were black with swimming gawrs, and the entire end of the marsh had been turned into a vast community of fur-covered dwellings.

Challenged by a strange flying guard, Jerry gave the password, "On to Raliad," and was permitted to alight in the square before his hut. Here the guards and officers recognized his disguise, and rushed up to greet him. Among them was Yewd.

"You are back sooner than we expected you, my Viljen," said the giant.

"Find Koha," Jerry replied, "and bring him to me. I would hold council with you two."

Two guards parted the silver curtains that veiled the doorway of the black hut, and Jerry went in. Since the need for his disguise was at an end, he removed it, and exchanged his huntsman's garments for a commoner's black and silver. A slave brought pulcho, set it on a taboret at his elbow, and withdrew. And a moment later Yewd strode in with Koha waddling behind him.

"What news, master?" asked the dwarf. "Do we join the Vil's army today?"

"Not today, or ever," replied Jerry dejectedly, pushing the pulcho flask toward his two sturdy henchmen. "I have failed in my mission-failed miserably and completely. The Vil would have none of me as an officer. He has made an alliance with Manith Zovil, marital as well as martial. And to top it all, my disguise was penetrated by one of his courtiers, so that I barely escaped with my life-he still deeming me the murderer of his son."

"Why, then, that leaves us free to harass the Torturer in our own way," said Yewd, drinking deeply. "And with the new weapons we should be able to more than hold our own."

"You forget that the Torturer and his puppet sit in Raliad," said Jerry. "He is no longer an outlaw, but the power behind the throne. Numin Vil, if he does not retake his capital, will himself be the outlaw. And even with the help of Manith Zovil, I do not believe he can do it. With our assistance it might be done, but he would renounce his kingdom forever rather than accept my aid."

"If we could only find the man who slew Shiev Zovil," said Koha, "the rest should be easy."

"Ah, but the irony of fate prevents even that!" exclaimed Jerry.

Then what are we to do?"

"Do? Why, I will found a city of outlaws, here on this spot, that will defy all the armies of Mars. So long as Thoor remains Vil of Kalsivar with the Torturer pulling the strings, we shall be a thorn in their sides. We will. . ."

He was interrupted by a guard, who drew back a silver curtain and said: Algo the spy is here with an important message."

"Admit him," said Jerry.

The spy, resplendent in his uniform of the imperial guards, hurried in.

"What news, Algo?" Jerry asked.

"The princess has been abducted."

"What!" Jerry sprang to his feet. "When? By whom?"

"Only a short time ago. And by agents of the Torturer."

"Impossible! Wasn't Neem the black dalf with her? And was she not surrounded by the Vil's army?"

"Neither," Algo replied. "She was circling above the camp on the swift gawr you gave her, accompanied by two guards. Suddenly four brown warriors plunged down from high above them. Three slew the guards with their javelins. The fourth dropped a noose around the neck of her highness's gawr, so that it was forced to follow his bird-beast or strangle. Then he flew off in the direction of Raliad, followed by his three companions. I managed to bring you this message by pretending to follow the abductors."

"Back to your post, then, Algo," said Jerry. "And from now on you rank a jendus for bringing this news."

The spy saluted smartly and departed.

The Earthman whirled on Koha.

"Have the saddles been prepared with the chains and hooks, as I ordered?"

"They have, master; four thousand of them."

"Good. See that the gawrs are saddled, and their riders ready. And have two thousand more flying warriors prepared to join them."

As Koha waddled away, Yewd asked: "What are you going to do?"

"First I will lead a raid upon the canal excavating crew," he said. "Then our watchword shall become our war cry: 'On to Raliad!'"

CHAPTER XXVI

SEATED in his black but, Jerry summoned his officers and called for a scroll, brush and ink. Then he wrote the following note:

TO SARKIS THE TORTURER, THOOR THE FALSE VIL, AND THE PEOPLE OF RALIAD:

Today, when the sun reaches the zenith, my army will enter Raliad through the Gate of Victory, march down the Avenue of Triumph, and take over the Imperial Palace. All citizens are warned of the danger of congregating at any of these places at that hour.

THE COMMONER.

"Cause five hundred copies of this notice to be made," he told his jendus of fliers, "and see that they are dropped along the Avenue of Triumph and upon the roof of the Imperial Palace, at once."

"I hear and obey, my Viljen," replied the officer, saluting.

Jerry turned to his jendus of cavalry. "Mobilize all riders at once, and start for Raliad. By hurrying, you will be able to meet the flying contingent in front of the Gate of Victory, shortly before noon. See that the riders who carry grenades are in the front ranks."

"To hear is to obey, O Viljen," the officer answered.

Having given detailed instructions to his other officers, Jerry went out on a brief tour of inspection. The turrets which had been manufactured in the cave were being rolled out into the sunlight and stacked. Fire-powder grenades were being issued to both flying warriors and members of the first contingent of rodal cavalry. The heavier bombs were passed out to a picked group of fliers, who were also given a few small grenades.

His inspection completed, Jerry mounted his gawr, took his place at the head of the raiding party, and set off for the canal work-camp. An hour's flight brought them directly above their objective.

As soon as the party of raiders was sighted a general alarm was sounded. The digging machines stopped work and their drivers were ordered off of them and into the work-camp, where they were surrounded by the guards, for it was believed that this was a slave raid. It suited Jerry's purpose to let them think so. And so he continued to circle until all of the slaves had been herded into the compound with their guards massed around them.

Then be swooped down, and with a thousand riders armed with grenades, formed a line between the camp and the abandoned machines. Another thousand riders dismounted behind them, and each ran to a machine. Meanwhile, the four thousand remaining riders maneuvered until four gawrs hovered above each machine. Then the riders each dropped two hooks suspended on heavy chains fifty feet in length. The men on the ground swiftly fastened the hooks to the sides of the digging machines.

As soon as the guards realized what the raiders were about, they charged the line of warriors which Jerry had posted on guard. But a few fire-powder grenades hurled among them wrought such havoc that they beat a hasty retreat.

Before they could rally, a thousand of the machines were dangling high above their heads, each carried by four gawrs. And in a moment more the rest of the raiders, led by Jerry, had taken to the air.

Straight back to the camp they flew. Here the machines were lowered to the sand, their supporting gawrs still hovering above them, and were swiftly fitted with the turrets which had been built to their exact dimensions to protect the drivers.

In less than a half hour every turret was in place with its shelves lined with grenades and an experienced driver in the saddle.

And now, at a command from the Earthman, the entire flying force took to the air. Jerry flew in the lead, flanked on either side by Yewd and Koha, and immediately followed by the contingent of fliers who carried the heavy bombs. Those who carried the converted digging machines were in the center, and were guarded on either side and at the rear by warriors armed with grenades. Behind these came the large metal flying machines carrying foot soldiers.

The sun was two-thirds of the way to the meridian when Jerry caught up with his cavalry, about two jahuds from the Gate of Victory. As he had anticipated, a heavy force of the Torturer's fliers circled above the gate. And the walls were lined with warriors, ready for the attack.

The Earthman sent his flying orderlies to carry his final commands to his various officers, then urged his bird-beast forward. Instantly, those who carried heavy bombs fell in behind him, forming an immense triangle in the sky. About five hundred feet above them, and leading them by approximately the same distance, flew a similar triangle of those who carried grenades.

At this, the flying warriors of the Torturer formed a single wedge, much larger than either of his, and came hurtling toward them. In accordance with their instructions, Jerry's men in the upper wedge did not throw their grenades until the foremost enemy was within javelin range. Then they began hurling them with deadly accuracy. The fire-powder exploded with sharp detonations like those of cordite, and the havoc wrought among the enemy fliers was appalling.

There was, however, a drawback to this mode of warfare in the air. Some of the shell fragments did considerable damage in his own ranks. He was about to order his warriors to cease throwing grenades and use their javelins when the command was made unnecessary by the enemy warriors themselves, their swift charge was turned to an ignominious and disastrous rout.

A moment more and Jerry was passing above the Gate of Victory at a height of about two thousand feet. The force above him still retained its V formation, but the bombers now drew together in a long, straight line, with the Earthman at the head. As he had expected, the Torturer had virtually packed the Avenue of Triumph with his cavalry and foot-soldiers arranged in succession so he could hurl them in alternate waves at any enemy that might be able to pass the gate.

He flew on, his bombers strung out behind him at intervals of about five hundred feet, following the Avenue of Triumph straight to the palace.

In the meantime, the Torturer's flying force continued its disorderly retreat, until it reached the palace, where Sarkis himself was waiting. Jerry saw the glint of his jeweled golden mask and armor on the roof, and a moment later saw him take the air on the back of a gawr.

He instantly reformed his forces, but Jerry had attained his objective.

Unhooking a bomb from its rack in the front of his saddle, he dropped it to the packed street below, then awaited the result. It struck between two warriors. There was a terrific detonation, and the warriors, together with those around them, disappeared in a cloud of dust, smoke and debris.

The concussion was quickly followed by a series of similar explosions, which, in the space of a few seconds, traveled clear back to the Gate of Victory. And when the smoke and dust cleared away, no living thing, either man or beast, was left on the entire length of the avenue. There were only huge craters in the paving where the bombs had struck.

Leaving his bombers to hold their position above the Avenue of Triumph, Jerry now soared upward to lead the other contingent against the hosts of the Torturer. But this time he cautioned his warriors to fly above the foe.

There was a brisk, sharp engagement, and again the forces of Sarkis were broken up. But the main body was driven back to the palace roof, and with them was the Torturer himself. Jerry hurled a grenade at him, but he forgot to set the time mechanism; it struck the neck of Sarkis's mount, it bounded off and rolled harmlessly to the roof.

A moment later the Torturer dismounted and disappeared into the mouth of one of the tunnels which led to the lower levels, followed by several hundred of his officers and men. Others of his force found haven in other tunnel mouths. But at least half of those who alighted on the roof never lived to reach them.

Leaving the main body of his men to guard the room and tunnels, Jerry, accompanied by Yewd, Koha and a score of his best fighters, flew straight to the balcony of Junia. As his bird-beast came to rest on the balcony, he heard the scream of a girl in mortal terror.

Springing from the saddle, he sprinted through the open window just in time to see Junia carried through the door on the back of a hideous, masked figure, clothed in woven gold links. The door slammed shut, there was the sound of a bolt sliding into place, followed by the noise of retreating footsteps in the hallway.

Yewd and Koha came through the window, and the other warriors began crowding in after them. But Jerry ordered them all back. Then, standing just outside the window, he hurled a percussion grenade at the door, and dropped below the sill. There was a sharp explosion; when the Earthman raised his eyes above the sill he saw that a jagged hole had been blown in the door. Dashing forward, he plunged through that hole, followed by Yewd, Koha, and the other warriors.

In the meantime, back at the Gate of Victory, Jerry's officers were carrying out his orders. As soon as the last heavy bomb had exploded, clearing the avenue of the Torturer's warriors, a small squad of gawr riders flew low over the gate and adjacent walls, hurling grenades which swiftly wiped out the massed defenders.

Following them came the gawrs carrying digging machines at the ends of long chains. These were set down in the street, four abreast, and the hooks released.

Behind them, two huge flying machines discharged foot soldiers upon the walls and into the gate towers. These quickly drove out the remnants of the defenders, and taking charge of the control levers, swung the gates wide just as the sun reached the zenith. At this, Jerry's fierce desert tribesmen, mounted on their rodals, poured through. Half of them followed the converted digging machines in their march along the Avenue of Triumph to the palace.

Sarkis had stationed warriors in the windows and upon the roofs of the buildings on either side to burl javelins down upon the army of the Commoner. But as fast as these showed themselves they were treated to grenades, hurled by the Earthman's fliers.

The other half of the rodal cavalry split in two parts, and accompanied by the large metal flying machines containing the foot soldiers, began a systematic circuit of the wall, killing or capturing the guards who did not flee, and installing the men of the Commoner in their places.

Swiftly, the blood-red pennon of the Torturer was torn down from each captured gate tower. And in its place was hoisted the black standard of the Commoner, with its single silver star. At the points where the numerous canals entered the city, solid walls were built up from the terraces to a common level, and there were tremendous barred gates which could be dropped in the channels to block navigation.

All these had to be captured and invested, as well as the land gates and sentinel towers.

As the last armed rider passed through the Gate of Victory, the jen in charge ordered it closed. Then, chancing to look out of the tower window, he uttered an exclamation of surprise and turned to the warrior who stood at the control levers.

"Look, Tarjus!" he exclaimed. "A vast host approaches across the Plains of Lav! And the sky above it is black with gawrs! Who do you think that could be? Now who could that be?"

Tarjus looked out of the window for a moment, then cried out in dismay. "We are in for it now, Deza help us!" he exclaimed. "A force the size of that one can be none other than the combined armies of Numin Vil and Manith Zovil!"

CHAPTER XXVII

WHEN the first cross street was reached by the improvised tanks, there was a fierce charge of rodal cavalry from both sides against the advancing machines. The drivers of the machines hurled grenades into the foremost ranks of enemy cavalry, then made a swift countercharge.

The huge steel jaws which had been designed to bite through solid rock now snapped like living animals at the fighting men and their mounts. Warriors were bitten completely in two, and a single snap was sufficient to kill or maim a rodal. Around the edges of the melee the flying warriors of the Commoner continued to hurl their grenades, harmless to the men in the metal turrets.

The sanguinary engagement was soon ended, with the scattered remnants of the Torturer's forces dashing off down the side streets.

At the next cross street a charge of foot soldiers met the advancing forces. But these were even more easily scattered than the cavalry. After that there was no more opposition until the palace was reached. Here Sarkis had concentrated the bulk of his most seasoned fighting men.

The army of the Commoner did not attack at once. Instead, it split into two columns, which went to the right and left, circling the palace until it was completely surrounded. Now a thousand metal fighting machines faced the building from all sides.

When all was in readiness, the machines advanced first. Some of them charged up to doorways, others straight up to the wall. But no matter what was in front of them, they went to work to remove it, biting out and swallowing great chunks of the wall, and eating away the tremendous arches that framed the metal doors.

Swiftly, machines excavated tunnels through the base of the wall. And as rapidly, others tore away the door frames and arches. Presently one machine ripped out a huge metal door, and charged through into a closely packed mass of defenders. Behind it came Jerry's foot-soldiers, hurling grenades as they went. As soon as they were through the doorway, the rodal cavalry charged in after them and deployed to the right and left. At almost the same time other machines were breaking through the walls and tearing down the doors, to encounter similar resistance and employ like measures. And soon the greatest battle ever fought in all Kalsivar was raging within the huge palace itself.

In the meantime Jerry, followed by Yewd, Koha and a score of his warriors, met with a check as he plunged through the hole in the door of Junia's apartment in pursuit of her masked abductor. For Sarkis had posted a considerable body of fighting men in the corridor, and these outnumbered the Earthman's little band at least five to one.

Jerry, wielding his sword, was in the front and center as the two forces clashed. At his side was the giant Yewd, using by preference in these close quarters, a short, thick-shafted spear. At Yewd's left, Koha the black dwarf swung his huge mace with great, smashing blows that snapped swordblades, crushed skulls like eggshells, and bit through bone and sinew alike. Behind them the small squad of the Earthman's picked fighters used such weapons as best met the emergency or suited their fancy.

231

Fully half of their number were cut down before the Sarkis warriors realized that it was sure death to step in front of the spear of the white giant, the sword of the Commoner, or the mace of the black dwarf. But once this realization came to them, they fled more swiftly than they had come to the encounter a short time before.

Bleeding from half a dozen small wounds, and panting from his exertions, Jerry paused and leaned on his dripping sword, while one of his warriors applied jembal to his injuries. Yewd and Koha also had their wounds dressed. Then his eyes chanced to fall on one of the brown warriors who had been felled by the mace of Koha.

Apparently it had only struck him a glancing blow, for he was moaning and attempting to rise. "Fetch me that warrior," Jerry ordered.

Two of his men removed the fellow's weapons, picked him up, and laid him at the feet of the Earthman.

"Give him pulcho," said Jerry.

A soldier produced a flask and put it to the man's lips. He drank deeply and brightened perceptibly.

"Get up," the Earthman ordered.

He got to his feet, swaying unsteadily.

"Where has the Torturer gone?"

"I don't know."

"You lie!" grated Jerry. "Throw him on his back and open his mouth."

Swiftly, the warriors carried out his orders. Jerry took a small bottle of fire-powder from his belt pouch, and standing over the prisoner, leisurely removed the stopper.

"A few grains in the eyes might make you talk," he said. "I will try that first. If it fails then the mouth."

Jerry let a single grain of the powder fall upon his perspiring cheek. It flared up, and the man screamed as it seared his skin.

"Stop! Wait! I'll tell you!" he shrieked.

"Ah, that is better," Jerry told him. "I am more than just, for I am merciful. If you tell me the truth this time, you will be spared."

"Before he went," said the prisoner, "I heard the Lord Sarkis tell our jen to meet him in the central audience chamber."

"Is that all he said?" asked Jerry.

"He said that in case the battle went against us, he had a hostage for the sake of whose safety the Commoner would grant us all our freedom."

Jerry corked the fire-powder and replaced it in his belt pouch.

"To the central audience chamber," he said, "and bring the prisoner with us, until we make sure he has told us the truth."

When they reached the main floor platform they heard the sudden deafening clamor of battle. Jerry went cautiously to the door to reconnoiter, and saw that his fighting machines had broken into the palace. Behind them, his foot-soldiers were hurling grenades into the massed defenders, creating fearful carnage among them. And a moment later his rodal cavalry charged in. From that time on, only cold steel was used.

In a moment the wave of battle had reached the door where the Earthman stood, as the forces of the Torturer fell back before the fierce onslaught of the desert tribesmen. Foot by foot, the forces of the Torturer were cut down or forced back, until Jerry's men were at the very doors of the audience chamber, and the remnant of Sarkis's army was inside it.

Suddenly the clarion notes of a trumpet sounded from the center of the vast room. In the military language of Mars, they were a request for a truce.

Looking up, Jerry saw the herald standing on the lower step of the central dais. But at the top stood the masked Torturer. He was supporting Junia with his left arm. And in his right hand gleamed a dagger.

Instantly the Earthman called for a herald, and when he came running up, ordered him to sound the "Truce granted."

As the silver tones broke over that vast assemblage, the din of battle ceased as if by magic. Then the sepulchral tones of the Torturer floated across the room to Jerry, sitting his rodal in the doorway.

"Desperate situations call for desperate remedies. We do not ordinarily sacrifice women with the dagger, but the moment one armed enemy sets foot within this room, Junia Sovil dies."

"My men will respect the truce so long as yours do," said Jerry. "What do you want?"

"Freedom," replied the Torturer. "You will immediately order that a gawr for me, and one for each of my men be saddled, provisioned and made ready on the palace roof at once. And in earnest of your own good intentions you will lay down your arms and join my other prisoner, to be kept as a hostage until we are ready to depart."

"Release the princess now, and I pledge you my word that you and your warriors shall all go free and unharmed," said Jerry.

"Do you take me for a fool?" the Torturer roared. "I am not so gullible as all that."

"Very well," said Jerry, "I will accept your terms. But if you attempt any tricks, you and those with you will never leave this palace alive."

Vaulting down from his saddle, he removed his weapons and handed them, one by one, by Koha and Yewd. While he did so he rapidly issued instructions to them. Then, as he handed his dagger to the black dwarf, a courier came running up.

"What is it?" asked Jerry.

"Numin Vil and Manith Zovil are at the Gate of Victory with a vast army," said the messenger. "They demand that we immediately throw the gates open to them, and say that failing in this, they will take the city by assault and slay all of us."

"Tell them," the Earthman replied, "that pressing business here at the palace prevents my meeting them and escorting them hither. Tell them I have weapons that would destroy their armies as easily as they did that of the Torturer. But say that I invite them to come here and meet me for a friendly conference, guaranteeing them safe conduct. Then, if they consent to come, bring them in my swiftest metal flier. But see that none of their flying warriors are permitted to pass above the walls."

Jerry whispered a final, "Don't forget the signal," to Yewd and Koha. Then he turned and marched weaponless through the doorway.

The Torturer's warriors opened their ranks to let him pass, and fearlessly he strode up to the dais.

CHAPTER XXVIII

As JERRY walked up to the dais on which the Torturer stood with Junia, he saw that the princess was tightly bound, hand and foot.

Sarkis greeted him with a chuckle from the depths of his hideous mask.

Now I have you both where I can kill you. I will die content."

"What do you mean?" asked Jerry. "Do you think you could do that and get out of here alive?"

"Since this defeat, I have nothing left to live for," said the Torturer. "I lured you here only for the purpose of revenge. First you shall see your beloved die; then you shall share her fate."

He raised his dagger aloft, clutching the princess by her glossy black hair as she struggled in his grasp. At the same instant Jerry lifted his hand to his head-a signal his men would understand. Then he sprang straight for the top of the dais.

The Earthman's remarkable jumping powers were something Sarkis had overlooked; the startled Torturer turned to defend himself. As Jerry alighted he gripped the dagger wrist of Sarkis with his left hand, and with his right dealt him such a buffet on the side of the head as must have made his ears ring inside the golden helmet.

The Torturer released the girl and focused all his attention on the Earthman. The two struggled for a moment on the narrow top of the dais, then lost their balance at the edge, and toppling, rolled over and over to the floor.

At the same instant pandemonium broke loose within that vast chamber. Jerry's men opened hostilities by hurling grenades into the packed mass of their foes. Then they charged. At this, some of the Torturer's men turned and ran toward the dais. But to their utter astonishment they saw that a square section of the floor, supported on four metal shafts, had risen in front of the throne. Through the opening squirmed a white giant, followed by a black dwarf.

And after them poured a steady stream of the Commoner's fierce fighting men.

In a few seconds the dais was completely surrounded by a ring of Jerry's soldiers, whose numbers were constantly augmented by those who poured through from beneath. And now, the pitiful remnant of the Torturer's army threw down their arms and surrendered.

Not so the Torturer. He wrenched himself free from Jerry's grasp and with his dagger aimed a blow at his heart.

But the Earthman kicked the weapon from his hand and sprang back.

"Give me a sword," he told Koha, "then cut the princess free and stand guard over her. But see that no one molests the Torturer. He is mine alone to deal with."

As the black dwarf pressed his sword into the Earthman's hand, Sarkis drew his own weapon.

"Some days ago," said Jerry, "you challenged me to a duel, but did not appear. Though I slew your substitute, I do not consider the affair settled. What is your opinion?"

"It will be settled when I have killed you," grated Sarkis, lunging.

Jerry deflected the lunge with ease then before his opponent could recover, raked him across the chest with his point, cutting a long gash in his garment of golden mesh and revealing an expanse of shining steel beneath.

"Ah, a breastplate!" said Jerry. "We must remove it."

Again they engaged, and again Jerry slit his enemy's golden covering, so that one corner hung down. A third slash, and Sarkis wore a golden apron which flopped about his legs as he moved.

But Jerry had only begun. Systematically, he began undressing his opponent with his point. At the fourth slash, the Torturer was plainly revealed as a brown-skinned man. With his golden disguise cut away from him, his torso was naked save for the breastplate. Then the Earthman cut the straps that held it and it clattered to the floor.

At this Jerry heard a hearty laugh behind him, and turning for an instant, saw Manith Zovil, who had just come up with Numin Vil. The Vil was clutching the collar of a great black dalf, who was growling thunderously and seemed anxious to leap forward to the aid of the Earthman.

"Back, Neem," said Jerry quickly.

Though the Torturer fought desperately, he was now badly hampered by his heavy golden garments, which he was compelled to hold up with one hand to keep them from slipping down around his legs and tripping him.

Suddenly Jerry avoided a lunge, and springing in, struck upward so that his pommel caught beneath the hooked nose of the hideous mask. It flew off revealing the features of Thoor Movil. Before his enemy could recover, Jerry turned and brought his blade down upon that of the brown prince with such force that the weapon was knocked from his grasp.

At this sudden revelation of the identity of the Torturer there were cries of amazement from the onlookers, and shouts of "Kill the false Vil! Slay the Torturer! Pierce his rotten heart!"

"Yield or die," said Jerry, presenting his point to his enemy's breast.

"I yield," replied Thoor Movil.

"Take charge of the prisoner," said Jerry, sheathing his sword. Two of his warriors sprang forward to do his bidding, and he turned to salute his royal guests. Junia had joined her father, and the Vil stood with his arm around her slight figure, while she fondled the head of Neem, the dalf.

Manith Zovil smiled broadly as he acknowledged Jerry's salute.

"That was rare entertainment you just afforded us, my friend," he said. "I'm glad you invited us here to witness it.

"But I didn't," replied Jerry. "I hoped to have it over with by the time you arrived."

"Then Deza be thanked that you miscalculated. I wouldn't have missed it for a million tayzos."

Numin Vil was more brusque. "Now that you have seized my capital, what do you intend doing with it?"

"I believe you offered the hand of your daughter to the man who would recapture it for you," Jerry replied.

"That offer was made to my friend Manith Zovil, and not to the murderer of my son," thundered the Vil.

"One moment, majesty," interrupted Manith Zovil. "It seems that between us we have done my friend Jerry Morgan a grave injustice. He did not kill your son."

"Then who did?"

"I slew Shiev Zovil in self-defense," replied the Prince. "I met him in the corridor near Jerry Morgan's apartment, and he lunged at me without a word of warning, when my sword was sheathed. I leaped back, and only the fact that the point was stopped by my breastbone saved my life.

"Then I drew my own weapon, and we had it out."

The poker face of Numin Vil showed nothing of his feelings, but his rumbling voice grew suddenly tremulous. "II cannot understand why Shiev attacked you thus."

"I can explain that, also," replied Manith Zovil. "Thoor Movil poisoned his mind against me. He wished to marry Junia himself, and after putting you and the crown prince out of the way, to make himself Vil of Kalsivar. As you see, his plans underwent some slight changes through circumstances, but his central purpose has ever been the same."

"It seems," rumbled Numin Vil, turning and fixing the prisoner with his expressionless eyes, "that my nephew is responsible not only for the death of my son, but for all of our troubles and misunderstandings. Were he my prisoner . . ."

"He is your prisoner, majesty," interrupted Jerry. "I wish to turn him over to you, along with your capital and your empire, which I will tell you frankly that I do not want. All I ask is that you legally free those of my followers who have been slaves, pardon those who have broken your laws, and permit us all to go in peace."

"Then you have no ambition to rule Kalsivar?"

"None whatever."

The Vil again regarded his treacherous nephew. "Thoor Movil," he said, "I sentence you. . ."

At this moment there was an interruption. No one had paid any attention to the slight, brown-skinned girl attired in a gray slave habit, who had unobtrusively wormed her way through the crowd to a position behind Thoor Movil. Jerry's first inkling of what was taking place was when he saw the glint of light on the blade of a dagger which she slipped into the prince's right hand.

The feel of that weapon galvanized the desperate prince to sudden action: Before the two warriors who stood guard at either side of him had any idea what was taking place, he sprang forward, seized the Vil by his braided beard, and raised his dagger to plunge it into the monarch's heart.

To all save Jerry this development was so unexpected, that they could only stand, gasping and helpless. But the Earthman had caught the glint of the dagger just in time. And so, when Thoor Movil leaped, Jerry was but a fraction of a second behind him. With a single, sweeping motion, his sword flashed from its scabbard and described a glittering arc. One moment the bystanders saw the brown prince standing with dagger raised for the death thrust; the next, they saw the upraised arm and sneering head leap upward and fly through the air, both severed by the same terrific blow.

Behind him Jerry heard a female voice screaming-cursing. He turned and saw Nisha Novil, wearing the gray of a slave girl, struggling in the grip of two of his warriors.

"What is this?" thundered Numin Vil. "Has my niece become a slave?"

"It was she who passed the dagger to Thoor Movil, majesty," volunteered one of the men.

"Then she shall have the sentence I intended for her traitorous brother," rumbled the monarch. "Nisha Novil, you are stripped of your royal rank, your wealth and lands. You have chosen to wear the habit of a slave girl as a disguise. Wear it now as your future apparel. And tomorrow you go on the auction block."

He waved his hand, and the two warriors dragged her away, still kicking, cursing, biting and scratching.

"Deza help the man who buys her," said Manith Zovil dryly.

The Vil turned to the Earthman.

"Jerry Morgan," he said, "you have not only restored my daughter and my empire, but have saved my life. The rewards which I promised you on the Plains of Lav shall now be yours. A million tayzos and the Raddek of Dhoor."

At this Jerry's heart turned bitter within him. For a moment he was minded to hold the empire which lay within his grasp-to make Junia his own, despite the evident reluctance of the Vil to give his daughter to a commoner. But he remembered that the princess had agreed to marry Manith Zovil, and he did not want the empire; it was only Junia he wanted-Junia and his freedom.

"I care not for your riches nor your titles," he said. "The free, adventurous life of your deserts and marshes suits me better than your crowded city existence. I would sooner sleep beneath the jeweled vault of heaven than in a palace with a golden roof set with the most precious gems; would rather watch the sun rise over the sand dunes or through the morning mists that hang over the Atabah Marsh, than over the most ornate building in your vast city. I want to go back to my wild tribesmen-to ride and hunt and live and. . ."

"And love?" asked Junia, coming quickly to his side and looking up at him with starry eyes, eloquent with a meaning which he could not mistake.

"And love!" he replied, taking her in his arms and possessing himself of her eager, upturned lips.

"Then take me with you, my Commoner," she murmured.

He looked up at the Vil.

"On my world," he said, "it is a custom for outlaws to say, 'Your money or your life!' You know that I hold all Kalsivar in the hollow of my hand. And I, the outlaw of Mars, now say to you, 'Your empire or your daughter!' It is up to you to choose."

For a moment the Vil glared at him, speechless. Then the suspicion of a twinkle came to his usually expressionless eyes as he replied: "Since she, herself, has chosen you, take her, my boy, and may Deza bless you both."

So Jerry Morgan, though he had renounced the throne of the greatest empire on all Mars, was very well content.

www.ingramcontent.com/pod-product-compliance
Lightning Source LLC
Chambersburg PA
CBHW020833260626
47169CB00003B/968